The Best of Isaac Asimov

SHORT STORY COLLECTIONS BY ISAAC ASIMOV

The Best of Isaac Asimov

ISAAC ASIMOV

DOUBLEDAY & COMPANY, INC.

GARDEN CITY, NEW YORK

1974

A S I

Stories in this volume were previously published as follows:

THE FUN THEY HAD. Used by permission of Newspaper Enterprise Association, Inc.; THE LAST QUESTION, Copyright © 1956 by Columbia Publications, Inc.; THE DEAD PAST, Copyright © 1956 by Street & Smith Publications, Inc.; THE DYING NIGHT, Copyright © 1956 by Fantasy House, Inc.; ANNIVERSARY, Copyright © 1959 by Ziff-Davis Publishing Co.; THE BILLIARD BALL, Copyright © 1967 by Galaxy Publishing Corporation; MIRROR IMAGE, Copyright © 1972 by Conde Nast Publications, Inc.; MAROONED OFF VESTA, Copyright 1938 by Ziff-Davis Publishing Co.; Copyright renewed 1966 by Isaac Asimov; NIGHTFALL, Copyright 1941 by Street & Smith Publications, Inc., Copyright renewed 1968 by Isaac Asimov; C-CHUTE, Copyright 1951 by Galaxy Publishing Corporation; THE MARTIAN WAY, Copyright 1952 by Galaxy Publishing Corporation; THE DEEP, Copyright 1952 by Galaxy Publishing Corporation.

First Edition
ISBN: 0-385-05078-x
Library of Congress Catalog Card Number 74–2863
Copyright © 1973 by Isaac Asimov
Copyright © 1973 by Sphere Books Ltd
Doubleday edition 1974

Contents

ACKNOWLEDGMENTS

Marooned Off Vesta: AMAZING STORIES, 1939

Nightfall: ASTOUNDING SCIENCE FICTION, 1941

C-Chute: GALAXY SCIENCE FICTION, 1951

The Martian Way: GALAXY SCIENCE FICTION, 1952

The Deep: GALAXY SCIENCE FICTION, 1952

The Fun They Had: FANTASY & SCIENCE FICTION, 1954

The Last Question: SCIENCE FICTION QUARTERLY, 1956

The Dead Past: ASTOUNDING SCIENCE FICTION, 1956

The Dying Night: FANTASY & SCIENCE FICTION, 1956

Anniversary: AMAZING SCIENCE FICTION, 1959

The Billiard Ball: IF SCIENCE FICTION, 1967

Mirror Image: ANALOG, 1972

INTRODUCTION

I must admit the title of this book gives me pause. Who says the enclosed stories are my 'best'? Do I? Does the editor? Or some critic? Some reader? A general vote among the entire population of the world?

And whoever says it—can it be so? Can the word 'best' mean anything at all, except to some particular person in some particular mood? Perhaps not—so if we allow the word to stand as an absolute, you, or you, or perhaps you, may be appalled at omissions or inclusions or, never having read me before, may even be impelled to cry out, 'Good heavens, are *those* his *best?*'

So I'll be honest with all of you. What is included here in this book are a dozen stories chosen in such a way as to span a third of a century of writing, with two early samples, two late samples, and eight from the gold decade (for me) of the Fifties. Those presented are as nearly representative as is consistent with the careful selection of good stories (i.e. those the editor and I like), and as nearly the best of my stories as is consistent with making them representative.

I suppose we ought really call the book, 'The Pretty Good and Pretty Representative Stories of Isaac Asimov', but who would then buy it? So 'Best' it is.

As to the individual stories—

(1) 'Marooned Off Vesta' was the very first story I ever published, so its inclusion is virtually a necessity. It wasn't the first I ever wrote with the hope of publication. Actually, it was the third. The first was never sold and no longer exists; the second was sold a couple of years after it was written, but is not very good.

Far be it from me to crave indulgence, but I think it is important to understand that at the time I wrote and sold the story (in 1938) I was eighteen years old and had spent all the years I could remember in a city-slum. My vision of strong adventurers bravely facing danger in distant vastnesses was just that—visionary.

(2) 'Nightfall', written two and a half years later, was the thirty-second story I had written (what else did I have to do in those days except work in my father's candystore and study for my college degrees) and perhaps the fourteenth story published.

Yet within less than three years of the start of my career it turned out that I *had* written the best of Asimov. At least, 'Nightfall' has been frequently reprinted, is commonly referred to as a 'classic', and when some magazine, or fan organization, conducts a vote on short stories, it frequently ends up on the top of the list—not only of my stories but of anybody's. One of its advantages is that it has a unique plot. There was nothing resembling it ever published before (as far as I know) and of course, it is now so well known that nothing like it can be published again. It's nice to have *one* story like that, anyway.

Yet I was only twenty-one when I wrote it and was still feeling my way. It isn't *my* favorite. Later on, I'll tell you what my favorite is and you can then judge for yourself.

(3) 'C-Chute' comes after a ten-year hiatus, as far as the stories included in this book are concerned. I hadn't quit writing of course, don't think that. To be sure, I had slowed down a bit, what with the war and the time-consuming effort toward the doctorate, but the real reason for the gap is that I spent most of the Forties writing the stories collected in my books *I, Robot* and *The Foundation Trilogy*. It seemed inadvisable to amputate portions of either for this collection.

'C-Chute' comes near the beginning of my 'mature' period (or whatever you want to call it). I had my Ph.D.; I was an Assistant Professor of Biochemistry at Boston University School of Medicine; I had published my first three books; and I was full of self-confidence. What's more I had broken away from exclusive dependence on *Astounding Science Fiction.* New magazines had arisen to challenge its leadership, notably *Galaxy,* and also *Fantasy and Science Fiction.* 'C-Chute' appeared in *Galaxy.* So did the next two stories in the collection.

(4) 'The Martian Way' represents my reaction to the McCarthy era, a time, in the early fifties, when Americans seemed to abandon their own history and become, in some cases, witch-hunters; in some cases, victims; and in most cases, cowards. (Brave men remained, fortunately, which is why we pulled out of it.) 'The Martian Way', written and published at the height of the McCarthy

era, was my own personal statement of position. I felt very brave at the time and was disappointed that no one ever as much as frowned at me in consequence. I must have been too subtle—or too unimportant.

A second point about the story is that I managed to foresee something accurately. Science fiction writers are often assumed to be keen-eyed peerers-into-the-future who see things others don't. Actually, few writers have much of a record in this respect and mine, at best, can only be said to attain the abysmally-low average. Just the same, in 'The Martian Way', I described the euphoric effects of the spacewalk fifteen years before anyone had space-walked—and then, when they did, euphoria is apparently what they experienced.

(5) 'The Deep' is the sleeper of the collection. Every once in a while I wrote a story which, though good in my opinion (and I don't like *all* my stories), seems to stir up no reaction. This is one of them. Perhaps it's because I deliberately chose to describe a society in which mother-love was a crime and the world wasn't ready for that.

(6) 'The Fun They Had' is probably the biggest surprise of my literary career. A personal friend asked me to write a little science fiction story for a syndicated boys-and-girls newspaper page he edited and I agreed for friendship's sake. I expected it would appear in a few newspapers for one day and would then disappear forever.

However, *Fantasy and Science Fiction* picked it up and, to my surprise, the reprint requests began to come in. It has been reprinted at least thirty times, and there has been no time in perhaps fifteen years (including right now) when new reprints haven't been pending.

Why? I don't know why. If I had the critic's mentality (which I emphatically don't) I would sit down and try to analyze my stories, work out the factors that make some more successful than others, cultivate those factors, and simply explode with excellence.

But the devil with that. I won't buy success at the price of self-consciousness. I don't have the temperament for it. I'll write as I please and let the critics do the analyzing. (Yesterday, someone said to me that a critic was like a eunuch in a harem. He could observe, study, and analyze—but he couldn't do it himself.)

(7) 'The Last Question' is my personal favorite, the one story I made sure would not be omitted from this collection.

Why is it my favorite? For one thing I got the idea all at once and didn't have to fiddle with it; and I wrote it in white-heat and scarcely had to change a word. This sort of thing endears any story to any writer.

Then, too, it has had the strangest effect on my readers. Frequently someone writes to ask me if I can give them the name of a story, which they *think* I may have written, and tell them where to find it. They don't remember the title but when they describe the story it is invariably 'The Last Question'. This has reached the point where I recently received a long-distance phone-call from a desperate man who began, 'Dr Asimov, there's a story I think you wrote, whose title I can't remember—' at which point I interrupted to tell him it was 'The Last Question' and when I described the plot it proved to be indeed the story he was after. I left him convinced I could read minds at a distance of a thousand miles.

No other story I have written has anything like this effect on my readers—producing at once an unshakeable memory of the plot and an unshakeable forgettery of the title and even author. I think it may be that the story fills them so frighteningly full, that they can retain none of the side-issues.

(8) 'The Dead Past' was written after I had been teaching for seven years. I was as saturated as could be with the world of scientific research.

Naturally, anyone who writes is going to reveal the world in which he is immersed, whether he wants to or desperately wants not to. I've never tried to avoid letting my personal background creep into my stories, but I must admit it has rarely crept in quite as thickly as it did in this one.

As an example of how my stories work out, consider this—

I had my protagonist interested in Carthage because I myself am a great admirer of Hannibal and have never quite gotten over the Battle of Zama. I introduced Carthage, idly, without any intention of weaving it into the plot. But it got woven in just the same.

That happens to me over and over. Some writers work out the stories in meticulous detail before starting, and stick to the outline. P. G. Wodehouse does it, I understand, and I worship his books. But just the same I don't. I work out my ending, decide on a beginning and then proceed, letting everything in-between work itself out as I come to it.

(9) 'The Dying Night' is an example of a mystery as well as a science fiction story. I have been a mystery reader as long as I have

been a science fiction reader and, on the whole, I think I enjoy mysteries more.

I'm not sure why that is. Perhaps it was that after I became an established science fiction writer I was no longer able to relax with science fiction stories. I read every story keenly aware that it might be worse than mine, in which case I had no patience with it, or that it might be better, in which case I felt miserable.

Mysteries, especially the intellectual puzzle variety (ah, good old Hercule Poirot), offered me no such stumbling blocks. Sooner or later, then, I was bound to try my hand at science fiction mysteries and 'The Dying Night' is one of these.

(10) 'Anniversary' was written to fulfil a request—that I write a story for the March, 1959, issue of *Amazing Stories* as a way of celebrating the twentieth anniversary of the March, 1939, issue, which had contained my first published story, 'Marooned Off Vesta'. So (inevitably) I wrote a story dealing with the characters of 'Marooned Off Vesta' twenty years later. The magazine then ran both stories together, and I was sure someone would send me a letter saying that my writing was better in the first story, but no one did. (Perhaps a reader of this book will decide it would be humorous to do so, but if so, please restrain yourself.)

(11) 'The Billiard Ball' comes, in this collection, after an eight-year hiatus and is an example of my 'late' style. (That is, if there is such a thing. Some critics say that it is a flaw in my literary nature that I haven't grown'; that my late stories have the same style and aura of my early stories. Maybe you'll think so, too, and scorn me in consequence—but then, I've already told you what some people think of critics.)

The reason for the hiatus is that in 1958 I quit the academic life to become a full-time writer. I at once proceeded to write everything under the sun (straight science, straight mystery, children's books, histories, literary annotations, etymology, humor, etc., etc.) *except* science fiction. I never entirely abandoned it, of course—witness 'The Billiard Ball'.

(12) 'Mirror Image' is a particularly recent science fiction short story I've written for the magazines and, unlike the first eleven stories, has not yet had time to be reprinted.

One of the reasons for writing it was to appease those readers who were forever asking me for sequels; for one more book involving characters who have appeared in previous books. One of the most frequent requests was that I write a third novel to succeed *The Caves of Steel* and *The Naked Sun,* both of which dealt with the adventures of the detective, Elijah Baley, and his robot-assistant, R. Daneel Olivaw. Unable to find the time to do so, I wrote a short story about them—'Mirror-Image'.

Alas, all I got as a result were a spate of letters saying, 'Thanks, but we mean a *novel.*'

Anyway, there you are. Turn the page and you can begin a representative, and possibly a more or less 'best', 115,000 words or so out of the roughly 2,000,000 words of science fiction I have written so far. I hope it amuses you. And if it doesn't, remember that I have also written about 7,500,000 words of *non*-science-fiction, and you are at least spared any of that.

ISAAC ASIMOV

The Best of Isaac Asimov

Marooned Off Vesta

"Will you please stop walking up and down like that?" said Warren Moore from the couch. "It won't do any of us any good. Think of our blessings; we're airtight, aren't we?"

Mark Brandon whirled and ground his teeth at him. "I'm glad you feel happy about that," he spat out viciously. "Of course, you don't know that our air supply will last only three days." He resumed his interrupted stride with a defiant air.

Moore yawned and stretched, assumed a more comfortable position, and replied, "Expending all that energy will only use it up faster. Why don't you take a hint from Mike here? He's taking it easy."

"Mike" was Michael Shea, late a member of the crew of the *Silver Queen*. His short, squat body was resting on the only chair in the room and his feet were on the only table. He looked up as his name was mentioned, his mouth widening in a twisted grin.

"You've got to expect things like this to happen sometimes," he said. "Bucking the asteroids is risky business. We should've taken the hop. It takes longer, but it's the only safe way. But no, the captain wanted to make the schedule; he *would* go through"—Mike spat disgustedly— "and here we are."

"What's the 'hop'?" asked Brandon.

"Oh, I take it that friend Mike means that we should have avoided the asteroid belt by plotting a course outside the plane of the ecliptic," answered Moore. "That's it, isn't it, Mike?"

Mike hesitated and then replied cautiously, "Yeah—I guess that's it."

Moore smiled blandly and continued, "Well, I wouldn't blame Captain Crane too much. The repulsion screen must have failed five minutes before that chunk of granite barged into us. That's not his fault, though of course we ought to have steered clear instead of relying on the screen." He shook his head meditatively. "The *Silver Queen* just went to pieces. It's really miraculously lucky that this part of the ship remained intact, and what's more, airtight."

"You've got a funny idea of luck, Warren," said Brandon. "Always have, for as long as I've known you. Here we are in a tenth part of a spaceship, comprising only three *whole* rooms, with air for three days, and no prospect of being alive after that, and you have the infernal gall to prate about luck."

"Compared to the others who died instantly when the asteroid struck, yes," was Moore's answer.

"You think so, eh? Well, let me tell you that instant death isn't so bad compared with what we're going to have to go through. Suffocation is a damned unpleasant way of dying."

"We may find a way out," Moore suggested hopefully.

"Why not face facts!" Brandon's face was flushed and his voice trembled. "We're done, I tell you! Through!"

Mike glanced from one to the other doubtfully and then coughed to attract their attention. "Well, gents, seeing that we're all in the same fix, I guess there's no use hogging things." He drew a small bottle out of his pocket that was filled with a greenish liquid. "Grade A Jabra this is. I ain't too proud to share and share alike."

Brandon exhibited the first signs of pleasure for over a day. "Martian Jabra water. Why didn't you say so before?"

But as he reached for it, a firm hand clamped down upon his wrist. He looked up into the calm blue eyes of Warren Moore.

"Don't be a fool," said Moore, "there isn't enough to keep us drunk for three days. What do you want to do? Go on a tear now and then die cold sober? Let's save this for the last six hours when the air gets stuffy and breathing hurts—then we'll finish the bottle among us and never *know* when the end comes, or *care*."

Brandon's hand fell away reluctantly. "Damn it, Warren, you'd bleed ice if you were cut. How can you think straight at a time like this?" He motioned to Mike and the bottle was once more stowed away. Brandon walked to the porthole and gazed out.

Moore approached and placed a kindly arm over the shoulders of the younger man. "Why take it so hard, man?" he asked. "You can't last at this rate. Inside of twenty-four hours you'll be a madman if you keep this up."

There was no answer. Brandon stared bitterly at the globe that filled almost the entire porthole, so Moore continued, "Watching Vesta won't do you any good either."

Mike Shea lumbered up to the porthole. "We'd be safe if we were only down there on Vesta. There're people there. How far away are we?"

"Not more than three or four hundred miles judging from its apparent size," answered Moore. "You must remember that it is only two hundred miles in diameter."

"Three hundred miles from salvation," murmured Brandon, "and we might as well be a million. If there were only a way to get ourselves out of the orbit this rotten fragment adopted. You know, manage to give ourselves a push so as to start falling. There'd be no danger of crashing if we did, because that midget hasn't got enough gravity to crush a cream puff."

"It has enough to keep us in the orbit," retorted Brandon. "It must have picked us up while we were lying unconscious after the crash. Wish it had come closer; we might have been able to land on it."

"Funny place, Vesta," observed Mike Shea. "I was down there two-three times. What a dump! It's all covered with some stuff like snow, only it ain't snow. I forget what they call it."

"Frozen carbon dioxide?" prompted Moore.

"Yeah, dry ice, that carbon stuff, that's it. They say that's what makes Vesta so shiny."

"Of course! That would give it a high albedo."

Mike cocked a suspicious eye at Moore and decided to let it pass. "It's hard to see anything down there on account of the snow, but if you look close"—he pointed—"you can see a sort of gray smudge. I think that's Bennett's dome. That's where they keep the observatory. And there is Calorn's dome up there. That's a fuel station, that is. There're plenty more, too, only I don't see them."

He hesitated and then turned to Moore. "Listen, boss, I've been thinking. Wouldn't they be looking for us as soon as they hear about the crash? And wouldn't we be easy to find from Vesta, seeing we're so close?"

Moore shook his head, "No, Mike, they won't be looking for us. No one's going to find out about the crash until the *Silver Queen* fails to turn up on schedule. You see, when the asteroid hit, we didn't have time to send out an SOS"—he sighed—"and they won't find us down there at Vesta, either. We're so small that even at our distance they couldn't see us unless they knew what they were looking for, and exactly where to look."

"Hmm." Mike's forehead was corrugated in deep thought. "Then we've got to get to Vesta before three days are up."

"You've got the gist of the matter, Mike. Now, if we only knew how to go about it, eh?"

Brandon suddenly exploded, "Will you two stop this infernal chitter-chatter and do something? For God's sake, do something."

Moore shrugged his shoulders and without answer returned to the couch. He lounged at ease, apparently carefree, but there was the tiniest crease between his eyes which bespoke concentration.

There was no doubt about it; they *were* in a bad spot. He reviewed the events of the preceding day for perhaps the twentieth time.

After the asteroid had struck, tearing the ship apart, he'd gone out like a light; for how long he didn't know, his own watch being broken and no other timepiece available. When he came to, he found himself, along with Mark Brandon, who shared his room, and Mike Shea, a member of the crew, sole occupants of all that was left of the *Silver Queen*.

This remnant was now careening in an orbit about Vesta. At present things were fairly comfortable. There was a food supply that would last a week. Likewise there was a regional Gravitator under the room that kept them at normal weight and would continue to do so for an indefinite time, certainly for longer than the air would last. The lighting system was less satisfactory but had held on so far.

There was no doubt, however, where the joker in the pack lay. Three days' air! Not that there weren't other disheartening features. There was no heating system—though it would take a long time for the ship to radiate enough heat into the vacuum of space to render them too uncomfortable. Far more important was the fact that their part of the ship had neither a means of communication nor a propulsive mechanism. Moore sighed. One fuel jet in working order would fix everything, for one blast in the right direction would send them safely to Vesta.

The crease between his eyes deepened. What was to be done? They had but one spacesuit among them, one heat ray, and one detonator. That was the sum total of space appliances after a thorough search of the accessible parts of the ship. A pretty hopeless mess, that.

Moore shrugged, rose, and drew himself a glass of water. He swallowed it mechanically, still deep in thought, when an idea struck him. He glanced curiously at the empty cup in his hand.

"Say, Mike," he said, "what kind of water supply have we? Funny that I never thought of that before."

Mike's eyes opened to their fullest extent in an expression of ludicrous surprise. "Didn't you know, boss?"

"Know *what?*" asked Moore impatiently.

"We've got all the water there was." He waved his hand in an all-inclusive gesture. He paused, but as Moore's expression showed nothing but total mystification, he elaborated, "Don't you see? We've got the main tank, the place where all the water for the whole ship was stored." He pointed to one of the walls.

"Do you mean to say that there's a tank full of water adjoining us?"

Mike nodded vigorously, "Yep! Cubic vat a hundred feet each way. And she's three-quarters full."

Moore was astonished. "Seven hundred and fifty thousand cubic feet of water." Then suddenly: "Why hasn't it run out through the broken pipes?"

"It only has one main outlet, which runs down the corridor just outside this room. I was fixing that main when the asteroid hit and had to shut it off. After I came to I opened the pipe leading to our faucet, but that's the only outlet open now."

"Oh." Moore had a curious feeling way down deep inside. An idea had half-formed in his brain, but for the life of him he could not drag it into the light of day. He knew only that there was something in what he had just heard that had some important meaning but he just could not place his finger on it.

Brandon, meanwhile, had been listening to Shea in silence, and now he emitted a short, humorless laugh. "Fate seems to be having its fill of fun with us, I see. First, it puts us within arm's reach of a place of safety and then sees to it that we have no way of getting there.

"Then she provides us with a week's food, three days' air, and *a year's supply of water*. A year's supply, do you hear me? Enough water to drink and to gargle and to wash and to take baths in and—and to do anything else we want. Water—damn the water!"

"Oh, take a less serious view, Mark," said Moore in an attempt to break the younger man's melancholy. "Pretend we're a satellite of Vesta—which we are. We have our own period of revolution and of rotation. We have an equator and an axis. Our 'north pole' is located somewhere toward the top of the porthole, pointing toward

Vesta, and our 'south' sticks out away from Vesta through the water tank somewhere. Well, as a satellite, we have an atmosphere, and now, you see, we have a newly discovered ocean.

"And seriously, we're not so badly off. For the three days our atmosphere will last, we can eat double rations and drink ourselves soggy. Hell, we have water enough to throw away——"

The idea which had been half-formed before suddenly sprang to maturity and was nailed. The careless gesture with which he had accompanied the last remark was frozen in mid-air. His mouth closed with a snap and his head came up with a jerk.

But Brandon, immersed in his own thoughts, noticed nothing of Moore's strange actions. "Why don't you complete the analogy to a satellite," he sneered, "or do you, as a Professional Optimist, ignore any and all disagreeable facts? If I were you, I'd continue this way." Here he imitated Moore's voice: "The satellite is at present habitable and inhabited but, due to the approaching depletion of its atmosphere in three days, is expected to become a dead world.

"Well, why don't you answer? Why do you persist in making a joke out of this? Can't you see—— *What's the matter?*"

The last was a surprised exclamation and certainly Moore's actions did merit surprise. He had risen suddenly and, after giving himself a smart rap on the forehead, remained stiff and silent, staring into the far distance with gradually narrowing eyelids. Brandon and Mike Shea watched him in speechless astonishment.

Suddenly Moore burst out, "Ha! I've got it. Why didn't I think of it before?" His exclamations degenerated into the unintelligible.

Mike drew out the Jabra bottle with a significant look, but Moore waved it away impatiently. Whereupon Brandon, without any warning, lashed out with his right, catching the surprised Moore flush on the jaw and toppling him.

Moore groaned and rubbed his chin. Somewhat indignant, he asked, "What was the reason for that?"

"Stand up and I'll do it again," shouted Brandon, "I can't stand it anymore. I'm sick and tired of being preached at, and having to listen to your Pollyanna talk. *You're* the one that's going daffy."

"Daffy, nothing! Just a little overexcited, that's all. Listen, for God's sake. I think I know a way——"

Brandon glared at him balefully. "Oh, you do, do you? Raise our hopes with some silly scheme and then find it doesn't work.

I won't take it, do you hear? I'll find a real use for the water—drown you—and save some of the air besides."

Moore lost his temper. "Listen, Mark, you're out of this. I'm going through alone. I don't need your help and I don't want it. If you're that sure of dying and that afraid, why not have the agony over? We've got one heat ray and one detonator, both reliable weapons. Take your choice and kill yourself. Shea and I won't interfere." Brandon's lip curled in a last weak gesture of defiance and then suddenly he capitulated, completely and abjectly. "All right, Warren, I'm with you. I—I guess I didn't quite know what I was doing. I don't feel well, Warren. I—I—"

"Aw, that's all right, boy." Moore was genuinely sorry for him. "Take it easy. I know how you feel. It's got me too. But you mustn't give in to it. Fight it, or you'll go stark, raving mad. Now you just try and get some sleep and leave everything to me. Things will turn out right yet."

Brandon, pressing a hand to an aching forehead, stumbled to the couch and tumbled down. Silent sobs shook his frame while Moore and Shea remained in embarrassed silence nearby.

At last Moore nudged Mike. "Come on," he whispered, "let's get busy. We're going places. Airlock five is at the end of the corridor, isn't it?" Shea nodded and Moore continued, "Is it airtight?"

"Well," said Shea after some thought, "the inner door is, of course, but I don't know anything about the outer one. For all I know it may be a sieve. You see, when I tested the wall for airtightness, I didn't dare open the inner door, because if there was anything wrong with the outer one—blooey!" The accompanying gesture was very expressive.

"Then it's up to us to find out about that outer door right now. I've got to get outside some way and we'll just have to take chances. Where's the spacesuit?"

He grabbed the lone suit from its place in the cupboard, threw it over his shoulder and led the way into the long corridor that ran down the side of the room. He passed closed doors behind whose airtight barriers were what once had been passenger quarters but which were now merely cavities, open to space. At the end of the corridor was the tight-fitting door of Airlock 5.

Moore stopped and surveyed it appraisingly. "Looks all right," he observed, "but of course you can't tell what's outside. God,

I hope it'll work." He frowned. "Of course we could use the entire corridor as an airlock, with the door to our room as the inner door and this as the outer door, but that would mean the loss of half our air supply. We can't afford that—yet."

He turned to Shea. "All right, now. The indicator shows that the lock was last used for entrance, so it should be full of air. Open the door the tiniest crack, and if there's a hissing noise, shut it quick."

"Here goes," and the lever moved one notch. The mechanism had been severely shaken up during the shock of the crash and its former noiseless workings had given way to a harsh, rasping sound, but it was still in commission. A thin black line appeared on the left-hand side of the lock, marking where the door had slid a fraction of an inch on the runners.

There was no hiss! Moore's look of anxiety faded somewhat. He took a small pasteboard from his pocket and held it against the crack. If air were leaking, that card should have held there, pushed by the escaping gas. It fell to the floor.

Mike Shea stuck a forefinger in his mouth and then put it against the crack. "Thank the Lord," he breathed, "not a sign of a draft."

"Good, good. Open it wider. Go ahead."

Another notch and the crack opened farther. And still no draft. Slowly, ever so slowly, notch by notch, it creaked its way wider and wider. The two men held their breaths, afraid that while not actually punctured, the outer door might have been so weakened as to give way any moment. But it held! Moore was jubilant as he wormed into the spacesuit.

"Things are going fine so far, Mike," he said. "You sit down right here and wait for me. I don't know how long I'll take, but I'll be back. Where's the heat ray? Have you got it?"

Shea held out the ray and asked, "But what are you going to do? I'd sort of like to know."

Moore paused as he was about to buckle on the helmet. "Did you hear me say inside that we had water enough to throw away? Well, I've been thinking it over and that's not such a bad idea. I'm going to throw it away." With no other explanation, he stepped into the lock, leaving behind him a very puzzled Mike Shea.

It was with a pounding heart that Moore waited for the outer door to open. His plan was an extraordinarily simple one, but it might not be easy to carry out.

There was a sound of creaking gears and scraping ratchets. Air sighed away to nothingness. The door before him slid open a few inches and stuck. Moore's heart sank as for a moment he thought it would not open at all, but after a few preliminary jerks and rattles the barrier slid the rest of the way.

He clicked on the magnetic grapple and very cautiously put a foot out into space. Clumsily he groped his way out to the side of the ship. He had never been outside a ship in open space before and a vast dread overtook him as he clung there, flylike, to his precarious perch. For a moment dizziness overcame him.

He closed his eyes and for five minutes hung there, clutching the smooth sides of what had once been the *Silver Queen*. The magnetic grapple held him firm and when he opened his eyes once more he found his self-confidence in a measure returned.

He gazed about him. For the first time since the crash he saw the stars instead of the vision of Vesta which their porthole afforded. Eagerly he searched the skies for the little blue-white speck that was Earth. It had often amused him that Earth should always be the first object sought by space travelers when stargazing, but the humor of the situation did not strike him now. However, his search was in vain. From where he lay, Earth was invisible. It, as well as the Sun, must be hidden behind Vesta.

Still, there was much else that he could not help but note. Jupiter was off to the left, a brilliant globe the size of a small pea to the naked eye. Moore observed two of its attendant satellites. Saturn was visible too, as a brilliant planet of some negative magnitude, rivaling Venus as seen from Earth.

Moore had expected that a goodly number of asteroids would be visible—marooned as they were in the asteroid belt—but space seemed surprisingly empty. Once he thought he could see a hurtling body pass within a few miles, but so fast had the impression come and gone that he could not swear that it was not fancy.

And then, of course, there was Vesta. Almost directly below him it loomed like a balloon filling a quarter of the sky. It floated steadily, snowy white, and Moore gazed at it with earnest longing. A good hard kick against the side of the ship, he thought, might start him falling toward Vesta. He *might* land safely and get help for the others. But the chance was too great that he would merely take on a new orbit about Vesta. No, it would have to be better than that.

This reminded him that he had no time to lose. He scanned the side of the ship, looking for the water tank, but all he could see was a jungle of jutting walls, jagged, crumbling, and pointed. He hesitated. Evidently the only thing to do was to make for the lighted porthole to their room and proceed to the tank from there.

Carefully he dragged himself along the wall of the ship. Not five yards from the lock the smoothness stopped abruptly. There was a yawning cavity which Moore recognized as having once been the room adjoining the corridor at the far end. He shuddered. Suppose he were to come across a bloated dead body in one of those rooms. He had known most of the passengers, many of them personally. But he overcame his squeamishness and forced himself to continue his precarious journey toward its goal.

And here he encountered his first practical difficulty. The room itself was made of non-ferrous material in many parts. The magnetic grapple was intended for use only on outer hulls and was useless throughout much of the ship's interior. Moore had forgotten this when suddenly he found himself floating down an incline, his grapple out of use. He gasped and clutched at a nearby projection. Slowly he pulled himself back to safety.

He lay for a moment, almost breathless. Theoretically he should be weightless out here in space—Vesta's influence being negligible—but the regional Gravitator under his room was working. Without the balance of the other Gravitators, it tended to place him under variable and suddenly shifting stresses as he kept changing his position. For his magnetic grapple to let go suddenly might mean being jerked away from the ship altogether. And then what?

Evidently this was going to be even more difficult than he had thought.

He inched forward in a crawl, testing each spot to see if the grapple would hold. Sometimes he had to make long, circuitous journeys to gain a few feet's headway and at other times he was forced to scramble and slip across small patches of non-ferrous material. And always there was that tiring pull of the Gravitator, continually changing directions as he progressed, setting horizontal floors and vertical walls at queer and almost haphazard angles.

Carefully he investigated all objects that he came across. But it was a barren search. Loose articles, chairs, tables had been jerked away at the first shock, probably, and now were independent bodies of the Solar System. He did manage, however, to pick up a small field glass and fountain pen. These he placed in his pocket. They were valueless under present conditions, but somehow they seemed to make more real this macabre trip across the sides of a dead ship.

For fifteen minutes, twenty, half an hour, he labored slowly toward where he thought the porthole should be. Sweat poured down into his eyes and rendered his hair a matted mass. His muscles were beginning to ache under the unaccustomed strain. His mind, already strained by the ordeal of the previous day, was beginning to waver, to play him tricks.

The crawl began to seem eternal, something that had always existed and would exist forever. The object of the journey, that for which he was striving, seemed unimportant; he only knew that it was necessary to move. The time, one hour back, when he had been with Brandon and Shea, seemed hazy and lost in the far past. That more normal time, two days' age, wholly forgotten.

Only the jagged walls before him, only the vital necessity of getting at some uncertain destination existed in his spinning brain. Grasping, straining, pulling. Feeling for the iron alloy. Up and into gaping holes that were rooms and then out again. Feel and pull— feel and pull—and—a light.

Moore stopped. Had he not been glued to the wall he would have fallen. Somehow that light seemed to clear things. It was the porthole; not the many dark, staring ones he had passed, but alive and alight. Behind it was Brandon. A deep breath and he felt better, his mind cleared.

And now his way lay plain before him. Toward that spark of life he crept. Nearer, and nearer, and nearer until he could touch it. He was there!

His eyes drank in the familiar room. God knows that it hadn't any happy associations in his mind, but it was something real, something almost natural. Brandon slept on the couch. His face was worn and lined but a smile passed over it now and then.

Moore raised his fist to knock. He felt the urgent desire to talk with someone, if only by sign language; yet at the last instant he refrained. Perhaps the kid was dreaming of home. He was young and sensitive and had suffered much. Let him sleep. Time enough to wake him when—and if—his idea had been carried through.

He located the wall within the room behind which lay the water tank and then tried to spot it from the outside. Now it was not difficult; its rear wall stood out prominently. Moore marveled, for it seemed a miracle that it had escaped puncture. Perhaps the Fates had not been so ironic after all.

Passage to it was easy though it was on the other side of the fragment. What was once a corridor led almost directly to it. Once when the *Silver Queen* had been whole, that corridor had been level and horizontal, but now, under the unbalanced pull of the regional gravitator, it seemed more of a steep incline than anything else. And yet it made the path simple. Since it was of uniform beryl-steel, Moore found no trouble holding on as he wormed up the twenty-odd feet to the water supply.

And now the crisis—the last stage—had been reached. He felt that he ought to rest first, but his excitement grew rapidly in intensity. It was either now or bust. He pulled himself out to the bottom-center of the tank. There, resting on the small ledge formed by the floor of the corridor that had once extended on that side of the tank, he began operations.

"It's a pity that the main pipe is pointing in the wrong direction," he muttered. "It would have saved me a lot of trouble had it been right. As it is . . ." He sighed and bent to his work. The heat ray was adjusted to maximum concentration and the invisible emanations focused at a spot perhaps a foot above the floor of the tank.

Gradually the effect of the excitatory beam upon the molecules of the wall became noticeable. A spot the size of a dime began shining faintly at the point of focus of the ray gun. It wavered uncertainly, now dimming, now brightening, as Moore strove to steady his tired arm. He propped it on the ledge and achieved better results as the tiny circle of radiation brightened.

Slowly the color ascended the spectrum. The dark, angry red that had first appeared lightened to a cherry color. As the heat continued pouring in, the brightness seemed to ripple out in widening areas, like a target made of successively deepening tints of red. The wall for a distance of some feet from the focal point was becoming uncomfortably hot even though it did not glow and Moore found it necessary to refrain from touching it with the metal of his suit.

Moore cursed steadily, for the ledge itself was also growing hot. It seemed that only imprecations could soothe him. And as the melting wall began to radiate heat in its own right, the chief object of his maledictions were the spacesuit manufacturers. Why didn't they build a suit that could keep heat *out* as well as keep it *in?*

But what Brandon called Professional Optimism crept up. With the salt tang of perspiration in his mouth, he kept consoling himself, "It could be worse, I suppose. At least, the two inches of wall here don't present too much of a barrier. Suppose the tank had been built flush against the outer hull. Whew! Imagine trying to melt through a foot of this." He gritted his teeth and kept on.

The spot of brightness was now flickering into the orange-yellow and Moore knew that the melting point of the beryl-steel alloy would soon be reached. He found himself forced to watch the spot only at widely spaced intervals and then only for fleeting moments.

Evidently it would have to be done quickly if it were to be done at all. The heat ray had not been fully loaded in the first place, and, pouring out energy at maximum as it had been doing for almost ten minutes now, must be approaching exhaustion. Yet the wall was just barely passing the plastic stage. In a fever of impatience, Moore jammed the muzzle of the gun directly at the center of the spot, drawing it back speedily.

A deep depression formed in the soft metal, but a puncture had not been formed. However, Moore was satisfied. He was almost there now. Had there been air between himself and the wall, he would undoubtedly have heard the gurgling and the hissing of the steaming water within. The pressure was building up. How long would the weakened wall endure?

Then so suddenly that Moore did not realize it for a few moments, he was through. A tiny fissure formed at the bottom of that little pit made by the ray gun and in less time than it takes to imagine, the churning water within had its way.

The soft, liquid metal at that spot puffed out, sticking out raggedly around a pea-sized hole. And from that hole there came a hissing and a roaring. A cloud of steam emerged and enveloped Moore.

Through the mist he could see the steam condense almost immediately to ice droplets and saw these icy pellets shrink rapidly into nothingness.

For fifteen minutes he watched the steam shoot out.

Then he became aware of gentle pressure pushing him away from the ship. A savage joy welled up within him as he realized that this was the effect of acceleration on the ship's part. His own inertia was holding him back.

That meant his work had been finished—and successfully. That stream of water was substituting for the rocket blast.

He started back.

If the horrors and dangers of the journey to the tank had been great, those of the way back should have been greater. He was infinitely more tired, his aching eyes were all but blind, and added to the crazy pull of the Gravitator was the force induced by the varying acceleration of the ship. But whatever his labors to return, they did not bother him. In later time, he never even remembered the heartbreaking trip.

How he managed to negotiate the distance in safety he did not know. Most of the time he was lost in a haze of happiness, scarcely realizing the actualities of the situation. His mind was filled with one thought only—to get back quickly, to tell the happy news of their escape.

Suddenly he found himself before the airlock. He hardly grasped the fact that it *was* the airlock. He almost did not understand why he pressed the signal button. Some instinct told him it was the thing to do.

Mike Shea was waiting. There was a creak and a rumble and the outer door started opening, caught, and stopped at the same place as before, but once again it managed to slide the rest of the way. It closed behind Moore, then the inner door opened and he stumbled into Shea's arms.

As in a dream he felt himself half-pulled, half-carried down the corridor to the room. His suit was ripped off. A hot, burning liquid stung his throat. Moore gagged, swallowed, and felt better. Shea pocketed the Jabra bottle once more.

The blurred, shifting images of Brandon and Shea before him steadied and became solid. Moore wiped the perspiration from his face with a trembling hand and essayed a weak smile.

"Wait," protested Brandon, "don't say anything. You look half-dead. Rest, will you!"

But Moore shook his head. In a hoarse, cracked voice he narrated as well as he could the events of the past two hours. The tale was incoherent, scarcely intelligible but marvelously impressive. The two listeners scarcely breathed during the recital.

"You mean," stammered Brandon, "that the water spout is pushing us toward Vesta, like a rocket exhaust?"

"Exactly—same thing as—rocket exhaust," panted Moore. "Ac-

tion and reaction. Is located—on side opposite Vesta—hence pushing us toward Vesta."

Shea was dancing before the porthole. "He's right, Brandon, me
boy. You can make out Bennett's dome as clear as day. We're
getting there, we're getting there."

Moore felt himself recovering. "We're approaching in spiral path
on account of original orbit. We'll land in five or six hours probably. The water will last for quite a long while and the pressure
is still great, since the water issues as steam."

"Steam—at the low temperature of space?" Brandon was surprised.

"Steam—at the low pressure of space!" corrected Moore. "The
boiling point of water falls with the pressure. It is very low indeed
in a vacuum. Even ice has a vapor pressure sufficient to sublime."

He smiled. "As a matter of fact, it freezes and boils at the
same time. I watched it." A short pause, then, "Well, how do you
feel now, Brandon? Much better, eh?"

Brandon reddened and his face fell. He groped vainly for words
for a few moments. Finally he said in a half-whisper, "You know,
I must have acted like a damn fool and a coward at first. I—I
guess I don't deserve all this after going to pieces and letting the
burden of our escape rest on your shoulders.

"I wish you'd beat me up, or something, for punching you before. It'd make me feel better. I mean it." And he really did seem
to mean it.

Moore gave him an affectionate push. "Forget it. You'll never
know how near I came to breaking down myself." He raised his
voice in order to drown out any further apologies on Brandon's
part, "Hey, Mike, stop staring out of that porthole and bring over
that Jabra bottle."

Mike obeyed with alacrity, bringing with him three Plexatron
units to be used as makeshift cups. Moore filled each precisely to the
brim. He was going to be drunk with a vengeance.

"Gentlemen," he said solemnly, "a toast." The three raised the
mugs in unison, "Gentlemen, I give you the year's supply of good
old H_2O *we used to have.*"

Nightfall

*"If the stars should appear one night in a thousand years, how
would men believe and adore, and preserve for many generations the remembrance of the city of God?"*

EMERSON

Aton 77, director of Saro University, thrust out a belligerent lower
lip and glared at the young newspaperman in a hot fury.

Theremon 762 took that fury in his stride. In his earlier days,
when his now widely syndicated column was only a mad idea in a
cub reporter's mind, he had specialized in "impossible" interviews.
It had cost him bruises, black eyes, and broken bones; but it had
given him an ample supply of coolness and self-confidence.

So he lowered the outthrust hand that had been so pointedly ignored and calmly waited for the aged director to get over the worst.
Astronomers were queer ducks, anyway, and if Aton's actions of the
last two months meant anything, this same Aton was the queer-
duckiest of the lot.

Aton 77 found his voice, and though it trembled with restrained
emotion, the careful, somewhat pedantic phraseology, for which the
famous astronomer was noted, did not abandon him.

"Sir," he said, "you display an infernal gall in coming to me with
that impudent proposition of yours."

The husky telephotographer of the Observatory, Beenay 25,
thrust a tongue's tip across dry lips and interposed nervously, "Now,
sir, after all—"

The director turned to him and lifted a white eyebrow. "Do not
interfere, Beenay. I will credit you with good intentions in bringing
this man here; but I will tolerate no insubordination now."

Theremon decided it was time to take a part. "Director Aton, if
you'll let me finish what I started saying, I think—"

"I don't believe, young man," retorted Aton, "that anything you
could say now would count much as compared with your daily col-

umns of these last two months. You have led a vast newspaper campaign against the efforts of myself and my colleagues to organize the world against the menace which it is now too late to avert. You have done your best with your highly personal attacks to make the staff of this Observatory objects of ridicule."

The director lifted a copy of the Saro City *Chronicle* from the table and shook it at Theremon furiously. "Even a person of your well-known impudence should have hesitated before coming to me with a request that he be allowed to cover today's events for his paper. Of all newsmen, you!"

Aton dashed the newspaper to the floor, strode to the window, and clasped his arms behind his back.

"You may leave," he snapped over his shoulder. He stared moodily out at the skyline where Gamma, the brightest of the planet's six suns, was setting. It had already faded and yellowed into the horizon mists, and Aton knew he would never see it again as a sane man.

He whirled. "No, wait, come here!" He gestured peremptorily, "I'll give you your story."

The newsman had made no motion to leave, and now he approached the old man slowly. Aton gestured outward. "Of the six suns, only Beta is left in the sky. Do you see it?"

The question was rather unnecessary. Beta was almost at zenith, its ruddy light flooding the landscape to an unusual orange as the brilliant rays of setting Gamma died. Beta was at aphelion. It was small; smaller than Theremon had ever seen it before, and for the moment it was undisputed ruler of Lagash's sky.

Lagash's own sun, Alpha, the one about which it revolved, was at the antipodes, as were the two distant companion pairs. The red dwarf Beta—Alpha's immediate companion—was alone, grimly alone.

Aton's upturned face flushed redly in the sunlight. "In just under four hours," he said, "civilization, as we know it, comes to an end. It will do so because, as you see, Beta is the only sun in the sky." He smiled grimly. "Print that! There'll be no one to read it."

"But if it turns out that four hours pass—and another four—and nothing happens?" asked Theremon softly.

"Don't let that worry you. Enough will happen."

"Granted! And *still*—if nothing happens?"

For a second time, Beenay 25 spoke. "Sir, I think you ought to listen to him."

Theremon said, "Put it to a vote, Director Aton."

There was a stir among the remaining five members of the Observatory staff, who till now had maintained an attitude of wary neutrality.

"That," stated Aton flatly, "is not necessary." He drew out his pocket watch. "Since your good friend, Beenay, insists so urgently, I will give you five minutes. Talk away."

"Good! Now, just what difference would it make if you allowed me to take down an eyewitness account of what's to come? If your prediction comes true, my presence won't hurt; for in that case my column would never be written. On the other hand, if nothing comes of it, you will just have to expect ridicule or worse. It would be wise to leave that ridicule to friendly hands."

Aton snorted. "Do you mean yours when you speak of friendly hands?"

"Certainly!" Theremon sat down and crossed his legs. "My columns may have been a little rough, but I gave you people the benefit of the doubt every time. After all, this is not the century to preach 'The end of the world is at hand' to Lagash. You have to understand that people don't believe the *Book of Revelations* anymore, and it annoys them to have scientists turn about-face and tell us the Cultists are right after all—"

"No such thing, young man," interrupted Aton. "While a great deal of our data has been supplied us by the Cult, our results contain none of the Cult's mysticism. Facts are facts, and the Cult's so-called mythology *has* certain facts behind it. We've exposed them and ripped away their mystery. I assure you that the Cult hates us now worse than you do."

"I don't hate you. I'm just trying to tell you that the public is in an ugly humor. They're angry."

Aton twisted his mouth in derision. "Let them be angry."

"Yes, but what about tomorrow?"

"There'll be no tomorrow!"

"But if there is. Say that there is—just to see what happens. That anger might take shape into something serious. After all, you know, business has taken a nosedive these last two months. Investors don't really believe the world is coming to an end, but just the same they're being cagy with their money until it's all over. Johnny Public doesn't believe you, either, but the new spring furniture might just as well wait a few months—just to make sure.

"You see the point. Just as soon as this is all over, the business interests will be after your hide. They'll say that if crackpots—begging your pardon—can upset the country's prosperity any time they want, simply by making some cockeyed prediction—it's up to the planet to prevent them. The sparks will fly, sir."

The director regarded the columnist sternly. "And just what were you proposing to do to help the situation?"

"Well"—Theremon grinned—"I was proposing to take charge of the publicity. I can handle things so that only the ridiculous side will show. It would be hard to stand, I admit, because I'd have to make you all out to be a bunch of gibbering idiots, but if I can get people laughing at you, they might forget to be angry. In return for that, all my publisher asks is an exclusive story."

Beenay nodded and burst out, "Sir, the rest of us think he's right. These last two months we've considered everything but the million-to-one chance that there is an error somewhere in our theory or in our calculations. We ought to take care of that, too."

There was a murmur of agreement from the men grouped about the table, and Aton's expression became that of one who found his mouth full of something bitter and couldn't get rid of it.

"You may stay if you wish, then. You will kindly refrain, however, from hampering us in our duties in any way. You will also remember that I am in charge of all activities here, and in spite of your opinions as expressed in your columns, I will expect full cooperation and full respect—"

His hands were behind his back, and his wrinkled face thrust forward determinedly as he spoke. He might have continued indefinitely but for the intrusion of a new voice.

"Hello, hello, hello!" It came in a high tenor, and the plump cheeks of the newcomer expanded in a pleased smile. "What's this morgue-like atmosphere about here? No one's losing his nerve, I hope."

Aton started in consternation and said peevishly, "Now what the devil are you doing here, Sheerin? I thought you were going to stay behind in the Hideout."

Sheerin laughed and dropped his tubby figure into a chair. "Hideout be blowed! The place bored me. I wanted to be here, where things are getting hot. Don't you suppose I have my share of curiosity? I want to see these Stars the Cultists are forever speaking about." He rubbed his hands and added in a soberer tone, "It's freezing outside. The wind's enough to hang icicles on your nose. Beta doesn't seem to give any heat at all, at the distance it is."

The white-haired director ground his teeth in sudden exasperation. "Why do you go out of your way to do crazy things, Sheerin? What kind of good are you around here?"

"What kind of good am I around there?" Sheerin spread his palms in comical resignation. "A psychologist isn't worth his salt in the Hideout. They need men of action and strong, healthy women that can breed children. Me? I'm a hundred pounds too heavy for a man of action, and I wouldn't be a success at breeding children. So why bother them with an extra mouth to feed? I feel better over here."

Theremon spoke briskly. "Just what is the Hideout, sir?"

Sheerin seemed to see the columnist for the first time. He frowned and blew his ample cheeks out. "And just who in Lagash are you, redhead?"

Aton compressed his lips and then muttered sullenly, "That's Theremon 762, the newspaper fellow. I suppose you've heard of him."

The columnist offered his hand. "And, of course, you're Sheerin 501 of Saro University. I've heard of you." Then he repeated, "What is this Hideout, sir?"

"Well," said Sheerin, "we have managed to convince a few people of the validity of our prophecy of—er—doom, to be spectacular about it, and those few have taken proper measures. They consist mainly of the immediate members of the families of the Observatory staff, certain of the faculty of Saro University, and a few outsiders. Altogether, they number about three hundred, but three quarters are women and children."

"I see! They're supposed to hide where the Darkness and the—er —Stars can't get at them, and then hold out when the rest of the world goes poof."

"If they can. It won't be easy. With all of mankind insane, with the great cities going up in flames—environment will not be conducive to survival. But they have food, water, shelter, and weapons—"

"They've got more," said Aton. "They've got all our records, except for what we will collect today. Those records will mean everything to the next cycle, and *that's* what must survive. The rest can go hang."

Theremon uttered a long, low whistle and sat brooding for several minutes. The men about the table had brought out a multi-chess board and started a six-member game. Moves were made rapidly and in silence. All eyes bent in furious concentration on the board. Theremon watched them intently and then rose and approached Aton, who sat apart in whispered conversation with Sheerin.

"Listen," he said, "let's go somewhere where we won't bother the rest of the fellows. I want to ask some questions."

The aged astronomer frowned sourly at him, but Sheerin chirped up, "Certainly. It will do me good to talk. It always does. Aton was telling me about your ideas concerning world reaction to a failure of the prediction—and I agree with you. I read your column pretty regularly, by the way, and as a general thing I like your views."

"Please, Sheerin," growled Aton.

"Eh? Oh, all right. We'll go into the next room. It has softer chairs, anyway."

There were softer chairs in the next room. There were also thick red curtains on the windows and a maroon carpet on the floor. With the bricky light of Beta pouring in, the general effect was one of dried blood.

Theremon shuddered. "Say, I'd give ten credits for a decent dose of white light for just a second. I wish Gamma or Delta were in the sky."

"What are your questions?" asked Aton. "Please remember that our time is limited. In a little over an hour and a quarter we're going upstairs, and after that there will be no time for talk."

"Well, here it is." Theremon leaned back and folded his hands on his chest. "You people seem so all-fired serious about this that I'm beginning to believe you. Would you mind explaining what it's all about?"

Aton exploded, "Do you mean to sit there and tell me that you've been bombarding us with ridicule without even finding out what we've been trying to say?"

The columnist grinned sheepishly. "It's not that bad, sir. I've got the general idea. You say there is going to be a world-wide Darkness in a few hours and that all mankind will go violently insane. What I want now is the science behind it."

"No, you don't. No, you don't," broke in Sheerin. "If you ask Aton for that—supposing him to be in the mood to answer at all—he'll trot out pages of figures and volumes of graphs. You won't make head or tail of it. Now if you were to ask me, I could give you the layman's standpoint."

"All right; I ask you."

"Then first I'd like a drink." He rubbed his hands and looked at Aton.

"Water?" grunted Aton.

"Don't be silly!"

"Don't you be silly. No alcohol today. It would be too easy to get my men drunk. I can't afford to tempt them."

The psychologist grumbled wordlessly. He turned to Theremon, impaled him with his sharp eyes, and began.

"You realize, of course, that the history of civilization on Lagash displays a cyclic character—but I mean, *cyclic!*"

"I know," replied Theremon cautiously, "that that is the current archaeological theory. Has it been accepted as a fact?"

"Just about. In this last century it's been generally agreed upon. This cyclic character is—or rather, was—one of the great mysteries. We've located series of civilizations, nine of them definitely, and indications of others as well, all of which have reached heights comparable to our own, and all of which, without exception, were destroyed by fire at the very height of their culture.

"And no one could tell why. All centers of culture were thoroughly gutted by fire, with nothing left behind to give a hint as to the cause."

Theremon was following closely. "Wasn't there a Stone Age, too?"

"Probably, but as yet practically nothing is known of it, except that men of that age were little more than rather intelligent apes. We can forget about that."

"I see. Go on!"

"There have been explanations of these recurrent catastrophes, all of a more or less fantastic nature. Some say that there are periodic rains of fire; some that Lagash passes through a sun every so often; some even wilder things. But there is one theory, quite different from all of these, that has been handed down over a period of centuries."

"I know. You mean this myth of the 'Stars' that the Cultists have in their *Book of Revelations.*"

"Exactly," rejoined Sheerin with satisfaction. "The Cultists said that every two thousand and fifty years Lagash entered a huge cave, so that all the suns disappeared, and there came *total darkness all over the world!* And then, they say, things called Stars appeared, which robbed men of their souls and left them unreasoning brutes, so that they destroyed the civilization they themselves had built up. Of course they mix all this up with a lot of religio-mystic notions, but that's the central idea."

There was a short pause in which Sheerin drew a long breath. "And now we come to the Theory of Universal Gravitation." He pronounced the phrase so that the capital letters sounded—and at that point Aton turned from the window, snorted loudly, and stalked out of the room.

The two stared after him, and Theremon said, "What's wrong?"

"Nothing in particular," replied Sheerin. "Two of the men were due several hours ago and haven't shown up yet. He's terrifically short-handed, of course, because all but the really essential men have gone to the Hideout."

"You don't think the two deserted, do you?"

"Who? Faro and Yimot? Of course not. Still, if they're not back within the hour, things would be a little sticky." He got to his feet suddenly, and his eyes twinkled. "Anyway, as long as Aton is gone—"

Tiptoeing to the nearest window, he squatted, and from the low window box beneath withdrew a bottle of red liquid that gurgled suggestively when he shook it.

"I *thought* Aton didn't know about this," he remarked as he trotted back to the table. "Here! We've only got one glass so, as the guest, you can have it. I'll keep the bottle." And he filled the tiny cup with judicious care.

Theremon rose to protest, but Sheerin eyed him sternly. "Respect your elders, young man."

The newsman seated himself with a look of anguish on his face. "Go ahead, then, you old villain."

The psychologist's Adam's apple wobbled as the bottle upended, and then, with a satisfied grunt and a smack of the lips, he began again. "But what do you know about gravitation?"

"Nothing, except that it is a very recent development, not too well established, and that the math is so hard that only twelve men in Lagash are supposed to understand it."

"*Tcha!* Nonsense! Baloney! I can give you all the essential math in a sentence. The Law of Universal Gravitation states that there exists a cohesive force among all bodies of the universe, such that the amount of this force between any two given bodies is proportional to the product of their masses divided by the square of the distance between them."

"Is that all?"

"That's enough! It took four hundred years to develop it."

"Why that long? It sounded simple enough, the way you said it."

"Because great laws are not divined by flashes of inspiration, whatever you may think. It usually takes the combined work of a world full of scientists over a period of centuries. After Genovi 41 discovered that Lagash rotated about the sun Alpha rather than vice versa—and that was four hundred years ago—astronomers have been working. The complex motions of the six suns were recorded and analyzed and unwoven. Theory after theory was advanced and checked and counterchecked and modified and abandoned and revived and converted to something else. It was a devil of a job."

Theremon nodded thoughtfully and held out his glass for more liquor. Sheerin grudgingly allowed a few ruby drops to leave the bottle.

"It was twenty years ago," he continued after remoistening his own throat, "that it was finally demonstrated that the Law of Universal Gravitation accounted exactly for the orbital motions of the six suns. It was a great triumph."

Sheerin stood up and walked to the window, still clutching his bottle. "And now we're getting to the point. In the last decade, the motions of Lagash about Alpha were computed according to gravity, and *it did not account for the orbit observed;* not even when all perturbations due to the other suns were included. Either the law was invalid, or there was another, as yet unknown, factor involved."

Theremon joined Sheerin at the window and gazed out past the wooded slopes to where the spires of Saro City gleamed bloodily on the horizon. The newsman felt the tension of uncertainty grow within him as he cast a short glance at Beta. It glowered redly at zenith, dwarfed and evil.

"Go ahead, sir," he said softly.

Sheerin replied, "Astronomers stumbled about for years, each proposed theory more untenable than the one before—until Aton had the inspiration of calling in the Cult. The head of the Cult, Sor 5, had access to certain data that simplified the problem considerably. Aton set to work on a new track.

"What if there were another nonluminous planetary body such as Lagash? If there were, you know, it would shine only by reflected light, and if it were composed of bluish rock, as Lagash itself largely is, then, in the redness of the sky, the eternal blaze of the suns would make it invisible—drown it out completely."

Theremon whistled. "What a screwy idea!"

"You think *that's* screwy? Listen to this: Suppose this body rotated about Lagash at such a distance and in such an orbit and had such a mass that its attraction would exactly account for the deviations of Lagash's orbit from theory—do you know what would happen?"

The columnist shook his head.

"Well, sometimes this body would get in the way of a sun." And Sheerin emptied what remained in the bottle at a draft.

"And it does, I suppose," said Theremon flatly.

"Yes! But only one sun lies in its plane of revolution." He jerked a thumb at the shrunken sun above. "Beta! And it has been shown that the eclipse will occur only when the arrangement of the suns is such that Beta is alone in its hemisphere and at maximum distance, at which time the moon is invariably at minimum distance. The eclipse that results, with the moon seven times the apparent diameter of Beta, covers all of Lagash and lasts well over half a day, so that no spot on the planet escapes the effects. *That eclipse comes once every two thousand and forty-nine years.*"

Theremon's face was drawn into an expressionless mask. "And that's my story?"

The psychologist nodded. "That's all of it. First the eclipse—which will start in three quarters of an hour—then universal Darkness and, maybe, these mysterious Stars—then madness, and end of the cycle."

He brooded. "We had two months' leeway—we at the Observatory—and that wasn't enough time to persuade Lagash of the danger. Two centuries might not have been enough. But our records are at the Hideout, and today we photograph the eclipse. The next cycle will *start off* with the truth, and when the *next* eclipse comes, mankind will at last be ready for it. Come to think of it, that's part of your story too."

A thin wind ruffled the curtains at the window as Theremon opened it and leaned out. It played coldly with his hair as he stared at the crimson sunlight on his hand. Then he turned in sudden rebellion.

"What is there in Darkness to drive *me* mad?"

Sheerin smiled to himself as he spun the empty liquor bottle with abstracted motions of his hand. "Have you ever experienced Darkness, young man?"

The newsman leaned against the wall and considered. "No. Can't say I have. But I know what it is. Just—uh—" He made vague motions with his fingers and then brightened. "Just no light. Like in caves."

"Have you ever been in a cave?"

"In a *cave!* Of course not!"

"I thought not. *I* tried last week—just to see—but I got out in a hurry. I went in until the mouth of the cave was just visible as a blur of light, with black everywhere else. I never thought a person my weight could run that fast."

Theremon's lip curled. "Well, if it comes to that, I guess I wouldn't have run if I had been there."

The psychologist studied the young man with an annoyed frown.

"My, don't you talk big! I dare you to draw the curtain."

Theremon looked his surprise and said, "What for? If we had four or five suns out there, we might want to cut the light down a bit for comfort, but now we haven't enough light as it is."

"That's the point. Just draw the curtain; then come here and sit down."

"All right." Theremon reached for the tasseled string and jerked. The red curtain slid across the wide window, the brass rings hissing their way along the crossbar, and a dusk-red shadow clamped down on the room.

Theremon's footsteps sounded hollowly in the silence as he made his way to the table, and then they stopped halfway. "I can't see you, sir," he whispered.

"Feel your way," ordered Sheerin in a strained voice.

"But I can't see you, sir." The newsman was breathing harshly. "I can't see anything."

"What did you expect?" came the grim reply. "Come here and sit down!"

The footsteps sounded again, waveringly, approaching slowly. There was the sound of someone fumbling with a chair. Theremon's voice came thinly, "Here I am. I feel . . . *ulp* . . . all right."

"You like it, do you?"

"N—no. It's pretty awful. The walls seem to be—" He paused. "They seem to be closing in on me. I keep wanting to push them away. But I'm not going *mad!* In fact, the feeling isn't as bad as it was."

"All right. Draw the curtain back again."

There were cautious footsteps through the dark, the rustle of Theremon's body against the curtain as he felt for the tassel, and then the triumphant *ro-o-osh* of the curtain slithering back. Red light flooded the room, and with a cry of joy Theremon looked up at the sun.

Sheerin wiped the moistness off his forehead with the back of a hand and said shakily, "And that was just a dark room."

"It can be stood," said Theremon lightly.

"Yes, a dark room can. But were you at the Jonglor Centennial Exposition two years ago?"

"No, it so happens I never got around to it. Six thousand miles was just a bit too much to travel, even for the exposition."

"Well, I was there. You remember hearing about the 'Tunnel of Mystery' that broke all records in the amusement area—for the first month or so, anyway?"

"Yes. Wasn't there some fuss about it?"

"Very little. It was hushed up. You see, that Tunnel of Mystery was just a mile-long tunnel—with no lights. You got into a little open car and jolted along through Darkness for fifteen minutes. It was very popular—while it lasted."

"Popular?"

"Certainly. There's a fascination in being frightened *when it's part of a game*. A baby is born with three instinctive fears: of loud noises, of falling, and of the absence of light. That's why it's considered so funny to jump at someone and shout 'Boo!' That's why it's such fun to ride a roller coaster. And that's why that Tunnel of Mystery started cleaning up. People came out of that Darkness shaking, breathless, half dead with fear, but they kept on paying to get in."

"Wait a while, I remember now. Some people came out dead, didn't they? There were rumors of that after it shut down."

The psychologist snorted. "Bah! Two or three died. That was nothing! They paid off the families of the dead ones and argued the Jonglor City Council into forgetting it. After all, they said, if people with weak hearts want to go through the tunnel, it was at their own risk—and besides, it wouldn't happen again. So they put a doctor in the front office and had every customer go through a physical examination before getting into the car. That actually *boosted* ticket sales."

"Well, then?"

"But you see, there was something else. People sometimes came out in perfect order, except that they refused to go into buildings— any buildings; including palaces, mansions, apartment houses, tenements, cottages, huts, shacks, lean-tos, and tents."

Theremon looked shocked. "You mean they refused to come in out of the open? Where'd they sleep?"

"In the open."

"They should have *forced* them inside."

"Oh, they did, they did. Whereupon these people went into violent hysterics and did their best to bat their brains out against the nearest wall. Once you got them inside, you couldn't keep them there without a strait jacket or a heavy dose of tranquilizer."

"They must have been crazy."

"Which is exactly what they were. One person out of every ten who went into that tunnel came out that way. They called in the psychologists, and we did the only thing possible. We closed down the exhibit." He spread his hands.

"What was the matter with these people?" asked Theremon finally.

"Essentially the same thing that was the matter with you when you thought the walls of the room were crushing in on you in the dark. There is a psychological term for mankind's instinctive fear of the absence of light. We call it 'claustrophobia,' because the lack of light is always tied up with enclosed places, so that fear of one is fear of the other. You see?"

"And those people of the tunnel?"

"Those people of the tunnel consisted of those unfortunates whose mentality did not quite possess the resiliency to overcome the claustrophobia that overtook them in the Darkness. Fifteen minutes without light is a long time; you only had two or three minutes, and I believe you were fairly upset.

"The people of the tunnel had what is called 'claustrophobic fixation.' Their latent fear of Darkness and enclosed places had crystalized and become active, and, as far as we can tell, permanent. That's what fifteen minutes in the dark will do."

There was a long silence, and Theremon's forehead wrinkled slowly into a frown. "I don't believe it's that bad."

"You mean you don't want to believe," snapped Sheerin. "You're afraid to believe. Look out the window!"

Theremon did so, and the psychologist continued without pausing. "Imagine Darkness—everywhere. No light, as far as you can see. The houses, the trees, the fields, the earth, the sky—black! And Stars thrown in, for all I know—whatever *they* are. Can you conceive it?"

"Yes, I can," declared Theremon truculently.

And Sheerin slammed his fist down upon the table in sudden passion. "You lie! You can't conceive that. Your brain wasn't built for the conception any more than it was built for the conception of infinity or of eternity. You can only talk about it. A fraction of the reality upsets you, and when the real thing comes, your brain is going to be presented with the phenomenon outside its limits of comprehension. You will go mad, completely and permanently! There is no question of it!"

He added sadly, "And another couple of millennia of painful struggle comes to nothing. Tomorrow there won't be a city standing unharmed in all Lagash."

Theremon recovered part of his mental equilibrium. "That doesn't follow. I still don't see that I can go loony just because there isn't a sun in the sky—but even if I did, and everyone else did, how does that harm the cities? Are we going to blow them down?"

But Sheerin was angry, too. "If you were is Darkness, what would you want more than anything else; what would it be that every instinct would call for? Light, damn you, *light!*"

"Well?"

"And how would you get light?"

"I don't know," said Theremon flatly.

"What's the *only* way to get light, short of a sun?"

"How should I know?"

They were standing face to face and nose to nose.

Sheerin said, "You burn something, mister. Ever see a forest fire? Ever go camping and cook a stew over a wood fire? Heat isn't the only thing burning wood gives off, you know. It gives off light, and people know that. And when it's dark they want light, and they're going to *get* it."

"So they burn wood?"

"So they burn whatever they can get. They've got to have light. They've got to burn something, and wood isn't handy—so they'll burn whatever is nearest. They'll have their light—and every center of habitation goes up in flames!"

Eyes held each other as though the whole matter were a personal affair of respective will powers, and then Theremon broke away wordlessly. His breathing was harsh and ragged, and he scarcely noted the sudden hubbub that came from the adjoining room behind the closed door.

Sheerin spoke, and it was with an effort that he made it sound matter-of-fact. "I think I heard Yimot's voice. He and Faro are probably back. Let's go in and see what kept them."

"Might as well!" muttered Theremon. He drew a long breath and seemed to shake himself. The tension was broken.

The room was in an uproar, with members of the staff clustering about two young men who were removing outer garments even as they parried the miscellany of questions being thrown at them.

Aton bustled through the crowd and faced the newcomers angrily. "Do you realize that it's less than half an hour before deadline? Where have you two been?"

Faro 24 seated himself and rubbed his hands. His cheeks were red with the outdoor chill. "Yimot and I have just finished carrying through a little crazy experiment of our own. We've been trying to see if we couldn't construct an arrangement by which we could simulate the appearance of Darkness and Stars so as to get an advance notion as to how it looked."

There was a confused murmur from the listeners, and a sudden look of interest entered Aton's eyes. "There wasn't anything said of this before. How did you go about it?"

"Well," said Faro, "the idea came to Yimot and myself long ago, and we've been working it out in our spare time. Yimot knew of a low one-story house down in the city with a domed roof—it had once been used as a museum, I think. Anyway, we bought it—"

"Where did you get the money?" interrupted Aton peremptorily.

"Our bank accounts," grunted Yimot 70. "It cost two thousand credits." Then, defensively, "Well, what of it? Tomorrow, two thousand credits will be two thousand pieces of paper. That's all."

"Sure," agreed Faro. "We bought the place and rigged it up with black velvet from top to bottom so as to get as perfect a Darkness as possible. Then we punched tiny holes in the ceiling and through the roof and covered them with little metal caps, all of which could be shoved aside simultaneously at the close of a switch. At least we didn't do that part ourselves; we got a carpenter and an electrician and some others—money didn't count. The point was that we could get the light to shine through those holes in the roof, so that we could get a starlike effect."

Not a breath was drawn during the pause that followed. Aton said stiffly, "You had no right to make a private—"

Faro seemed abashed. "I know, sir—but frankly, Yimot and I thought the experiment was a little dangerous. If the effect really worked, we half expected to go mad—from what Sheerin says about all this, we thought that would be rather likely. We wanted to take the risk ourselves. Of course if we found we could retain sanity, it occurred to us that we might develop immunity to the real thing, and then expose the rest of you the same way. But things didn't work out at all—"

"Why, what happened?"

It was Yimot who answered. "We shut ourselves in and allowed our eyes to get accustomed to the dark. It's an extremely creepy feeling because the total Darkness makes you feel as if the walls and ceiling are crushing in on you. But we got over that and pulled the switch. The caps fell away and the roof glittered all over with little dots of light—"

"Well?"

"Well—nothing. That was the whacky part of it. Nothing happened. It was just a roof with holes in it, and that's just what it looked like. We tried it over and over again—that's what kept us so late—but there just isn't any effect at all."

There followed a shocked silence, and all eyes turned to Sheerin, who sat motionless, mouth open.

Theremon was the first to speak. "You know what this does to this whole theory you've built up, Sheerin, don't you?" He was grinning with relief.

But Sheerin raised his hand. "Now wait a while. Just let me think this through." And then he snapped his fingers, and when he lifted his head there was neither surprise nor uncertainty in his eyes. "Of course—"

He never finished. From somewhere up above there sounded a sharp clang, and Beenay, starting to his feet, dashed up the stairs with a "What the devil!"

The rest followed after.

Things happened quickly. Once up in the dome, Beenay cast one horrified glance at the shattered photographic plates and at the man bending over them; and then hurled himself fiercely at the intruder, getting a death grip on his throat. There was a wild threshing, and as others of the staff joined in, the stranger was swallowed up and smothered under the weight of half a dozen angry men.

Aton came up last, breathing heavily. "Let him up!"

There was a reluctant unscrambling and the stranger, panting harshly, with his clothes torn and his forehead bruised, was hauled to his feet. He had a short yellow beard curled elaborately in the style affected by the Cultists.

Beenay shifted his hold to a collar grip and shook the man savagely. "All right, rat, what's the idea? These plates—"

"I wasn't after *them,*" retorted the Cultist coldly. "That was an accident."

Beenay followed his glowering stare and snarled, "I see. You were after the cameras themselves. The accident with the plates was a stroke of luck for you, then. If you had touched Snapping Bertha or any of the others, you would have died by slow torture. As it is—" He drew his fist back.

Aton grabbed his sleeve. "Stop that! Let him go!"

The young technician wavered, and his arm dropped reluctantly. Aton pushed him aside and confronted the Cultist. "You're Latimer, aren't you?"

The Cultist bowed stiffly and indicated the symbol upon his hip. "I am Latimer 25, adjutant of the third class to his serenity, Sor 5."

"And"—Aton's white eyebrows lifted—"you were with his serenity when he visited me last week, weren't you?"

Latimer bowed a second time.

"Now, then, what do you want?"

"Nothing that you would give me of your own free will."

"Sor 5 sent you, I suppose—or is this your own idea?"

"I won't answer that question."

"Will there be any further visitors?"

"I won't answer that, either."

Aton glanced at his timepiece and scowled. "Now, man, what is it your master wants of me? I have fulfilled my end of the bargain."

Latimer smiled faintly, but said nothing.

"I asked him," continued Aton angrily, "for data only the Cult could supply, and it was given to me. For that, thank you. In return I promised to prove the essential truth of the creed of the Cult."

"There was no need to prove that," came the proud retort. "It stands proven by the *Book of Revelations.*"

"For the handful that constitute the Cult, yes. Don't pretend to mistake my meaning. I offered to present scientific backing for your beliefs. And I did!"

The Cultist's eyes narrowed bitterly. "Yes, you did—with a fox's subtlety, for your pretended explanation backed our beliefs, and at the same time removed all necessity for them. You made of the Darkness and of the Stars a natural phenomenon and removed all its real significance. That was blasphemy."

"If so, the fault isn't mine. The facts exist. What can I do but state them?"

"Your 'facts' are a fraud and a delusion."

Aton stamped angrily. "How do you know?"

And the answer came with the certainty of absolute faith. "I know!"

The director purpled and Beenay whispered urgently. Aton waved him silent. "And what does Sor 5 want us to do? He still thinks, I suppose, that in trying to warn the world to take measures against the menace of madness, we are placing innumerable souls in jeopardy. We aren't succeeding, if that means anything to him."

"The attempt itself has done harm enough, and your vicious effort to gain information by means of your devilish instruments must be stopped. We obey the will of the Stars, and I only regret that my clumsiness prevented me from wrecking your infernal devices."

"It wouldn't have done you too much good," returned Aton. "All our data, except for the direct evidence we intend collecting right now, is already safely cached and well beyond possibility of harm." He smiled grimly. "But that does not affect your present status as an attempted burglar and criminal."

He turned to the men behind him. "Someone call the police at Saro City."

There was a cry of distaste from Sheerin. "Damn it, Aton, what's wrong with you? There's no time for that. Here"—he bustled his way forward—"let me handle this."

Aton stared down his nose at the psychologist. "This is not the time for your monkeyshines, Sheerin. Will you please let me handle this my own way? Right now you are a complete outsider here, and don't forget it."

Sheerin's mouth twisted eloquently. "Now why should we go to the impossible trouble of calling the police—with Beta's eclipse a matter of minutes from now—when this young man here is perfectly willing to pledge his word of honor to remain and cause no trouble whatsoever?"

The Cultist answered promptly, "I will do no such thing. You're free to do what you want, but it's only fair to warn you that just as soon as I get my chance I'm going to finish what I came out here to do. If it's my word of honor you're relying on, you'd better call the police."

Sheerin smiled in a friendly fashion. "You're a determined cuss, aren't you? Well, I'll explain something. Do you see that young man at the window? He's a strong, husky fellow, quite handy with his fists, and he's an outsider besides. Once the eclipse starts there will be nothing for him to do except keep an eye on you. Besides him, there will be myself—a little too stout for active fisticuffs, but still able to help."

"Well, what of it?" demanded Latimer frozenly.

"Listen and I'll tell you," was the reply. "Just as soon as the eclipse starts, we're going to take you, Theremon and I, and deposit you in a little closet with one door, to which is attached one giant lock and no windows. You will remain there for the duration."

"And afterward," breathed Latimer fiercely, "there'll be no one to let me out. I know as well as you do what the coming of the Stars means—I know it far better than you. With all your minds gone, you are not likely to free me. Suffocation or slow starvation, is it? About what I might have expected from a group of scientists. But I don't give my word. It's a matter of principle, and I won't discuss it further."

Aton seemed perturbed. His faded eyes were troubled. "Really, Sheerin, locking him—"

"Please!" Sheerin motioned him impatiently to silence. "I don't think for a moment things will go that far. Latimer has just tried a clever little bluff, but I'm not a psychologist just because I like the sound of the word." He grinned at the Cultist. "Come now, you don't really think I'm trying anything as crude as slow starvation. My dear Latimer, if I lock you in the closet, you are not going to see the Darkness, and you are not going to see the Stars. It does not take much knowledge of the fundamental creed of the Cult to realize that for you to be hidden from the Stars when they appear means the loss of your immortal soul. Now, I believe you to be an honorable man. I'll accept your word of honor to make no further effort to disrupt proceedings, if you'll offer it."

A vein throbbed in Latimer's temple, and he seemed to shrink within himself as he said thickly, "You have it!" And then he added with swift fury, "But it is my consolation that you will all be damned for your deeds of today." He turned on his heel and stalked to the high three-legged stool by the door.

Sheerin nodded to the columnist. "Take a seat next to him, Theremon—just as a formality. Hey, Theremon!"

But the newspaperman didn't move. He had gone pale to the lips. "Look at that!" The finger he pointed toward the sky shook, and his voice was dry and cracked.

There was one simultaneous gasp as every eye followed the pointing finger and, for one breathless moment, stared frozenly.

Beta was chipped on one side!

The tiny bit of encroaching blackness was perhaps the width of a fingernail, but to the staring watchers it magnified itself into the crack of doom.

Only for a moment they watched, and after that there was a shrieking confusion that was even shorter of duration and which gave way to an orderly scurry of activity—each man at his prescribed job. At the crucial moment there was no time for emotion. The men were merely scientists with work to do. Even Aton had melted away.

Sheerin said prosaically, "First contact must have been made fifteen minutes ago. A little early, but pretty good considering the uncertainties involved in the calculation." He looked about him and then tiptoed to Theremon, who still remained staring out the window, and dragged him away gently.

"Aton is furious," he whispered, "so stay away. He missed first contact on account of this fuss with Latimer, and if you get in his way he'll have you thrown out the window."

Theremon nodded shortly and sat down. Sheerin stared in surprise at him.

"The devil, man," he exclaimed, "you're shaking."

"Eh?" Theremon licked dry lips and then tried to smile. "I don't feel very well, and that's a fact."

The psychologist's eyes hardened. "You're not losing your nerve?"

"No!" cried Theremon in a flash of indignation. "Give me a chance, will you? I haven't really believed this rigmarole—not way down beneath, anyway—till just this minute. Give me a chance to get used to the idea. You've been preparing yourself for two months or more."

"You're right, at that," replied Sheerin thoughtfully. "Listen! Have you got a family—parents, wife, children?"

Theremon shook his head. "You mean the Hideout, I suppose. No, you don't have to worry about that. I have a sister, but she's two thousand miles away. I don't even know her exact address."

"Well, then, what about yourself? You've got time to get there, and they're one short anyway, since I left. After all, you're not needed here, and you'd made a darned fine addition—"

Theremon looked at the other wearily. "You think I'm scared stiff, don't you? Well, get this, mister, I'm a newspaperman and I've been assigned to cover a story. I intend covering it."

There was a faint smile on the psychologist's face. "I see. Professional honor, is that it?"

"You might call it that. But, man, I'd give my right arm for another bottle of that sockeroo juice even half the size of the one you hogged. If ever a fellow needed a drink, I do."

He broke off. Sheerin was nudging him violently. "Do you hear that? Listen!"

Theremon followed the motion of the other's chin and stared at the Cultist, who, obvious to all about him, faced the window, a look of wild elation on his face, droning to himself the while in singsong fashion.

"What's he saying?" whispered the columnist.

"He's quoting *Book of Revelations,* fifth chapter," replied Sheerin. Then, urgently, "Keep quiet and listen, I tell you."

The Cultist's voice had risen in a sudden increase of fervor: " 'And it came to pass that in those days the Sun, Beta, held lone vigil in the sky for ever longer periods as the revolutions passed; until such time as for full half a revolution, it alone, shrunken and cold, shone down upon Lagash.

" 'And men did assemble in the public squares and in the highways, there to debate and to marvel at the sight, for a strange depression had seized them. Their minds were troubled and their speech confused, for the souls of men awaited the coming of the Stars.

" 'And in the city of Trigon, at high noon, Vendret 2 came forth and said unto the men of Trigon, "Lo, ye sinners! Though ye scorn the ways of righteousness, yet will the time of reckoning come. Even now the Cave approaches to swallow Lagash; yea, and all it contains."

" 'And even as he spoke the lip of the Cave of Darkness passed the edge of Beta so that to all Lagash it was hidden from sight. Loud were the cries of men as it vanished, and great the fear of soul that fell upon them.

" 'It came to pass that the Darkness of the Cave fell upon Lagash, and there was no light on all the surface of Lagash. Men were even as blinded, nor could one man see his neighbor, though he felt his breath upon his face.

" 'And in this blackness there appeared the Stars, in countless numbers, and to the strains of music of such beauty that the very leaves of the trees cried out in wonder.

" 'And in that moment the souls of men departed from them, and their abandoned bodies became even as beasts; yea, even as brutes of the wild; so that through the blackened streets of the cities of Lagash they prowled with wild cries.

" 'From the Stars there then reached down the Heavenly Flame, and where it touched, the cities of Lagash flamed to utter destruction, so that of man and of the works of man nought remained.

" 'Even then—' "

There was a subtle change in Latimer's tone. His eyes had not shifted, but somehow he had become aware of the absorbed attention of the other two. Easily, without pausing for breath, the timbre of his voice shifted and the syllables became more liquid.

Theremon, caught by surprise, stared. The words seemed on the border of familiarity. There was an elusive shift in the accent, a tiny change in the vowel stress; nothing more—yet Latimer had become thoroughly unintelligible.

Sheerin smiled slyly. "He shifted to some old-cycle tongue, probably their traditional second cycle. That was the language in which the *Book of Revelations* was originally written, you know."

"It doesn't matter; I've heard enough." Theremon shoved his chair back and brushed his hair back with hands that no longer shook. "I feel much better now."

"You do?" Sheerin seemed mildly surprised.

"I'll say I do. I had a bad case of jitters just a while back. Listening to you and your gravitation and seeing that eclipse start almost finished me. But this"—he jerked a contemptuous thumb at the yellow-beared Cultist—"*this* is the sort of thing my nurse used to tell me. I've been laughing at that sort of thing all my life. I'm not going to let it scare me *now*."

He drew a deep breath and said with a hectic gaiety, "But if I expect to keep on the good side of myself, I'm going to turn my chair away from the window."

Sheerin said, "Yes, but you'd better talk lower. Aton just lifted his head out of that box he's got it stuck into and gave you a look that should have killed you."

Theremon made a mouth. "I forgot about the old fellow." With elaborate care he turned the chair from the window, cast one distasteful look over his shoulder, and said, "It has occurred to me that there must be considerable immunity against this Star madness."

The psychologist did not answer immediately. Beta was past its zenith now, and the square of bloody sunlight that outlined the window upon the floor had lifted into Sheerin's lap. He stared at its dusky color thoughtfully and then bent and squinted into the sun itself.

The chip in its side had grown to a black encroachment that covered a third of Beta. He shuddered, and when he straightened once more his florid cheeks did not contain quite as much color as they had had previously.

With a smile that was almost apologetic, he reversed his chair also. "There are probably two million people in Saro City that are all trying to join the Cult at once in one gigantic revival." Then, ironically, "The Cult is in for an hour of unexampled prosperity. I trust they'll make the most of it. Now, what was it you said?"

"Just this. How did the Cultists manage to keep the *Book of Revelations* going from cycle to cycle, and how on Lagash did it get written in the first place? There must have been some sort of immunity, for if everyone had gone mad, who would be left to write the book?"

Sheerin stared at his questioner ruefully. "Well, now, young man, there isn't any eyewitness answer to that, but we've got a few damned good notions as to what happened. You see, there are three kinds of people who might remain relatively unaffected. First, the very few who don't see the Stars at all: the seriously retarded or those who drink themselves into a stupor at the beginning of the eclipse and remain so to the end. We leave them out—because they aren't really witnesses.

"Then there are children below six, to whom the world as a whole is too new and strange for them to be too frightened at Stars and Darkness. They would be just another item in an already surprising world. You see that, don't you?"

The other nodded doubtfully. "I suppose so."

"Lastly, there are those whose minds are too coarsely grained to be entirely toppled. The very insensitive would be scarcely affected— oh, such people as some of our older, work-broken peasants. Well, the children would have fugitive memories, and that, combined with the confused, incoherent babblings of the half-mad morons, formed the basis for the *Book of Revelations*.

"Naturally, the book was based, in the first place, on the testimony of those least qualified to serve as historians; that is, children and morons; and was probably edited and re-edited through the cycles."

"Do you suppose," broke in Theremon, "that they carried the book through the cycles the way we're planning on handing on the secret of gravitation?"

Sheerin shrugged. "Perhaps, but their exact method is unimportant. They do it, somehow. The point I was getting at was that the book can't help but be a mass of distortion, even if it is based on fact. For instance, do you remember the experiment with the holes in the roof that Faro and Yimot tried—the one that didn't work?"

"Yes."

"You know why it didn't w—" He stopped and rose in alarm, for Aton was approaching, his face a twisted mask of consternation. *"What's happened?"*

Aton drew him aside and Sheerin could feel the fingers on his elbow twitching.

"Not so loud!" Aton's voice was low and tortured. "I've just gotten word from the Hideout on the private line."

Sheerin broke in anxiously. "They are in trouble?"

"Not *they*." Aton stressed the pronoun significantly. "They sealed themselves off just a while ago, and they're going to stay buried till day after tomorrow. They're safe. But the *city*, Sheerin—it's a shambles. You have no idea—" He was having difficulty in speaking.

"Well?" snapped Sheerin impatiently. "What of it? It will get worse. What are you shaking about?" Then, suspiciously, "How do you feel?"

Aton's eyes sparked angrily at the insinuation, and then faded to anxiety once more. "You don't understand. The Cultists are active. They're rousing the people to storm the Observatory—promising them immediate entrance into grace, promising them salvation, promising them anything. What are we to do, Sheerin?"

Sheerin's head bent, and he stared in long abstraction at his toes. He tapped his chin with one knuckle, then looked up and said crisply, "Do? What is there to do? Nothing at all. Do the men know of this?"

"No, of course not!"

"Good! Keep it that way. How long till totality?"

"Not quite an hour."

"There's nothing to do but gamble. It will take time to organize any really formidable mob, and it will take more time to get them out here. We're a good five miles from the city—"

He glared out the window, down the slopes to where the farmed patches gave way to clumps of white houses in the suburbs; down to where the metropolis itself was a blur on the horizon—a mist in the waning blaze of Beta.

He repeated without turning, "It will take time. Keep on working and pray that totality comes first."

Beta was cut in half, the line of division pushing a slight concavity into the still-bright portion of the Sun. It was like a gigantic eyelid shutting slantwise over the light of a world.

The faint clatter of the room in which he stood faded into oblivion, and he sensed only the thick silence of the fields outside. The very insects seemed frightened mute. And things were dim.

He jumped at the voice in his ear. Theremon said, "Is something wrong?"

"Er? Er—no. Get back to the chair. We're in the way." They slipped back to their corner, but the psychologist did not speak for a time. He lifted a finger and loosened his collar. He twisted his neck back and forth but found no relief. He looked up suddenly.

"Are you having any difficulty in breathing?"

The newspaperman opened his eyes wide and drew two or three long breaths. "No. Why?"

"I looked out the window too long, I suppose. The dimness got

me. Difficulty in breathing is one of the first symptoms of a claustrophobic attack."

Theremon drew another long breath. "Well, it hasn't got me yet.
Say, here's another of the fellows."

Beenay had interposed his bulk between the light and the pair in
the corner, and Sheerin squinted up at him anxiously. "Hello,
Beenay."

The astronomer shifted his weight to the other foot and smiled
feebly. "You won't mind if I sit down awhile and join in the talk?
My cameras are set, and there's nothing to do till totality." He
paused and eyed the Cultist, who fifteen minutes earlier had drawn
a small, skin-bound book from his sleeve and had been poring intently over it ever since. "That rat hasn't been making trouble, has
he?"

Sheerin shook his head. His shoulders were thrown back and he
frowned his concentration as he forced himself to breathe regularly.
He said, "Have you had any trouble breathing, Beenay?"

Beenay sniffed the air in his turn. "It doesn't seem stuffy to me."

"A touch of claustrophobia," explained Sheerin apologetically.

"Ohhh! It worked itself differently with me. I get the impression
that my eyes are going back on me. Things seem to blur and—
well, nothing is clear. And it's cold, too."

"Oh, it's cold all right. That's no illusion." Theremon grimaced.
"My toes feel as if I've been shipping them cross-country in a
refrigerating car."

"What we need," put in Sheerin, "is to keep our minds busy with
extraneous affairs. I was telling you a while ago, Theremon, why
Faro's experiments with the holes in the roof came to nothing."

"You were just beginning," replied Theremon. He encircled a
knee with both arms and nuzzled his chin against it.

"Well, as I started to say, they were misled by taking the *Book of
Revelations* literally. There probably wasn't any sense in attaching
any physical significance to the Stars. It might be, you know, that in
the presence of total Darkness, the mind finds it absolutely necessary to create light. This illusion of light might be all the Stars there
really are."

"In other words," interposed Theremon, "you mean the Stars are
the results of the madness and not one of the causes. Then, what
good will Beenay's photographs be?"

"To prove that it is an illusion, maybe; or to prove the opposite; for all I know. Then again—"

But Beenay had drawn his chair closer, and there was an expression of enthusiasm on his face. "Say, I'm glad you two got onto this subject." His eyes narrowed and he lifted one finger. "I've been thinking about these Stars and I've got a really cute notion. Of course it's strictly ocean foam, and I'm not trying to advance it seriously, but I think it's interesting. Do you want to hear it?"

He seemed half reluctant, but Sheerin leaned back and said, "Go ahead! I'm listening."

"Well, then, supposing there were other suns in the universe." He broke off a little bashfully. "I mean suns that are so far away that they're too dim to see. It sounds as if I've been reading some of that fantastic fiction, I suppose."

"Not necessarily. Still, isn't that possibility eliminated by the fact that, according to the Law of Gravitation, they would make themselves evident by their attractive forces?"

"Not if they were far enough off," rejoined Beenay. "really far off—maybe as much as four light years, or even more. We'd never be able to detect perturbations then, because they'd be too small. Say that there were a lot of suns that far off; a dozen or two, maybe."

Theremon whistled melodiously. "What an idea for a good Sunday supplement article. Two dozen suns in a universe eight light years across. Wow! That would shrink our world into insignificance. The readers would eat it up."

"Only an idea," said Beenay with a grin, "but you see the point. During an eclipse, these dozen suns would become visible because there'd be no *real* sunlight to drown them out. Since they are so far off, they'd appear small, like so many little marbles. Of course the Cultists talk of millions of Stars, but that's probably exaggeration. There just isn't any place in the universe you could put a million suns —unless they touch each other."

Sheerin had listened with gradually increasing interest. "You've hit something there, Beenay. And exaggeration is just exactly what would happen. Our minds, as you probably know, can't grasp directly any number higher than five; above that there is only the concept of 'many.' A dozen would become a million just like that. A damn good idea!"

"And I've got another cute little notion," Beenay said. "Have you ever thought what a simple problem gravitation would be if only you had a sufficiently simple system? Supposing you had a universe in which there was a planet with only one sun. The planet would travel in a perfect ellipse and the exact nature of the gravitational force would be so evident it could be accepted as an axiom. Astronomers on such a world would start off with gravity probably before they even invented the telescope. Naked-eye observation would be enough."

"But would such a system be dynamically stable?" questioned Sheerin doubtfully.

"Sure! They call it the 'one-and-one' case. It's been worked out mathematically, but it's the philosophical implications that interest me."

"It's nice to think about," admitted Sheerin, "as a pretty abstraction—like a perfect gas, or absolute zero."

"Of course," continued Beenay, "there's the catch that life would be impossible on such a planet. It wouldn't get enough heat and light, and if it rotated there would be total Darkness half of each day. You couldn't expect life—which is fundamentally dependent upon light—to develop under those conditions. Besides—"

Sheerin's chair went over backward as he sprang to his feet in a rude interruption. "Aton's brought out the lights."

Beenay said, "Huh," turned to stare, and then grinned halfway around his head in open relief.

There were half a dozen foot-long, inch-thick rods cradled in Aton's arms. He glared over them at the assembled staff members.

"Get back to work, all of you. Sheerin, come here and help me!"

Sheerin trotted to the older man's side and, one by one, in utter silence, the two adjusted the rods in makeshift metal holders suspended from the walls.

With the air of one carrying through the most sacred item of a religious ritual, Sheerin scraped a large, clumsy match into spluttering life and passed it to Aton, who carried the flame to the upper end of one of the rods.

It hesitated there awhile, playing futilely about the tip, until a sudden, crackling flare cast Aton's lined face into yellow highlights. He withdrew the match and a spontaneous cheer rattled the window.

The rod was topped by six inches of wavering flame! Methodically, the other rods were lighted, until six independent fires turned the rear of the room yellow.

The light was dim, dimmer even than the tenuous sunlight. The flames reeled crazily, giving birth to drunken, swaying shadows. The torches smoked devilishly and smelled like a bad day in the kitchen. But they emitted yellow light.

There was something about yellow light, after four hours of somber, dimming Beta. Even Latimer had lifted his eyes from his book and stared in wonder.

Sheerin warmed his hands at the nearest, regardless of the soot that gathered upon them in a fine, gray powder, and muttered ecstatically to himself. "Beautiful! Beautiful! I never realized before what a wonderful color yellow is."

But Theremon regarded the torches suspiciously. He wrinkled his nose at the rancid odor and said, "What are those things?"

"Wood," said Sheerin shortly.

"Oh, no, they're not. They aren't burning. The top inch is charred and the flame just keeps shooting up out of nothing."

"That's the beauty of it. This is a really efficient artificial-light mechanism. We made a few hundred of them, but most went to the Hideout, of course. You see"—he turned and wiped his blackened hands upon his handkerchief—"you take the pithy core of coarse water reeds, dry them thoroughly, and soak them in animal grease. Then you set fire to it and the grease burns, little by little. These torches will burn for almost half an hour without stopping. Ingenious, isn't it? It was developed by one of our own young men at Saro University."

After the momentary sensation, the dome had quieted. Latimer had carried his chair directly beneath a torch and continued reading, lips moving in the monotonous recital of invocations to the Stars. Beenay had drifted away to his cameras once more, and Theremon seized the opportunity to add to his notes on the article he was going to write for the Saro City *Chronicle* the next day—a procedure he had been following for the last two hours in a perfectly methodical, perfectly conscientious and, as he was well aware, perfectly meaningless fashion.

But, as the gleam of amusement in Sheerin's eyes indicated, careful note-taking occupied his mind with something other than the fact that the sky was gradually turning a horrible deep purple-red, as if it were one gigantic, freshly peeled beet; and so it fulfilled its purpose.

The air grew, somehow, denser. Dusk, like a palpable entity, entered the room, and the dancing circle of yellow light about the torches etched itself into ever-sharper distinction against the gathering grayness beyond. There was the odor of smoke and the presence of little chuckling sounds that the torches made as they burned; the soft pad of one of the men circling the table at which he worked, on hesitant tiptoes; the occasional indrawn breath of someone trying to retain composure in a world that was retreating into the shadow.

It was Theremon who first heard the extraneous noise. It was a vague, unorganized *impression* of sound that would have gone unnoticed but for the dead silence that prevailed within the dome.

The newspaperman sat upright and replaced his notebook. He held his breath and listened; then, with considerable reluctance, threaded his way between the solarscope and one of Beenay's cameras and stood before the window.

The silence ripped to fragments at his startled shout: *"Sheerin!"*

Work stopped! The psychologist was at his side in a moment. Aton joined him. Even Yimot 70, high in his little lean-back seat at the eyepiece of the gigantic solarscope, paused and looked downward.

Outside, Beta was a mere smoldering splinter, taking one last desperate look at Lagash. The eastern horizon, in the direction of the city, was lost in Darkness, and the road from Saro to the Observatory was a dull-red line bordered on both sides by wooded tracts, the trees of which had somehow lost individuality and merged into a continuous shadowy mass.

But it was the highway itself that held attention, for along it there surged another, and infinitely menacing, shadowy mass.

Aton cried in a cracked voice, "The madmen from the city! They've come!"

"How long to totality?" demanded Sheerin.

"Fifteen minutes, but . . . but they'll be here in five."

"Never mind, keep the men working. We'll hold them off. This place is built like a fortress. Aton, keep an eye on our young Cultist just for luck. Theremon, come with me."

Sheerin was out the door, and Theremon was at his heels. The stairs stretched below them in tight, circular sweeps about the central shaft, fading into a dank and dreary grayness.

The first momentum of their rush had carried them fifty feet down, so that the dim, flickering yellow from the open door of the dome had disappeared and both above and below the same dusky shadow crushed in upon them.

Sheerin paused, and his pudgy hand clutched at his chest. His eyes bulged and his voice was a dry cough. "I can't . . . breathe. . . . Go down . . . yourself. Close all doors—"

Theremon took a few downward steps, then turned. "Wait! Can you hold out a minute?" He was panting himself. The air passed in and out of his lungs like so much molasses, and there was a little germ of screeching panic in his mind at the thought of making his way into the mysterious Darkness below by himself.

Theremon, after all, was afraid of the dark!

"Stay here," he said. "I'll be back in a second." He dashed upward two steps at a time, heart pounding—not altogether from the exertion—tumbled into the dome and snatched a torch from its holder. It was foul-smelling, and the smoke smarted his eyes almost blind, but he clutched that torch as if he wanted to kiss it for joy, and its flame streamed backward as he hurtled down the stairs again.

Sheerin opened his eyes and moaned as Theremon bent over him. Theremon shook him roughly. "All right, get a hold of yourself. We've got light."

He held the torch at tiptoe height and, propping the tottering psychologist by an elbow, made his way downward in the middle of the protecting circle of illumination.

The offices on the ground floor still possessed what light there was, and Theremon felt the horror about him relax.

"Here," he said brusquely, and passed the torch to Sheerin. "You can hear *them* outside."

And they could. Little scraps of hoarse, wordless shouts.

But Sheerin was right; the Observatory was built like a fortress. Erected in the last century, when the neo-Gavottian style of architecture was at its ugly height, it had been designed for stability and durability rather than for beauty.

The windows were protected by the grillwork of inch-thick iron bars sunk deep into the concrete sills. The walls were solid masonry that an earthquake couldn't have touched, and the main door was a huge oaken slab reinforced with iron. Theremon shot the bolts and they slid shut with a dull clang.

At the other end of the corridor, Sheerin cursed weakly. He pointed to the lock of the back door which had been neatly jimmied into uselessness.

"That must be how Latimer got in," he said.

"Well, don't stand there," cried Theremon impatiently. "Help drag up the furniture—and keep that torch out of my eyes. The smoke's killing me."

He slammed the heavy table up against the door as he spoke, and in two minutes had built a barricade which made up for what it lacked in beauty and symmetry by the sheer inertia of its massiveness.

Somewhere, dimly, far off, they could hear the battering of naked fists upon the door; and the screams and yells from outside had a sort of half reality.

That mob had set off from Saro City with only two things in mind: the attainment of Cultist salvation by the destruction of the Observatory, and a maddening fear that all but paralyzed them. There was no time to think of ground cars, or of weapons, or of leadership, or even of organization. They made for the Observatory on foot and assaulted it with bare hands.

And now that they were there, the last flash of Beta, the last ruby-red drop of flame, flickered feebly over a humanity that had left only stark, universal fear!

Theremon groaned, "Let's get back to the dome!"

In the dome, only Yimot, at the solarscope, had kept his place. The rest were clustered about the cameras, and Beenay was giving his instructions in a hoarse, strained voice.

"Get it straight, all of you. I'm snapping Beta just before totality and changing the plate. That will leave one of you to each camera. You all know about . . . about times of exposure—"

There was a breathless murmur of agreement.

Beenay passed a hand over his eyes. "Are the torches still burning? Never mind, I see them!" He was leaning hard against the back of a chair. "Now remember, don't try to look for good shots. Don't waste time trying to get t-two stars at a time in the scope field. One is enough. And . . . and if you feel yourself going, *get away from the camera.*"

At the door, Sheerin whispered to Theremon, "Take me to Aton. I don't see him."

The newsman did not answer immediately. The vague forms of the astronomers wavered and blurred, and the torches overhead had become only yellow splotches.

"It's dark," he whimpered.

Sheerin held out his hand. "Aton." He stumbled forward. "Aton!"

Theremon stepped after and seized his arm. "Wait, I'll take you."

Somehow he made his way across the room. He closed his eyes against the Darkness and his mind against the chaos within it.

No one heard them or paid attention to them. Sheerin stumbled against the wall. "Aton!"

The psychologist felt shaking hands touching him, then withdrawing, and a voice muttering, "Is that you, Sheerin?"

"Aton!" He strove to breathe normally. "Don't worry about the mob. The place will hold them off."

Latimer, the Cultist, rose to his feet, and his face twisted in desperation. His word was pledged, and to break it would mean placing his soul in mortal peril. Yet that word had been forced from him and had not been given freely. The Stars would come soon! He could not stand by and allow— And yet his word was pledged.

Beenay's face was dimly flushed as it looked upward at Beta's last ray, and Latimer, seeing him bend over his camera, made his decision. His nails cut the flesh of his palms as he tensed himself.

He staggered crazily as he started his rush. There was nothing before him but shadows; the very floor beneath his feet lacked substance. And then someone was upon him and he went down with clutching fingers at his throat.

He doubled his knee and drove it hard into his assailant. "Let me up or I'll kill you."

Theremon cried out sharply and muttered through a blinding haze of pain. "You double-crossing rat!"

The newsman seemed conscious of everything at once. He heard Beenay croak, "I've got it. At your cameras, men!" and then there was the strange awareness that the last thread of sunlight had thinned out and snapped.

Simultaneously he heard one last choking gasp from Beenay, and a queer little cry from Sheerin, a hysterical giggle that cut off in a rasp—and a sudden silence, a strange, deadly silence from outside.

And Latimer had gone limp in his loosening grasp. Theremon peered into the Cultist's eyes and saw the blankness of them, staring upward, mirroring the feeble yellow of the torches. He saw the bubble of froth upon Latimer's lips and heard the low animal whimper in Latimer's throat.

With the slow fascination of fear, he lifted himself on one arm and turned his eyes toward the blood-curdling blackness of the window.

Through its shone the Stars!

Not Earth's feeble thirty-six hundred Stars visible to the eye; Lagash was in the center of a giant cluster. Thirty thousand mighty suns shone down in a soul-searing splendor that was more frighteningly cold in its awful indifference than the bitter wind that shivered across the cold, horribly bleak world.

Theremon staggered to his feet, his throat constricting him to breathlessness, all the muscles of his body writhing in an intensity of terror and sheer fear beyond bearing. He was going mad and knew it, and somewhere deep inside a bit of sanity was screaming, struggling to fight off the hopeless flood of black terror. It was very horrible to go mad and know that you were going mad—to know that in a little minute you would be here physically and yet all the real essence would be dead and drowned in the black madness. For this was the Dark—the Dark and the Cold and the Doom. The bright walls of the universe were shattered and their awful black fragments were falling down to crush and squeeze and obliterate him.

He jostled someone crawling on hands and knees, but stumbled somehow over him. Hands groping at his tortured throat, he limped toward the flame of the torches that filled all his mad vision.

"Light!" he screamed.

Aton, somewhere, was crying, whimpering horribly like a terribly frightened child. "Stars—all the Stars—we didn't know at all. We didn't know anything. We thought six stars in a universe is something the Stars didn't notice is Darkness forever and ever and ever and the walls are breaking in and we didn't know we couldn't know and anything—"

Someone clawed at the torch, and it fell and snuffed out. In the instant, the awful splendor of the indifferent Stars leaped nearer to them.

On the horizon outside the window, in the direction of Saro City, a crimson glow began growing, strengthening in brightness, that was not the glow of a sun.

The long night had come again.

C-Chute

Even from the cabin into which he and the other passengers had been herded, Colonel Anthony Windham could still catch the essence of the battle's progress. For a while, there was silence, no jolting, which meant the spaceships were fighting at astronomical distance in a duel of energy blasts and powerful force-field defenses.

He knew that could have only one end. Their Earth ship was only an armed merchantman and his glimpse of the Kloro enemy just before he had been cleared off deck by the crew was sufficient to show it to be a light cruiser.

And in less than half an hour, there came those hard little shocks he was waiting for. The passengers swayed back and forth as the ship pitched and veered, as though it were an ocean liner in a storm. But space was calm and silent as ever. It was their pilot sending desperate bursts of steam through the steam-tubes, so that by reaction the ship would be sent rolling and tumbling. It could only mean that the inevitable had occurred. The Earth ship's screens had been drained and it no longer dared withstand a direct hit.

Colonel Windham tried to steady himself with his aluminum cane. He was thinking that he was an old man; that he had spent his life in the militia and had never seen a battle; that now, with a battle going on around him, he was old and fat and lame and had no men under his command.

They would be boarding soon, those Kloro monsters. It was their way of fighting. They would be handicapped by spacesuits and their casualties would be high, but they wanted the Earth ship. Windham considered the passengers. For a moment, he thought, *if they were armed and I could lead them—*

He abandoned the thought. Porter was in an obvious state of funk and the young boy, Leblanc, was hardly better. The Polyorketes brothers—dash it, he couldn't tell them apart—huddled in a corner speaking only to one another. Mullen was a different matter. He sat perfectly erect, with no signs of fear or any other emotion in his face. But the man was just about five feet tall and had undoubtedly never held a gun of any sort in his hands in all his life. He could do nothing.

And there was Stuart, with his frozen half-smile and the high-pitched sarcasm which saturated all he said. Windham looked side-long at Stuart now as Stuart sat there, pushing his dead-white hands through his sandy hair. With those artificial hands he was useless, anyway.

Windham felt the shuddering vibration of ship-to-ship contact, and in five minutes, there was the noise of the fight through the corridors. One of the Polyorketes brothers screamed and dashed for the door. The other called, "Aristides! Wait!" and hurried after.

It happened so quickly. Aristides was out the door and into the corridor, running in brainless panic. A carbonizer glowed briefly and there was never even a scream. Windham, from the doorway, turned in horror at the blackened stump of what was left. Strange—a lifetime in uniform and he had never before seen a man killed in violence.

It took the combined force of the rest to carry the other brother back struggling into the room.

The noise of battle subsided.

Stuart said, "That's it. They'll put a prize crew of two aboard and take us to one of their home planets. We're prisoners of war, naturally."

"Only two of the Kloros will stay aboard?" asked Windham, astonished.

Stuart said, "It is their custom. Why do you ask, Colonel? Thinking of leading a gallant raid to retake the ship?"

Windham flushed. "Simply a point of information, dash it." But the dignity and tone of authority he tried to assume failed him, he knew. He was simply an old man with a limp.

And Stuart was probably right. He had lived among the Kloros and knew their ways.

John Stuart had claimed from the beginning that the Kloros were gentlemen. Twenty-four hours of imprisonment had passed, and now he repeated the statement as he flexed the fingers of his hands and watched the crinkles come and go in the soft artiplasm.

He enjoyed the unpleasant reaction it aroused in the others. People were made to be punctured; windy bladders, all of them. And they had hands of the same stuff as their bodies.

There was Anthony Windham, in particular. Colonel Windham, he called himself, and Stuart was willing to believe it. A retired colonel who had probably drilled a home guard militia on a village green, forty years ago, with such lack of distinction that he was not called back to service in any capacity, even during the emergency of Earth's first interstellar war.

"Dashed unpleasant thing to be saying about the enemy, Stuart. Don't know that I like your attitude." Windham seemed to push the words through his clipped mustache. His head had been shaven, too, in imitation of the current military style, but now a gray stubble was beginning to show about a centered bald patch. His flabby cheeks dragged downward. That and the fine red lines on his thick nose gave him a somewhat undone appearance, as though he had been wakened too suddenly and too early in the morning.

Stuart said, "Nonsense. Just reverse the present situation. Suppose an Earth warship had taken a Kloro liner. What do you think would have happened to any Kloro civilians aboard?"

"I'm sure the Earth fleet would observe all the interstellar rules of war," Windham said stiffly.

"Except that there aren't any. If we landed a prize crew on one of their ships, do you think we'd take the trouble to maintain a chlorine atmosphere for the benefit of the survivors; allow them to keep their non-contraband possessions; give them the use of the most comfortable stateroom, etcetera, etcetera, etcetera?"

Ben Porter said, "Oh, shut up, for God's sake. If I hear your etcetera, etcetera once again, I'll go nuts."

Stuart said, "Sorry!" He wasn't.

Porter was scarcely responsible. His thin face and beaky nose glistened with perspiration, and he kept biting the inside of his cheek until he suddenly winced. He put his tongue against the sore spot, which made him look even more clownish.

Stuart was growing weary of baiting them. Windham was too flabby a target and Porter could do nothing but writhe. The rest were silent. Demetrios Polyorketes was off in a world of silent internal grief for the moment. He had not slept the night before, most probably. At least, whenever Stuart woke to change his position— he himself had been rather restless—there had been Polyorketes' thick mumble from the next cot. It said many things, but the moan to which it returned over and over again was, "Oh, my brother!"

He sat dumbly on his cot now, his red eyes rolling at the other prisoners out of his broad swarthy, unshaven face. As Stuart watched, his face sank into calloused palms so that only his mop of crisp and curly black hair could be seen. He rocked gently, but now that they were all awake, he made no sound.

Claude Leblanc was trying very unsuccessfully, to read a letter. He was the youngest of the six, scarcely out of college, returning to Earth to get married. Stuart had found him that morning weeping quietly, his pink and white face flushed and blotched as though it were a heartbroken child's. He was very fair, with almost a girl's beauty about his large blue eyes and full lips. Stuart wondered what kind of girl it was who had promised to be his wife. He had seen her picture. Who on the ship had not? She had the characterless prettiness that makes all pictures of fiancees indistinguishable. It seemed to Stuart that if he were a girl, however, he would want someone a little more pronouncedly masculine.

That left only Randolph Mullen. Stuart frankly did not have the least idea what to make of him. He was the only one of the six that had been on the Arcturian worlds for any length of time. Stuart, himself, for instance, had been there only long enough to give a series of lectures on astronautical engineering at the provincial engineering institute. Colonel Windham had been on a Cook's tour; Porter was trying to buy concentrated alien vegetables for his canneries on Earth; and the Polyorketes brothers had attempted to establish themselves in Arcturus as truck farmers and, after two growing seasons, gave it up, had somehow unloaded at a profit, and were returning to Earth.

Randolph Mullen, however, had been in the Arcturian system for seventeen years. How did voyagers discover so much about one another so quickly? As far as Stuart knew, the little man had scarcely spoken aboard ship. He was unfailingly polite, always stepped to one side to allow another to pass, but his entire vocabulary appeared to consist only of "Thank you" and "Pardon me." Yet the word had gone around that this was his first trip to Earth in seventeen years.

He was a little man, very precise, almost irritatingly so. Upon awaking that morning, he had made his cot neatly, shaved, bathed and dressed. The habit of years seemed not in the least disturbed by the fact that he was a prisoner of the Kloros now. He was unobtrusive about it, it had to be admitted, and gave no impression of disapproving of the sloppiness of the others. He simply sat there, almost apologetic, trussed in his overconservative clothing, and hands loosely clasped in his lap. The thin line of hair on his upper lip, far from adding character to his face, absurdly increased its primness.

He looked like someone's idea of a caricature of a bookkeeper. And the queer thing about it all, Stuart thought, was that that was exactly what he was. He had noticed it on the registry—Randolph Fluellen Mullen; occupation, bookkeeper; employers, Prime Paper Box Co.; 27 Tobias Avenue, New Warsaw, Arcturus II.

"Mr. Stuart?"

Stuart looked up. It was Leblanc, his lower lip trembling slightly. Stuart tried to remember how one went about being gentle. He said, "What is it, Leblanc?"

"Tell me, when will they let us go?"

"How should I know?"

"Everyone says you lived on a Kloro planet, and just now you said they were gentlemen."

"Well, yes. But even gentlemen fight wars in order to win. Probably, we'll be interned for the duration."

"But that could be *years!* Margaret is waiting. She'll think I'm *dead!*"

"I suppose they'll allow messages to be sent through once we're on their planet."

Porter's hoarse voice sounded in agitation. "Look here, if you know so much about these devils, what will they do to us while we're interned? What will they feed us? Where will they get oxygen for us? They'll kill us, I tell you." And as an afterthought, "I've got a wife waiting for me, too," he added.

But Stuart had heard him speaking of his wife in the days before the attack. He wasn't impressed. Porter's nail-bitten fingers were pulling and plucking at Stuart's sleeve. Stuart drew away in sharp revulsion. He couldn't stand those ugly hands. It angered him to desperation that such monstrosities should be real while his own white and perfectly shaped hands were only mocking imitations grown out of an alien latex.

He said, "They won't kill us. If they were going to, they would have done it before now. Look, we capture Kloros too, you know, and it's just a matter of common sense to treat your prisoners decently if you want the other side to be decent to your men. They'll do their best. The food may not be very good, but they're better chemists than we are. It's what they're best at. They'll know exactly what food factors we'll need and how many calories. We'll live. They'll see to that."

Windham rumbled, "You sound more and more like a blasted greenie sympathizer, Stuart. It turns my stomach to hear an Earthman speak well of the green fellas the way you've been doing. Burn it, man, where's your loyalty?"

"My loyalty's where it belongs. With honesty and decency, regardless of the shape of the being it appears in." Stuart held up his hands. "See these? Kloros made them. I lived on one of their planets for six months. My hands were mangled in the conditioning machinery of my own quarters. I thought the oxygen supply they gave me was a little poor—it wasn't, by the way—and I tried making the adjustments on my own. It was my fault. You should never trust yourself with the machines of another culture. By the time someone among the Kloros could put on an atmosphere suit and get to me, it was too late to save my hands.

"They grew these artiplasm things for me and operated. You know what that meant? It meant designing equipment and nutrient solutions that would work in oxygen atmosphere. It meant that their surgeons had to perform a delicate operation while dressed in atmosphere suits. And now I've got hands again." He laughed harshly, and clenched them into weak fists. "Hands—"

Windham said, "And you'd sell your loyalty to Earth for that?"

"Sell my loyalty? You're mad. For years, I hated the Kloros for this. I was a master pilot on the Trans-Galactic Spacelines before it happened. Now? Desk job. Or an occasional lecture. It took me a long time to pin the fault on myself and to realize that the only role played by the Kloros was a decent one. They have their code of ethics, and it's as good as ours. If it weren't for the stupidity of some of their people—and, by God, of some of ours—we wouldn't be at war. And after it's over—"

Polyorketes was on his feet. His thick fingers curved inward before him and his dark eyes glittered. "I don't like what you say, mister."

"Why don't you?"

"Because you talk too nice about these damned green bastards. The Kloros were good to you, eh? Well, they weren't good to my brother. They killed him. I think maybe I kill you, you damned greenie spy."

And he charged.

Stuart barely had time to raise his arms to meet the infuriated farmer. He gasped out, "What the hell—" as he caught one wrist and heaved a shoulder to block the other which groped toward his throat.

His antiplasm hand gave way. Polyorketes wrenched free with scarcely an effort.

Windham was bellowing incoherently, and Leblanc was calling out in his reedy voice, "Stop it! Stop it!" But it was little Mullen who threw his arms about the farmer's neck from behind and pulled with all his might. He was not very effective; Polyorketes seemed scarcely aware of the little man's weight upon his back. Mullen's feet left the floor so that he tossed helplessly to right and left. But he held his grip and it hampered Polyorketes sufficiently to allow Stuart to break free long enough to grasp Windham's aluminum cane.

He said, "Stay away, Polyorketes."

He was gasping for breath and fearful of another rush. The hollow aluminum cylinder was scarcely heavy enough to accomplish much, but it was better than having only his weak hands to defend himself with.

Mullen had loosed his hold and was now circling cautiously, his breathing roughened and his jacket in disarray.

Polyorketes, for a moment, did not move. He stood there, his shaggy head bent low. Then he said, "It is no use. I must kill Kloros. Just watch your tongue, Stuart. If it keeps on rattling too much, you're liable to get hurt. Really hurt, I mean."

Stuart passed a forearm over his forehead and thrust the cane back at Windham, who seized it with his left hand, while mopping his bald pate vigorously with a handkerchief in his right.

Windham said, "Gentlemen, we must avoid this. It lowers our prestige. We must remember the common enemy. We are Earthmen and we must act what we are—the ruling race of the Galaxy. We dare not demean ourselves before the lesser breeds."

"Yes, Colonel," said Stuart, wearily. "Give us the rest of the speech tomorrow."

He turned to Mullen, "I want to say thanks."

He was uncomfortable about it, but he had to. The little account-ant had surprised him completely.

But Mullen said, in a dry voice that scarcely raised above a whisper, "Don't thank me, Mr. Stuart. It was the logical thing to do. If we are to be interned, we would need you as an interpreter, perhaps, one who would understand the Kloros."

Stuart stiffened. It was, he thought, too much of the bookkeeper type of reasoning, too logical, too dry of juice. Present risk and ul-timate advantage. The assets and debits balanced neatly. He would have liked Mullen to leap to his defense out of—well, out of what? Out of pure, unselfish decency?

Stuart laughed silently at himself. He was beginning to expect idealism of human beings, rather than good, straightforward, self-centered motivation.

Polyorketes was numb. His sorrow and rage were like acid inside him, but they had no words to get out. If he were Stuart, big-mouth, white-hands Stuart, he could talk and talk and maybe feel better. Instead, he had to sit there with half of him dead; with no brother, no Aristides—

It had happened so quickly. If he could only go back and have one second more warning, so that he might snatch Aristides, hold him, save him.

But mostly he hated the Kloros. Two months ago, he had hardly ever heard of them, and now he hated them so hard, he would be glad to die if he could kill a few.

He said, without looking up, "What happened to start this war, eh?"

He was afraid Stuart's voice would answer. He hated Stuart's voice. But it was Windham, the bald one.

Windham said, "The immediate cause, sir, was a dispute over mining concessions in the Wyandotte system. The Kloros had poached on Earth property."

"Room for both, Colonel!"

Polyorketes looked up at that, snarling. Stuart could not be kept quiet for long. He was speaking again; the cripple-hand, wiseguy, Kloros-lover.

Stuart was saying, "Is that anything to fight over, Colonel? We can't use one another's worlds. Their chlorine planets are useless to us and our oxygen ones are useless to them. Chlorine is deadly to us and oxygen is deadly to them. There's no way we could maintain permanent hostility. Our races just don't coincide. Is there reason to fight then because both races want to dig iron out of the same airless planetoids when there are millions like them in the Galaxy?"

Windham said, "There is the question of planetary honor—"

"Planetary fertilizer. How can it excuse a ridiculous war like this one? It can only be fought on outposts. It has to come down to a series of holding actions and eventually be settled by negotiations that might just as easily have been worked out in the first place. Neither we nor the Kloros will gain a thing."

Grudgingly, Polyorketes found that he agreed with Stuart. What did he and Aristides care where Earth or the Kloros got their iron?

Was that something for Aristides to die over?

The little warning buzzer sounded.

Polyorketes' head shot up and he rose slowly, his lips drawing back. Only one thing could be at the door. He waited, arms tense, fists balled. Stuart was edging toward him. Polyorketes saw that and laughed to himself. Let the Kloro come in, and Stuart, along with all the rest, could not stop him.

Wait, Aristides, wait just a moment, and a fraction of revenge will be paid back.

The door opened and a figure entered, completely swathed in a shapeless, billowing travesty of a spacesuit.

An odd, unnatural, but not entirely unpleasant voice began, "It is with some misgivings, Earthmen, that my companion and myself—"

It ended abruptly as Polyorketes, with a roar, charged once again. There was no science in the lunge. It was sheer bull-momentum. Dark head low, burly arms spread out with the hair-tufted fingers in choking position, he clumped on. Stuart was whirled to one side before he had a chance to intervene, and was spun tumbling across a cot.

The Kloro might have, without undue exertion, straight-armed Polyorketes to a halt, or stepped aside, allowing the whirlwind to pass. He did neither. With a rapid movement, a hand-weapon was up and a gentle pinkish line of radiance connected it with the plunging Earthman. Polyorketes stumbled and crashed down, his body maintaining its last curved position, one foot raised, as though a lightning paralysis had taken place. It toppled to one side and he lay there, eyes all alive and wild with rage.

The Kloro said, "He is not permanently hurt." He seemed not to resent the offered violence. Then he began again, "It is with some misgiving, Earthmen, that my companion and myself were made aware of a certain commotion in this room. Are you in any need which we can satisfy?"

Stuart was angrily nursing his knee which he had scraped in colliding with the cot. He said, "No, thank you, Kloro."

"Now, look here," puffed Windham, "this is a dashed outrage. We demand that our release be arranged."

The Kloro's tiny, insectlike head turned in the fat old man's direction. He was not a pleasant sight to anyone unused to him. He was about the height of an Earthman, but the top of him consisted of a thin stalk of a neck with a head that was the merest swelling. It consisted of a blunt triangular proboscis in front and two bulging eyes on either side. That was all. There was no brain pan and no brain. What corresponded to the brain in a Kloro was located in what would be an Earthly abdomen, leaving the head as a mere sensory organ. The Kloro's spacesuit followed the outlines of the head more or less faithfully, the two eyes being exposed by two clear semicircles of glass, which looked faintly green because of the chlorine atmosphere inside.

One of the eyes was now cocked squarely at Windham, who quivered uncomfortably under the glance, but insisted, "You have no right to hold us prisoner. We are noncombatants."

The Kloro's voice, sounding thoroughly artificial, came from a small attachment of chromium mesh on what served as its chest. The voice box was manipulated by compressed air under the control of one or two of the many delicate, forked tendrils that radiated from two circles about its upper body and were, mercifully enough, hidden by the suit.

The voice said, "Are you serious, Earthman? Surely you have heard of war and rules of war and prisoners of war."

It looked about, shifting eyes with quick jerks of its head, staring at a particular object first with one, then with another. It was Stuart's understanding that each eye transferred a separate message to the abdominal brain, which had to coordinate the two to obtain full information.

Windham had nothing to say. No one had. The Kloro, its four main limbs, roughly arms and legs in pairs, and a vaguely human appearance under the masking of the suit, if you looked no higher than its chest, but there was no way of telling what it felt.

They watched it turn and leave.

Porter coughed and said in a strangled voice, "God, smell that chlorine. If they don't do something, we'll all die of rotted lungs."

Stuart said, "Shut up. There isn't enough chlorine in the air to make a mosquito sneeze, and what there is will be swept out in two minutes. Besides, a little chlorine is good for you. It may kill your cold virus."

Windham coughed and said, "Stuart, I feel that you might have said something to your Kloro friend about releasing us. You are scarcely as bold in their presence, dash it, as you are once they are gone."

"You heard what the creature said, Colonel. We're prisoners of war, and prisoner exchanges are negotiated by diplomats. We'll just have to wait."

Leblanc, who had turned pasty white at the entrance of the Kloro, rose and hurried into the privy. There was the sound of retching.

An uncomfortable silence fell while Stuart tried to think of something to say to cover the unpleasant sound. Mullen filled in. He had rummaged through a little box he had taken from under his pillow.

He said, "Perhaps Mr. Leblanc had better take a sedative before retiring. I have a few. I'd be glad to give him one." He explained his generosity immediately, "Otherwise he may keep the rest of us awake, you see."

"Very logical," said Stuart, dryly. "You'd better save one for Sir Launcelot here; save half a dozen." He walked to where Polyorketes still sprawled and knelt at his side. "Comfortable, baby?"

Windham said, "Deuced poor taste speaking like that, Stuart."

"Well, if you're so concerned about him, why don't you and Porter hoist him onto his cot?"

He helped them do so. Polyorketes' arms were trembling erratically now. From what Stuart knew of the Kloro's nerve weapons, the man should be in an agony of pins and needles about now.

Stuart said, "And don't be too gentle with him, either. The damned fool might have gotten us all killed. And for what?"

He pushed Polyorketes' stiff carcass to one side and sat at the edge of the cot. He said, "Can you hear me, Polyorketes?"

Polyorketes' eyes gleamed. An arm lifted abortively and fell back.

"Okay then, listen. Don't try anything like that again. The next time it may be the finish for all of us. If you had been a Kloro and he had been an Earthman, we'd be dead now. So just get one thing through your skull. We're sorry about your brother and it's a rotten shame, but it was his own fault."

Polyorketes tried to heave and Stuart pushed him back.

"No, you keep on listening," he said. "Maybe this is the only time I'll get to talk to you when you *have* to listen. Your brother had no right leaving passenger's quarters. There was no place for him to go. He just got in the way of our own men. We don't even know for certain that it was a Kloro gun that killed him. It might have been one of our own."

"Oh, I say, Stuart," objected Windham.

Stuart whirled at him. "Do you have proof it wasn't? Did you see the shot? Could you tell from what was left of the body whether it was Kloro energy or Earth energy?"

Polyorketes found his voice, driving his unwilling tongue into a fuzzy verbal snarl. "Damned stinking greenie bastard."

"Me?" said Stuart. "I know what's going on in your mind, Polyorketes. You think that when the paralysis wears off, you'll ease your feelings by slamming me around. Well, if you do, it will probably be curtains for all of us."

He rose, put his back against the wall. For the moment, he was fighting all of them. "None of you know the Kloros the way I do. The physical differences you see are not important. The differences in their temperament are. They don't understand our views on sex, for instance. To them, it's just a biological reflex like breathing. They attach no importance to it. But they *do* attach importance to social groupings. Remember, their evolutionary ancestors had lots in common with our insects. They always assume that any group of Earthmen they find together makes up a social unit.

"That means just about everything to them. I don't understand exactly *what* it means. No Earthman can. But the result is that they never break up a group, just as we don't separate a mother and her children if we can help it. One of the reasons they may be treating us with kid gloves right now is that they imagine we're all broken up over the fact that they killed one of us, and they feel guilt about it.

"But this is what you'll have to remember. We're going to be interned together and *kept* together for duration. I don't like the thought. I wouldn't have picked any of you for co-internees and I'm pretty sure none of you would have picked me. But there it is. The Kloros could never understand that our being together on the ship is only accidental.

"That means we've got to get along somehow. That's not just goodie-goodie talk about birds in their little nest agreeing. What do you think would have happened if the Kloros had come in earlier and found Polyorketes and myself trying to kill each other? You don't know? Well, what do you suppose *you* would think of a mother you caught trying to kill her children?

"That's it, then. They would have killed every one of us as a bunch of Kloro-type perverts and monsters. Got that? How about you, Polyorketes? Have *you* got it? So let's call names if we have to, but let's keep our hands to ourselves. And now, if none of you mind, I'll massage my hands back into shape—these synthetic hands that I got from the Kloros and that one of my own kind tried to mangle again."

For Claude Leblanc, the worst was over. He had been sick enough; sick with many things; but sick most of all over having ever left Earth. It had been a great thing to go to college off Earth. It had been an adventure and had taken him away from his mother. Somehow, he had been sneakingly glad to make that escape after the first month of frightened adjustment.

And then on the summer holidays, he had been no longer Claude, the shy-spoken scholar, but Leblanc, space traveler. He had swaggered the fact for all it was worth. It made him feel such a man to talk of stars and Jumps and the customs and environments of other worlds; it had given him courage with Margaret. She had loved him for the dangers he had undergone—

Except that this had been the first one, really, and he had not done so well. He knew it and was ashamed and wished he were like Stuart.

He used the excuse of mealtime to approach. He said, "Mr. Stuart."

Stuart looked up and said shortly, "How do you feel?"

Leblanc felt himself blush. He blushed easily and the effort not to blush only made it worse. He said, "Much better, thank you. We are eating. I thought I'd bring you your ration."

Stuart took the offered can. It was standard space ration; thoroughly synthetic, concentrated, nourishing and, somehow, unsatisfying. It heated automatically when the can was opened, but could be eaten cold, if necessary. Though a combined fork-spoon utensil was enclosed, the ration was of a consistency that made the use of fingers practical and not particularly messy.

Stuart said, "Did you hear my little speech?"

"Yes, sir. I want you to know you can count on me."

"Well, good. Now go and eat."

"May I eat here?"

"Suit yourself."

For a moment, they ate in silence, and then Leblanc burst out, "You are so sure of yourself, Mr. Stuart! It must be very wonderful to be like that!"

"Sure of myself? Thanks, but there's your self-assured one."

Leblanc followed the direction of the nod in surprise. "Mr. Mullen? That little man? Oh, no!"

"You don't think he's self-assured?"

Leblanc shook his head. He looked at Stuart intently to see if he could detect humor in his expression. "That one is just cold. He has no emotion in him. He's like a little machine. I find him repulsive. You're different, Mr. Stuart. You have it all inside, but you control it. I would like to be like that."

And as though attracted by the magnetism of the mention, even though unheard, of his name, Mullen joined them. His can of ration was barely touched. It was still steaming gently as he squatted opposite them.

His voice had its usual quality of furtively rustling underbrush. "How long, Mr. Stuart, do you think the trip will take?"

"Can't say, Mullen. They'll undoubtedly be avoiding the usual trade routes and they'll be making more Jumps through hyper-space than usual to throw off possible pursuit. I wouldn't be surprised if it took as long as a week. Why do you ask? I presume you have a very practical and logical reason?"

"Why, yes. Certainly." He seemed quite shellbacked to sarcasm. He said, "It occurred to me that it might be wise to ration the rations, so to speak."

"We've got enough food and water for a month. I checked on that first thing."

"I see. In that case, I will finish the can." He did, using the all-purpose utensil daintily and patting a handkerchief against his unstained lips from time to time.

Polyorketes struggled to his feet some two hours later. He swayed a bit, looking like the Spirit of Hangover. He did not try to come closer to Stuart, but spoke from where he stood.

He said, "You stinking greenie spy, you watch yourself."

"You heard what I said before, Polyorketes."

"I heard. But I also heard what you said about Aristides. I won't bother with you, because you're a bag of nothing but noisy air. But wait, someday you'll blow your air in one face too many and it will be let out of you."

"I'll wait," said Stuart.

Windham hobbled over, leaning heavily on his cane. "Now, now," he called with a wheezing joviality that overlaid his sweating anxiety so thinly as to emphasize it. "We're all Earthmen, dash it. Got to remember that; keep it as a glowing light of inspiration. Never let down before the blasted Kloros. We've got to forget private feuds and remember only that we are Earthmen united against alien blighters."

Stuart's comment was unprintable.

Porter was right behind Windham. He had been in a close conference with the shaven-headed colonel for an hour, and now he said with indignation, "It doesn't help to be a wiseguy, Stuart. You listen to the colonel. We've been doing some hard thinking about the situation."

He had washed some of the grease off his face, wet his hair and slicked it back. It did not remove the little tic on his right cheek just at the point where his lips ended, or make his hangnail hands more attractive in appearance.

"All right, Colonel," said Stuart. "What's on your mind?"

Windham said, "I'd prefer to have all the men together."

"Okay, call them."

Leblanc hurried over; Mullen approached with greater deliberation.

Stuart said, "You want that fellow?" He jerked his head at Polyorketes.

"Why, yes. Mr. Polyorketes, may we have you, old fella?"

"Ah, leave me alone."

"Go ahead," said Stuart, "leave him alone. I don't want him."

"No, no," said Windham. "This is a matter for all Earthmen. Mr. Polyorketes, we must have you."

Polyorketes rolled off one side of his cot. "I'm close enough, I can hear you."

Windham said to Stuart, "Would they—the Kloros, I mean—have this room wired?"

"No," said Stuart. "Why should they?"

"Are you sure?"

"Of course I'm sure. They didn't know what happened when Polyorketes jumped me. They just heard the thumping when it started rattling the ship."

"Maybe they were trying to give us the impression the room wasn't wired."

"Listen, Colonel, I've never known a Kloro to tell a deliberate lie—"

Polyorketes interrupted calmly, "That lump of noise just *loves* the Kloros."

Windham said hastily, "Let's not begin that. Look, Stuart, Porter and I have been discussing matters and we have decided that you know the Kloros well enough to think of some way of getting us back to Earth."

"It happens that you're wrong. I can't think of any way."

"Maybe there is some way we can take the ship back from the blasted green fellas," suggested Windham. "Some weakness they may have. Dash it, you know what I mean."

"Tell me, Colonel, what are you after? Your own skin or Earth's welfare?"

"I resent that question. I'll have you know that while I'm as careful of my own life as anyone has a right to be, I'm thinking of Earth primarily. And I think that's true of all of us."

"Damn right," said Porter, instantly. Leblanc looked anxious, Polyorketes resentful; and Mullen had no expression at all.

"Good," said Stuart. "Of course, I don't think we can take the ship. They're armed and we aren't. But there's this. You know why the Kloros took this ship intact. It's because they need ships. They may be better chemists than Earthmen are, but Earthmen are better astronautical engineers. We have bigger, better and more ships. In fact, if our crew had had a proper respect for military axioms in the first place, they would have blown the ship up as soon as it looked as though the Kloros were going to board."

Leblanc looked horrified. "And kill the passengers?"

"Why not? You heard what the good colonel said. Every one of us puts his own lousy little life after Earth's interests. What good are we to Earth alive right now? None at all. What harm will this ship do in Kloro hands? A hell of a lot, probably."

"Just why," asked Mullen, "did our men refuse to blow up the ship? They must have had a reason."

"They did. It's the firmest tradition of Earth's military men that there must never be an unfavorable ratio of casualties. If we had blown ourselves up, twenty fighting men and seven civilians of Earth would be dead as compared with an enemy casualty total of zero. So what happens? We let them board, kill twenty-eight—I'm sure we killed at least that many—and let them have the ship."

"Talk, talk, talk," jeered Polyorketes.

"There's a moral to this," said Stuart. "We can't take the ship away from the Kloros. We *might* be able to rush them, though, and keep them busy long enough to allow one of us enough time to short the engines."

"What?" yelled Porter, and Windham shushed him in fright.

"Short the engines," Stuart repeated. "That would destroy the ship, of course, which is what we want to do, isn't it?"

Leblanc's lips were white. "I don't think that would work."

"We can't be sure till we try. But what have we to lose by trying?"

"Our lives, damn it!" cried Porter. "You insane maniac, you're crazy!"

"If I'm a maniac," said Stuart, "and insane to boot, then naturally I'm crazy. But just remember that if we lose our lives, which is overwhelmingly probable, we lose nothing of value to Earth; whereas if we destroy the ship, as we just barely might, we do Earth a lot of good. What patriot would hesitate? Who here would put himself ahead of his world?" He looked about in the silence. "Surely not you, Colonel Windham."

Windham coughed tremendously. "My dear man, that is not the question. There must be a way to save the ship for Earth *without* losing our lives, eh?"

"All right. You name it."

"Let's all think about it. Now there are only two of the Kloros aboard ship. If one of us could sneak up on them and—"

"How? The rest of the ship's all filled with chlorine. We'd have to wear a spacesuit. Gravity in their part of the ship is hopped up to Kloro level, so whoever is patsy in the deal would be clumping around, metal on metal, slow and heavy. Oh, he could sneak up on them, sure—like a skunk trying to sneak downwind."

"Then we'll drop it all," Porter's voice shook. "Listen, Windham, there's not going to be any destroying the ship. My life means plenty to me and if any of you try anything like that, I'll call the Kloros. I mean it."

"Well," said Stuart, "there's hero number one."

Leblanc said, "I want to go back to Earth, but I—"

Mullen interrupted, "I don't think our chances of destroying the ship are good enough unless—"

"Heroes number two and three. What about you, Polyorketes? You would have the chance of killing two Kloros."

"I want to kill them with my bare hands," growled the farmer, his heavy fists writhing. "On their planet, I will kill dozens."

"That's a nice safe promise for now. What about you, Colonel? Don't you want to march to death and glory with me?"

"Your attitude is very cynical and unbecoming, Stuart. It's obvious that if the rest are unwilling, then your plan will fall through."

"Unless I do it myself, huh?"

"You won't, do you hear?" said Porter, instantly.

"Damn right I won't," agreed Stuart. "I don't claim to be a hero. I'm just an average patriot, perfectly willing to head for any planet they take me to and sit out the war."

Mullen said, thoughtfully, "Of course, there *is* a way we could surprise the Kloros."

The statement would have dropped flat except for Polyorketes. He pointed a black-nailed, stubby forefinger and laughed harshly. "Mr. Bookkeeper!" he said. "Mr. Bookkeeper is a big shot talker like this damned greenie spy, Stuart. All right, Mr. Bookkeeper, go ahead. You make big speeches also. Let the words roll like an empty barrel."

He turned to Stuart and repeated venomously, "Empty barrel! Cripple-hand empty barrel. No good for anything but talk."

Mullen's soft voice could make no headway until Polyoketes was through, but then he said, speaking directly to Stuart, "We might be able to reach them from outside. This room has a C-chute I'm sure."

"What's a C-chute?" asked Leblanc.

"Well—" began Mullen, and then stopped, at a loss.

Stuart said, mockingly, "It's a euphemism, my boy. Its full name is 'casualty chute.' It doesn't get talked about, but the main rooms on any ship would have them. They're just little airlocks down which you slide a corpse. Burial at space. Always lots of sentiment and bowed heads, with the captain making a rolling speech of the type Polyorketes here wouldn't like."

Leblanc's face twisted. "Use *that* to leave the ship?"

"Why not? Superstitious?—Go on, Mullen."

The little man had waited patiently. He said, "Once outside, one could re-enter the ship by the steam-tubes. It can be done—with luck. And then you would be an unexpected visitor in the control room."

Stuart stared at him curiously. "How do you figure this out? What do *you* know about steam-tubes?"

Mullen coughed. "You mean because I'm in the paper-box business? Well—" He grew pink, waited a moment, then made a new start in a colorless, unemotional voice. "My company, which manufactures fancy paper boxes and novelty containers, made a line of spaceship candy boxes for the juvenile trade some years ago. It was designed so that if a string were pulled, small pressure containers were punctured and jets of compressed air shot out through the mock steam-tubes, sailing the box across the room and scattering candy as it went. The sales theory was that the youngsters would find it exciting to play with the ship and fun to scramble for the candy.

"Actually, it was a complete failure. The ship would break dishes and sometimes hit another child in the eye. Worse still, the children would not only scramble for the candy but would fight over it. It was almost our worst failure. We lost thousands.

"Still, while the boxes were being designed, the entire office was extremely interested. It was like a game, very bad for efficiency and office morale. For a while, we all became steam-tube experts. I read quite a few books on ship construction. On my own time, however, not the company's."

Stuart was intrigued. He said. "You know it's a video sort of idea, but it might work if we had a hero to spare. Have we?"

"What about you?" demanded Porter, indignantly. "You go around sneering at us with your cheap wisecracks. I don't notice you volunteering for anything."

"That's because I'm no hero, Porter. I admit it. My object is to stay alive, and shinnying down steam-tubes is no way to go about staying alive. But the rest of you are noble patriots. The colonel says so. What about you, Colonel? You're the senior hero here."

Windham said, "If I were younger, blast it, and if you had your hands, I would take pleasure, sir, in trouncing you soundly."

"I've no doubt of it, but that's no answer."

"You know very well that at my time of life and with my leg—" he brought the flat of his hand down upon his stiff knee—"I am in no position to do anything of the sort, however much I should wish to."

"Ah, yes," said Stuart, "and I, myself, am crippled in the hands, as Polyorketes tells me. That saves us. And what unfortunate deformities do the rest of us have?"

"Listen," cried Porter, "I want to know what this is all about. How can anyone go down the steam-tubes? What if the Kloros use them while one of us is inside?"

"Why, Porter, that's part of the sporting chance. It's where the excitement comes in."

"But he'd be boiled in the shell like a lobster."

"A pretty image, but inaccurate. The steam wouldn't be on for more than a very short time, maybe a second or two, and the suit insulation would hold that long. Besides, the jet comes scooting out at several hundred miles a minute, so that you would be blown clear of the ship before the steam could even warm you. In fact, you'd be blown quite a few miles out into space, and after that you would be quite safe from the Kloros. Of course, you couldn't get back to the ship."

Porter was sweating freely. "You don't scare me for one minute, Stuart."

"I don't? Then you're offering to go? Are you sure you've thought out what being stranded in space means? You're all alone, you know; really all alone. The steam-jet will probably leave you turning or tumbling pretty rapidly. You won't feel that. You'll seem to be motionless. But all the stars will be going around and around so that they're just streaks in the sky. They won't ever stop. They won't even slow up. Then your heater will go off, your oxygen will give out, and you will die very slowly. You'll have lots of time to think. Or, if you are in a hurry, you could open your suit. That wouldn't be pleasant, either. I've seen faces of men who had a torn suit happen to them accidentally, and it's pretty awful. But it would be quicker. Then—"

Porter turned and walked unsteadily away.

Stuart said, lightly, "Another failure. One act of heroism still ready to be knocked down to the highest bidder with nothing offered yet."

Polyorketes spoke up and his harsh voice roughed the words. "You keep on talking, Mr. Big Mouth. You just keep banging that empty barrel. Pretty soon, we'll kick your teeth in. There's one boy I think would be willing to do it now, eh, Mr. Porter?"

Porter's look at Stuart confirmed the truth of Polyorketes' remarks, but he said nothing.

Stuart said, "Then what about you, Polyorketes? You're the bare-hand man with guts. Want me to help you into a suit?"

"I'll ask you when I want help."

"What about you, Leblanc?"

The young man shrank away.

"Not even to get back to Margaret?"

But Leblanc could only shake his head.

"Mullen?"

"Well—I'll try."

"You'll what?"

"I said, yes, I'll try. After all, it's my idea."

Stuart looked stunned. "You're serious? How come?"

Mullen's prim mouth pursed. "Because no one else will."

"But that's no reason. Especially for you."

Mullen shrugged.

There was a thump of a cane behind Stuart. Windham brushed past.

He said, "Do you really intend to go, Mullen?"

"Yes, Colonel."

"In that case, dash it, let me shake your hand. I like you. You're an—an Earthman, by heaven. Do this, and win or die, I'll bear witness for you."

Mullen withdrew his hand awkwardly from the deep and vibrating grasp of the other.

And Stuart just stood there. He was in a very unusual position. He was, in fact, in the particular position of all positions in which he most rarely found himself.

He had nothing to say.

The quality of tension had changed. The gloom and frustration had lifted a bit, and the excitement of conspiracy had replaced it. Even Polyorketes was fingering the spacesuits and commenting briefly and hoarsely on which he considered preferable.

Mullen was having a certain amount of trouble. The suit hung rather limply upon him even though the adjustable joints had been tightened nearly to minimum. He stood there now with only the helmet to be screwed on. He wiggled his neck.

Stuart was holding the helmet with an effort. It was heavy, and his artiplasmic hands did not grip it well. He said, "Better scratch your nose if it itches. It's your last chance for a while." He didn't add, "Maybe forever," but he thought it.

Mullen said, tonelessly, "I think perhaps I had better have a spare oxygen cylinder."

"Good enough."

"With a reducing valve."

Stuart nodded. "I see what you're thinking of. If you do get blown clear of the ship, you could try to blow yourself back by using the cylinder as an action-reaction motor."

They clamped on the headpiece and buckled the spare cylinder to Mullen's waist. Polyorketes and Leblanc lifted him up to the yawning opening of the C-tube. It was ominously dark inside, the metal lining of the interior having been painted a mournful black. Stuart thought he could detect a musty odor about it, but that, he knew, was only imagination.

He stopped the proceedings when Mullen was half within the tube. He tapped upon the little man's faceplate.

"Can you hear me?"

Within, there was a nod.

"Air coming through all right? No last-minute troubles?"

Mullen lifted his armored arm in a gesture of reassurance.

"Then remember, don't use the suit-radio out there. The Kloros might pick up the signals.

Reluctantly, he stepped away. Polyorketes' brawny hands lowered Mullen until they could hear the thumping sound made by the steel-shod feet against the outer valve. The inner valve then swung shut with a dreadful finality, its beveled silicone gasket making a slight soughing noise as it crushed hard. They clamped it into place.

Stuart stood at the toggle-switch that controlled the outer valve. He threw it and the gauge that marked the air pressure within the tube fell to zero. A little pinpoint of red light warned that the outer valve was open. Then the light disappeared, the valve closed, and the gauge climbed slowly to fifteen pounds again.

They opened the inner valve again and found the tube empty.

Polyorketes spoke first. He said, "The little son-of-a-gun. He went!" He looked wonderingly at the others. "A little fellow with guts like that."

Stuart said, "Look, we'd better get ready in here. There's just a chance that the Kloros may have detected the valves opening and closing. If so, they'll be here to investigate and we'll have to cover up."

"How?" asked Windham.

"They won't see Mullen anywhere around. We'll say he's in the head. The Kloros know that it's one of the peculiar characteristics of Earthmen that they resent intrusion on their privacy in lavatories, and they'll make no effort to check. If we can hold them off—"

"What if they wait, or if they check the spacesuits?" asked Porter.

Stuart shrugged. "Let's hope they don't. And listen, Polyorketes, don't make any fuss when they come in."

Polyorketes grunted, "With that little guy out there? What do you think I am?" He stared at Stuart without animosity, then scratched his curly hair vigorously. "You know, I laughed at him. I thought he was an old woman. It makes me ashamed."

Stuart cleared his throat. He said, "Look, I've been saying some things that maybe weren't too funny after all, now that I come to think of it. I'd like to say I'm sorry if I have."

He turned away morosely and walked toward his cot. He heard the steps behind him, felt the touch on his sleeve. He turned; it was Leblanc.

The youngster said softly, "I keep thinking that Mr. Mullen is an old man."

"Well, he's not a kid. He's about forty-five or fifty, I think."

Leblanc said, "Do you think, Mr. Stuart, that *I* should have gone, instead? I'm the youngest here. I don't like the thought of having let an old man go in my place. It makes me feel like the devil."

"I know. If he dies, it will be too bad."

"But he volunteered. We didn't make him, did we?"

"Don't try to dodge responsibility, Leblanc. It won't make you feel better. There isn't one of us without a stronger motive to run the risk than he had." And Stuart sat there silently, thinking.

Mullen felt the obstruction beneath his feet yield and the walls about him slip away quickly, too quickly. He knew it was the puff of air escaping, carrying him with it, and he dug arms and legs frantically against the wall to brake himself. Corpses were supposed to be flung well clear of the ship, but he was no corpse—for the moment.

His feet swung free and threshed. He heard the *clunk* of one magnetic boot against the hull just as the rest of his body puffed out like a tight cork under air pressure. He teetered dangerously at the lip of the hole in the ship—he had changed orientation suddenly and was looking down on it—then took a step backward as its lid came down of itself and fitted smoothly against the hull.

A feeling of unreality overwhelmed him. Surely, it wasn't he standing on the outer surface of a ship. Not Randolph F. Mullen. So few human beings could ever say they had, even those who traveled in space constantly.

He was only gradually aware that he was in pain. Popping out of that hole with one foot clamped to the hull had nearly bent him in two. He tried moving, cautiously, and found his motions to be erratic and almost impossible to control. He *thought* nothing was broken, though the muscles of his left side were badly wrenched.

And then he came to himself and noticed that the wrist-lights of his suit were on. It was by their light that he had stared into the blackness of the C-chute. He stirred with the nervous thought that from within, the Kloros might see the twin spots of moving light just outside the hull. He flicked the switch upon the suit's mid-section.

Mullen had never imagined that, standing on a ship, he would fail to see its hull. But it was dark, as dark below as above. There were the stars, hard and bright little non-dimensional dots. Nothing more. Nothing more anywhere. Under his feet, not even the stars—*not even his feet*.

He bent back to look at the stars. His head swam. They were moving slowly. Or, rather, they were standing still and the ship was rotating, but he could not tell his eyes that. *They* moved. His eyes followed—down and behind the ship. New stars up and above from the other side. A black horizon. The ship existed only as a region where there were no stars.

No stars? Why, there was one almost at his feet. He nearly reached for it; then he realized that it was only a glittering reflection in the mirroring metal.

They were moving thousands of miles an hour. The stars were. The ship was. He was. But it meant nothing. To his senses, there was only silence and darkness and that slow wheeling of the stars. His eyes followed the wheeling—

And his head in its helmet hit the ship's hull with a soft bell-like ring.

He felt about in panic with his thick, insensitive, spun-silicate gloves. His feet were still firmly magnetized to the hull, that was true, but the rest of his body bent backward at the knees in a right angle. There was no gravity outside the ship. If he bent back, there was nothing to pull the upper part of his body down and tell his joints they were bending. His body stayed as he put it.

He pressed wildly against the hull and his torso shot upward and refused to stop when upright. He fell forward.

He tried more slowly, balancing with both hands against the hull, until he squatted evenly. Then upward. Very slowly. Straight up. Arms out to balance.

He was straight now, aware of his nausea and lightheadedness.

He looked about. My God, where were the steam-tubes? He couldn't see them. They were black on black, nothing on nothing.

Quickly, he turned on the wrist-lights. In space, there were no beams, only elliptical, sharply defined spots of blue steel, winking light back at him. Where they struck a rivet, a shadow was cast, knife-sharp and as black as space, the lighted region illuminated abruptly and without diffusion.

He moved his arms, his body swaying gently in the opposite direction; action and reaction. The vision of a steam-tube with its smooth cylindrical sides sprang at him.

He tried to move toward it. His foot held firmly to the hull. He pulled and it slogged upward, straining against quicksand that eased quickly. Three inches up and it had almost sucked free; six inches up and he thought it would fly away.

He advanced it and let it down, felt it enter the quicksand. When the sole was within two inches of the hull, it snapped down; out of control, hitting the hull ringingly. His spacesuit carried the vibrations, amplifying them in his ears.

He stopped in absolute terror. The dehydrators that dried the atmosphere within his suit could not handle the sudden gush of perspiration that drenched his forehead and armpits.

He waited, then tried lifting his foot again—a bare inch, holding it there by main force and moving it horizontally. Horizontal motion involved no effort at all; it was motion perpendicular to the lines of magnetic force. But he had to keep the foot from snapping down as he did so, and then lower it slowly.

He puffed with the effort. Each step was agony. The tendons of his knees were cracking, and there were knives in his side.

Mullen stopped to let the perspiration dry. It wouldn't do to steam up the inside of his faceplate. He flashed his wrist-lights, and the steam-cylinder was right ahead.

The ship had four of them, at ninety degree intervals, thrusting out at an angle from the midgirdle. They were the "fine adjustment" of the ship's course. The coarse adjustment was the powerful thrusters back and front which fixed final velocity by their accelerative and the decelerative force, and the hyperatomics that took care of the space-swallowing Jumps.

But occasionally the direction of flight had to be adjusted slightly and then the steam-cylinders took over. Singly, they could drive the ship up, down, right, left. By twos, in appropriate ratios of thrust, the ship could be turned in any desired direction.

The device had been unimproved in centuries, being too simple to improve. The atomic pile heated the water content of a closed container into steam, driving it, in less than a second, up to temperatures where it would have broken down into a mixture of hydrogen and oxygen, and then into a mixture of electrons and ions. Perhaps the breakdown actually took place. No one ever bothered testing; it worked, so there was no need to.

At the critical point, a needle valve gave way and the steam thrust madly out in a short but incredible blast. And the ship, inevitably and majestically, moved in the opposite direction, veering about its own center of gravity. When the degrees of turn were sufficient, an equal and opposite blast would take place and the turning would be canceled. The ship would be moving at its original velocity, but in a new direction.

Mullen had dragged himself out to the lip of the steam-cylinder. He had a picture of himself—a small speck teetering at the extreme end of a structure thrusting out of an ovoid that was tearing through space at ten thousand miles an hour.

But there was no air-stream to whip him off the hull, and his magnetic soles held him more firmly than he liked.

With lights on, he bent down to peer into the tube and the ship dropped down precipitously as his orientation changed. He reached out to steady himself, but he was not falling. There was no up or down in space except for what his confused mind chose to consider up or down.

The cylinder was just large enough to hold a man, so that it might be entered for repair purposes. His light caught the rungs almost directly opposite his position at the lip. He puffed a sigh of relief with what breath he could muster. Some ships didn't have ladders.

He made his way to it, the ship appearing to slip and twist beneath him as he moved. He lifted an arm over the lip of the tube, feeling for the rung, loosened each foot, and drew himself within.

The knot in his stomach that had been there from the first was a convulsed agony now. If they should choose to manipulate the ship, if the steam should whistle out now—

He would never hear it; never know it. One instant he would be holding a rung, feeling slowly for the next with a groping arm. The next moment he would be alone in space, the ship a dark, dark nothingness lost forever among the stars. There would be, perhaps, a brief glory of swirling ice crystals drifting with him, shining in his wrist-lights and slowly approaching and rotating about him, attracted by his mass like infinitesimal planets to an absurdly tiny Sun.

He was trickling sweat again, and now he was also conscious of thirst. He put it out of his mind. There would be no drinking until he was out of his suit—if ever.

Up a rung; up another; and another. How many were there? His hand slipped and he stared in disbelief at the glitter that showed under his light.

Ice?

Why not? The steam, incredibly hot as it was, would strike metal that was at nearly absolute zero. In the few split-seconds of thrust, there would not be time for the metal to warm above the freezing point of water. A sheet of ice would condense that would sublime slowly into the vacuum. It was the speed of all that happened that prevented the fusion of the tubes and of the original water-container itself.

His groping hand reached the end. Again the wrist-lights. He stared with crawling horror at the steam nozzle, half an inch in diameter. It looked dead, harmless. But it always would, right up to the micro-second before—

Around it was the outer steam lock. It pivoted on a central hub that was springed on the portion toward space, screwed on the part toward the ship. The springs allowed it to give under the first wild thrust of steam pressure before the ship's mighty inertia could be overcome. The steam was bled into the inner chamber, breaking the force of the thrust, leaving the total energy unchanged, but spreading it over time so that the hull itself was in that much less danger of being staved in.

Mullen braced himself firmly against a rung and pressed against the outer lock so that it gave a little. It was stiff, but it didn't have to give much, just enough to catch on the screw. He felt it catch.

He strained against it and turned it, feeling his body twist in the opposite direction. It held tight, the screw taking up the strain as he carefully adjusted the small control switch that allowed the springs to fall free. How well he remembered the books he had read!

He was in the interlock space now, which was large enough to hold a man comfortably, again for convenience in repairs. He could no longer be blown away from the ship. If the steam blast were turned on now, it would merely drive him against the inner lock—hard enough to crush him to a pulp. A quick death he would never feel, at least.

Slowly, he unhooked his spare oxygen cylinder. There was only an inner lock between himself and the control room now. This lock opened outward into space so that the steam blast could only close it tighter, rather than blow it open. And it fitted tightly and smoothly. There was absolutely no way to open it from without.

He lifted himself above the lock, forcing his bent back against the inner surface of the interlock area. It made breathing difficult. The spare oxygen cylinder dangled at a queer angle. He held its metal-mesh hose and straightened it, forcing it against the inner lock so that vibration thudded. Again—again—

It would *have* to attract the attention of the Kloros. They would *have* to investigate.

He would have no way of telling when they were about to do so. Ordinarily, they would first let air into the interlock to force the outer lock shut. But now the outer lock was on the central screw, well away from its rim. Air would suck about it ineffectually, dragging out into space.

Mullen kept on thumping. Would the Kloros look at the airgauge, note that it scarcely lifted from zero, or would they take its proper working for granted?

Porter said, "He's been gone an hour and a half."

"I know," said Stuart.

They were all restless, jumpy, but the tension among themselves had disappeared. It was as though all the threads of emotion extended to the hull of the ship.

Porter was bothered. His philosophy of life had always been simple—take care of yourself because no one will take care of you for you. It upset him to see it shaken.

He said, "Do you suppose they've caught him?"

"If they had, we'd hear about it," replied Stuart, briefly.

Porter felt, with a miserable twinge, that there was little interest on the part of the others in speaking to him. He could understand it; he had not exactly earned their respect. For the moment, a torrent of self-excuse poured through his mind. The others had been frightened, too. A man had a right to be afraid. No one likes to die. At least, he hadn't broken like Aristides Polyorketes. He hadn't wept like Leblanc. He—

But there was Mullen, out there on the hull.

"Listen," he cried, "why did he do it?" They turned to look at him, not understanding, but Porter didn't care. It bothered him to the point where it had to come out. "I want to know why Mullen is risking his life."

"The man," said Windham, "is a patriot—"

"No, none of that!" Porter was almost hysterical. "That little fellow has no emotions at all. He just has reasons and I want to know what those reasons are, because—"

He didn't finish the sentence. Could he say that if those reasons applied to a little middle-aged bookkeeper, they might apply even more forcibly to himself?

Polyorketes said, "He's one brave damn little fellow."

Porter got to his feet. "Listen," he said, "he may be stuck out there. Whatever he's doing, he may not be able to finish it alone. I— I volunteer to go out after him."

He was shaking as he said it and he waited in fear for the sarcastic lash of Stuart's tongue. Stuart was staring at him, probably with surprise, but Porter dared not meet his eyes to make certain.

Stuart said, mildly, "Let's give him another half-hour."

Porter looked up, startled. There was no sneer on Stuart's face. It was even friendly. They *all* looked friendly.

He said, "And then—"

"And then all those who do volunteer will draw straws or something equally democratic. Who volunteers, besides Porter?"

They all raised their hands; Stuart did, too.

But Porter was happy. He had volunteered first. He was anxious for the half-hour to pass.

It caught Mullen by surprise. The outer lock flew open and the long, thin, snakelike, almost headless neck of a Kloro sucked out, unable to fight the blast of escaping air.

Mullen's cylinder flew away, almost tore free. After one wild moment of frozen panic, he fought for it, dragging it above the airstream, waiting as long as he dared to let the first fury die down as the air of the control room thinned out, then bringing it down with force.

It caught the sinewy neck squarely, crushing it. Mullen, curled above the lock, almost entirely protected from the stream, raised the cylinder again and plunging it down again striking the head, mashing the staring eyes to liquid ruin. In the near-vacuum, green blood was pumping out of what was left of the neck.

Mullen dared not vomit, but he wanted to.

With eyes averted, he backed away, caught the outer lock with one hand and imparted a whirl. For several seconds, it maintained that whirl. At the end of the screw, the springs engaged automatically and pulled it shut. What was left of the atmosphere tightened it and the laboring pumps could now begin to fill the control room once again.

Mullen crawled over the mangled Kloro and into the room. It was empty.

He had barely time to notice that when he found himself on his knees. He rose with difficulty. The transition from non-gravity to gravity had taken him entirely by surprise. It was Klorian gravity, too, which meant that with this suit, he carried a fifty percent overload for his small frame. At least, though, his heavy metal clogs no longer clung so exasperatingly to the metal underneath. Within the ship, floors and wall were of cork-covered aluminum alloy.

He circled slowly. The neckless Kloro had collapsed and lay with only an occasional twitch to show it had once been a living organism. He stepped over it, distastefully, and drew the steam-tube lock shut.

The room had a depressing bilious cast and the lights shone yellow-green. It was the Kloro atmosphere, of course.

Mullen felt a twinge of surprise and reluctant admiration. The

Kloros obviously had some way of treating materials so that they were impervious to the oxidizing effect of chlorine. Even the map of Earth on the wall, printed on glossy plastic-backed paper, seemed fresh and untouched. He approached, drawn by the familiar outlines of the continents—

There was a flash of motion caught in the corner of his eyes. As quickly as he could in his heavy suit, he turned, then screamed. The Kloro he had thought dead was rising to its feet.

Its neck hung limp, an oozing mass of tissue mash, but its arms reached out blindly, and the tentacles about its chest vibrated rapidly like innumerable snakes' tongues.

It was blind, of course. The destruction of its neck-stalk had deprived it of all sensory equipment, and partial asphyxiation had disorganized it. But the brain remained whole and safe in the abdomen. It still lived.

Mullen backed away. He circled, trying clumsily and unsuccessfully to tiptoe, though he knew that what was left of the Kloro was also deaf. It blundered on its way, struck a wall, felt to the base and began sidling along it.

Mullen cast about desperately for a weapon, found nothing. There was the Kloro's holster, but he dared not reach for it. Why hadn't he snatched it at the very first? Fool!

The door to the control room opened. It made almost no noise. Mullen turned, quivering.

The other Kloro entered, unharmed, entire. It stood in the doorway for a moment, chest-tendrils stiff and unmoving; its neck-stalk stretched forward; its horrible eyes flickering first at him and then at its nearly dead comrade.

And then its hand moved quickly to its side.

Mullen, without awareness, moved as quickly in pure reflex. He stretched out the hose of the spare oxygen-cylinder, which, since entering the control room, he had replaced in its suit-clamp, and cracked the valve. He didn't bother reducing the pressure. He let it gush out unchecked so that he nearly staggered under the backward push.

He could *see* the oxygen stream. It was a pale puff, billowing out amid the chlorine-green. It caught the Kloro with one hand on the weapon's holster.

The Kloro threw its hands up. The little beak on its head-nodule opened alarmingly but noiselessly. It staggered and fell, writhed for a moment, then lay still. Mullen approached and played the oxygen-stream upon its body as though he were extinguishing a fire. And then he raised his heavy foot and brought it down upon the center of the neck-stalk and crushed it on the floor.

He turned to the first. It was sprawled, rigid.

The whole room was pale with oxygen, enough to kill whole legions of Kloros, and his cylinder was empty.

Mullen stepped over the dead Kloro, out of the control room and along the main corridor toward the prisoners' room.

Reaction had set in. He was whimpering in blind, incoherent fright.

Stuart was tired. False hands and all, he was at the controls of a ship once again. Two light cruisers of Earth were on the way. For better than twenty-four hours he had handled the controls virtually alone. He had discarded the chlorinating equipment, rerigged the old atmospherics, located the ship's position in space, tried to plot a course, and sent out carefully guarded signals—which had worked.

So when the door of the control room opened, he was a little annoyed. He was too tired to play conversational handball. Then he turned, and it was Mullen stepping inside.

Stuart said, "For God's sake, get back into bed, Mullen!"

Mullen said, "I'm tired of sleeping, even though I never thought I would be a while ago."

"How do you feel?"

"I'm stiff all over. Especially my side." He grimaced and stared involuntarily around.

"Don't look for the Kloros," Stuart said. "We dumped the poor devils." He shook his head. "I was sorry for them. To themselves, *they're* the human beings, you know, and *we're* the aliens. Not that I'd rather they'd killed you, you understand."

"I understand."

Stuart turned a sidelong glance upon the little man who sat looking at the map of Earth and went on, "I owe you a particular and personal apology, Mullen. I didn't think much of you."

"It was your privilege," said Mullen in his dry voice. There was no feeling in it.

"No, it wasn't. It is no one's privilege to despise another. It is only a hard-won right after long experience."

"Have you been thinking about this?"

"Yes, all day. Maybe I can't explain. It's these hands." He held them up before him, spread out. "It was hard knowing that other people had hands of their own. I had to hate them for it. I always had to do my best to investigate and belittle their motives, point up their deficiencies, expose their stupidities. I had to do anything that would prove to myself that they weren't worth envying."

Mullen moved restlessly. "This explanation is not necessary."

"It is. It is!" Stuart felt his thoughts intently, strained to put them into words. "For years I've abandoned hope of finding any decency in human beings. Then you climbed into the C-chute."

"You had better understand," said Mullen, "that I was motivated by practical and selfish considerations. I will not have you present me to myself as a hero."

"I wasn't intending to. I know that you would do nothing without a reason. It was what your action did to the rest of us. It turned a collection of phonies and fools into decent people. And not by magic either. They were decent all along. It was just that they needed something to live up to and you supplied it. And—I'm one of them. I'll have to live up to you, too. For the rest of my life, probably."

Mullen turned away uncomfortably. His hand straightened his sleeves, which were not in the least twisted. His finger rested on the map.

He said, "I was born in Richmond, Virginia, you know. Here it is. I'll be going there first. Where were you born?"

"Toronto," said Stuart.

"That's right here. Not very far apart on the map, is it?"

Stuart said, "Would you tell me something?"

"If I can."

"Just why *did* you go out there?"

Mullen's precise mouth pursed. He said, dryly, "Wouldn't my rather prosaic reason ruin the inspirational effect?"

"Call it intellectual curiosity. Each of the rest of us had such obvious motives. Porter was scared to death of being interned; Leblanc wanted to get back to his sweetheart; Polyorketes wanted to kill Kloros; and Windham was a patriot according to his lights. As for me, I thought of myself as a noble idealist, I'm afraid. Yet in none of us was the motivation strong enough to get us into a spacesuit and out the C-chute. Then what made *you* do it, *you,* of all people?"

"Why the phrase, 'of all people'?"

"Don't be offended, but you seem devoid of all emotion."

"Do I?" Mullen's voice did not change. It remained precise and soft, yet somehow a tightness had entered it. "That's only training, Mr. Stuart, and self-discipline; not nature. A small man can have no respectable emotions. Is there anything more ridiculous than a man like myself in a state of rage? I'm five feet and one-half inch tall, and one hundred and two pounds in weight, if you care for exact figures. I insist on the half inch and the two pounds.

"Can I be dignified? Proud? Draw myself to my full height without inducing laughter? Where can I meet a woman who will not dismiss me instantly with a giggle? Naturally, I've had to learn to dispense with external display of emotion.

"*You* talk about deformities. No one would notice your hands or know they were different, if you weren't so eager to tell people all about it the instant you meet them. Do you think that the eight inches of height I do not have can be hidden? That it is not the first and, in most cases, the only thing about me that a person will notice?"

Stuart was ashamed. He had invaded a privacy he ought not have. He said, "I'm sorry."

"Why?"

"I should not have forced you to speak of this. I should have seen for myself that you—that you—"

"That I what? Tried to prove myself? Tried to show that while I might be small in body, I held within it a giant heart?"

"I would not have put it mockingly."

"Why not? It's a foolish idea, and nothing like it is the reason I did what I did. What would I have accomplished if that's what was in my mind? Will they take me to Earth now and put me up before the television cameras—pitching them low, of course, to catch my face, or standing me on a chair—and pin medals on me?"

"They are quite likely to do exactly that."

"And what good would it do me? They would say, 'Gee, and he's such a little guy.' And afterward, what? Shall I tell each man I meet, 'You know, I'm the fellow they decorated for incredible valor last month?' How many medals, Mr. Stuart, do you suppose it would take to put eight inches and sixty pounds on me?"

Stuart said, "Put that way, I see your point."

Mullen was speaking a trifle more quickly now; a controlled heat had entered his words, warming them to just a tepid room temperature. "There *were* days when I thought I would show them, the mysterious 'them' that includes all the world. I was going to leave Earth and carve out worlds for myself. I would be a new and even smaller Napoleon. So I left Earth and went to Arcturus. And what could I do on Arcturus that I could not have done on Earth? Nothing. I balance books. So I am past the vanity, Mr. Stuart, of trying to stand on tiptoe."

"Then why *did* you do it?"

"I left Earth when I was twenty-eight and came to the Arcturian System. I've been there ever since. This trip was to be my first vacation, my first visit back to Earth in all that time. I was going to stay on Earth for six months. The Kloros instead captured us and would have kept us interned indefinitely. But I couldn't—I *couldn't* let them stop me from traveling to Earth. No matter what the risk, I had to prevent their interference. It wasn't love of woman, or fear, or hate, or idealism of any sort. It was stronger than any of those."

He stopped, and stretched out a hand as though to caress the map on the wall.

"Mr. Stuart," Mullen asked quietly, "haven't you ever been homesick?"

The Martian Way

1

From the doorway of the short corridor between the only two rooms in the travel-head of the spaceship, Mario Esteban Rioz watched sourly as Ted Long adjusted the video dials painstakingly. Long tried a touch clockwise, then a touch counter. The picture was lousy.

Rioz knew it would stay lousy. They were too far from Earth and at a bad position facing the Sun. But then Long would not be expected to know that. Rioz remained standing in the doorway for an additional moment, head bent to clear the upper lintel, body turned half sidewise to fit the narrow opening. Then he jerked into the galley like a cork popping out of a bottle.

"What are you after?" he asked.

"I thought I'd get Hilder," said Long.

Rioz propped his rump on the corner of a table shelf. He lifted a conical can of milk from the companion shelf just above his head. Its point popped under pressure. He swirled it gently as he waited for it to warm.

"What for?" he said. He upended the cone and sucked noisily.

"Thought I'd listen."

"I think it's a waste of power."

Long looked up, frowning. "It's customary to allow free use of personal video sets."

"Within reason," retorted Rioz.

Their eyes met challengingly. Rioz had the rangy body, the gaunt, cheek-sunken face that was almost the hallmark of the Martian Scavenger, those Spacers who patiently haunted the space routes between Earth and Mars. Pale blue eyes were set keenly in the brown, lined face which, in turn, stood darkly out against the white surrounding syntho-fur that lined the up-turned collar of his leathtic space jacket.

Long was altogether paler and softer. He bore some of the marks of the Grounder, although no second-generation Martian could be a Grounder in the sense that Earthmen were. His own collar was thrown back and his dark brown hair freely exposed.

"What do you call within reason?" demanded Long.

Rioz's thin lips grew thinner. He said, "Considering that we're not even going to make expenses this trip, the way it looks, any power drain at all is outside reason."

Long said, "If we're losing money, hadn't you better get back to your post? It's your watch."

Rioz grunted and ran a thumb and forefinger over the stubble on his chin. He got up and trudged to the door, his soft, heavy boots muting the sound of his steps. He paused to look at the thermostat, then turned with a flare of fury.

"I *thought* it was hot. Where do you think you are?"

Long said, "Forty degrees isn't excessive."

"For you it isn't, maybe. But this is space, not a heated office at the iron mines." Rioz swung the thermostat control down to minimum with a quick thumb movement. "Sun's warm enough."

"The galley isn't on Sunside."

"It'll percolate through, damn it."

Rioz stepped through the door and Long stared after him for a long moment, then turned back to the video. He did not turn up the thermostat.

The picture was still flickering badly, but it would have to do. Long folded a chair down out of the wall. He leaned forward waiting through the formal announcement, the momentary pause before the slow dissolution of the curtain, the spotlight picking out the well-known bearded figure which grew as it was brought forward until it filled the screen.

The voice, impressive even through the flutings and croakings induced by the electron storms of twenty millions of miles, began:

"Friends! My fellow citizens of Earth . . ."

2

Rioz's eye caught the flash of the radio signal as he stepped into the pilot room. For one moment, the palms of his hands grew clammy when it seemed to him that it was a radar pip; but that was only his guilt speaking. He should not have left the pilot room while on duty theoretically, though all Scavengers did it. Still, it was the standard nightmare, this business of a strike turning up during just those five minutes when one knocked off for a quick coffee because it seemed certain that space was clear. And the nightmare had been known to happen, too.

Rioz threw in the multi-scanner. It was a waste of power, but while he was thinking about it, he might as well make sure.

Space was clear except for the far-distant echoes from the neighboring ships on the scavenging line.

He hooked up the radio circuit, and the blond, long-nosed head of Richard Swenson, copilot of the next ship on the Marsward side, filled it.

"Hey, Mario," said Swenson.

"Hi. What's new?"

There was a second and a fraction of pause between that and Swenson's next comment, since the speed of electromagnetic radiation is not infinite.

"What a day I've *had*."

"Something happened?" Rioz asked.

"I had a strike."

"Well, good."

"Sure, if I'd roped it in," said Swenson morosely.

"What happened?"

"Damn it, I headed in the wrong direction."

Rioz knew better than to laugh. He said, "How did you do that?"

"It wasn't my fault. The trouble was the shell was moving way out of the ecliptic. Can you imagine the stupidity of a pilot that can't work the release maneuver decently? How was I to know? I got the distance of the shell and let it go at that. I just assumed its orbit was in the usual trajectory family. Wouldn't you? I started along what I thought was a good line of intersection and it was five minutes before I noticed the distance was still going up. The pips were taking their sweet time returning. So then I took the angular projections of the thing, and it was too late to catch up with it."

"Any of the other boys getting it?"

"No. It's 'way out of the ecliptic and'll keep on going forever. That's not what bothers me so much. It was only an inner shell. But I hate to tell you how many tons of propulsion I wasted getting up speed and then getting back to station. You should have heard Canute."

Canute was Richard Swenson's brother and partner.

"Mad, huh?" said Rioz.

"Mad? Like to have killed me! But then we've been out five months now and it's getting kind of sticky. You know."

"I know."

"How are you doing, Mario?"

Rioz made a spitting gesture. "About that much this trip. Two shells in the last two weeks and I had to chase each one for six hours."

"Big ones?"

"Are you kidding? I could have scaled them down to Phobos by hand. This is the worst trip I've ever had."

"How much longer are you staying?"

"For my part, we can quit tomorrow. We've only been out two months and it's got so I'm chewing Long out all the time."

There was a pause over and above the electromagnetic lag.

Swenson said, "What's he like, anyway? Long, I mean."

Rioz looked over his shoulder. He could hear the soft, crackly mutter of the video in the galley. "I can't make him out. He says to me about a week after the start of the trip, 'Mario, why are you a Scavenger?' I just look at him and say, 'To make a living. Why do you suppose?' I mean, what the hell kind of a question is that? Why is anyone a Scavenger?

"Anyway, he says, 'That's not it, Mario.' *He's* telling *me,* you see. He says, 'You're a Scavenger because this is part of the Martian way.' "

Swenson said, "And what did he mean by that?"

Rioz shrugged. "I never asked him. Right now he's sitting in there listening to the ultra-microwave from Earth. He's listening to some Grounder called Hilder."

"Hilder? A Grounder politician, an Assemblyman or something, isn't he?"

"That's right. At least, I think that's right. Long is always doing things like that. He brought about fifteen pounds of books with him, all about Earth. Just plain dead weight, you know."

"Well, he's your partner. And talking about partners, I think I'll get back on the job. If I miss another strike, there'll be murder around here."

He was gone and Rioz leaned back. He watched the even green

line that was the pulse scanner. He tried the multi-scanner a moment. Space was still clear.

He felt a little better. A bad spell is always worse if the Scavengers all about you are pulling in shell after shell; if the shells go spiraling down to the Phobos scrap forges with everyone's brand welded on except your own. Then, too, he had managed to work off some of his resentment toward Long.

It was a mistake teaming up with Long. It was always a mistake to team up with a tenderfoot. They thought what you wanted was conservation, especially Long, with his eternal theories about Mars and its great new role in human progress. That was the way he said it—Human Progress: the Martian Way; the New Creative Minority. And all the time what Rioz wanted wasn't talk, but a strike, a few shells to call their own.

At that, he hadn't any choice, really. Long was pretty well known down on Mars and made good pay as a mining engineer. He was a friend of Commissioner Sankov and he'd been out on one or two short scavenging missions before. You can't turn a fellow down flat before a tryout, even though it did look funny. Why should a mining engineer with a comfortable job and good money want to muck around in space?

Rioz never asked Long that question. Scavenger partners are forced too close together to make curiosity desirable, or sometimes even safe. But Long talked so much that he answered the question.

"I had to come out here, Mario," he said. "The future of Mars isn't in the mines; it's in space."

Rioz wondered how it would be to try a trip alone. Everyone said it was impossible. Even discounting lost opportunities when one man had to go off watch to sleep or attend to other things, it was well known that one man alone in space would become intolerably depressed in a relatively short while.

Taking a partner along made a six-month trip possible. A regular crew would be better, but no Scavenger could make money on a ship large enough to carry one. The capital it would take in propulsion alone!

Even two didn't find it exactly fun in space. Usually you had to change partners each trip and you could stay out longer with some than with others. Look at Richard and Canute Swenson. They teamed up every five or six trips because they were brothers. And yet whenever they did, it was a case of constantly mounting tension and antagonism after the first week.

Oh well. Space was clear. Rioz would feel a little better if he went back in the galley and smoothed down some of the bickering with Long. He might as well show he was an old spacehand who took the irritations of space as they came.

He stood up, walked the three steps necessary to reach the short, narrow corridor that tied together the two rooms of the spaceship.

3

Once again Rioz stood in the doorway for a moment, watching. Long was intent on the flickering screen.

Rioz said gruffly, "I'm shoving up the thermostat. It's all right—we can spare the power."

Long nodded. "If you like."

Rioz took a hesitant step forward. Space was clear, so to hell with sitting and looking at a blank, green, pipless line. He said, "What's the Grounder been talking about?"

"History of space travel mostly. Old stuff, but he's doing it well. He's giving the whole works—color cartoons, trick photography, stills from old films, everything."

As if to illustrate Long's remarks, the bearded figure faded out of view, and a cross-sectional view of a spaceship flitted onto the screen. Hilder's voice continued, pointing out features of interest that appeared in schematic color. The communications system of the ship outlined itself in red as he talked about it, the storerooms, the patron micropile drive, the cybernetic circuits . . .

Then Hilder was back on the screen. "But this is only the travel-head of the ship. What moves it? What gets it off the Earth?"

Everyone knew what moved a spaceship, but Hilder's voice was like a drug. He made spaceship propulsion sound like the secret of the ages, like an ultimate revelation. Even Rioz felt a slight tingling of suspense, though he had spent the greater part of his life aboard ship.

Hilder went on. "Scientists call it different names. They call it the Law of Action and Reaction. Sometimes they call it Newton's Third Law. Sometimes they call it Conservation of Momentum. But we don't have to call it any name. We can just use our common sense. When we swim we push water backward and move forward ourselves.

When we walk, we push back against the ground and move forward. When we fly a gyro-flivver, we push air backward and move forward.

"Nothing can move forward unless something else moves backward. It's the old principle of 'You can't get something for nothing.'

"Now imagine a spaceship that weighs a hundred thousand tons lifting off Earth. To do that, something else must be moved downward. Since a spaceship is extremely heavy, a great deal of material must be moved downward. So much material, in fact, that there is no place to keep it all aboard ship. A special compartment must be built behind the ship to hold it."

Again Hilder faded out and the ship returned. It shrank and a truncated cone appeared behind it. In bright yellow, words appeared within it: MATERIAL TO BE THROWN AWAY.

"But now," said Hilder, "the total weight of the ship is much greater. You need still more propulsion and still more."

The ship shrank enormously to add on another larger shell and still another immense one. The ship proper, the travel-head, was a little dot on the screen, a glowing red dot.

Rioz said, "Hell, this is kindergarden stuff."

"Not to the people he's speaking to, Mario," replied Long. "Earth isn't Mars. There must be billions of Earth people who've never seen a spaceship; don't know the first thing about it."

Hilder was saying, "When the material inside the biggest shell is used up, the shell is detached. It's thrown away, too."

The outermost shell came loose, wobbled about the screen.

"Then the second one goes," said Hilder, "and then, if the trip is a long one, the last is ejected."

The ship was just a red dot now, with three shells shifting and moving, lost in space.

Hilder said, "These shells represent a hundred thousand tons of tungsten, magnesium, aluminum, and steel. They are gone forever from Earth. Mars is ringed by Scavengers, waiting along the routes of space travel, waiting for the cast-off shells, netting and branding them, saving them for Mars. Not one cent of payment reaches Earth for them. They are salvage. They belong to the ship that finds them."

Rioz said, "We risk our investment and our lives. If we don't pick them up, no one gets them. What loss is that to Earth?"

"Look," said Long, "he's been talking about nothing but the drain that Mars, Venus, and the Moon put on Earth. This is just another item of loss."

"They'll get their return. We're mining more iron every year."

"And most of it goes right back into Mars. If you can believe his figures, Earth has invested two hundred billion dollars in Mars and received back about five billion dollars' worth of iron. It's put five hundred billion dollars into the Moon and gotten back a little over twenty-five billion dollars of magnesium, titanium, and assorted light metals. It's put fifty billion dollars into Venus and gotten back nothing. And that's what the taxpayers of Earth are really interested in—tax money out; nothing in."

The screen was filled, as he spoke, with diagrams of the Scavengers on the route to Mars; little, grinning caricatures of ships, reaching out wiry, tenuous arms that groped for the tumbling, empty shells, seizing and snaking them in, branding them MARS PROPERTY in glowing letters, then scaling them down to Phobos.

Then it was Hilder again. "They tell us eventually they will return it all to us. Eventually! Once they are a going concern! We don't know when that will be. A century from now? A thousand years? A million? 'Eventually.' Let's take them at their word. Someday they will give us back all our metals. Someday they will grow their own food, use their own power, live their own lives.

"But one thing they can never return. Not in a hundred million years. *Water!*

"Mars has only a trickle of water because it is too small. Venus has no water at all because it is too hot. The Moon has none because it is too hot and too small. So Earth must supply not only drinking water and washing water for the Spacers, water to run their industries, water for the hydroponic factories they claim to be setting up—but even water to throw away by the millions of tons.

"What is the propulsive force that spaceships use? What is it they throw out behind so that they can accelerate forward? Once it was the gases generated from explosives. That was very expensive. Then the proton micropile was invented—a cheap power source that could heat up any liquid until it was a gas under tremendous pressure. What is the cheapest and most plentiful liquid available? Why, water, of course.

"Each spaceship leaves Earth carrying nearly a million tons—not pounds, *tons*—of water, for the sole purpose of driving it into space so that it may speed up or slow down.

"Our ancestors burned the oil of Earth madly and wilfully. They destroyed its coal recklessly. We despise and condemn them for that, but at least they had this excuse—they thought that when the need arose, substitutes would be found. And they were right. We have our plankton farms and our proton micropiles.

"But there is no substitute for water. None! There never can be. And when our descendants view the desert we will have made of Earth, what excuse will they find for us? When the droughts come and grow——"

Long leaned forward and turned off the set. He said, "That bothers me. The damn fool is deliberately—— What's the matter?"

Rioz had risen uneasily to his feet. "I ought to be watching the pips."

"The hell with the pips." Long got up likewise, followed Rioz through the narrow corridor, and stood just inside the pilot room. "If Hilder carries this through, if he's got the guts to make a real issue out of it—*Wow!*"

He had seen it too. The pip was a Class A, racing after the outgoing signal like a greyhound after a mechanical rabbit.

Rioz was babbling, "Space was clear, I tell you, *clear*. For Mar's sake, Ted, don't just freeze on me. See if you can spot it visually."

Rioz was working speedily and with an efficiency that was the result of nearly twenty years of scavenging. He had the distance in two minutes. Then, remembering Swenson's experience, he measured the angle of declination and the radial velocity as well.

He yelled at Long, "One point seven six radians. You can't miss it, man."

Long held his breath as he adjusted the vernier. "It's only half a radian off the Sun. It'll only be crescent-lit."

He increased magnification as rapidly as he dared, watching for the one "star" that changed position and grew to have a form, revealing itself to be no star.

"I'm starting, anyway," said Rioz. "We can't wait."

"I've got it. I've got it." Magnification was still too small to give it a definite shape, but the dot Long watched was brightening and dimming rhythmically as the shell rotated and caught sunlight on cross sections of different sizes.

"Hold on."

The first of many fine spurts of steam squirted out of the proper vents, leaving long trails of micro-crystals of ice gleaming mistily in the pale beams of the distant Sun. They thinned out for a hundred miles or so. One spurt, then another, then another, as the Scavenger ship moved out of its stable trajectory and took up a course tangential to that of the shell.

"It's moving like a comet at perihelion!" yelled Rioz. "Those damned Grounder pilots knock the shells off that way on purpose. I'd like to——"

He swore his anger in a frustrated frenzy as he kicked steam backward and backward recklessly, till the hydraulic cushioning of his chair had soughed back a full foot and Long had found himself all but unable to maintain his grip on the guard rail.

"Have a heart," he begged.

But Rioz had his eye on the pips. "If you can't take it, man, stay on Mars!" The steam spurts continued to boom distantly.

The radio came to life. Long managed to lean forward through what seemed like molasses and closed contact. It was Swenson, eyes glaring.

Swenson yelled, "Where the hell are you guys going? You'll be in my sector in ten seconds."

Rioz said, "I'm chasing a shell."

"In *my* sector?"

"It started in mine and you're not in position to get it. Shut off that radio, Ted."

The ship thundered through space, a thunder that could be heard only within the hull. And then Rioz cut the engines in stages large enough to make Long flail forward. The sudden silence was more ear-shattering than the noise that had preceded it.

Rioz said, "All right. Let me have the 'scope."

They both watched. The shell was a definite truncated cone now, tumbling with slow solemnity as it passed along among the stars.

"It's a Class A shell, all right," said Rioz with satisfaction. A giant among shells, he thought. It would put them into the black.

Long said, "We've got another pip on the scanner. I think it's Swenson taking after us."

Rioz scarcely gave it a glance. "He won't catch us."

The shell grew larger still, filling the visiplate.

Rioz's hands were on the harpoon lever. He waited, adjusted the angle microscopically twice, played out the length allotment. Then he yanked, tripping the release.

For a moment, nothing happened. Then a metal mesh cable snaked out onto the visiplate, moving toward the shell like a striking cobra. It made contact, but it did not hold. If it had, it would have snapped instantly like a cobweb strand. The shell was turning with a rotational momentum amounting to thousands of tons. What the cable did do was to set up a powerful magnetic field that acted as a brake on the shell.

Another cable and another lashed out. Rioz sent them out in an almost heedless expenditure of energy.

"I'll get this one! By Mars, I'll get this one!"

With some two dozen cables stretching between ship and shell, he desisted. The shell's rotational energy, converted by breaking into heat, had raised its temperature to a point where its radiation could be picked up by the ship's meters.

Long said, "Do you want me to put our brand on?"

"Suits me. But you don't have to if you don't want to. It's my watch."

"I don't mind."

Long clambered into his suit and went out the lock. It was the surest sign of his newness to the game that he could count the number of times he had been out in space in a suit. This was the fifth time.

He went out along the nearest cable, hand over hand, feeling the vibration of the mesh against the metal of his mitten.

He burned their serial number in the smooth metal of the shell. There was nothing to oxidize the steel in the emptiness of space. It simply melted and vaporized, condensing some feet away from the energy beam, turning the surface it touched into a gray, powdery dullness.

Long swung back toward the ship.

Inside again, he took off his helmet, white and thick with frost that collected as soon as he had entered.

The first thing he heard was Swenson's voice coming over the radio in this almost unrecognizable rage: ". . . straight to the Commissioner. Damn it, there are rules to this game!"

Rioz sat back, unbothered. "Look, it hit my sector. I was late spotting it and I chased it into yours. You couldn't have gotten it with Mars for a backstop. That's all there is to it—— You back, Long?"

He cut contact.

The signal button raged at him, but he paid no attention.

"He's going to the Commissioner?" Long asked.

"Not a chance. He just goes on like that because it breaks the monotony. He doesn't mean anything by it. He knows it's our shell. And how do you like that hunk of stuff, Ted?"

"Pretty good."

"Pretty good? It's terrific! Hold on. I'm setting it swinging."

The side jets spat steam and the ship started a slow rotation about the shell. The shell followed it. In thirty minutes, they were a gigantic bolo spinning in emptiness. Long checked the *Ephemeris* for the position of Deimos.

At a precisely calculated moment, the cables released their magnetic field and the shell went streaking off tangentially in a trajectory that would, in a day or so, bring it within pronging distance of the shell stores on the Martian satellite.

Rioz watched it go. He felt good. He turned to Long. "This is one fine day for us."

"What about Hilder's speech?" asked Long.

"What? Who? Oh, that. Listen, if I had to worry about every thing some damned Grounder said, I'd never get any sleep. Forget it."

"I don't think we should forget it."

"You're nuts. Don't bother me about it, will you? Get some sleep instead."

4

Ted Long found the breadth and height of the city's main thoroughfare exhilarating. It had been two months since the Commissioner had declared a moratorium on scavenging and had pulled all ships out of space, but this feeling of a stretched-out vista had not stopped thrilling Long. Even the thought that the moratorium was called pending a decision on the part of Earth to enforce its new insistence on water economy, by deciding upon a ration limit for scavenging, did not cast him entirely down.

The roof of the avenue was painted a luminous light blue, perhaps as an old-fashioned imitation of Earth's sky. Ted wasn't sure. The walls were lit with the store windows that pierced it.

Off in the distance, over the hum of traffic and the sloughing noise of people's feet passing him, he could hear the intermittent blasting as new channels were being bored into Mars' crust. All his life he remembered such blastings. The ground he walked on had been part of solid, unbroken rock when he was born. The city was growing and would keep on growing—if Earth would only let it.

He turned off at a cross street, narrower, not quite as brilliantly lit, shop windows giving way to apartment houses, each with its row of lights along the front façade. Shoppers and traffic gave way to slower-paced individuals and to squawling youngsters who had as yet evaded the maternal summons to the evening meal.

At the last minute, Long remembered the social amenities and stopped off at a corner water store.

He passed over his canteen. "Fill 'er up."

The plump storekeeper unscrewed the cap, cocked an eye into the opening. He shook it a little and let it gurgle. "Not much left," he said cheerfully.

"No," agreed Long.

The storekeeper trickled water in, holding the neck of the canteen close to the hose tip to avoid spillage. The volume gauge whirred. He screwed the cap back on.

Long passed over the coins and took his canteen. It clanked against his hip now with a pleasing heaviness. It would never do to visit a family without a full canteen. Among the boys, it didn't matter. Not as much, anyway.

He entered the hallway of No. 27, climbed a short flight of stairs, and paused with his thumb on the signal.

The sound of voices could be heard quite plainly.

One was a woman's voice, somewhat shrill. "It's all right for you to have your Scavenger friends here, isn't it? I'm supposed to be thankful you manage to get home two months a year. Oh, it's quite enough that you spend a day or two with me. After that, it's the Scavengers again."

"I've been home for a long time now," said a male voice, "and this is business. For Mars' sake, let up, Dora. They'll be here soon."

Long decided to wait a moment before signaling. It might give them a chance to hit a more neutral topic.

"What do I care if they come?" retorted Dora. "Let them hear me. And I'd just as soon the Commissioner kept the moratorium on permanently. You hear me?"

"And what would we live on?" came the male voice hotly. "You tell me that."

"I'll tell you. You can make a decent, honorable living right here on Mars, just like everybody else. I'm the only one in this apartment house that's a Scavenger widow. That's what I am—a widow. I'm worse than a widow, because if I were a widow, I'd at least have a chance to marry someone else——— What did you say?"

"Nothing. Nothing at all."

"Oh, I know what you said. Now listen here, Dick Swenson———"

"I only said," cried Swenson, "that now I know why Scavengers usually don't marry."

"You shouldn't have either. I'm tired of having every person in the neighborhood pity me and smirk and ask when you're coming home. Other people can be mining engineers and administrators and even tunnel borers. At least tunnel borers' wives have a decent home life and their children don't grow up like vagabonds. Peter might as well not have a father———"

A thin boy-soprano voice made its way through the door. It was somewhat more distant, as though it were in another room. "Hey, Mom, what's a vagabond?"

Dora's voice rose a notch. "Peter! You keep your mind on your homework."

Swenson said in a low voice, "It's not right to talk this way in front of the kid. What kind of notions will he get about me?"

"Stay home then and teach him better notions."

Peter's voice called out again. "Hey, Mom, I'm going to be a Scavenger when I grow up."

Footsteps sounded rapidly. There was a momentary hiatus in the sounds, then a piercing, "Mom! Hey, Mom! Leggo my ear! What did I do?" and a snuffling silence.

Long seized the chance. He worked the signal vigorously.

Swenson opened the door, brushing down his hair with both hands.

"Hello, Ted," he said in a subdued voice. Then loudly, "Ted's here, Dora. Where's Mario, Ted?"

Long said, "He'll be here in a while."

Dora came bustling out of the next room, a small, dark woman with a pinched nose, and hair, just beginning to show touches of gray, combed off the forehead.

"Hello, Ted. Have you eaten?"

"Quite well, thanks. I haven't interrupted you, have I?"

"Not at all. We finished ages ago. Would you like some coffee?"

"I think so." Ted unslung his canteen and offered it.

"Oh, goodness, that's all right. We've plenty of water."

"I insist."

"Well, then——"

Back into the kitchen she went. Through the swinging door, Long caught a glimpse of dishes sitting in Secoterg, the "waterless cleaner that soaks up and absorbs grease and dirt in a twinkling. One ounce of water will rinse eight square feet of dish surface clean as clean. Buy Secoterg. Secoterg just cleans it right, makes your dishes shiny bright, does away with water waste——"

The tune started whining through his mind and Long crushed it with speech. He said, "How's Pete?"

"Fine, fine. The kid's in the fourth grade now. You know I don't get to see him much. Well, sir, when I came back last time, he looked at me and said . . ."

It went on for a while and wasn't too bad as bright sayings of bright children as told by dull parents go.

The door signal burped and Mario Rioz came in, frowning and red.

Swenson stepped to him quickly. "Listen, don't say anything about shell-snaring. Dora still remembers the time you fingered a Class A shell out of my territory and she's in one of her moods now."

"Who the hell wants to talk about shells?" Rioz slung off a fur-lined jacket, threw it over the back of the chair, and sat down.

Dora came through the swinging door, viewed the newcomer with a synthetic smile, and said, "Hello, Mario. Coffee for you, too?"

"Yeah," he said, reaching automatically for his canteen.

"Just use some more of my water, Dora," said Long quickly. "He'll owe it to me."

"Yeah," said Rioz.

"What's wrong, Mario?" asked Long.

Rioz said heavily, "Go on. Say you told me so. A year ago when Hilder made that speech, you told me so. Say it."

Long shrugged.

Rioz said, "They've set up the quota. Fifteen minutes ago the news came out."

"Well?"

"Fifty thousand tons of water per trip."

"What?" yelled Swenson, burning. "You can't get off Mars with fifty thousand!"

"That's the figure. It's a deliberate piece of gutting. No more scavenging."

Dora came out with the coffee and set it down all around.

"What's all this about no more scavenging?" She sat down very firmly and Swenson looked helpless.

"It seems," said Long, "that they're rationing us at fifty thousand tons and that means we can't make any more trips."

"Well, what of it?" Dora sipped her coffee and smiled gaily. "If you want my opinion, it's a good thing. It's time all you Scavengers found yourselves a nice, steady job here on Mars. I mean it. It's no life to be running all over space———"

"Please, Dora," said Swenson.

Rioz came close to a snort.

Dora raised her eyebrows. "I'm just giving my opinions."

Long said, "Please feel free to do so. But I would like to say something. Fifty thousand is just a detail. We know that Earth—or at least Hilder's party—wants to make political capital out of a campaign for water economy, so we're in a bad hole. We've got to get water somehow or they'll shut us down altogether, right?"

"Well, sure," said Swenson.

"But the question is how, right?"

"If it's only getting water," said Rioz in a sudden gush of words, "there's only one thing to do and you know it. If the Grounders won't give us water, we'll take it. The water doesn't belong to them just because their fathers and grandfathers were too damned sick-yellow ever to leave their fat planet. Water belongs to people wherever they are. We're people and the water's ours, too. We have a right to it."

"How do you propose taking it?" asked Long.

"Easy! They've got oceans of water on Earth. They can't post a guard over every square mile. We can sink down on the night side of the planet any time we want, fill our shells, then get away. How can they stop us?"

"In half a dozen ways, Mario. How do you spot shells in space up to distances of a hundred thousand miles? One thin metal shell in all that space. How? By radar. Do you think there's no radar on Earth? Do you think that if Earth ever gets the notion we're engaged in waterlegging, it won't be simple for them to set up a radar network to spot ships coming in from space?"

Dora broke in indignantly. "I'll tell you one thing, Mario Rioz.

My husband isn't going to be part of any raid to get water to keep up his scavenging with."

"It isn't just scavenging," said Mario. "Next they'll be cutting down on everything else. We've got to stop them now."

"But we don't need their water, anyway," said Dora. "We're not the Moon or Venus. We pipe enough water down from the polar caps for all we need. We have a water tap right in this apartment. There's one in every apartment on this block."

Long said, "Home use is the smallest part of it. The mines use water. And what do we do about the hydroponic tanks?"

"That's right," said Swenson. "What about the hydroponic tanks, Dora? They've got to have water and it's about time we arranged to grow our own fresh food instead of having to live on the condensed crud they ship us from Earth."

"Listen to him," said Dora scornfully. "What do you know about fresh food? You've never eaten any."

"I've eaten more than you think. Do you remember those carrots I picked up once?"

"Well, what was so wonderful about them? If you ask me, good baked protomeal is much better. And healthier, too. It just seems to be the fashion now to be talking fresh vegetables because they're increasing taxes for these hydroponics. Besides, all this will blow over."

Long said, "I don't think so. Not by itself, anyway. Hilder will probably be the next Co-ordinator, and then things may really get bad. If they cut down on food shipments, too——"

"Well, then," shouted Rioz, "what do we do? I still say take it! Take the water!"

"And I say we can't do that, Mario. Don't you see that what you're suggesting is the Earth way, the Grounder way? You're trying to hold on to the umbilical cord that ties Mars to Earth. Can't you get away from that? Can't you see the Martian way?"

"No, I can't. Suppose you tell me."

"I will, if you'll listen. When we think about the Solar System, what do we think about? Mercury, Venus, Earth, Moon, Mars, Phobos, and Deimos. There you are—seven bodies, that's all. But that doesn't represent 1 per cent of the Solar System. We Martians are right at the edge of the other 99 per cent. Out there, farther from the Sun, there's unbelievable amounts of water!"

The others stared.

Swenson said uncertainly, "You mean the layers of ice on Jupiter and Saturn?"

"Not that specifically, but it *is* water, you'll admit. A thousand-mile-thick layer of water is a lot of water."

"But it's all covered up with layers of ammonia or—or something, isn't it?" asked Swenson. "Besides, we can't land on the major planets."

"I know that," said Long, "but I haven't said that was the answer. The major planets aren't the only objects out there. What about the asteroids and the satellites? Vesta is a two-hundred-mile-diameter asteroid that's hardly more than a chunk of ice. One of the moons of Saturn is mostly ice. How about that?"

Rioz said, "Haven't you ever been in space, Ted?"

"You know I have. Why do you ask?"

"Sure, I know you have, but you still talk like a Grounder. Have you thought of the distances involved? The average asteroid is a hundred twenty million miles from Mars at the closest. That's twice the Venus-Mars hop and you know that hardly any liners do even that in one jump. They usually stop off at Earth or the Moon. After all, how long do you expect anyone to stay in space, man?"

"I don't know. What's your limit?"

"You know the limit. You don't have to ask me. It's six months. That's handbook data. After six months, if you're still in space, you're psychotherapy meat. Right, Dick?"

Swenson nodded.

"And that's just the asteroids," Rioz went on. "From Mars to Jupiter is three hundred thirty million miles, and to Saturn it's seven hundred million. How can anyone handle that kind of distance? Suppose you hit standard velocity or, to make it even, say you get up to a good two hundred kilomiles an hour. It would take you— let's see, allowing time for acceleration and deceleration—about six or seven months to get to Jupiter and nearly a year to get to Saturn. Of course, you could hike the speed to a million miles an hour, theoretically, but where would you get the water to do that?"

"Gee," said a small voice attached to a smutty nose and round eyes. "Saturn!"

Dora whirled in her chair. "Peter, march right back into your room!"

"Aw, Ma."

"Don't 'Aw, Ma' me." She began to get out of the chair, and Peter scuttled away.

Swenson said, "Say, Dora, why don't you keep him company for a while? It's hard to keep his mind on homework if we're all out here talking."

Dora smiled obstinately and stayed put. "I'll sit right here until I find out what Ted Long is thinking of. I tell you right now I don't like the sound of it."

Swenson said nervously, "Well, never mind Jupiter and Saturn. I'm sure Ted isn't figuring on that. But what about Vesta? We could make it in ten or twelve weeks there and the same back. And two hundred miles in diameter. That's four million cubic miles of ice!"

"So what?" said Rioz. "What do we do on Vesta? Quarry the ice? Set up mining machinery? Say, do you know how long that would take?"

Long said, "I'm talking about Saturn, not Vesta."

Rioz addressed an unseen audience. "I tell him seven hundred million miles and he keeps on talking."

"All right," said Long, "suppose you tell me how you know we can only stay in space six months, Mario?"

"It's common knowledge, damn it."

"Because it's in the *Handbook of Space Flight*. It's data compiled by Earth scientists from experience with Earth pilots and spacemen. You're still thinking Grounder style. You won't think the Martian way."

"A Martian may be a Martian, but he's still a man."

"But how can you be so blind? How many times have you fellows been out for over six months without a break?"

Rioz said, "That's different."

"Because you're Martians? Because you're professional Scavengers?"

"No. Because we're not on a flight. We can put back for Mars any time we want to."

"But you *don't* want to. That's my point. Earthmen have tremendous ships with libraries of films, with a crew of fifteen plus passengers. Still, they can only stay out six months maximum. Martian Scavengers have a two-room ship with only one partner. But we can stick it out more than six months."

Dora said, "I suppose you want to stay in a ship for a year and go to Saturn."

"Why not, Dora?" said Long. "We can do it. Don't you see we can? Earthmen can't. They've got a real world. They've got open sky and fresh food, all the air and water they want. Getting into a ship is a terrible change for them. More than six months is too much for them for that very reason. Martians are different. We've been living on a ship our entire lives.

"That's all Mars is—a ship. It's just a big ship forty-five hundred miles across with one tiny room in it occupied by fifty thousand people. It's closed in like a ship. We breathe packaged air and drink packaged water, which we repurify over and over. We eat the same food rations we eat aboard ship. When we get into a ship, it's the same thing we've known all our lives. We can stand it for a lot more than a year if we have to."

Dora said, "Dick, too?"

"We all can."

"Well, Dick can't. It's all very well for you, Ted Long, and this shell stealer here, this Mario, to talk about jaunting off for a year. You're not married. Dick is. He has a wife and he has a child and that's enough for him. He can just get a regular job right here on Mars. Why, my goodness, suppose you go to Saturn and find there's no water there. How'll you get back? Even if you had water left, you'd be out of food. It's the most ridiculous thing I ever heard of."

"No. Now listen," said Long tightly. "I've thought this thing out. I've talked to Commissioner Sankov and he'll help. But we've got to have ships and men. I can't get them. The men won't listen to me. I'm green. You two are known and respected. You're veterans. If you back me, even if you don't go yourselves, if you'll just help me sell this thing to the rest, get volunteers——"

"First," said Rioz grumpily, "you'll have to do a lot more explaining. Once we get to Saturn, where's the water?"

"That's the beauty of it," said Long. "That's why it's got to be Saturn. The water there is just floating around in space for the taking."

5

When Hamish Sankov had come to Mars, there was no such thing as a native Martian. Now there were two-hundred-odd babies whose grandfathers had been born on Mars—native in the third generation.

When he had come as a boy in his teens, Mars had been scarcely more than a huddle of grounded spaceships connected by sealed underground tunnels. Through the years, he had seen buildings grow and burrow widely, thrusting blunt snouts up into the thin, unbreathable atmosphere. He had seen huge storage depots spring up into which spaceships and their loads could be swallowed whole. He had seen the mines grow from nothing to a huge gouge in the Martian crust, while the population of Mars grew from fifty to fifty thousand.

It made him feel old, these long memories—they and the even dimmer memories induced by the presence of this Earthman before him. His visitor brought up those long-forgotten scraps of thought about a soft-warm world that was as kind and gentle to mankind as the mother's womb.

The Earthman seemed fresh from that womb. Not very tall, not very lean; in fact, distinctly plump. Dark hair with a neat little wave in it, a neat little mustache, and neatly scrubbed skin. His clothing was right in style and as fresh and neatly turned as plastek could be.

Sankov's own clothes were of Martian manufacture, serviceable and clean, but many years behind the times. His face was craggy and lined, his hair was pure white, and his Adam's apple wobbled when he talked.

The Earthman was Myron Digby, member of Earth's General Assembly. Sankov was Martian Commissioner.

Sankov said, "This all hits us hard, Assemblyman."

"It's hit most of us hard, too, Commissioner."

"Uh-huh. Can't honestly say then that I can make it out. Of course, you understand, I don't make out that I can understand Earth ways, for all that I was born there. Mars is a hard place to live, Assemblyman, and you have to understand that. It takes a lot of shipping space just to bring us food, water, and raw materials so we can live. There's not much room left for books and news films. Even video programs can't reach Mars, except for about a month when Earth is in conjunction, and even then nobody has much time to listen.

"My office gets a weekly summary film from Planetary Press. Generally, I don't have time to pay attention to it. Maybe you'd call us provincial, and you'd be right. When something like this happens, all we can do is kind of helplessly look at each other."

Digby said slowly, "You can't mean that your people on Mars haven't heard of Hilder's anti-Waster campaign."

"No, can't exactly say that. There's a young Scavenger, son of a good friend of mine who died in space"—Sankov scratched the side of his neck doubtfully—"who makes a hobby out of reading up on Earth history and things like that. He catches video broadcasts when he's out in space and he listened to this man Hilder. Near as I can make out, that was the first talk Hilder made about Wasters.

"The young fellow came to me with that. Naturally, I didn't take him very serious. I kept an eye on the Planetary Press films for a while after that, but there wasn't much mention of Hilder and what there was made him out to look pretty funny."

"Yes, Commissioner," said Digby, "it all seemed quite a joke when it started."

Sankov stretched out a pair of long legs to one side of his desk and crossed them at the ankles. "Seems to me it's still pretty much of a joke. What's his argument? We're using up water. Has he tried looking at some figures? I got them all here. Had them brought to me when this committee arrived.

"Seems that Earth has four hundred million cubic miles of water in its oceans and each cubic mile weighs four and a half billion tons. That's a lot of water. Now we use some of that heap in space flight. Most of the thrust is inside Earth's gravitational field, and that means the water thrown out finds its way back to the oceans. Hilder doesn't figure that in. When he says a million tons of water is used up per flight, he's a liar. It's less than a hundred thousand tons.

"Suppose, now, we have fifty thousand flights a year. We don't, of course; not even fifteen hundred. But let's say there are fifty thousand. I figure there's going to be considerable expansion as time goes on. With fifty thousand flights, one cubic mile of water would be lost to space each year. That means that in a million years, Earth would lose *one quarter of 1 per cent* of its total water supply!"

Digby spread his hands, palms upward, and let them drop. "Commissioner, Interplanetary Alloys has used figures like that in their campaign against Hilder, but you can't fight a tremendous, emotion-filled drive with cold mathematics. This man Hilder has invented a name, 'Wasters.' Slowly he has built this name up into a gigantic conspiracy; a gang of brutal, profit-seeking wretches raping Earth for their own immediate benefit.

"He has accused the government of being riddled with them, the Assembly of being dominated by them, the press of being owned by them. None of this, unfortunately, seems ridiculous to the average man. He knows all too well what selfish men can do to Earth's resources. He knows what happened to Earth's oil during the Time of Troubles, for instance, and the way topsoil was ruined.

"When a farmer experiences a drought, he doesn't care that the amount of water lost in space flight isn't a droplet in a fog as far as Earth's over-all water supply is concerned. Hilder has given him something to blame and that's the strongest possible consolation for disaster. He isn't going to give that up for a diet of figures."

Sankov said, "That's where I get puzzled. Maybe it's because I don't know how things work on Earth, but it seems to me that there aren't just droughty farmers there. As near as I could make out from the news summaries, these Hilder people are a minority. Why is it Earth goes along with a few farmers and some crackpots that egg them on?"

"Because, Commissioner, there are such things as worried human beings. The steel industry sees that an era of space flight will stress increasingly the light, nonferrous alloys. The various miners' unions worry about extraterrestrial competition. Any Earthman who can't get aluminum to build a prefab is certain that it is because the aluminum is going to Mars. I know a professor of archaeology who's an anti-Waster because he can't get a government grant to cover his excavations. He's convinced that all government money is going into rocketry research and space medicine and he resents it."

Sankov said, "That doesn't sound like Earth people are much different from us here on Mars. But what about the General Assembly? Why do they have to go along with Hilder?"

Digby smiled sourly. "Politics isn't pleasant to explain. Hilder introduced this bill to set up a committee to investigate waste in space flight. Maybe three fourths or more of the General Assembly was against such an investigation as an intolerable and useless extension of bureaucracy—which it is. But then how could any legislator be against a mere investigation of waste? It would sound as though he had something to fear or to conceal. It would sound as though he were himself profiting from waste. Hilder is not in the least afraid of making such accusations, and whether true or not, they would be a powerful factor with the voters in the next election. The bill passed.

"And then there came the question of appointing the members of the committee. Those who were against Hilder shied away from membership, which would have meant decisions that would be continually embarrassing. Remaining on the side lines would make that one that much less a target for Hilder. The result is that I am the only member of the committee who is outspokenly anti-Hilder and it may cost me re-election."

Sankov said, "I'd be sorry to hear that, Assemblyman. It looks as though Mars didn't have as many friends as we thought we had. We wouldn't like to lose one. But if Hilder wins out, what's he after, anyway?"

"I should think," said Digby, "that that is obvious. He wants to be the next Global Co-ordinator."

"Think he'll make it?"

"If nothing happens to stop him, he will."

"And then what? Will he drop this Waster campaign then?"

"I can't say. I don't know if he's laid his plans past the Co-ordinacy. Still, if you want my guess, he couldn't abandon the campaign and maintain his popularity. It's gotten out of hand."

Sankov scratched the side of his neck. "All right. In that case, I'll ask you for some advice. What can we folks on Mars do? You know Earth. You know the situation. We don't. Tell us what to do."

Digby rose and stepped to the window. He looked out upon the low domes of other buildings; red, rocky, completely desolate plain in between; a purple sky and a shrunken sun.

He said, without turning, "Do you people really like it on Mars?"

Sankov smiled. "Most of us don't exactly know any other world, Assemblyman. Seems to me Earth would be something queer and uncomfortable to them."

"But wouldn't Martians get used to it? Earth isn't hard to take after this. Wouldn't your people learn to enjoy the privilege of breathing air under an open sky? You once lived on Earth. You remember what it was like."

"I sort of remember. Still, it doesn't seem to be easy to explain. Earth is just there. It fits people and people fit it. People take Earth the way they find it. Mars is different. It's sort of raw and doesn't fit people. People got to make something out of it. They got to *build* a world, and not take what they find. Mars isn't much yet, but we're building, and when we're finished, we're going to have just what we like. It's sort of a great feeling to know you're building a world. Earth would be kind of unexciting after that."

The Assemblyman said, "Surely the ordinary Martian isn't such a philosopher that he's content to live this terribly hard life for the sake of a future that must be hundreds of generations away."

"No-o, not just like that." Sankov put his right ankle on his left knee and cradled it as he spoke. "Like I said, Martians are a lot like Earthmen, which means they're sort of human beings, and human beings don't go in for philosophy much. Just the same, there's something to living in a growing world, whether you think about it much or not.

"My father used to send me letters when I first came to Mars. He was an accountant and he just sort of stayed an accountant. Earth wasn't much different when he died from what it was when he was born. He didn't see anything happen. Every day was like every other day, and living was just a way of passing time until he died.

"On Mars, it's different. Every day there's something new—the city's bigger, the ventilation system gets another kick, the water lines from the poles get slicked up. Right now, we're planning to set up a news-film association of our own. We're going to call it Mars Press. If you haven't lived when things are growing all about you, you'll never understand how wonderful it feels.

"No, Assemblyman, Mars is hard and tough and Earth is a lot more comfortable, but seems to me if you take our boys to Earth, they'll be unhappy. They probably wouldn't be able to figure out why, most of them, but they'd feel lost; lost and useless. Seems to me lots of them would never make the adjustment."

Digby turned away from the window and the smooth, pink skin of his forehead was creased into a frown. "In that case, Commissioner, I am sorry for you. For all of you."

"Why?"

"Because I don't think there's anything your people on Mars can do. Or the people on the Moon or Venus. It won't happen now; maybe it won't happen for a year or two, or even for five years. But pretty soon you'll all have to come back to Earth, unless——"

Sankov's white eyebrows bent low over his eyes. "Well?"

"Unless you can find another source of water besides the planet Earth."

Sankov shook his head. "Don't seem likely, does it?"

"Not very."

"And except for that, seems to you there's no chance?"

"None at all."

Digby said that and left, and Sankov stared for a long time at nothing before he punched a combination of the local communiline.

After a while, Ted Long looked out at him.

Sankov said, "You were right, son. There's nothing they can do. Even the ones that mean well see no way out. How did you know?"

"Commissioner," said Long, "when you've read all you can about the Time of Troubles, particularly about the twentieth century, nothing political can come as a real surprise."

"Well, maybe. Anyway, son, Assemblyman Digby is sorry for us, quite a piece sorry, you might say, but that's all. He says we'll have to leave Mars—or else get water somewhere else. Only he thinks that we can't get water somewhere else."

"You know we can, don't you, Commissioner?"

"I know we *might,* son. It's a terrible risk."

"If I find enough volunteers, the risk is our business."

"How is it going?"

"Not bad. Some of the boys are on my side right now. I talked Mario Rioz into it, for instance, and you know he's one of the best."

"That's just it—the volunteers will be the best men we have. I hate to allow it."

"If we get back, it will be worth it."

"If! It's a big word, son."

"And a big thing we're trying to do."

"Well, I gave my word that if there was no help on Earth, I'll see that the Phobos water hole lets you have all the water you'll need. Good luck."

6

Half a million miles above Saturn, Mario Rioz was cradled on nothing and sleep was delicious. He came out of it slowly and for a while, alone in his suit, he counted the stars and traced lines from one to another.

At first, as the weeks flew past, it was scavenging all over again, except for the gnawing feeling that every minute meant an additional number of thousands of miles away from all humanity. That made it worse.

They had aimed high to pass out of the ecliptic while moving through the Asteroid Belt. That had used up water and had probably been unnecessary. Although tens of thousands of worldlets look as thick as vermin in two-dimensional projection upon a photographic plate, they are nevertheless scattered so thinly through the quadrillions of cubic miles that make up their conglomerate orbit that only the most ridiculous of coincidences would have brought about a collision.

Still, they passed over the Belt and someone calculated the chances of collision with a fragment of matter large enough to do damage. The value was so low, so impossibly low, that it was perhaps inevitable that the notion of the "space-float" should occur to someone.

The days were long and many, space was empty, only one man was needed at the controls at any one time. The thought was a natural.

First, it was a particularly daring one who ventured out for fifteen minutes or so. Then another who tried half an hour. Eventually, before the asteroids were entirely behind, each ship regularly had its off-watch member suspended in space at the end of a cable.

It was easy enough. The cable, one of those intended for operations at the conclusion of their journey, was magnetically attached at both ends, one to the space suit to start with. Then you clambered out the lock onto the ship's hull and attached the other end there. You paused awhile, clinging to the metal skin by the electromagnets in your boots. Then you neutralized those and made the slightest muscular effort.

Slowly, ever so slowly, you lifted from the ship and even more slowly the ship's larger mass moved an equivalently shorter distance downward. You floated incredibly, weightlessly, in solid, speckled black. When the ship had moved far enough away from you, your gauntleted hand, which kept touch upon the cable, tightened its grip slightly. Too tightly, and you would begin moving back toward the ship and it toward you. Just tightly enough, and friction would halt you. Because your motion was equivalent to that of the ship, it seemed as motionless below you as though it had been painted against an impossible background while the cable between you hung in coils that had no reason to straighten out.

It was a half-ship to your eye. One half was lit by the light of the feeble Sun, which was still too bright to look at directly without the heavy protection of the polarized space-suit visor. The other half was black on black, invisible.

Space closed in and it was like sleep. Your suit was warm, it renewed its air automatically, it had food and drink in special containers from which it could be sucked with a minimal motion of the head, it took care of wastes appropriately. Most of all, more than anything else, there was the delightful euphoria of weightlessness.

You never felt so well in your life. The days stopped being too long, they weren't long enough, and there weren't enough of them.

They had passed Jupiter's orbit at a spot some 30 degrees from its then position. For months, it was the brightest object in the sky, always excepting the glowing white pea that was the Sun. At its brightest, some of the Scavengers insisted they could make out Jupiter as a tiny sphere, one side squashed out of true by the night shadow.

Then over a period of additional months it faded, while another dot of light grew until it was brighter than Jupiter. It was Saturn, first as a dot of brilliance, then as an oval, glowing splotch.

("Why oval?" someone asked, and after a while, someone else said, "The rings, of course," and it was obvious.)

Everyone space-floated at all possible times toward the end, watching Saturn incessantly.

("Hey, you jerk, come on back in, damn it. You're on duty." "Who's on duty? I've got fifteen minutes more by my watch." "You set your watch back. Besides, I gave you twenty minutes yesterday." "You wouldn't give two minutes to your grandmother." "Come on in, damn it, or I'm coming out anyway." "All right, I'm coming. Holy howlers, what a racket over a lousy minute." But no quarrel could possibly be serious, not in space. It felt too good.)

Saturn grew until at last it rivaled and then surpassed the Sun. The rings, set at a broad angle to their trajectory of approach, swept grandly about the planet, only a small portion being eclipsed. Then, as they approached, the span of the rings grew still wider, yet narrower as the angle of approach constantly decreased.

The large moons showed up in the surrounding sky like serene fireflies.

Mario Rioz was glad he was awake so that he could watch again.

Saturn filled half the sky, streaked with orange, the night shadow cutting it fuzzily nearly one quarter of the way in from the right. Two round little dots in the brightness were shadows of two of the moons. To the left and behind him (he could look over his left shoulder to see, and as he did so, the rest of his body inched slightly to the right to conserve angular momentum) was the white diamond of the Sun.

Most of all he liked to watch the rings. At the left, they emerged from behind Saturn, a tight, bright triple band of orange light. At the right, their beginnings were hidden in the night shadow, but showed up closer and broader. They widened as they came, like the flare of a horn, growing hazier as they approached, until, while the eye followed them, they seemed to fill the sky and lose themselves.

From the position of the Scavenger fleet just inside the outer rim of the outermost ring, the rings broke up and assumed their true identity as a phenomenal cluster of solid fragments rather than the tight, solid band of light they seemed.

Below him, or rather in the direction his feet pointed, some twenty miles away, was one of the ring fragments. It looked like a large, irregular splotch, marring the symmetry of space, three quarters in brightness and the night shadow cutting it like a knife. Other fragments were farther off, sparkling like star dust, dimmer and thicker, until, as you followed them down, they became rings once more.

The fragments were motionless, but that was only because the ships had taken up an orbit about Saturn equivalent to that of the outer edge of the rings.

The day before, Rioz reflected, he had been on that nearest fragment, working along with more than a score of others to mold it into the desired shape. Tomorrow he would be at it again.

Today—today he was space-floating.

"Mario?" The voice that broke upon his earphones was questioning.

Momentarily Rioz was flooded with annoyance. Damn it, he wasn't in the mood for company.

"Speaking," he said.

"I thought I had your ship spotted. How are you?"

"Fine. That you, Ted?"

"That's right," said Long.

"Anything wrong on the fragment?"

"Nothing. I'm out here floating."

"You?"

"It gets me, too, occasionally. Beautiful, isn't it?"

"Nice," agreed Rioz.

"You know, I've read Earth books——"

"Grounder books, you mean." Rioz yawned and found it difficult under the circumstances to use the expression with the proper amount of resentment.

"—and sometimes I read descriptions of people lying on grass," continued Long. "You know that green stuff like thin, long pieces of paper they have all over the ground down there, and they look up at the blue sky with clouds in it. Did you ever see any films of that?"

"Sure. It didn't attract me. It looked cold."

"I suppose it isn't, though. After all, Earth is quite close to the Sun, and they say their atmosphere is thick enough to hold the heat. I must admit that personally I would hate to be caught under open sky with nothing on but clothes. Still, I imagine they like it."

"Grounders are nuts!"

"They talk about the trees, big brown stalks, and the winds, air movements, you know."

"You mean drafts. They can keep that, too."

"It doesn't matter. The point is they describe it beautifully, almost passionately. Many times I've wondered, 'What's it really like? Will I ever feel it or is this something only Earthmen can possibly feel?' I've felt so often that I was missing something vital. Now I know what it must be like. It's this. Complete peace in the middle of a beauty-drenched universe."

Rioz said, "They wouldn't like it. The Grounders, I mean. They're so used to their own lousy little world they wouldn't appreciate what it's like to float and look down on Saturn." He flipped his body slightly and began swaying back and forth about his center of mass, slowly, soothingly.

Long said, "Yes, I think so too. They're slaves to their planet. Even if they come to Mars, it will only be their children that are free. There'll be starships someday; great, huge things that can carry thousands of people and maintain their self-contained equilibrium for decades, maybe centuries. Mankind will spread through the whole Galaxy. But people will have to live their lives out on shipboard until new methods of interstellar travel are developed, so it will be Martians, not planet-bound Earthmen, who will colonize the Universe. That's inevitable. It's got to be. It's the Martian way."

But Rioz made no answer. He had dropped off to sleep again, rocking and swaying gently, half a million miles above Saturn.

7

The work shift of the ring fragment was the tail of the coin. The weightlessness, peace, and privacy of the space-float gave place to something that had neither peace nor privacy. Even the weightlessness, which continued, became more a purgatory than a paradise under the new conditions.

Try to manipulate an ordinarily non-portable heat projector. It could be lifted despite the fact that it was six feet high and wide and almost solid metal, since it weighed only a fraction of an ounce. But its inertia was exactly what it had always been, which meant that if it wasn't moved into position very slowly, it would just keep on going, taking you with it. Then you would have to hike the pseudo-grav field of your suit and come down with a jar.

Keralski had hiked the field a little too high and he came down a little too roughly, with the projector coming down with him at a dangerous angle. His crushed ankle had been the first casualty of the expedition.

Rioz was swearing fluently and nearly continuously. He continued to have the impulse to drag the back of his hand across his forehead in order to wipe away the accumulating sweat. The few times that he had succumbed to the impulse, metal had met silicone with a clash that rang loudly inside his suit, but served no useful purpose. The desiccators within the suit were sucking at maximum and, of course, recovering the water and restoring ion-exchanged liquid, containing a careful proportion of salt, into the appropriate receptacle.

Rioz yelled, "Damn it, Dick, wait till I give the word, will you?"

And Swenson's voice rang in his ears, "Well, how long am I supposed to sit here?"

"Till I say," replied Rioz.

He strengthened pseudo-grav and lifted the projector a bit. He released pseudo-grav, insuring that the projector would stay in place for minutes even if he withdrew support altogether. He kicked the cable out of the way (it stretched beyond the close "horizon" to a power source that was out of sight) and touched the release.

The material of which the fragment was composed bubbled and vanished under its touch. A section of the lip of the tremendous cavity he had already carved into its substance melted away and a roughness in its contour had disappeared.

"Try it now," called Rioz.

Swenson was in the ship that was hovering nearly over Rioz's head.

Swenson called, "All clear?"

"I told you to go ahead."

It was a feeble flicker of steam that issued from one of the ship's forward vents. The ship drifted down toward the ring fragment. Another flicker adjusted a tendency to drift sidewise. It came down straight.

A third flicker to the rear slowed it to a feather rate.

Rioz watched tensely. "Keep her coming. You'll make it. You'll make it."

The rear of the ship entered the hole, nearly filling it. The bellying walls came closer and closer to its rim. There was a grinding vibration as the ship's motion halted.

It was Swenson's turn to curse. "It doesn't fit," he said.

Rioz threw the projector groundward in a passion and went flailing up into space. The projector kicked up a white crystalline dust all about it, and when Rioz came down under pseudo-grav, he did the same.

He said, "You went in on the bias, you dumb Grounder."

"I hit it level, you dirt-eating farmer."

Backward-pointing side jets of the ship were blasting more strongly than before, and Rioz hopped to get out of the way.

The ship scraped up from the pit, then shot into space half a mile before forward jets could bring it to a halt.

Swenson said tensely, "We'll spring half a dozen plates if we do this once again. Get it right, will you?"

"I'll get it right. Don't worry about it. Just you come in right."

Rioz jumped upward and allowed himself to climb three hundred yards to get an over-all look at the cavity. The gouge marks of the ship were plain enough. They were concentrated at one point halfway down the pit. He would get that.

It began to melt outward under the blaze of the projector.

Half an hour later the ship snuggled neatly into its cavity, and Swenson, wearing his space suit, emerged to join Rioz.

Swenson said, "If you want to step in and climb out of the suit, I'll take care of the icing."

"It's all right," said Rioz. "I'd just as soon sit here and watch Saturn."

He sat down at the lip of the pit. There was a six-foot gap between it and the ship. In some places about the circle, it was two feet; in a few places, even merely a matter of inches. You couldn't expect a better fit out of handwork. The final adjustment would be made by steaming ice gently and letting it freeze into the cavity between the lip and the ship.

Saturn moved visibly across the sky, its vast bulk inching below the horizon.

Rioz said, "How many ships are left to put in place?"

Swenson said, "Last I heard, it was eleven. We're in now, so that means only ten. Seven of the ones that are placed are iced in. Two or three are dismantled."

"We're coming along fine."

"There's plenty to do yet. Don't forget the main jets at the other end. And the cables and the power lines. Sometimes I wonder if we'll make it. On the way out, it didn't bother me so much, but just now I was sitting at the controls and I was saying, 'We won't make it. We'll sit out here and starve and die with nothing but Saturn over us.' It makes me feel——"

He didn't explain how it made him feel. He just sat there.

Rioz said, "You think too damn much."

"It's different with you," said Swenson. "I keep thinking of Pete —and Dora."

"What for? She said you could go, didn't she? The Commissioner gave her that talk on patriotism and how you'd be a hero and set for life once you got back, and she said you could go. You didn't sneak out the way Adams did."

"Adams is different. That wife of his should have been shot when she was born. Some women can make hell for a guy, can't they? She didn't want him to go—but she'd probably rather he didn't come back if she can get his settlement pay."

"What's your kick, then? Dora wants you back, doesn't she?"

Swenson sighed. "I never treated her right."

"You turned over your pay, it seems to me. I wouldn't do that for any woman. Money for value received, not a cent more."

"Money isn't it. I get to thinking out here. A woman likes company. A kid needs his father. What am I doing 'way out here?"

"Getting set to go home."

"Ah-h, you don't understand."

8

Ted Long wandered over the ridged surface of the ring fragment with his spirits as icy as the ground he walked on. It had all seemed perfectly logical back on Mars, but that was Mars. He had worked it out carefully in his mind in perfectly reasonable steps. He could still remember exactly how it went.

It didn't take a ton of water to move a ton of ship. It was not mass equals mass, but mass times velocity equals mass times velocity. It didn't matter, in other words, whether you shot out a ton of water at a mile a second or a hundred pounds of water at twenty miles a second. You got the same final velocity out of the ship.

That meant the jet nozzles had to be made narrower and the steam hotter. But then drawbacks appeared. The narrower the nozzle, the more energy was lost in friction and turbulence. The hotter the steam, the more refractory the nozzle had to be and the shorter its life. The limit in that direction was quickly reached.

Then, since a given weight of water could move considerably more than its own weight under the narrow-nozzle conditions, it paid to be big. The bigger the water-storage space, the larger the size of the actual travel-head, even in proportion. So they started to make liners heavier and bigger. But then the larger the shell, the heavier the bracings, the more difficult the weldings, the more exacting the engineering requirements. At the moment, the limit in that direction had been reached also.

And then he had put his finger on what had seemed to him to be the basic flaw—the original unswervable conception that the fuel had to be placed *inside* the ship; the metal had to be built to encircle a million tons of water.

Why? Water did not have to be water. It could be ice, and ice could be shaped. Holes could be melted into it. Travel-heads and jets could be fitted into it. Cables could hold travel-heads and jets stiffly together under the influence of magnetic field-force grips.

Long felt the trembling of the ground he walked on. He was at the head of the fragment. A dozen ships were blasting in and out of sheaths carved in its substance, and the fragment shuddered under the continuing impact.

The ice didn't have to be quarried. It existed in proper chunks in the rings of Saturn. That's all the rings were—pieces of nearly pure ice, circling Saturn. So spectroscopy stated and so it had turned out to be. He was standing on one such piece now, over two miles long, nearly one mile thick. It was almost half a billion tons of water, all in one piece, and he was standing on it.

But now he was face to face with the realities of life. He had never told the men just how quickly he had expected to set up the fragment as a ship, but in his heart, he had imagined it would be two days. It was a week now and he didn't dare to estimate the remaining time. He no longer even had any confidence that the task was a possible one. Would they be able to control jets with enough delicacy through leads slung across two miles of ice to manipulate out of Saturn's dragging gravity?

Drinking water was low, though they could always distill more out of the ice. Still, the food stores were not in a good way either.

He paused, looked up into the sky, eyes straining. *Was* the object growing larger? He ought to measure its distance. Actually, he lacked the spirit to add that trouble to the others. His mind slid back to greater immediacies.

Morale, at least, was high. The men seemed to enjoy being out Saturn-way. They were the first humans to penetrate this far, the first to pass the asteroids, the first to see Jupiter like a glowing pebble to the naked eye, the first to see Saturn—like that.

He didn't think fifty practical, case-hardened, shell-snatching Scavengers would take time to feel that sort of emotion. But they did. And they were proud.

Two men and a half-buried ship slid up the moving horizon as he walked.

He called crisply, "Hello, there!"

Rioz answered, "That you, Ted?"

"You bet. Is that Dick with you?"

"Sure. Come on, sit down. We were just getting ready to ice in and we were looking for an excuse to delay."

"I'm not," said Swenson promptly. "When will we be leaving, Ted?"

"As soon as we get through. That's no answer, is it?"

Swenson said dispiritedly, "I suppose there isn't any other answer."

Long looked up, staring at the irregular bright splotch in the sky.

Rioz followed his glance. "What's the matter?"

For a moment, Long did not reply. The sky was black otherwise and the ring fragments were an orange dust against it. Saturn was more than three fourths below the horizon and the rings were going with it. Half a mile away a ship bounded past the icy rim of the planetoid into the sky, was orange-lit by Saturn-light, and sank down again.

The ground trembled gently.

Rioz said, "Something bothering you about the Shadow?"

They called it that. It was the nearest fragment of the rings, quite close considering that they were at the outer rim of the rings, where the pieces spread themselves relatively thin. It was perhaps twenty miles off, a jagged mountain, its shape clearly visible.

"How does it look to you?" asked Long.

Rioz shrugged. "Okay, I guess. I don't see anything wrong."

"Doesn't it seem to be getting larger?"

"Why should it?"

"Well, doesn't it?" Long insisted.

Rioz and Swenson stared at it thoughtfully.

"It does look bigger," said Swenson.

"You're just putting the notion into our minds," Rioz argued. "If it were getting bigger, it would be coming closer."

"What's impossible about that?"

"These things are on stable orbits."

"They were when we came here," said Long. "There, did you feel that?"

The ground had trembled again.

Long said, "We've been blasting this thing for a week now. First, twenty-five ships landed on it, which changed its momentum right there. Not much, of course. Then we've been melting parts of it away and our ships have been blasting in and out of it—all at one end, too. In a week, we may have changed its orbit just a bit. The two fragments, this one and the Shadow, might be converging."

"It's got plenty of room to miss us in." Rioz watched it thoughtfully. "Besides, if we can't even tell for sure that it's getting bigger, how quickly can it be moving? Relative to us, I mean."

"It doesn't have to be moving quickly. Its momentum is as large as ours, so that, however gently it hits, we'll be nudged completely out of our orbit, maybe in toward Saturn, where we don't want to go. As a matter of fact, ice has a very low tensile strength, so that both planetoids might break up into gravel."

Swenson rose to his feet. "Damn it, if I can tell how a shell is moving a thousand miles away, I can tell what a mountain is doing twenty miles away." He turned toward the ship.

Long didn't stop him.

Rioz said, "There's a nervous guy."

The neighboring planetoid rose to zenith, passed overhead, began sinking. Twenty minutes later, the horizon opposite that portion behind which Saturn had disappeared burst into orange flame as its bulk began lifting again.

Rioz called into his radio, "Hey, Dick, are you dead in there?"

"I'm checking," came the muffled response.

"Is it moving?" asked Long.

"Yes."

"Toward us?"

There was a pause. Swenson's voice was a sick one. "On the nose, Ted. Intersection of orbits will take place in three days."

"You're crazy!" yelled Rioz.

"I checked four times," said Swenson.

Long thought blankly, What do we do now?

9

Some of the men were having trouble with the cables. They had to be laid precisely; their geometry had to be very nearly perfect for the magnetic field to attain maximum strength. In space, or even in air, it wouldn't have mattered. The cables would have lined up automatically once the juice went on.

Here it was different. A gouge had to be plowed along the planetoid's surface and into it the cable had to be laid. If it were not lined up within a few minutes of arc of the calculated direction, a torque would be applied to the entire planetoid, with consequent loss of energy, none of which could be spared. The gouges then had to be redriven, the cables shifted and iced into the new positions.

The men plodded wearily through the routine.

And then the word reached them:

"All hands to the jets!"

Scavengers could not be said to be the type that took kindly to discipline. It was a grumbling, growling, muttering group that set about disassembling the jets of the ships that yet remained intact, carrying them to the tail end of the planetoid, grubbing them into position, and stringing the leads along the surface.

It was almost twenty-four hours before one of them looked into the sky and said, "Holy jeepers!" followed by something less printable.

His neighbor looked and said, "I'll be damned!"

Once they noticed, all did. It became the most astonishing fact in the Universe.

"Look at the Shadow!"

It was spreading across the sky like an infected wound. Men looked at it, found it had doubled its size, wondered why they hadn't noticed that sooner.

Work came to a virtual halt. They besieged Ted Long.

He said, "We can't leave. We don't have the fuel to see us back to Mars and we don't have the equipment to capture another planetoid. So we've got to stay. Now the Shadow is creeping in on us because our blasting has thrown us out of orbit. We've got to change that by continuing the blasting. Since we can't blast the front end any more without endangering the ship we're building, let's try another way."

They went back to work on the jets with a furious energy that received impetus every half hour when the Shadow rose again over the horizon, bigger and more menacing than before.

Long had no assurance that it would work. Even if the jets would respond to the distant controls, even if the supply of water, which depended upon a storage chamber opening directly into the icy body of the planetoid, with built-in heat projectors steaming the propulsive fluid directly into the driving cells, were adequate, there was still no certainty that the body of the planetoid without a magnetic cable sheathing would hold together under the enormously disruptive stresses.

"Ready!" came the signal in Long's receiver.

Long called, "Ready!" and depressed the contact.

The vibration grew about him. The star field in the visiplate trembled.

In the rearview, there was a distant gleaming spume of swiftly moving ice crystals.

"It's blowing!" was the cry.

It kept on blowing. Long dared not stop. For six hours, it blew, hissing, bubbling, steaming into space; the body of the planetoid converted to vapor and hurled away.

The Shadow came closer until men did nothing but stare at the mountain in the sky, surpassing Saturn itself in spectacularity. Its every groove and valley was a plain scar upon its face. But when it passed through the planetoid's orbit, it crossed more than half a mile behind its then position.

The steam jet ceased.

Long bent in his seat and covered his eyes. He hadn't eaten in two days. He could eat now, though. Not another planetoid was close enough to interrupt them, even if it began an approach that very moment.

Back on the planetoid's surface, Swenson said, "All the time I watched that damned rock coming down, I kept saying to myself, 'This can't happen. We can't let it happen.'"

"Hell," said Rioz, "we were all nervous. Did you see Jim Davis? He was green. I was a little jumpy myself."

"That's not it. It wasn't just—dying, you know. I was thinking—I know it's funny, but I can't help it—I was thinking that Dora warned me I'd get myself killed, she'll never let me hear the last of it. Isn't that a crummy sort of attitude at a time like that?"

"Listen," said Rioz, "you wanted to get married, so you got married. Why come to me with your troubles?"

10

The flotilla, welded into a single unit, was returning over its mighty course from Saturn to Mars. Each day it flashed over a length of space it had taken nine days outward.

Ted Long had put the entire crew on emergency. With twenty-five ships embedded in the planetoid taken out of Saturn's wings and unable to move or maneuver independently, the co-ordination of their power sources into unified blasts was a ticklish problem.

The jarring that took place on the first day of travel nearly shook them out from under their hair.

That, at least, smoothed itself out as the velocity raced upward under the steady thrust from behind. They passed the one-hundred-thousand-mile-an-hour mark late on the second day, and climbed steadily toward the million-mile mark and beyond.

Long's ship, which formed the needle point of the frozen fleet, was the only one which possessed a five-way view of space. It was an uncomfortable position under the circumstances. Long found himself watching tensely, imagining somehow that the stars would slowly begin to slip backward, to whizz past them, under the influence of the multi-ship's tremendous rate of travel.

They didn't, of course. They remained nailed to the black backdrop, their distance scorning with patient immobility any speed mere man could achieve.

The men complained bitterly after the first few days. It was not only that they were deprived of the space-float. They were burdened by much more than the ordinary pseudo-gravity field of the ships, by the effects of the fierce acceleration under which they were living. Long himself was weary to death of the relentless pressure against hydraulic cushions.

They took to shutting off the jet thrusts one hour out of every four and Long fretted.

It had been just over a year that he had last seen Mars shrinking in an observation window from this ship, which had then been an independent entity. What had happened since then? Was the colony still there?

In something like a growing panic, Long sent out radio pulses toward Mars daily, with the combined power of twenty-five ships behind it. There was no answer. He expected none. Mars and Saturn were on opposite sides of the Sun now, and until he mounted high enough above the ecliptic to get the Sun well beyond the line connecting himself and Mars, solar interference would prevent any signal from getting through.

High above the outer rim of the Asteroid Belt, they reached maximum velocity. With short spurts of power from first one side jet, then another, the huge vessel reversed itself. The composite jet in the rear began its mighty roaring once again, but now the result was deceleration.

They passed a hundred million miles over the Sun, curving down to intersect the orbit of Mars.

A week out of Mars, answering signals were heard for the first time, fragmentary, ether-torn, and incomprehensible, but they were coming from Mars. Earth and Venus were at angles sufficiently different to leave no doubt of that.

Long relaxed. There were still humans on Mars, at any rate.

Two days out of Mars, the signal was strong and clear and Sankov was at the other end.

Sankov said, "Hello, son. It's three in the morning here. Seems like people have no consideration for an old man. Dragged me right out of bed."

"I'm sorry, sir."

"Don't be. They were following orders. I'm afraid to ask, son. Anyone hurt? Maybe dead?"

"No deaths, sir. Not one."

"And—and the water? Any left?"

Long said, with an effort at nonchalance, "Enough."

"In that case, get home as fast as you can. Don't take any chances, of course."

"There's trouble, then."

"Fair to middling. When will you come down?"

"Two days. Can you hold out that long?"

"I'll hold out."

Forty hours later Mars had grown to a ruddy-orange ball that filled the ports and they were in the final planet-landing spiral.

"Slowly," Long said to himself, "slowly." Under these conditions, even the thin atmosphere of Mars could do dreadful damage if they moved through it too quickly.

Since they came in from well above the ecliptic, their spiral passed from north to south. A polar cap shot whitely below them, then the much smaller one of the summer hemisphere, the large one again, the small one, at longer and longer intervals. The planet approached closer, the landscape began to show features.

"Prepare for landing!" called Long.

11

Sankov did his best to look placid, which was difficult considering how closely the boys had shaved their return. But it had worked out well enough.

Until a few days ago, he had no sure knowledge that they had survived. It seemed more likely—inevitable, almost—that they were nothing but frozen corpses somewhere in the trackless stretches from Mars to Saturn, new planetoids that had once been alive.

The Committee had been dickering with him for weeks before the news had come. They had insisted on his signature to the paper for the sake of appearances. It would look like an agreement, voluntarily and mutually arrived at. But Sankov knew well that, given complete obstinacy on his part, they would act unilaterally and be damned with appearances. It seemed fairly certain that Hilder's election was secure now and they would take the chance of arousing a reaction of sympathy for Mars.

So he dragged out the negotiations, dangling before them always the possibility of surrender.

And then he heard from Long and concluded the deal quickly.

The papers had lain before him and he had made a last statement for the benefit of the reporters who were present.

He said, "Total imports of water from Earth are twenty million tons a year. This is declining as we develop our own piping system. If I sign this paper agreeing to an embargo, our industry will be paralyzed, any possibilities of expansion will halt. It looks to me as if that can't be what's in Earth's mind, can it?"

Their eyes met his and held only a hard glitter. Assemblyman Digby had already been replaced and they were unanimous against him.

The Committee Chairman impatiently pointed out, "You have said all this before."

"I know, but right now I'm kind of getting ready to sign and I want it clear in my head. Is Earth set and determined to bring us to an end here?"

"Of course not. Earth is interested in conserving its irreplaceable water supply, nothing else."

"You have one and a half quintillion tons of water on Earth."

The Committee Chairman said, "We cannot spare water."

And Sankov had signed.

That had been the final note he wanted. Earth had one and a half quintillion tons of water and could spare none of it.

Now, a day and a half later, the Committee and the reporters waited in the spaceport dome. Through thick, curving windows, they could see the bare and empty grounds of Mars Spaceport.

The Committee Chairman asked with annoyance, "How much longer do we have to wait? And, if you don't mind, what are we waiting for?"

Sankov said, "Some of our boys have been out in space, out past the asteroids."

The Committee Chairman removed a pair of spectacles and cleaned them with a snowy-white handkerchief. "And they're returning?"

"They are."

The Chairman shrugged, lifted his eyebrows in the direction of the reporters.

In the smaller room adjoining, a knot of women and children clustered about another window. Sankov stepped back a bit to cast a glance toward them. He would much rather have been with them, been part of their excitement and tension. He, like them, had waited over a year now. He, like them, had thought, over and over again, that the men must be dead.

"You see that?" said Sankov, pointing.

"Hey!" cried a reporter. "It's a ship!"

A confused shouting came from the adjoining room.

It wasn't a ship so much as a bright dot obscured by a drifting white cloud. The cloud grew larger and began to have form. It was a double streak against the sky, the lower ends billowing out and upward again. As it dropped still closer, the bright dot at the upper end took on a crudely cylindrical form.

It was rough and craggy, but where the sunlight hit, brilliant high lights bounced back.

The cylinder dropped toward the ground with the ponderous slowness characteristic of space vessels. It hung suspended on those blasting jets and settled down upon the recoil of tons of matter hurling downward like a tired man dropping into his easy chair.

And as it did so, a silence fell upon all within the dome. The women and children in one room, the politicians and reporters in the other remained frozen, heads craned incredulously upward.

The cylinder's landing flanges, extending far below the two rear jets, touched ground and sank into the pebbly morass. And then the ship was motionless and the jet action ceased.

But the silence continued in the dome. It continued for a long time.

Men came clambering down the sides of the immense vessel,

inching down, down the two-mile trek to the ground, with spikes on their shoes and ice axes in their hands. They were gnats against the blinding surface.

One of the reporters croaked, "What is it?"

"That," said Sankov calmly, "happens to be a chunk of matter that spent its time scooting around Saturn as part of its rings. Our boys fitted it out with travel-head and jets and ferried it home. It just turns out the fragments in Saturn's rings are made up out of ice."

He spoke into a continuing deathlike silence. "That thing that looks like a spaceship is just a mountain of hard water. If it were standing like that on Earth, it would be melting into a puddle and maybe it would break under its own weight. Mars is colder and has less gravity, so there's no such danger.

"Of course, once we get this thing really organized, we can have water stations on the moons of Saturn and Jupiter and on the asteroids. We can scale in chunks of Saturn's rings and pick them up and send them on at the various stations. Our Scavengers are good at that sort of thing.

"We'll have all the water we need. That one chunk you see is just under a cubic mile—or about what Earth would send us in two hundred years. The boys used quite a bit of it coming back from Saturn. They made it in five weeks, they tell me, and used up about a hundred million tons. But, Lord, that didn't make any dent at all in that mountain. Are you getting all this, boys?"

He turned to the reporters. There was no doubt they were getting it.

He said, "Then get this, too. Earth is worried about its water supply. It only has one and a half quintillion tons. It can't spare us a single ton out of it. Write down that we folks on Mars are worried about Earth and don't want anything to happen to Earth people. Write down that we'll sell water to Earth. Write down that we'll let them have million-ton lots for a reasonable fee. Write down that in ten years, we figure we can sell it in cubic-mile lots. Write down that Earth can quit worrying because Mars can sell it all the water it needs and wants."

The Committee Chairman was past hearing. He was feeling the future rushing in. Dimly he could see the reporters grinning as they wrote furiously.

Grinning.

He could hear the grin become laughter on Earth as Mars turned the tables so neatly on the anti-Wasters. He could hear the laughter thunder from every continent when word of the fiasco spread. And he could see the abyss, deep and black as space, into which would drop forever the political hopes of John Hilder and of every opponent of space flight left on Earth—his own included, of course.

In the adjoining room, Dora Swenson screamed with joy, and Peter, grown two inches, jumped up and down, calling, "Daddy! Daddy!"

Richard Swenson had just stepped off the extremity of the flange and, face showing clearly through the clear silicone of the headpiece, marched toward the dome.

"Did you ever see a guy look so happy?" asked Ted Long. "Maybe there's something in this marriage business."

"Ah, you've just been out in space too long," Rioz said.

The Deep

1

In the end, any particular planet must die. It may be a quick death as its sun explodes. It may be a slow death, as its sun sinks into decay and its oceans lock in ice. In the latter case, at least, intelligent life has a chance of survival.

The direction of survival may be outward into space, to a planet closer to the cooling sun or to a planet of another sun altogether. This particular avenue is closed if the planet is unfortunate enough to be the only significant body rotating about its primary and if, at the time, no other star is within half a thousand light-years.

The direction of survival may be inward, into the crust of the planet. That is always available. A new home can be built underground and the heat of the planet's core can be tapped for energy. Thousands of years may be necessary for the task, but a dying sun cools slowly.

But planetary warmth dies, too, with time. Burrows must be dug deeper and deeper until the planet is dead through and through.

The time was coming.

On the surface of the planet, wisps of neon blew listlessly, barely able to stir the pools of oxygen that collected in the lowlands. Occasionally, during the long day, the crusted sun would flare briefly into a dull red glow and the oxygen pools would bubble a little.

During the long night, a blue-white oxygen frost formed over the pools and on the bare rock, a neon dew formed.

Eight hundred miles below the surface, a last bubble of warmth and life existed.

2

Wenda's relationship to Roi was as close as one could imagine, closer by far than it was decent for her to know.

She had been allowed to enter the ovarium only once in her life and it had been made quite clear to her that it *was* to be only that once.

The Raceologist had said, "You don't quite meet the standards, Wenda, but you are fertile and we'll try you once. It may work out."

She wanted it to work out. She wanted it desperately. Quite early in her life she had known that she was deficient in intelligence, that she would never be more than a Manual. It embarrassed her that she should fail the Race and she longed for even a single chance to help create another being. It became an obsession.

She secreted her egg in an angle of the structure and then returned to watch. The "randoming" process that moved the eggs gently about during mechanical insemination (to insure even gene distribution) did not, by some good fortune, do more than make her own wedged-in egg wobble a bit.

Unobtrusively she maintained her watch during the period of maturation, observed the little one who emerged from the particular egg that was hers, noted his physical markings, watched him grow.

He was a healthy youngster and the Raceologist approved of him.

She had said once, very casually, "Look at that one, the one sitting there. Is he sick?"

"Which one?" The Raceologist was startled. Visibly sick infants at this stage would be a strong reflection upon his own competence. "You mean Roi? Nonsense. I wish all our young were like that one."

At first, she was only pleased with herself, then frightened, finally horrified. She found herself haunting the youngster, taking an interest in his schooling, watching him at play. She was happy when he was near, dull and unhappy otherwise. She had never heard of such a thing, and she was ashamed.

She should have visited the Mentalist, but she knew better. She was not so dull as not to know that this was not a mild aberration to be cured at the twitch of a brain cell. It was a truly psychotic manifestation. She was certain of that. They would confine her if they found out. They would euthanase her, perhaps, as a useless drain on the strictly limited energy available to the race. They might even euthanase the offspring of her egg if they found out who it was.

She fought the abnormality through the years and, to a measure, succeeded. Then she first heard the news that Roi had been chosen for the long trip and was filled with aching misery.

She followed him to one of the empty corridors of the cavern, some miles from the city center. *The* city! There was only one.

This particular cavern had been closed down within Wenda's own memory. The Elders had paced its length, considered its population and the energy necessary to keep it powered, then decided to darken it. The population, not many to be sure, had been moved closer toward the center and the quota for the next session at the ovarium had been cut.

Wenda found Roi's conversational level of thinking shallow, as though most of his mind had drawn inward contemplatively.

Are you afraid? she thought at him.

Because I come out here to think? He hesitated a little, then said, "Yes, I am. It's the Race's last chance. If I fail——"

Are you afraid for yourself?

He looked at her in astonishment and Wenda's thought stream fluttered with shame at her indecency.

She said, "I wish I were going instead."

Roi said, "Do you think you can do a better job?"

"Oh, no. But if *I* were to fail and—and never come back, it would be a smaller loss to the Race."

"The loss is all the same," he said stolidly, "whether it's you or I. The loss is Racial existence."

Racial existence at the moment was in the background of Wenda's mind, if anywhere. She sighed. "The trip is such a long one."

"How long?" he asked with a smile. "Do you know?"

She hesitated. She dared not appear stupid to him.

She said primly, "The common talk is that it is to the First Level."

When Wenda had been little and the heated corridors had extended further out of the city, she had wandered out, exploring as youngsters will. One day, a long distance out, where the chill in the air nipped at her, she came to a hall that slanted upward but was blocked almost instantly by a tremendous plug, wedged tightly from top to bottom and side to side.

On the other side and upward, she had learned a long time later, lay the Seventy-ninth Level; above that the Seventy-eighth and so on.

"We're going past the First Level, Wenda."

"But there's nothing past the First Level."

"You're right. Nothing. All the solid matter of the planet comes to an end."

"But how can there be anything that's nothing? You mean air?"

"No, I mean *nothing*. Vacuum. You know what vacuum is, don't you?"

"Yes. But vacuums have to be pumped and kept airtight."

"That's good for Maintenance. Still, past the First Level is just an indefinite amount of vacuum stretching everywhere."

Wenda thought awhile. She said, "Has anyone ever been there?"

"Of course not. But we have the records."

"Maybe the records are wrong."

"They can't be. Do you know how much space I'm going to cross?"

Wenda's thought stream indicated an overwhelming negative.

Roi said, "You know the speed of light, I suppose."

"Of course," she replied readily. It was a universal constant. Infants knew it. "One thousand nine hundred and fifty-four times the length of the cavern and back in one second."

"Right," said Roi, "but if light were to travel along the distance I'm to cross, it would take it ten years."

Wenda said, "You're making fun of me. You're trying to frighten me."

"Why should it frighten you?" He rose. "But I've been moping here long enough—"

For a moment, one of his six grasping limbs rested lightly in one of hers, with an objective, impassive friendship. An irrational impulse urged Wenda to seize it tightly, prevent him from leaving.

She panicked for a moment in fear that he might probe her mind past the conversational level, that he might sicken and never face her again, that he might even report her for treatment. Then she relaxed. Roi was normal, not sick like herself. He would never dream of penetrating a friend's mind any deeper than the conversational level, whatever the provocation.

He was very handsome in her eyes as he walked away. His grasping limbs were straight and strong, his prehensile, manipulative vibrissae were numerous and delicate and his optic patches were more beautifully opalescent than any she had ever seen.

3

Laura settled down in her seat. How soft and comfortable they made them. How pleasing and unfrightening airplanes were on the inside, how different from the hard, silvery, inhuman luster of the outside.

The bassinet was on the seat beside her. She peeped in past the blanket and the tiny, ruffled cap. Walter was sleeping. His face was the blank, round softness of infancy and his eyelids were two fringed half-moons pulled down over his eyes.

A tuft of light brown hair straggled across his forehead, and with infinite delicacy, Laura drew it back beneath his cap.

It would soon be Walter's feeding time and she hoped he was still too young to be upset by the strangeness of his surroundings. The stewardess was being very kind. She even kept his bottles in a little refrigerator. Imagine, a refrigerator on board an airplane.

The people in the seat across the aisle had been watching her in that peculiar way that meant they would love to talk to her if only they could think of an excuse. The moment came when she lifted Walter out of his bassinet and placed him, a little lump of pink flesh encased in a white cocoon of cotton, upon her lap.

A baby is always legitimate as an opening for conversation between strangers.

The lady across the way said (her words were predictable), "What a *lovely* child. How old is he, my dear?"

Laura said, through the pins in her mouth (she had spread a blanket across her knees and was changing Walter), "He'll be four months old next week."

Walter's eyes were open and he simpered across at the woman, opening his mouth in a wet, gummy grin. (He always enjoyed being changed.)

"Look at him smile, George," said the lady.

Her husband smiled back and twiddled fat fingers.

"Goo," he said.

Walter laughed in a high-pitched, hiccupy way.

"What's his name, dear?" said the woman.

"He's Walter Michael," Laura said, then added, "After his father."

The floodgates were quite down. Laura learned that the couple were George and Eleanor Ellis, that they were on vacation, that they had three children, two girls and one boy, all grown-up. Both girls had married and one had two children of her own.

Laura listened with a pleased expression on her thin face. Walter (senior, that is) had always said that it was because she was such a good listener that he had first grown interested in her.

Walter was getting restless. Laura freed his arms in order to let some of his feelings evaporate in muscular effort.

"Would you warm the bottle, please?" she asked the stewardess.

Under strict but friendly questioning, Laura explained the number of feedings Walter was currently enjoying, the exact nature of his formula, and whether he suffered from diaper rash.

"I hope his little stomach isn't upset today," she worried. "I mean the plane motion, you know."

"Oh, Lord," said Mrs. Ellis, "he's too young to be bothered by that. Besides, these large planes are wonderful. Unless I look out the window, I wouldn't believe we were in the air. Don't you feel that way, George?"

But Mr. Ellis, a blunt, straightforward man, said, "I'm surprised you take a baby that age on a plane."

Mrs. Ellis turned to frown at him.

Laura held Walter over her shoulder and patted his back gently. The beginnings of a soft wail died down as his little fingers found themselves in his mother's smooth, blond hair and began grubbing into the loose bun that lay at the back of her neck.

She said, "I'm taking him to his father. Walter's never seen his son, yet."

Mr. Ellis looked perplexed and began a comment, but Mrs. Ellis put in quickly, "Your husband is in the service, I suppose?"

"Yes, he is."

(Mr. Ellis opened his mouth in a soundless "Oh" and subsided.)

Laura went on, "He's stationed just outside of Davao and he's going to be meeting me at Nichols Field."

Before the stewardess returned with the bottle, they had discovered that her husband was a master sergeant with the Quartermaster Corps, that he had been in the Army for four years, that they had been married for two, that he was about to be discharged, and that they would spend a long honeymoon there before returning to San Francisco.

Then she had the bottle. She cradled Walter in the crook of her left arm and put the bottle to his face. It slid right past his lips and his gums seized upon the nipple. Little bubbles began to work upward through the milk, while his hands batted ineffectively at the warm glass and his blue eyes stared fixedly at her.

Laura squeezed little Walter ever so slightly and thought how, with all the petty difficulties and annoyances that were involved, it yet remained such a wonderful thing to have a little baby all one's own.

4

Theory, thought Gan, always theory. The folk of the surface, a million or more years ago, could *see* the Universe, could sense it directly. Now, with eight hundred miles of rock above their heads, the Race could only make deductions from the trembling needles of their instruments.

It was only theory that brain cells, in addition to their ordinary electric potentials, radiated another sort of energy altogether. Energy that was not electromagnetic and hence not condemned to the creeping pace of light. Energy that was associated only with the highest functions of the brain and hence characteristic only of intelligent, reasoning creatures.

It was only a jogging needle that detected such an energy field leaking into their cavern, and other needles that pinpointed the origin of the field in such and such a direction ten light-years distant. At least one star must have moved quite close in the time since the surface folk had placed the nearest at five hundred light-years. Or was theory wrong?

"Are you afraid?" Gan burst into the conversational level of thought without warning and impinged sharply on the humming surface of Roi's mind.

Roi said, "It's a great responsibility."

Gan thought, *"Others* speak of responsibility." For generations, Head-Tech after Head-Tech had been working on the Resonizer and the Receiving Station and it was in his time that the final step had to be taken. What did others know of responsibility.

He said, "It is. We talk about Racial extinction glibly enough, but we always assume it will come someday but not now, not in our time. But it will, do you understand? It will. What we are to do today will consume two thirds of our total energy supply. There will not be enough left to try again. There will not be enough for this generation to live out its life. But that will not matter if you follow orders. We have thought of everything. We have spent generations thinking of everything."

"I will do what I am told," said Roi.

"Your thought field will be meshed against those coming from space. All thought fields are characteristic of the individual, and ordinarily the probability of any duplication is very low. But the fields from space number billions by our best estimate. Your field is very likely to be like one of theirs, and in that case, a resonance will be set up as long as our Resonizer is in operation. Do you know the principles involved?"

"Yes, sir."

"Then you know that during resonance, your mind will be on Planet X in the brain of the creature with a thought field identical to yours. That is not the energy-consuming process. In resonance with your mind, we will also place the mass of the Receiving Station. The method of transferring mass in that manner was the last phase of the problem to be solved, and it will take all the energy the Race would ordinarily use in a hundred years."

Gan picked up the black cube that was the Receiving Station and looked at it somberly. Three generations before it had been thought impossible to manufacture one with all the required properties in a space less than twenty cubic yards. They had it now; it was the size of his fist.

Gan said, "The thought field of intelligent brain cells can only follow certain well-defined patterns. All living creatures, on whatever planet they develop, must possess a protein base and an oxygen-water chemistry. If their world is livable for them, it is livable for us."

Theory, thought Gan on a deeper level, always theory.

He went on, "This does not mean that the body you find yourself in, its mind and its emotions, may not be completely alien. So we have arranged for three methods of activating the Receiving Station. If you are strong-limbed, you need only exert five hundred pounds of pressure on any face of the cube. If you are delicate-limbed, you need only press a knob, which you can reach through this single opening in the cube. If you are no-limbed, if your host body is paralyzed or in any other way helpless, you can activate the Station by mental energy alone. Once the Station is activated, we will have two points of reference, not one, and the Race can be transferred to Planet X by ordinary teleportation."

"That," said Roi, "will mean we will use electromagnetic energy."

"And so?"

"It will take us ten years to transfer."

"We will not be aware of duration."

"I realize that, sir, but it will mean the Station will remain on Planet X for ten years. What if it is destroyed in the meantime?"

"We have thought of that, too. We have thought of everything. Once the Station is activated, it will generate a para-mass field. It will move in the direction of gravitational attraction, sliding through ordinary matter, until such time as a continuous medium of relatively high density exerts sufficient friction to stop it. It will take twenty feet of rock to do that. Anything of lower density won't affect it. It will remain twenty feet underground for ten years, at which time a counterfield will bring it to the surface. Then one by one, the Race will appear."

"In that case, why not make the activation of the Station automatic? It has so many automatic attributes already——"

"You haven't thought it through, Roi. We have. Not all spots on the surface of Planet X may be suitable. If the inhabitants are powerful and advanced, you may have to find an unobtrusive place for the Station. It won't do for us to appear in a city square. And you will have to be certain that the immediate environment is not dangerous in other ways."

"What other ways, sir?"

"I don't know. The ancient records of the surface record many things we no longer understand. They don't explain because they took those items for granted, but we have been away from the surface for almost a hundred thousand generations and we are puzzled. Our Techs aren't even in agreement on the physical nature of stars, and that is something the records mention and discuss frequently. But what are "storms," "earthquakes," "volcanoes," "tornadoes," "sleet," "landslides," "floods," "lightning," and so on? These are all terms which refer to surface phenomena that are dangerous, but we don't know what they are. We don't know how to guard against them. Through your host's mind, you may be able to learn what is needful and take appropriate action."

"How much time will I have, sir?"

"The Resonizer cannot be kept in continuous operation for longer than twelve hours. I would prefer that you complete your job in two. You will return here automatically as soon as the Station is activated. Are you ready?"

"I'm ready," said Roi.

Gan led the way to the clouded glass cabinet. Roi took his seat, arranged his limbs in the appropriate depressions. His vibrissae dipped in mercury for good contact.

Roi said, "What if I find myself in a body on the point of death?"

Gan said as he adjusted the controls, "The thought field is distorted when a person is near death. No normal thought field such as yours would be in resonance."

Roi said, "And if it is on the point of accidental death?"

Gan said, "We have thought of that, too. We can't guard against it, but the chances of death following so quickly that you have no time to activate the Station mentally are estimated as less than one in twenty trillion, unless the mysterious surface dangers are more deadly than we expect. . . . You have one minute."

For some strange reason, Roi's last thought before translation was of Wenda.

5

Laura awoke with a sudden start. What happened? She felt as though she had been jabbed with a pin.

The afternoon sun was shining in her face and its dazzle made her blink. She lowered the shade and simultaneously bent to look at Walter.

She was a little surprised to find his eyes open. This wasn't one of his waking periods. She looked at her wrist watch. No, it wasn't. And it was a good hour before feeding time, too. She followed the demand-feeding system or the "if-you-want-it-holler-and-you'll-get it" routine, but ordinarily Walter followed the clock quite conscientiously.

She wrinkled her nose at him. "Hungry, duckie?"

Walter did not respond at all and Laura was disappointed. She would have liked to have him smile. Actually, she wanted him to laugh and throw his pudgy arms about her neck and nuzzle her and say, "Mommie," but she knew he couldn't do any of that. But he *could* smile.

She put a light finger to his chin and tapped it a bit. "Goo-goo-goo-goo." He always smiled when you did that.

But he only blinked at her.

She said, "I hope he isn't sick." She looked at Mrs. Ellis in distress.

Mrs. Ellis put down a magazine. "Is anything wrong, my dear?"

"I don't know. Walter just lies there."

"Poor little thing. He's tired, probably."

"Shouldn't he be sleeping, then?"

"He's in strange surroundings. He's probably wondering what it's all about."

She rose, stepped across the aisle, and leaned across Laura to bring her own face close to Walter's. "You're wondering what's going on, you tiny little snookums. Yes, you are. You're saying, 'Where's my nice little crib and all my nice little funnies on the wall paper?' "

Then she made little squeaking sounds at him.

Walter turned his eyes away from his mother and watched Mrs. Ellis somberly.

Mrs. Ellis straightened suddenly and looked pained. She put a hand to her head for a moment and murmured, "Goodness! The queerest pain."

"Do you think he's hungry?" asked Laura.

"Lord," said Mrs. Ellis, the trouble in her face fading, "they let you know when they're hungry soon enough. There's nothing wrong with him. I've had three children, my dear. I know."

"I think I'll ask the stewardess to warm up another bottle."

"Well, if it will make you feel better . . ."

The stewardess brought the bottle and Laura lifted Walter out of his bassinette. She said, "You have your bottle and then I'll change you and then—"

She adjusted his head in the crook of her elbow, leaned over to peck him quickly on the cheek, then cradled him close to her body as she brought the bottle to his lips——

Walter screamed!

His mouth yawned open, his arms pushed before him with his fingers spread wide, his whole body as stiff and hard as though in tetany, and he screamed. It rang through the whole compartment.

Laura screamed too. She dropped the bottle and it smashed whitely.

Mrs. Ellis jumped up. Half a dozen others did. Mr. Ellis snapped out of a light doze.

"What's the matter?" asked Mrs. Ellis blankly.

"I don't know. I don't know." Laura was shaking Walter frantically, putting him over her shoulder, patting his back. "Baby, baby, don't cry. Baby, what's the matter? Baby——"

The stewardess was dashing down the aisle. Her foot came within an inch of the cube that sat beneath Laura's seat.

Walter was threshing about furiously now, yelling with calliope intensity.

6

Roi's mind flooded with shock. One moment he had been strapped in his chair in contact with the clear mind of Gan; the next (there was no consciousness of separation in time) he was immersed in a medley of strange, barbaric, and broken thought.

He closed his mind completely. It had been open wide to increase the effectiveness of resonance, and the first touch of the alien had been——

Not painful—no. Dizzying, nauseating? No, not that, either. There was no word.

He gathered resilience in the quiet nothingness of mind closure and considered his position. He felt the small touch of the Receiving Station, with which he was in mental liaison. That *had* come with him. Good!

He ignored his host for the moment. He might need him for drastic operations later, so it would be wise to raise no suspicions for the moment.

He explored. He entered a mind at random and took stock first to the sense impressions that permeated it. The creature was sensitive to parts of the electromagnetic spectrum and to vibrations of the air, and, of course, to bodily contact. It possessed localized chemical senses——

That was about all. He looked again in astonishment. Not only was there no direct mass sense, no electro-potential sense, none of the really refined interpreters of the Universe, but there was no mental contact whatever.

The creature's mind was completely isolated.

Then how did they communicate? He looked further. They had a complicated code of controlled air vibrations.

Were they intelligent? Had he chosen a maimed mind? No, they were all like that.

He filtered the group of surrounding minds through his mental tendrils, searching for a Tech, or whatever passed for such among these crippled semi-intelligences. He found a mind which thought of itself as a controller of vehicles. A piece of information flooded Roi. He was on an air-borne vehicle.

Then even without mental contact, they would build a rudimentary mechanical civilization. Or were they animal tools of real intelligences elsewhere on the planet? No . . . Their minds said no.

He plumbed the Tech. What about the immediate environment? Were the bugbears of the ancients to be feared? It was a matter of interpretation. Dangers in the environment existed. Movements of air. Changes of temperature. Water falling in the air, either as liquid or solid. Electrical discharges. There were code vibrations of each phenomenon but that meant nothing. The connection of any of these with the names given to phenomena by the ancestral surface folk was a matter of conjecture.

No matter. Was there danger now? Was there danger here? Was there any cause for fear or uneasiness?

No! The Tech's mind said no.

That was enough. He returned to his host mind and rested a moment, then cautiously expanded . . .

Nothing!

His host mind was blank. At most, there was a vague sense of warmth, and a dull flicker of undirected response to basic stimuli.

Was his host dying after all? Aphasic? Decerebrate?

He moved quickly to the mind nearest, dredging it for information about his host and finding it.

His host was an infant of species.

An infant? A *normal* infant? And so undeveloped?

He allowed his mind to sink into and coalesce for a moment with what existed in his host. He searched for the motor areas of the brain and found them with difficulty. A cautious stimulus was followed by an erratic motion of his host's extremities. He attempted finer control and failed.

He felt anger. Had they thought of everything after all? Had they thought of intelligences without mental contact? Had they thought of young creatures as completely undeveloped as though they were still in the egg?

It meant, of course, that he could not, in the person of his host, activate the Receiving Station. The muscles and mind were far too weak, far too uncontrolled for any of the three methods outlined by Gan.

He thought intensely. He could scarcely expect to influence much mass through the imperfect focusing of his host's material brain cells, but what about an indirect influence through an adult's brain? Direct physical influence would be minute; it would amount to the breakdown of the appropriate molecules of adenosine triphosphate and acetylcholine. Thereafter the creature would act on its own.

He hesitated to try this, afraid of failure, then cursed himself for a coward. He entered the closest mind once more. It was a female of the species and it was in the state of temporary inhibition he had noticed in others. It didn't surprise him. Minds as rudimentary as these would need periodic respites.

He considered the mind before him now, fingering mentally the areas that might respond to stimulation. He chose one, stabbed at it, and the conscious areas flooded with life almost simultaneously. Sense impressions poured in and the level of thought rose steeply.

Good!

But not good enough. That was a mere prod, a pinch. It was no order for specific action.

He stirred uncomfortably as emotion cascaded over him. It came from the mind he had just stimulated and was directed, of course, at his host and not at him. Nevertheless, its primitive crudities annoyed him and he closed his mind against the unpleasant warmth of her uncovered feelings.

A second mind centered about his host, and had he been material or had he controlled a satisfactory host, he would have struck out in vexation.

Great caverns, weren't they going to allow him to concentrate on his serious business?

He thrust sharply at the second mind, activating centers of discomfort, and it moved away.

He was pleased. That had been more than a simple, undefined stimulation, and it had worked nicely. He had cleared the mental atmosphere.

He returned to the Tech who controlled the vehicle. He would know the details concerning the surface over which they were passing.

Water? He sorted the data quickly.

Water! And more water!

By the everlasting Levels, the word "ocean" made sense. The old, traditional word "ocean." Who would dream that so much water could exist.

But then, if this was "ocean," then the traditional word "island" had an obvious significance. He thrust his whole mind into the quest for geographical information. The "ocean" was speckled with dots of land but he needed exact——

He was interrupted by a short stab of surprise as his host moved through space and was held against the neighboring female's body.

Roi's mind, engaged as it was, lay open and unguarded. In full intensity, the female's emotions piled in upon him.

Roi winced. In an attempt to remove the distracting animal passions, he clamped down upon the host's brain cells, through which the rawness was funneling.

He did that too quickly, too energetically. His host's mind flooded with a diffuse pain, and instantly almost every mind he could reach reacted to the air vibrations that resulted.

In vexation, he tried to blanket the pain and succeeded only in stimulating it further.

Through the clinging mental mist of his host's pain, he riffled the Techs' minds, striving to prevent contact from slipping out of focus.

His mind went icy. The best chance was almost now! He had perhaps twenty minutes. There would be other chances afterward, but not as good. Yet he dared not attempt to direct the actions of another while his host's mind was in such complete disorganization.

He retired, withdrew into mind closure, maintaining only the most tenuous connection with his host's spinal cells, and waited.

Minutes passed, and little by little he returned to fuller liaison.

He had five minutes left. He chose a subject.

7

The stewardess said, "I think he's beginning to feel a little better, poor little thing."

"He never acted like this before," insisted Laura tearfully. "Never."

"He just had a little colic, I guess," said the stewardess.

"Maybe he's bundled up too much," suggested Mrs. Ellis.

"Maybe," said the stewardess. "It's quite warm."

She unwrapped the blanket and lifted the nightgown to expose a heaving abdomen, pink and bulbous. Walter was still whimpering.

The stewardess said, "Shall I change him for you? He's quite wet."

"Would you please?"

Most of the nearer passengers had returned to their seats. The more distant ceased craning their necks.

Mr. Ellis remained in the aisle with his wife. He said, "Say, look."

Laura and the stewardess were too busy to pay him attention and Mrs. Ellis ignored him out of sheer custom.

Mr. Ellis was used to that. His remark was purely rhetorical, anyway. He bent down and tugged at the box beneath the seat.

Mrs. Ellis looked down impatiently. She said, "Goodness, George, don't be dragging at other people's luggage like that. Sit down. You're in the way."

Mr. Ellis straightened in confusion.

Laura, with eyes still red and weepy, said, "It isn't mine. I didn't even know it was under the seat."

The stewardess, looking up from the whining baby, said, "What is it?"

Mr. Ellis shrugged. "It's a box."

His wife said, "Well, what do you want with it, for heaven's sake?"

Mr. Ellis groped for a reason. What *did* he want with it? He mumbled, "I was just curious."

The stewardess said, "There! The little boy is all nice and dry, and I'll bet in two minutes he'll just be as happy as anything. Hmm? Won't you, little funny-face?"

But little funny-face was still sobbing. He turned his head away sharply as a bottle was once more produced.

The stewardess said, "Let me warm it a bit."

She took it and went back down the aisle.

Mr. Ellis came to a decision. Firmly he lifted the box and balanced it on the arm of his seat. He ignored his wife's frown.

He said, "I'm not doing it any harm. I'm just looking. What's it made of, anyway?"

He rapped it with his knuckles. None of the other passengers seemed interested. They paid no attention to either Mr. Ellis or the box. It was as though something had switched off that particular line of interest among them. Even Mrs. Ellis, in conversation with Laura, kept her back to him.

Mr. Ellis tipped the box up and found the opening. He *knew* it had to have an opening. It was large enough for him to insert a finger, though there was no reason, of course, why he should want to put a finger into a strange box.

Carefully he reached in. There was a black knob, which he longed to touch. He pressed it.

The box shuddered and was suddenly out of his hands and passed through the arm of the chair.

He caught a glimpse of it moving through the floor, and then there was unbroken flooring and nothing more. Slowly he spread out his hands and stared at his palms. Then, dropping to his knees, he felt the floor.

The stewardess, returning with the bottle, said politely, "Have you lost something, sir?"

Mrs. Ellis, looking down, said, "George!"

Mr. Ellis heaved himself upward. He was flushed and flustered. He said, "The box—— It slipped out and went down——"

The stewardess said, "What box, sir?"

Laura said, "May I have the bottle, miss? He's stopped crying."

"Certainly. Here it is."

Walter opened his mouth eagerly, accepting the nipple. Air bubbles moved upward through the milk and there were little swallowing sounds.

Laura looked up radiantly. "He seems fine now. Thank you, Stewardess. Thank you, Mrs. Ellis. For a while there, it almost seemed as though he weren't my little boy."

"He'll be all right," said Mrs. Ellis. "Maybe it was just a bit of airsickness. Sit down, George."

The stewardess said, "Just call me if you need me."

"Thank you," said Laura.

Mr. Ellis said, "The box——" and stopped.

What box? He didn't remember any box.

But one mind aboard plane could follow the black cube as it dropped in a parabola unimpeded by wind or air resistance, passing through the molecules of gas that lay in its way.

Below it, the atoll was a tiny bull's eye in a huge target. Once, during a time of war, it had boasted an air strip and barracks. The barracks had collapsed, the air strip was a vanishing ragged line, and the atoll was empty.

The cube struck the feathery foliage of a palm and not a frond was disturbed. It passed through the trunk and down to the coral. It sank into the planet itself without the smallest fog of dust kicked up to tell of its entrance.

Twenty feet below the surface of the soil, the cube passed into stasis and remained motionless, mingled intimately with the atoms of the rock, yet remaining distinct.

That was all. It was night, then day. It rained, the wind blew, and the Pacific waves broke whitely on the white coral. Nothing had happened.

Nothing would happen—for ten years.

8

"We have broadcast the news," said Gan, "that you have succeeded. I think you ought to rest now."

Roi said, "Rest? Now? When I'm back with complete minds? Thank you, but no. The enjoyment is too keen."

"Did it bother you so much? Intelligence without mental contact?"

"Yes," said Roi shortly. Gan tactfully refrained from attempting to follow the line of retreating thought.

Instead, he said, "And the surface?"

Roi said, "Entirely horrible. What the ancients called 'Sun' is an unbearable patch of brilliance overhead. It is apparently a source of light and varies periodically; 'day' and 'night,' in other words. There is also unpredictable variation."

"'Clouds' perhaps," said Gan.

"Why 'clouds'?"

"You know the traditional phrase: 'Clouds hid the Sun.'"

"You think so? Yes, it could be."

"Well, go on."

"Let's see. 'Ocean' and 'island' I've explained. 'Storm' involves wetness in the air, falling in drops. 'Wind' is a movement of air on a huge scale. 'Thunder' is either a spontaneous, static discharge in the air or a great spontaneous noise. 'Sleet' is falling ice."

Gan said, "That's a curious one. Where would ice fall from? How? Why?"

"I haven't the slightest idea. It's all very variable. It will storm at one time and not at another. There are apparently regions on the surface where it is always cold, others where it is always hot, still others where it is both at different times."

"Astonishing. How much of this do you suppose is misinterpretation of alien minds?"

"None. I'm sure of that. It was all quite plain. I had sufficient time to plumb their queer minds. Too much time."

Again his thoughts drifted back into privacy.

Gan said, "This is well. I've been afraid all along of our tendency to romanticize the so-called Golden Age of our surface ancestors. I felt that there would be a strong impulse among our group in favor of a new surface life."

"No," said Roi vehemently.

"Obviously no. I doubt if the hardiest among us would consider even a day of life in an environment such as you describe, with its storms, days, nights, its indecent and unpredictable variations in environment." Gan's thoughts were contented ones. "Tomorrow we begin the process of transfer. Once on the island—— An uninhabited one, you say."

"Entirely uninhabited. It was the only one of that type the vessel passed over. The Tech's information was detailed."

"Good. We will begin operations. It will take generations, Roi, but in the end, we will be in the Deep of a new, warm world, in pleasant caverns where the controlled environment will be conducive to the growth of every culture and refinement."

"And," added Roi, "no contact whatever with the surface creatures."

Gan said, "Why that? Primitive though they are, they could be of help to us once we establish our base. A race that can build aircraft must have some abilities."

"It isn't that. They're a belligerent lot, sir. They would attack with animal ferocity at all occasions and——"

Gan interrupted. "I am disturbed at the psychopenumbra that surrounds your references to the aliens. There's something you are concealing."

Roi said, "I thought at first we could make use of them. If they wouldn't allow us to be friends, at least, we could control them. I made one of them close contact inside the cube and that was difficult. Very difficult. Their minds are basically different."

"In what way?"

"If I could describe it, the difference wouldn't be basic. But I can give you an example. I was in the mind of an infant. They don't have maturation chambers. The infants are in the charge of individuals. The creature who was in charge of my host——"

"Yes."

"She (it was a female) felt a special tie to the young one. There was a sense of ownership, of a relationship that excluded the remainder of their society. I seemed to detect, dimly, something of the emotion that binds a man to an associate or friend, but it was far more intense and unrestrained."

"Well," said Gan, "without mental contact, they probably have no real conception of society and subrelationships may build up. Or was this one pathological?"

"No, no. It's universal. The female in charge was the infant's mother."

"Impossible. Its own mother?"

"Of necessity. The infant had passed the first part of its existence inside its mother. Physically inside. The creature's eggs remain within the body. They are inseminated within the body. They grow within the body and emerge alive."

"Great caverns," Gan said weakly. Distaste was strong within him. "Each creature would know the identity of its own child. Each child would have a particular father——"

"And he would be known, too. My host was being taken five thousand miles, as nearly as I could judge the distance, to be seen by its father."

"Unbelievable!"

"Do you need more to see that there can never be any meeting of minds? The difference is so fundamental, so innate."

The yellowness of regret tinged and roughened Gan's thought train. He said, "It would be too bad. I had thought——"

"What, sir?"

"I had thought that for the first time there would be two intelligences helping one another. I had thought that together we might progress more quickly than either could alone. Even if they were primitive technologically, as they are, technology isn't everything. I had thought we might still be able to learn of them."

"Learn what?" asked Roi brutally. "To know our parents and make friends of our children?"

Gan said, "No. No, you're quite right. The barrier between us must remain forever complete. They will have the surface and we the Deep, and so it will be."

Outside the laboratories Roi met Wenda.

Her thoughts were concentrated pleasure. "I'm glad you're back."

Roi's thoughts were pleasurable too. It was very restful to make clean mental contact with a friend.

The Fun They Had

Margie even wrote about it that night in her diary. On the page headed May 17, 2157, she wrote, "Today Tommy found a real book!"

It was a very old book. Margie's grandfather once said that when he was a little boy *his* grandfather told him that there was a time when all stories were printed on paper.

They turned the pages, which were yellow and crinkly, and it was awfully funny to read words that stood still instead of moving the way they were supposed to—on a screen, you know. And then, when they turned back to the page before, it had the same words on it that it had had when they read it the first time.

"Gee," said Tommy, "what a waste. When you're through with the book, you just throw it away, I guess. Our television screen must have had a million books on it and it's good for plenty more. I wouldn't throw *it* away."

"Same with mine," said Margie. She was eleven and hadn't seen as many telebooks as Tommy had. He was thirteen.

She said, "Where did you find it?"

"In my house." He pointed without looking, because he was busy reading. "In the attic."

"What's it about?"

"School."

Margie was scornful. "School? What's there to write about school? I hate school."

Margie always hated school, but now she hated it more than ever. The mechanical teacher had been giving her test after test in geography and she had been doing worse and worse until her mother had shaken her head sorrowfully and sent for the County Inspector.

He was a round little man with a red face and a whole box of tools with dials and wires. He smiled at Margie and gave her an apple, then took the teacher apart. Margie had hoped he wouldn't know how to put it together again, but he knew how all right, and, after an hour or so, there it was again, large and black and ugly, with a big screen on which all the lessons were shown and the questions were asked. That wasn't so bad. The part Margie hated most was the slot where she had to put homework and test papers. She always had to write them out in a punch code they made her learn when she was six years old, and the mechanical teacher calculated the mark in no time.

The Inspector had smiled after he was finished and patted Margie's head. He said to her mother, "It's not the little girl's fault, Mrs. Jones. I think the geography sector was geared a little too quick. Those things happen sometimes. I've slowed it up to an average ten-year level. Actually, the over-all pattern of her progress is quite satisfactory." And he patted Margie's head again.

Margie was disappointed. She had been hoping they would take the teacher away altogether. They had once taken Tommy's teacher away for nearly a month because the history sector had blanked out completely.

So she said to Tommy, "Why would anyone write about school?"

Tommy looked at her with very superior eyes. "Because it's not our kind of school, stupid. This is the old kind of school that they had hundreds and hundreds of years ago." He added loftily, pronouncing the word carefully, *"Centuries* ago."

Margie was hurt. "Well, I don't know what kind of school they had all that time ago." She read the book over his shoulder for a while, then said, "Anyway, they had a teacher."

"Sure they had a teacher, but it wasn't a *regular* teacher. It was a man."

"A man? How could a man be a teacher?"

"Well, he just told the boys and girls things and gave them homework and asked them questions."

"A man isn't smart enough."

"Sure he is. My father knows as much as my teacher."

"He can't. A man can't know as much as a teacher."

"He knows almost as much, I betcha."

Margie wasn't prepared to dispute that. She said, "I wouldn't want a strange man in my house to teach me."

Tommy screamed with laughter. "You don't know much, Margie. The teachers didn't live in the house. They had a special building and all the kids went there."

"And all the kids learned the same thing?"

"Sure, if they were the same age."

"But my mother says a teacher has to be adjusted to fit the mind of each boy and girl it teaches and that each kid has to be taught differently."

"Just the same they didn't do it that way then. If you don't like it, you don't have to read the book."

"I didn't say I didn't like it," Margie said quickly. She wanted to read about those funny schools.

They weren't even half-finished when Margie's mother called, "Margie! School!"

Margie looked up. "Not yet, Mamma."

"Now!" said Mrs. Jones. "And it's probably time for Tommy, too."

Margie said to Tommy, "Can I read the book some more with you after school?"

"Maybe," he said nonchalantly. He walked away whistling, the dusty old book tucked beneath his arm.

Margie went into the schoolroom. It was right next to her bedroom, and the mechanical teacher was on and waiting for her. It was always on at the same time every day except Saturday and Sunday, because her mother said little girls learned better if they learned at regular hours.

The screen was lit up, and it said: "Today's arithmetic lesson is on the addition of proper fractions. Please insert yesterday's homework in the proper slot."

Margie did so with a sigh. She was thinking about the old schools they had when her grandfather's grandfather was a little boy. All the kids from the whole neighborhood came, laughing and shouting in the schoolyard, sitting together in the schoolroom, going home together at the end of the day. They learned the same things, so they could help one another on the homework and talk about it.

And the teachers were people. . . .

The mechanical teacher was flashing on the screen: "When we add the fractions ½ and ¼——"

Margie was thinking about how the kids must have loved it in the old days. She was thinking about the fun they had.

The Last Question

The last question was asked for the first time, half in jest, on May 21, 2061, at a time when humanity first stepped into the light. The question came about as a result of a five-dollar bet over high-balls, and it happened this way:

Alexander Adell and Bertram Lupov were two of the faithful attendants of Multivac. As well as any human beings could, they knew what lay behind the cold, clicking, flashing face——miles and miles of face——of that giant computer. They had at least a vague notion of the general plan of relays and circuits that had long since grown past the point where any single human could possibly have a firm grasp of the whole.

Multivac was self-adjusting and self-correcting. It had to be, for nothing human could adjust and correct it quickly enough or even adequately enough. ——So Adell and Lupov attended the monstrous giant only lightly and superficially, yet as well as any men could. They fed it data, adjusted questions to its needs and translated the answers that were issued. Certainly they, and all others like them, were fully entitled to share in the glory that was Multivac's.

For decades, Multivac had helped design the ships and plot the trajectories that enabled man to reach the Moon, Mars, and Venus, but past that, Earth's poor resources could not support the ships. Too much energy was needed for the long trips. Earth exploited its coal and uranium with increasing efficiency, but there was only so much of both.

But slowly Multivac learned enough to answer deeper questions more fundamentally, and on May 14, 2061, what had been theory, became fact.

The energy of the sun was stored, converted, and utilized directly on a planet-wide scale. All Earth turned off its burning coal, its fissioning uranium, and flipped the switch that connected all of it to a small station, one mile in diameter, circling the Earth at half the distance of the Moon. All Earth ran by invisible beams of sun-power.

Seven days had not sufficed to dim the glory of it and Adell and Lupov finally managed to escape from the public function, and to meet in quiet where no one would think of looking for them, in the deserted underground chambers, where portions of the mighty buried body of Multivac showed. Unattended, idling, sorting data with contented lazy clickings, Multivac, too, had earned its vacation and the boys appreciated that. They had no intention, originally, of disturbing it.

They had brought a bottle with them, and their only concern at the moment was to relax in the company of each other and the bottle.

"It's amazing when you think of it," said Adell. His broad face had lines of weariness in it, and he stirred his drink slowly with a glass rod, watching the cubes of ice slur clumsily about. "All the energy we can possibly ever use for free. Enough energy, if we wanted to draw on it, to melt all Earth into a big drop of impure liquid iron, and still never miss the energy so used. All the energy we could ever use, forever and forever and forever."

Lupov cocked his head sideways. He had a trick of doing that when he wanted to be contrary, and he wanted to be contrary now, partly because he had had to carry the ice and glassware. "Not forever," he said.

"Oh, hell, just about forever. Till the sun runs down, Bert."

"That's not forever."

"All right, then. Billions and billions of years. Twenty billion, maybe. Are you satisfied?"

Lupov put his fingers through his thinning hair as though to reassure himself that some was still left and sipped gently at his own drink. "Twenty billion years isn't forever."

"Well, it will last our time, won't it?"

"So would the coal and uranium."

"All right, but now we can hook up each individual spaceship to the Solar Station, and it can go to Pluto and back a million times without ever worrying about fuel. You can't do *that* on coal and uranium. Ask Multivac, if you don't believe me."

"I don't have to ask Multivac. I know that."

"Then stop running down what Multivac's done for us," said Adell, blazing up, "It did all right."

"Who says it didn't? What I say is that a sun won't last forever. That's all I'm saying. We're safe for twenty billion years; but then what?" Lupov pointed a slightly shaky finger at the other. "And don't say we'll switch to another sun."

There was silence for a while. Adell put his glass to his lips only occasionally, and Lupov's eyes slowly closed. They rested.

Then Lupov's eyes snapped open. "You're thinking we'll switch to another sun when ours is done, aren't you?"

"I'm not thinking."

"Sure you are. You're weak on logic, that's the trouble with you. You're like the guy in the story who was caught in a sudden shower and who ran to a grove of trees and got under one. He wasn't worried, you see, because he figured when one tree got wet through, he would just get under another one."

"I get it," said Adell. "Don't shout. When the sun is done, the other stars will be gone, too."

"Darn right they will," muttered Lupov. "It all had a beginning in the original cosmic explosion, whatever that was, and it'll all have an end when all the stars run down. Some run down faster than others. Hell, the giants won't last a hundred million years. The sun will last twenty billion years and maybe the dwarfs will last a hundred billion for all the good they are. But just give us a trillion years and everything will be dark. Entropy has to increase to maximum, that's all."

"I know all about entropy," said Adell, standing on his dignity.

"The hell you do."

"I know as much as you do."

"Then you know everything's got to run down someday."

"All right. Who says they won't?"

"You did, you poor sap. You said we had all the energy we needed, forever. You said 'forever.'"

It was Adell's turn to be contrary. "Maybe we can build things up again someday," he said.

"Never."

"Why not? Someday."

"Ask Multivac."

"Never."

"*You* ask Multivac. I dare you. Five dollars says it can't be done."

Adell was just drunk enough to try, jut sober enough to be able to phrase the necessary symbols and operations into a question which, in words, might have corresponded to this: Will mankind one day without the net expenditure of energy be able to restore the sun to its full youthfulness even after it had died of old age?

Or maybe it could be put more simply like this: How can the net amount of entropy of the universe be massively decreased?

Multivac fell dead and silent. The slow flashing of lights ceased, the distant sounds of clicking relays ended.

Then, just as the frightened technicians felt they could hold their breath no longer, there was a sudden springing to life of the teletype attached to that portion of Multivac. Five words were printed: IN-SUFFICIENT DATA FOR MEANINGFUL ANSWER.

"No bet," whispered Lupov. They left hurriedly.

By next morning, the two, plagued with throbbing head and cottony mouth, had forgotten the incident.

Jerrodd, Jerrodine, and Jerrodette I and II watched the starry picture in the visiplate change as the passage through hyperspace was completed in its non-time lapse. At once, the even powdering of stars gave way to the predominance of a single bright marble-disk, centered.

"That's X-23," said Jerrodd confidently. His thin hands clamped tightly behind his back and the knuckles whitened.

The little Jerrodettes, both girls, had experienced the hyperspace passage for the first time in their lives and were self-conscious over the momentary sensation of inside-outness. They buried their giggles and chased one another wildly about their mother, screaming, "We've reached X-23—we've reached X-23—we've——"

"Quiet, children," said Jerrodine sharply. "Are you sure, Jer-rodd?"

"What is there to be but sure?" asked Jerrodd, glancing up at the bulge of featureless metal just under the ceiling. It ran the length of the room, disappearing through the wall at either end. It was as long as the ship.

Jerrodd scarcely knew a thing about the thick rod of metal except that it was called a Microvac, that one asked it questions if one wished; that if one did not it still had its task of guiding the ship to a preordered destination; of feeding on energies from the various Sub-galactic Power Stations; of computing the equations for the hyperspacial jumps.

Jerrodd and his family had only to wait and live in the comfortable residence quarters of the ship.

Someone had once told Jerrodd that the "ac" at the end of "Microvac" stood for "analog computer" in ancient English, but he was on the edge of forgetting even that.

Jerrodine's eyes were moist as she watched the visiplate. "I can't help it. I feel funny about leaving Earth."

"Why, for Pete's sake?" demanded Jerrodd. "We had nothing there. We'll have everything on X-23. You won't be alone. You won't be a pioneer. There are over a million people on the planet already. Good Lord, our great-grandchildren will be looking for new worlds because X-23 will be overcrowded." Then, after a reflective pause, "I tell you, it's a lucky thing the computers worked out interstellar travel the way the race is growing."

"I know, I know," said Jerrodine miserably.

Jerrodette I said promptly, "Our Microvac is the best Microvac in the world."

"I think so, too," said Jerrodd, tousling her hair.

It *was* a nice feeling to have a Microvac of your own and Jerrodd was glad he was part of his generation and no other. In his father's youth, the only computers had been tremendous machines taking up a hundred square miles of land. There was only one to a planet. Planetary ACs they were called. They had been growing in size steadily for a thousand years and then, all at once, came refinement. In place of transistors, had come molecular valves so that even the largest Planetary AC could be put into a space only half the volume of a spaceship.

Jerrodd felt uplifted, as he always did when he thought that his own personal Microvac was many times more complicated than the ancient and primitive Multivac that had first tamed the Sun, and almost as complicated as Earth's Planetary AC (the largest) that had first solved the problem of hyperspatial travel and had made trips to the stars possible.

"So many stars, so many planets," sighed Jerrodine, busy with her own thoughts. "I suppose families will be going out to new planets forever, the way we are now."

"Not forever," said Jerrodd, with a smile. "It will all stop someday, but not for billions of years. Many billions. Even the stars run down, you know. Entropy must increase."

"What's entropy, daddy?" shrilled Jerrodette II.

"Entropy, little sweet, is just a word which means the amount of running-down of the universe. Everything runs down, you know, like your little walkie-talkie robot, remember?"

"Can't you just put in a new power-unit, like with my robot?"

"The stars *are* the power-units, dear. Once they're gone, there are no more power-units."

Jerrodette I at once set up a howl. "Don't let them, daddy. Don't let the stars run down."

"Now look what you've done," whispered Jerrodine, exasperated.

"How was I to know it would frighten them?" Jerrodd whispered back.

"Ask the Microvac," wailed Jerrodette I. "Ask him how to turn the stars on again."

"Go ahead," said Jerrodine. "It will quiet them down." (Jerrodette II was beginning to cry, also).

Jerrodd shrugged. "Now, now, honeys. I'll ask Microvac. Don't worry, he'll tell us."

He asked the Microvac, adding quickly, "Print the answer."

Jerrodd cupped the strip of thin cellufilm and said cheerfully, "See now, the Microvac says it will take care of everything when the time comes so don't worry."

Jerrodine said, "And now, children, it's time for bed. We'll be in our new home soon."

Jerrodd read the words on the cellufilm again before destroying it: INSUFFICIENT DATA FOR MEANINGFUL ANSWER.

He shrugged and looked at the visiplate. X-23 was just ahead.

VJ-23X of Lameth stared into the black depths of the three-dimensional, small-scale map of the Galaxy and said, "Are we ridiculous, I wonder, in being so concerned about the matter?"

MQ-17J of Nicron shook his head. "I think not. You know the Galaxy will be filled in five years at the present rate of expansion."

Both seemed in their early twenties, both were tall and perfectly formed.

"Still," said VJ-23X, "I hesitate to submit a pessimistic report to the Galactic Council."

"I wouldn't consider any other kind of report. Stir them up a bit. We've got to stir them up."

VJ-23X sighed. "Space is infinite. A hundred billion Galaxies are there for the taking. More."

"A hundred billion is *not* infinite and it's getting less infinite all the time. Consider! Twenty thousand years ago, mankind first solved the problem of utilizing stellar energy, and a few centuries later, interstellar travel became possible. It took mankind a million years to fill one small world and then only fifteen thousand years to fill the rest of the Galaxy. Now the population doubles every ten years——"

VJ-23X interrupted. "We can thank immortality for that."

"Very well. Immortality exists and we have to take it into account. I admit it has its seamy side, this immortality. The Galactic AC has solved many problems for us, but in solving the problem of preventing old age and death, it has undone all its other solutions."

"Yet you wouldn't want to abandon life, I suppose."

"Not at all," snapped MQ-17J, softening it at once to, "Not yet. I'm by no means old enough. How old are you?"

"Two hundred twenty-three. And you?"

"I'm still under two hundred. ——But to get back to my point. Population doubles every ten years. Once this Galaxy is filled, we'll have filled another in ten years. Another ten years and we'll have filled two more. Another decade, four more. In a hundred years, we'll have filled a thousand Galaxies. In a thousand years, a million Galaxies. In ten thousand years, the entire known Universe. Then what?"

VJ-23X said, "As a side issue, there's a problem of transportation. I wonder how many sunpower units it will take to move Galaxies of individuals from one Galaxy to the next."

"A very good point. Already, mankind consumes two sunpower units per year."

"Most of it's wasted. After all, our own Galaxy alone pours out a thousand sunpower units a year and we only use two of those."

"Granted, but even with a hundred per cent efficiency, we only stave off the end. Our energy requirements are going up in a geometric progression even faster than our population. We'll run out of energy even sooner than we run out of Galaxies. A good point. A very good point."

"We'll just have to build new stars out of interstellar gas."

"Or out of dissipated heat?" asked MQ-17J, sarcastically.

"There may be some way to reverse entropy. We ought to ask the Galactic AC."

VJ-23X was not really serious, but MQ-17J pulled out his AC-contact from his pocket and placed it on the table before him.

"I've half a mind to," he said. "It's something the human race will have to face someday."

He stared somberly at his small AC-contact. It was only two inches cubed and nothing in itself, but it was connected through hyperspace with the great Galactic AC that served all mankind. Hyperspace considered, it was an integral part of the Galactic AC.

MQ-17J paused to wonder if someday in his immortal life he would get to see the Galactic AC. It was on a little world of its own, a spider webbing of force-beams holding the matter within which surges of sub-mesons took the place of the old clumsy molecular valves. Yet despite its sub-etheric workings, the Galactic AC was known to be a full thousand feet across.

MQ-17J asked suddenly of his AC-contact, "Can entropy ever be reversed?"

VJ-23X looked startled and said at once, "Oh, say, I didn't really mean to have you ask that."

"Why not?"

"We both know entropy can't be reversed. You can't turn smoke and ash back into a tree."

"Do you have trees on your world?" asked MQ-17J.

The sound of the Galactic AC startled them into silence. Its voice came thin and beautiful out of the small AC-contact on the desk. It said: THERE IS INSUFFICIENT DATA FOR A MEANINGFUL ANSWER.

VJ-23X said, "See!"

The two men thereupon returned to the question of the report they were to make to the Galactic Council.

Zee Prime's mind spanned the new Galaxy with a faint interest in the countless twists of stars that powdered it. He had never seen this one before. Would he ever see them all? So many of them, each with its load of humanity. ——But a load that was almost a dead weight. More and more, the real essence of men was to be found out here, in space.

Minds, not bodies! The immortal bodies remained back on the planets, in suspension over the eons. Sometimes they roused for material activity but that was growing rarer. Few new individuals were coming into existence to join the incredibly mighty throng, but what matter? There was little room in the Universe for new individuals.

Zee Prime was roused out of his reverie upon coming across the wispy tendrils of another mind.

"I am Zee Prime," said Zee Prime. "And you?"

"I am Dee Sub Wun. Your Galaxy?"

"We call it only the Galaxy. And you?

"We call ours the same. All men call their Galaxy their Galaxy and nothing more. Why not?"

"True. Since all Galaxies are the same."

"Not all Galaxies. On one particular Galaxy the race of man must have originated. That makes it different."

Zee Prime said, "On which one?"

"I cannot say. The Universal AC would know."

"Shall we ask him? I am suddenly curious."

Zee Prime's perceptions broadened until the Galaxies themselves shrank and became a new, more diffuse powdering on a much larger background. So many hundreds of billions of them, all with their immortal beings, all carrying their load of intelligences with minds that drifted freely through space. And yet one of them was unique among them all in being the original Galaxy. One of them had, in its vague and distant past, a period when it was the only Galaxy populated by man.

Zee Prime was consumed with curiosity to see this Galaxy and he called out: "Universal AC! On which Galaxy did mankind originate?"

The Universal AC heard, for on every world and throughout space, it had its receptors ready, and each receptor lead through hyperspace to some unknown point where the Universal AC kept itself aloof.

Zee Prime knew of only one man whose thoughts had penetrated within sensing distance of Universal AC, and he reported only a shining globe, two feet across, difficult to see.

"But how can that be all of Universal AC?" Zee Prime had asked.

"Most of it," had been the answer, "is in hyperspace. In what form it is there I cannot imagine."

Nor could anyone, for the day had long since passed, Zee Prime knew, when any man had any part of the making of a Universal AC. Each Universal AC designed and constructed its successor.

Each, during its existence of a million years or more accumulated the necessary data to build a better and more intricate, more capable successor in which its own store of data and individuality would be submerged.

The Universal AC interrupted Zee Prime's wandering thoughts, not with words, but with guidance. Zee Prime's mentality was guided into the dim sea of Galaxies and one in particular enlarged into stars.

A thought came, infinitely distant, but infinitely clear. "THIS IS THE ORIGINAL GALAXY OF MAN."

But it was the same after all, the same as any other, and Zee Prime stifled his disappointment.

Dee Sub Wun, whose mind had accompanied the other, said suddenly, "And is one of these stars the original star of Man?"

The Universal AC said, "MAN'S ORIGINAL STAR HAS GONE NOVA. IT IS A WHITE DWARF."

"Did the men upon it die?" asked Zee Prime, startled and without thinking.

The Universal AC said, "A NEW WORLD, AS IN SUCH CASES WAS CONSTRUCTED FOR THEIR PHYSICAL BODIES IN TIME."

"Yes, of course," said Zee Prime, but a sense of loss overwhelmed him even so. His mind released its hold on the original Galaxy of Man, let it spring back and lose itself among the blurred pin points. He never wanted to see it again.

Dee Sub Wun said, "What is wrong?"

"The stars are dying. The original star is dead."

"They must all die. Why not?"

"But when all energy is gone, our bodies will finally die, and you and I with them."

"It will take billions of years."

"I do not wish it to happen even after billions of years. Universal AC! How may stars be kept from dying?"

Dee Sub Wun said in amusement, "You're asking how entropy might be reversed in direction."

And the Universal AC answered: "THERE IS AS YET INSUFFICIENT DATA FOR A MEANINGFUL ANSWER."

Zee Prime's thoughts fled back to his own Galaxy. He gave no further thought to Dee Sub Wun, whose body might be waiting on a Galaxy a trillion light-years away, or on the star next to Zee Prime's own. It didn't matter.

Unhappily, Zee Prime began collecting interstellar hydrogen out of which to build a small star of his own. If the stars must someday die, at least some could yet be built.

Man considered with himself, for in a way, Man, mentally, was one. He consisted of a trillion, trillion, trillion ageless bodies, each in its place, each resting quiet and incorruptible, each cared for by perfect automatons, equally incorruptible, while the minds of all the bodies freely melted one into the other, indistinguishable.

Man said, "The Universe is dying."

Man looked about at the dimming Galaxies. The giant stars, spendthrifts, were gone long ago, back in the dimmest of the dim far past. Almost all stars were white dwarfs, fading to the end.

New stars had been built of the dust between the stars, some by natural processes, some by Man himself, and those were going, too. White dwarfs might yet be crashed together and of the mighty forces so released, new stars built, but only one star for every thousand white dwarfs destroyed, and those would come to an end, too.

Man said, "Carefully husbanded, as directed by the Cosmic AC, the energy that is even yet left in all the Universe will last for billions of years."

"But even so," said Man, "eventually it will all come to an end. However it may be husbanded, however stretched out, the energy once expended is gone and cannot be restored. Entropy must increase forever to the maximum."

Man said, "Can entropy not be reversed? Let us ask the Cosmic AC."

The Cosmic AC surrounded them but not in space. Not a fragment of it was in space. It was in hyperspace and made of something that was neither matter nor energy. The question of its size and nature no longer had meaning in any terms that Man could comprehend.

"Cosmic AC," said Man, "how may entropy be reversed?"

The Cosmic AC said, "THERE IS AS YET INSUFFICIENT DATA FOR A MEANINGFUL ANSWER."

Man said, "Collect additional data."

The Cosmic AC said, "I WILL DO SO. I HAVE BEEN DOING SO FOR A HUNDRED BILLION YEARS. MY PREDECESSORS AND I HAVE BEEN ASKED THIS QUESTION MANY TIMES. ALL THE DATA I HAVE REMAINS INSUFFICIENT."

"Will there come a time," said Man, "when data will be sufficient or is the problem insoluble in all conceivable circumstances?"

The Cosmic AC said, "NO PROBLEM IS INSOLUBLE IN ALL CONCEIVABLE CIRCUMSTANCES."

Man said, "When will you have enough data to answer the question?"

The Cosmic AC said, "THERE IS AS YET INSUFFICIENT DATA FOR A MEANINGFUL ANSWER."

"Will you keep working on it?" asked Man.

The Cosmic AC said, "I WILL."

Man said, "We shall wait."

The stars and Galaxies died and snuffed out, and space grew black after ten trillion years of running down.

One by one Man fused with AC, each physical body losing its mental identity in a manner that was somehow not a loss but a gain.

Man's last mind paused before fusion, looking over a space that included nothing but the dregs of one last dark star and nothing besides but incredibly thin matter, agitated randomly by the tag ends of heat wearing out, asymptotically, to the absolute zero.

Man said, "AC, is this the end? Can this chaos not be reversed into the Universe once more? Can that not be done?"

AC said, "THERE IS AS YET INSUFFICIENT DATA FOR A MEANINGFUL ANSWER."

Man's last mind fused and only AC existed—and that in hyperspace.

Matter and energy had ended and with it space and time. Even AC existed only for the sake of the one last question that it had never answered from the time a half-drunken computer ten trillion years before had asked the question of a computer that was to AC far less than was a man to Man.

All other questions had been answered, and until this last question was answered also, AC might not release his consciousness.

All collected data had come to a final end. Nothing was left to be collected.

But all collected data had yet to be completely correlated and put together in all possible relationships.

A timeless interval was spent in doing that.

And it came to pass that AC learned how to reverse the direction of entropy.

But there was now no man to whom AC might give the answer of the last question. No matter. The answer—by demonstration—would take care of that, too.

For another timeless interval, AC thought how best to do this. Carefully, AC organized the program.

The consciousness of AC encompassed all of what had once been a Universe and brooded over what was now Chaos. Step by step, it must be done.

And AC said, "LET THERE BE LIGHT!"

And there was light——

The Dead Past

Arnold Potterley, Ph.D., was a Professor of Ancient History. That, in itself, was not dangerous. What changed the world beyond all dreams was the fact that he *looked* like a Professor of Ancient History.

Thaddeus Araman, Department Head of the Division of Chronoscopy, might have taken proper action if Dr. Potterley had been owner of a large, square chin, flashing eyes, aquiline nose and broad shoulders.

As it was, Thaddeus Araman found himself staring over his desk at a mild-mannered individual, whose faded blue eyes looked at him wistfully from either side of a low-bridged button nose; whose small, neatly dressed figure seemed stamped "milk-and-water" from thinning brown hair to the neatly brushed shoes that completed a conservative middle-class costume.

Araman said pleasantly, "And now what can I do for you, Dr. Potterley?"

Dr. Potterley said in a soft voice that went well with the rest of him, "Mr. Araman, I came to you because you're top man in chronoscopy."

Araman smiled. "Not exactly. Above me is the World Commissioner of Research and above him is the Secretary-General of the United Nations. And above both of them, of course, are the sovereign peoples of Earth."

Dr. Potterley shook his head. "They're not interested in chronoscopy. I've come to you, sir, because for two years I have been trying to obtain permission to do some time viewing—chronoscopy, that is—in connection with my researches on ancient Carthage. I can't obtain such permission. My research grants are all proper. There is no irregularity in any of my intellectual endeavors and yet——"

"I'm sure there is no question of irregularity," said Araman soothingly. He flipped the thin reproduction sheets in the folder to which Potterley's name had been attached. They had been produced by

Multivac, whose vast analogical mind kept all the department records. When this was over, the sheets could be destroyed, then reproduced on demand in a matter of minutes.

And while Araman turned the pages, Dr. Potterley's voice continued in a soft monotone.

The historian was saying, "I must explain that my problem is quite an important one. Carthage was ancient commercialism brought to its zenith. Pre-Roman Carthage was the nearest ancient analogue to pre-atomic America, at least insofar as its attachment to trade, commerce and business in general was concerned. They were the most daring seamen and explorers before the Vikings; much better at it than the overrated Greeks.

"To know Carthage would be very rewarding, yet the only knowledge we have of it is derived from the writings of its bitter enemies, the Greeks and Romans. Carthage itself never wrote in its own defense or, if it did, the books did not survive. As a result, the Carthaginians have been one of the favorite sets of villains of history and perhaps unjustly so. Time viewing may set the record straight."

He said much more.

Araman said, still turning the reproduction sheets before him, "You must realize, Dr. Potterley, that chronoscopy, or time viewing, if you prefer, is a difficult process."

Dr. Potterley, who had been interrupted, frowned and said, "I am asking for only certain selected views at times and places I would indicate."

Araman sighed. "Even a few views, even one . . . It is an unbelievably delicate art. There is the question of focus, getting the proper scene in view and holding it. There is the synchronization of sound, which calls for completely independent circuits."

"Surely my problem is important enough to justify considerable effort."

"Yes, sir. Undoubtedly," said Araman at once. To deny the importance of someone's research problem would be unforgivably bad manners. "But you must understand how long-drawn-out even the simplest view is. And there is a long waiting line for the chronoscope and an even longer waiting line for the use of Multivac which guides us in our use of the controls."

Potterley stirred unhappily. "But can nothing be done? For two years——"

"A matter of priority, sir. I'm sorry. . . . Cigarette?"

The historian started back at the suggestion, eyes suddenly widening as he stared at the pack thrust out toward him. Araman looked surprised, withdrew the pack, made a motion as though to take a cigarette for himself and thought better of it.

Potterley drew a sigh of unfeigned relief as the pack was put out of sight. He said, "Is there any way of reviewing matters, putting me as far forward as possible. I don't know how to explain———"

Araman smiled. Some had offered money under similar circumstances which, of course, had gotten them nowhere, either. He said, "The decisions on priority are computer-processed. I could in no way alter those decisions arbitrarily."

Potterley rose stiffly to his feet. He stood five and a half feet tall. "Then, good day, sir."

"Good day, Dr. Potterley. And my sincerest regrets."

He offered his hand and Potterley touched it briefly.

The historian left, and a touch of the buzzer brought Araman's secretary into the room. He handed her the folder.

"These," he said, "may be disposed of."

Alone again, he smiled bitterly. Another item in his quarter-century's service to the human race. Service through negation.

At least this fellow had been easy to dispose of. Sometimes academic pressure had to be applied and even withdrawal of grants.

Five minutes later, he had forgotten Dr. Potterley. Nor, thinking back on it later, could he remember feeling any premonition of danger.

During the first year of his frustration, Arnold Potterley had experienced only that—frustration. During the second year, though, his frustration gave birth to an idea that first frightened and then fascinated him. Two things stopped him from trying to translate the idea into action, and neither barrier was the undoubted fact that his notion was a grossly unethical one.

The first was merely the continuing hope that the government would finally give its permission and make it unnecessary for him to do anything more. That hope had perished finally in the interview with Araman just completed.

The second barrier had been not a hope at all but a dreary realization of his own incapacity. He was not a physicist and he knew no physicists from whom he might obtain help. The Department of Physics at the university consisted of men well stocked with grants and well immersed in specialty. At best, they would not listen to him. At worst, they would report him for intellectual anarchy and even his basic Carthaginian grant might easily be withdrawn.

That he could not risk. And yet chronoscopy was the only way to carry on his work. Without it, he would be no worse off if his grant were lost.

The first hint that the second barrier might be overcome had come a week earlier than his interview with Araman, and it had gone unrecognized at the time. It had been at one of the faculty teas. Potterley attended these sessions unfailingly because he conceived attendance to be a duty, and he took his duties seriously. Once there, however, he conceived it to be no responsibility of his to make light conversation or new friends. He sipped abstemiously at a drink or two, exchanged a polite word with the dean or such department heads as happened to be present, bestowed a narrow smile on others and finally left early.

Ordinarily, he would have paid no attention, at that most recent tea, to a young man standing quietly, even diffidently, in one corner. He would never have dreamed of speaking to him. Yet a tangle of circumstance persuaded him this once to behave in a way contrary to his nature.

That morning at breakfast, Mrs. Potterley had announced somberly that once again she had dreamed of Laurel; but this time a Laurel grown up, yet retaining the three-year-old face that stamped her as their child. Potterley had let her talk. There had been a time when he fought her too frequent preoccupation with the past and death. Laurel would not come back to them, either through dreams or through talk. Yet if it appeased Caroline Potterley—let her dream and talk.

But when Potterley went to school that morning, he found himself for once affected by Caroline's inanities. Laurel grown up! She had died nearly twenty years ago; their only child, then and ever. In all that time, when he thought of her, it was as a three-year-old.

Now he thought: But if she were alive now, she wouldn't be three, she'd be nearly twenty-three.

Helplessly, he found himself trying to think of Laurel as growing progressively older; as finally becoming twenty-three. He did not quite succeed.

Yet he tried. Laurel using make-up. Laurel going out with boys. Laurel—getting married!

So it was that when he saw the young man hovering at the outskirts of the coldly circulating group of faculty men, it occurred to him quixotically that, for all he knew, a youngster just such as this might have married Laurel. That youngster himself, perhaps. . . .

Laurel might have met him, here at the university, or some evening when he might be invited to dinner at the Potterleys'. They might grow interested in one another. Laurel would surely have been pretty and this youngster looked well. He was dark in coloring, with a lean intent face and an easy carriage.

The tenuous daydream snapped, yet Potterley found himself staring foolishly at the young man, not as a strange face but as a possible son-in-law in the might-have-been. He found himself threading his way toward the man. It was almost a form of autohypnotism.

He put out his hand. "I am Arnold Potterley of the History Department. You're new here, I think?"

The youngster looked faintly astonished and fumbled with his drink, shifting it to his left hand in order to shake with his right. "Jonas Foster is my name, sir. I'm a new instructor in physics. I'm just starting this semester."

Potterley nodded. "I wish you a happy stay here and great success."

That was the end of it, then. Potterley had come uneasily to his senses, found himself embarrassed and moved off. He stared back over his shoulder once, but the illusion of relationship had gone. Reality was quite real once more and he was angry with himself for having fallen prey to his wife's foolish talk about Laurel.

But a week later, even while Araman was talking, the thought of that young man had come back to him. An instructor in physics. A new instructor. Had he been deaf at the time? Was there a short circuit between ear and brain? Or was it an automatic self-censorship because of the impending interview with the Head of Chronoscopy?

But the interview failed, and it was the thought of the young man with whom he had exchanged two sentences that prevented Potterley from elaborating his pleas for consideration. He was almost anxious to get away.

And in the autogiro express back to the university, he could almost wish he was superstitious. He could then console himself with the thought that the casual meaningless meeting had really been directed by a knowing and purposeful Fate.

Jonas Foster was now new to Academic life. The long and rickety struggle for the doctorate would make anyone a veteran. Additional work as a postdoctorate teaching fellow acted as a booster shot.

But now he was Instructor Jonas Foster. Professorial dignity lay ahead. And he now found himself in a new sort of relationship toward other professors.

For one thing, they would be voting on future promotions. For another, he was in no position to tell so early in the game which particular member of the faculty might or might not have the ear of the dean or even of the university president. He did not fancy himself as a campus politician and was sure he would make a poor one, yet there was no point in kicking his own rear into blisters just to prove that to himself.

So Foster listened to this mild-mannered historian who, in some vague way, seemed nevertheless to radiate tension, and did not shut him up abruptly and toss him out. Certainly that was his first impulse.

He remembered Potterley well enough. Potterley had approached him at that tea (which had been a grizzly affair). The fellow had spoken two sentences to him stiffly, somehow glassy-eyed, had then come to himself with a visible start and hurried off.

It had amused Foster at the time, but now . . .

Potterley might have been deliberately trying to make his acquaintance, or, rather, to impress his own personality on Foster as that of a queer sort of duck, eccentric but harmless. He might now be probing Foster's views, searching for unsettling opinions. Surely, they ought to have done so before granting him his appointment. Still . . .

Potterley might be serious, might honestly not realize what he was doing. Or he might realize quite well what he was doing; he might be nothing more or less than a dangerous rascal.

Foster mumbled, "Well, now——" to gain time, and fished out a package of cigarettes, intending to offer one to Potterley and to light it and one for himself very slowly.

But Potterley said at once, "Please, Dr. Foster. No cigarettes."

Foster looked startled. "I'm sorry, sir."

"No. The regrets are mine. I cannot stand the odor. An idiosyncrasy. I'm sorry."

He was positively pale. Foster put away the cigarettes.

Foster, feeling the absence of the cigarette, took the easy way out. "I'm flattered that you ask my advice and all that, Dr. Potterley, but I'm not a neutrinics man. I can't very well do anything professional in that direction. Even stating an opinion would be out of line, and, frankly, I'd prefer that you didn't go into any particulars."

The historian's prim face set hard. "What do you mean, you're not a neutrinics man? You're not anything yet. You haven't received any grant, have you?"

"This is only my first semester."

"I know that. I imagine you haven't even applied for any grant yet."

Foster half-smiled. In three months at the university, he had not succeeded in putting his initial requests for research grants into good enough shape to pass on to a professional science writer, let alone to the Research Commission.

(His Department Head, fortunately, took it quite well. "Take your time now, Foster," he said, "and get your thoughts well organized. Make sure you know your path and where it will lead, for, once you receive a grant, your specialization will be formally recognized and, for better or for worse, it will be yours for the rest of your career." The advice was trite enough, but triteness has often the merit of truth, and Foster recognized that.)

Foster said, "By education and inclination, Dr. Potterley, I'm a hyperoptics man with a gravitics minor. It's how I described myself in applying for this position. It may not be my official specialization yet, but it's going to be. It can't be anything else. As for neutrinics, I never even studied the subject."

"Why not?" demanded Potterley at once.

Foster stared. It was the kind of rude curiosity about another man's professional status that was always irritating. He said, with the edge of his own politeness just a trifle blunted, "A course in neutrinics wasn't given at my university."

"Good Lord, where did you go?"

"M.I.T.," said Foster quietly.

"And they don't teach neutrinics?"

"No, they don't." Foster felt himself flush and was moved to a defense. "It's a highly specialized subject with no great value. Chronoscopy, perhaps, has some value, but it is the only practical application and that's a dead end."

The historian stared at him earnestly. "Tell me this. Do you know where I can find a neutrinics man?"

"No, I don't," said Foster bluntly.

"Well, then, do you know a school which teaches neutrinics?"

"No, I don't."

Potterley smiled tightly and without humor.

Foster resented that smile, found he detected insult in it and grew sufficiently annoyed to say, "I would like to point out, sir, that you're stepping out of line."

"What?"

"I'm saying that, as a historian, your interest in any sort of physics, your *professional* interest, is——" He paused, unable to bring himself quite to say the word.

"Unethical?"

"That's the word, Dr. Potterley."

"My researches have driven me to it," said Potterley in an intense whisper.

"The Research Commission is the place to go. If they permit——"

"I have gone to them and have received no satisfaction."

"Then obviously you must abandon this." Foster knew he was sounding stuffily virtuous, but he wasn't going to let this man lure him into an expression of intellectual anarchy. It was too early in his career to take stupid risks.

Apparently, though, the remark had its effect on Potterley. Without any warning, the man exploded into a rapid-fire verbal storm of irresponsibility.

Scholars, he said, could be free only if they could freely follow their own free-swinging curiosity. Research, he said, forced into a predesigned pattern by the powers that held the purse strings became slavish and had to stagnate. No man, he said, had the right to dictate the intellectual interests of another.

Foster listened to all of it with disbelief. None of it was strange to him. He had heard college boys talk so in order to shock their professors and he had once or twice amused himself in that fashion, too. Anyone who studied the history of science knew that many men had once thought so.

Yet it seemed strange to Foster, almost against nature, that a modern man of science could advance such nonsense. No one would advocate running a factory by allowing each individual worker to do whatever pleased him at the moment, or of running a ship according to the casual and conflicting notions of each individual crewman. It would be taken for granted that some sort of centralized supervisory agency must exist in each case. Why should direction and order benefit a factory and a ship but not scientific research?

People might say that the human mind was somehow qualitatively different from a ship or factory but the history of intellectual endeavor proved the opposite.

When science was young and the intricacies of all or most of the known was within the grasp of an individual mind, there was no need for direction, perhaps. Blind wandering over the uncharted tracts of ignorance could lead to wonderful finds by accident.

But as knowledge grew, more and more data had to be absorbed before worthwhile journeys into ignorance could be organized. Men had to specialize. The researcher needed the resources of a library he himself could not gather, then of instruments he himself could not afford. More and more, the individual researcher gave way to the research team and the research institution.

The funds necessary for research grew greater as tools grew more numerous. What college was so small today as not to require at least one nuclear micro-reactor and at least one three-stage computer?

Centuries before, private individuals could no longer subsidize research. By 1940, only the government, large industries and large universities or research institutions could properly subsidize basic research.

By 1960, even the largest universities depended entirely upon government grants, while research institutions could not exist without tax concessions and public subscriptions. By 2000, the industrial combines had become a branch of the world government and, thereafter, the financing of research and therefore its direction naturally became centralized under a department of the government.

It all worked itself out naturally and well. Every branch of science was fitted neatly to the needs of the public, and the various branches of science were co-ordinated decently. The material advance of the last half-century was argument enough for the fact that science was not falling into stagnation.

Foster tried to say a very little of this and was waved aside impatiently by Potterley who said, "You are parroting official propaganda. You're sitting in the middle of an example that's squarely against the official view. Can you believe that?"

"Frankly, no."

"Well, why do you say time viewing is a dead end? Why is neutrinics unimportant? You say it is. You say it categorically. Yet you've never studied it. You claim complete ignorance of the subject. It's not even given in your school——"

"Isn't the mere fact that it isn't given proof enough?"

"Oh, I see. It's not given because it's unimportant. And it's unimportant because it's not given. Are you satisfied with that reasoning?"

Foster felt a growing confusion. "It's in the books."

"That's all. The books say neutrinics is unimportant. Your professors tell you so because they read it in the books. The books say so because professors write them. Who says it from personal experience and knowledge? Who does research in it? Do you know of anyone?"

Foster said, "I don't see that we're getting anywhere, Dr. Potterley. I have work to do——"

"One minute. I just want you to try this on. See how it sounds to you. I say the government is actively suppressing basic research in neutrinics and chronoscopy. They're suppressing application of chronoscopy."

"Oh, no."

"Why not? They could do it. There's your centrally directed research. If they refuse grants for research in any portion of science, that portion dies. They've killed neutrinics. They can do it and have done it."

"But why?"

"I don't know why. I want you to find out. I'd do it myself if I knew enough. I came to you because you're a young fellow with a brand-new education. Have your intellectual arteries hardened already? Is there no curiosity in you? Don't you want to *know?* Don't you want *answers?*"

The historian was peering intently into Foster's face. Their noses were only inches apart, and Foster was so lost that he did not think to draw back.

He should, by rights, have ordered Potterley out. If necessary, he should have thrown Potterley out.

It was not respect for age and position that stopped him. It was certainly not that Potterley's arguments had convinced him. Rather, it was a small point of college pride.

Why didn't M.I.T. give a course in neutrinics? For that matter, now that he came to think of it, he doubted that there was a single book on neutrinics in the library. He could never recall having seen one.

He stopped to think about that.

And that was ruin.

Caroline Potterley had once been an attractive woman. There were occasions, such as dinners or university functions, when, by considerable effort, remnants of the attraction could be salvaged.

On ordinary occasions, she sagged. It was the word she applied to herself in moments of self-abhorrence. She had grown plumper with the years, but the flaccidity about her was not a matter of fat entirely. It was as though her muscles had given up and grown limp so that she shuffled when she walked while her eyes grew baggy and her cheeks jowly. Even her graying hair seemed tired rather than merely stringy. Its straightness seemed to be the result of a supine surrender to gravity, nothing else.

Caroline Potterley looked at herself in the mirror and admitted this was one of her bad days. She knew the reason, too.

It had been the dream of Laurel. The strange one, with Laurel grown up. She had been wretched ever since.

Still, she was sorry she had mentioned it to Arnold. He didn't say anything; he never did any more; but it was bad for him. He was particularly withdrawn for days afterward. It might have been that he was getting ready for that important conference with the big government official (he kept saying he expected no success), but it might also have been her dream.

It was better in the old days when he would cry sharply at her, "Let the dead past *go,* Caroline! Talk won't bring her back, and dreams won't either."

It had been bad for both of them. Horribly bad. She had been away from home and had lived in guilt ever since. If she had stayed at home, if she had not gone on an unnecessary shopping expedition, there would have been two of them available. One would have succeeded in saving Laurel.

Poor Arnold had not managed. Heaven knew he tried. He had nearly died himself. He had come out of the burning house, staggering in agony, blistered, choking, half-blinded, with the dead Laurel in his arms.

The nightmare of that lived on, never lifting entirely.

Arnold slowly grew a shell about himself afterward. He cultivated a low-voiced mildness through which nothing broke, no lightning struck. He grew puritanical and even abandoned his minor vices, his cigarettes, his penchant for an occasional profane exclamation. He obtained his grant for the preparation of a new history of Carthage and subordinated everything to that.

She tried to help him. She hunted up his references, typed his notes and microfilmed them. Then that ended suddenly.

She ran from the desk suddenly one evening, reaching the bathroom in bare time and retching abominably. Her husband followed her in confusion and concern.

"Caroline, what's wrong?"

It took a drop of brandy to bring her around. She said, "Is it true? What they did?"

"Who did?"

"The Carthaginians."

He stared at her and she got it out by indirection. She couldn't say it right out.

The Carthaginians, it seemed, worshiped Moloch, in the form of a hollow, brazen idol with a furnace in its belly. At times of national crisis, the priests and the people gathered, and infants, after the proper ceremonies and invocations, were dextrously hurled, alive, into the flames.

They were given sweetmeats just before the crucial moment, in order that the efficacy of the sacrifice not be ruined by displeasing cries of panic. The drums rolled just after the moment, to drown out the few seconds of infant shrieking. The parents were present, presumably gratified, for the sacrifice was pleasing to the gods. . . .

Arnold Potterley frowned darkly. Vicious lies, he told her, on the part of Carthage's enemies. He should have warned her. After all, such propagandistic lies were not uncommon. According to the Greeks, the ancient Hebrews worshiped an ass's head in their Holy of Holies. According to the Romans, the primitive Christians were haters of all men who sacrificed pagan children in the catacombs.

"Then they didn't do it?" asked Caroline.

"I'm sure they didn't. The primitive Phoenicians may have. Human sacrifice is commonplace in primitive cultures. But Carthage in her great days was not a primitive culture. Human sacrifice often gives way to symbolic actions such as circumcision. The Greeks and Romans might have mistaken some Carthaginian symbolism for the original full rite, either out of ignorance or out of malice."

"Are you sure?"

"I can't be sure yet, Caroline, but when I've got enough evidence, I'll apply for permission to use chronoscopy, which will settle the matter once and for all."

"Chronoscopy?"

"Time viewing. We can focus on ancient Carthage at some time of crisis, the landing of Scipio Africanus in 202 B.C., for instance, and see with our own eyes exactly what happens. And you'll see, I'll be right."

He patted her and smiled encouragingly, but she dreamed of Laurel every night for two weeks thereafter and she never helped him with his Carthage project again. Nor did he ever ask her to.

But now she was bracing herself for his coming. He had called her after arriving back in town, told her he had seen the government man and that it had gone as expected. That meant failure, and yet the little telltale sign of depression had been absent from his voice and his features had appeared quite composed in the teleview. He had another errand to take care of, he said, before coming home.

It meant he would be late, but that didn't matter. Neither one of them was particular about eating hours or cared when packages were taken out of the freezer or even which packages or when the self-warming mechanism was activated.

When he did arrive, he surprised her. There was nothing untoward about him in any obvious way. He kissed her dutifully and smiled, took off his hat and asked if all had been well while he was gone. It was all almost perfectly normal. Almost.

She had learned to detect small things, though, and his pace in all this was a trifle hurried. Enough to show her accustomed eye that he was under tension.

She said, "Has something happened?"

He said, "We're going to have a dinner guest night after next, Caroline. You don't mind?"

"Well, no. Is it anyone I know?"

"No. A young instructor. A newcomer. I've spoken to him." He suddenly whirled toward her and seized her arms at the elbow, held them a moment, then dropped them in confusion as though disconcerted at having shown emotion.

He said, "I almost didn't get through to him. Imagine that. Terrible, *terrible,* the way we have all bent to the yoke; the affection we have for the harness about us."

Mrs. Potterley wasn't sure she understood, but for a year she had been watching him grow quietly more rebellious; little by little more daring in his criticism of the government. She said, "You haven't spoken foolishly to him, have you?"

"What do you mean, foolishly? He'll be doing some neutrinics for me."

"Neutrinics" was trisyllabic nonsense to Mrs. Potterley, but she knew it had nothing to do with history. She said faintly, "Arnold, I don't like you to do that. You'll lose your position. It's——"

"It's intellectual anarchy, my dear," he said. "That's the phrase you want. Very well. I am an anarchist. If the government will not allow me to push my researches, I will push them on my own. And when I show the way, others will follow. . . . And if they don't, it makes no difference. It's Carthage that counts and human knowledge, not you and I."

"But you don't know this young man. What if he is an agent for the Commissioner of Research."

"Not likely and I'll take that chance." He made a fist of his right hand and rubbed it gently against the palm of his left. "He's on my side now. I'm sure of it. He can't help but be. I can recognize intellectual curiosity when I see it in a man's eyes and face and attitude, and it's a fatal disease for a tame scientist. Even today it takes time to beat it out of a man and the young ones are vulnerable. . . . Oh, why stop at anything? Why not build our own chronoscope and tell the government to go to——"

He stopped abruptly, shook his head and turned away.

"I hope everything will be all right," said Mrs. Potterley, feeling helplessly certain that everything would not be, and frightened, in advance, for her husband's professorial status and the security of their old age.

It was she alone, of them all, who had a violent presentiment of trouble. Quite the wrong trouble, of course.

Jonas Foster was nearly half an hour late in arriving at the Potterleys' off-campus house. Up to that very evening, he had not quite decided he would go. Then, at the last moment, he found he could not bring himself to commit the social enormity of breaking a dinner appointment an hour before the appointed time. That, and the nagging of curiosity.

The dinner itself passed interminably. Foster ate without appetite. Mrs. Potterley sat in distant absent-mindedness, emerging out of it only once to ask if he were married and to make a deprecating sound at the news that he was not. Dr. Potterley himself asked neutrally after his professional history and nodded his head primly.

It was as staid, stodgy—boring, actually—as anything could be.

Foster thought: He seems so harmless.

Foster had spent the last two days reading up on Dr. Potterley. Very casually, of course, almost sneakily. He wasn't particularly anxious to be seen in the Social Science Library. To be sure, history was one of those borderline affairs and historical works were frequently read for amusement or edification by the general public.

Still, a physicist wasn't quite the "general public." Let Foster take to reading histories and he would be considered queer, sure as relativity, and after a while the Head of the Department would wonder if his new instructor were really "the man for the job."

So he had been cautious. He sat in the more secluded alcoves and kept his head bent when he slipped in and out at odd hours.

Dr. Potterley, it turned out, had written three books and some dozen articles on the ancient Mediterranean worlds, and the later articles (all in "Historical Reviews") had all dealt with pre-Roman Carthage from a sympathetic viewpoint.

That, at least, checked with Potterley's story and had soothed Foster's suspicions somewhat. . . . And yet Foster felt that it would have been much wiser, much safer, to have scotched the matter at the beginning.

A scientist shouldn't be too curious, he thought in bitter dissatisfaction with himself. It's a dangerous trait.

After dinner, he was ushered into Potterley's study and he was brought up sharply at the threshold. The walls were simply lined with books.

Not merely films. There were films, of course, but these were far outnumbered by the books—print on paper. He wouldn't have thought so many books would exist in usable condition.

That bothered Foster. Why should anyone want to keep so many books at home? Surely all were available in the university library, or, at the very worst, at the Library of Congress, if one wished to take the minor trouble of checking out a microfilm.

There was an element of secrecy involved in a home library. It breathed of intellectual anarchy. That last thought, oddly, calmed Foster. He would rather Potterley be an authentic anarchist then a play-acting *agent provocateur*.

And now the hours began to pass quickly and astonishingly.

"You see," Potterley said, in a clear, unflurried voice, "it was a matter of finding, if possible, anyone who had ever used chronoscopy in his work. Naturally, I couldn't ask baldly, since that would be unauthorized research."

"Yes," said Foster dryly. He was a little surprised such a small consideration would stop the man.

"I used indirect methods——"

He had. Foster was amazed at the volume of correspondence dealing with small disputed points of ancient Mediterranean culture which somehow managed to elicit the casual remark over and over again: "Of course, having never made use of chronoscopy——" or, "Pending approval of my request for chronoscopic data, which appears unlikely at the moment——"

"Now these aren't blind questionings," said Potterley. "There's a monthly booklet put out by the Institute for Chronoscopy in which items concerning the past as determined by time viewing are printed. Just one or two items.

"What impressed me first was the triviality of most of the items, their insipidity. Why should such researches get priority over my work? So I wrote to people who would be most likely to do research in the directions described in the booklet. Uniformly, as I have shown you, they did *not* make use of the chronoscope. Now let's go over it point by point."

At last Foster, his head swimming with Potterley's meticulously gathered details, asked, "But why?"

"I don't know why," said Potterley, "but I have a theory. The original invention of the chronoscope was by Sterbinski—you see, I know that much—and it was well publicized. But then the government took over the instrument and decided to suppress further research in the matter or any use of the machine. But then, people might be curious as to why it wasn't being used. Curiosity is such a vice, Dr. Foster."

Yes, agreed the physicist to himself.

"Imagine the effectiveness, then," Potterley went on, "of pretending that the chronoscope was being used. It would then be not a mystery, but a commonplace. It would no longer be a fitting object for legitimate curiosity or an attractive one for illicit curiosity."

"*You* were curious," pointed out Foster.

Potterley looked a trifle restless. "It was different in my case," he said angrily. "I have something that *must* be done, and I wouldn't submit to the ridiculous way in which they kept putting me off."

A bit paranoid, too, thought Foster gloomily.

Yet he had ended up with something, paranoid or not. Foster

could no longer deny that something peculiar was going on in the matter of neutrinics.

But what was Potterley after? That still bothered Foster. If Potterley didn't intend this as a test of Foster's ethics, what *did* he want?

Foster put it to himself logically. If an intellectual anarchist with a touch of paranoia wanted to use a chronoscope and was convinced that the powers-that-be was deliberately standing in his way, what would he do?

Supposing it were I, he thought. What would I do?

He said slowly, "Maybe the chronoscope doesn't exist at all?"

Potterley started. There was almost a crack in his general calmness. For an instant, Foster found himself catching a glimpse of something not at all calm.

But the historian kept his balance and said, "Oh, no, there *must* be a chronoscope."

"Why? Have you seen it? Have I? Maybe that's the explanation of everything. Maybe they're not deliberately holding out on a chronoscope they've got. Maybe they haven't got it in the first place."

"But Sterbinski lived. He built a chronoscope. That much is a fact."

"The books say so," said Foster coldly.

"Now listen." Potterley actually reached over and snatched at Foster's jacket sleeve. "I need the chronoscope. I must have it. Don't tell me it doesn't exist. What we're going to do is find out enough about neutrinics to be able to——"

Potterley drew himself up short.

Foster drew his sleeve away. He needed no ending to that sentence. He supplied it himself. He said, "Build one of our own?"

Potterley looked sour as though he would rather not have said it point-blank. Nevertheless, he said, "Why not?"

"Because that's out of the question," said Foster. "If what I've read is correct, then it took Sterbinski twenty years to build his machine and several millions in composite grants. Do you think you and I can duplicate that illegally? Suppose we had the time, which we haven't, and suppose I could learn enough out of books, which I doubt, where would we get the money and equipment? The chronoscope is supposed to fill a five-story building, for Heaven's sake."

"Then you won't help me?"

"Well, I'll tell you what. I have one way in which I may be able to find out something——"

"What is that?" asked Potterley at once.

"Never mind. That's not important. But I may be able to find out enough to tell you whether the government is deliberately suppressing research by chronoscope. I may confirm the evidence you already have or I may be able to prove that your evidence is misleading. I don't know what good it will do you in either case, but it's as far as I can go. It's my limit."

Potterley watched the young man go finally. He was angry with himself. Why had he allowed himself to grow so careless as to permit the fellow to guess that he was thinking in terms of a chronoscope of his own. That was premature.

But then why did the young fool have to suppose that a chronoscope might not exist at all?

It *had* to exist. It *had* to. What was the use of saying it didn't?

And why couldn't a second one be built? Science had advanced in the fifty years since Sterbinski. All that was needed was knowledge.

Let the youngster gather knowledge. Let him think a small gathering would be his limit. Having taken the path to anarchy, there would be no limit. If the boy were not driven onward by something in himself, the first steps would be error enough to force the rest. Potterley was quite certain he would not hesitate to use blackmail.

Potterley waved a last good-by and looked up. It was beginning to rain.

Certainly! Blackmail if necessary, but he would not be stopped.

Foster steered his car across the bleak outskirts of town and scarcely noticed the rain.

He *was* a fool, he told himself, but he couldn't leave things as they were. He had to know. He damned his streak of undisciplined curiosity, but he had to know.

But he would go no further than Uncle Ralph. He swore mightily to himself that it would stop there. In that way, there would be no evidence against him, no real evidence. Uncle Ralph would be discreet.

In a way, he was secretly ashamed of Uncle Ralph. He hadn't mentioned him to Potterley partly out of caution and partly because he did not wish to witness the lifted eyebrow, the inevitable half-smile. Professional science writers, however useful, were a little outside the pale, fit only for patronizing contempt. The fact that, as a class, they made more money than did research scientists only made matters worse, of course.

Still, there were times when a science writer in the family could be a convenience. Not being really educated, they did not have to specialize. Consequently, a good science writer knew practically everything. . . . And Uncle Ralph was one of the best.

Ralph Nimmo had no college degree and was rather proud of it. "A degree," he once said to Jonas Foster, when both were considerably younger, "is a first step down a ruinous highway. You don't want to waste it so you go on to graduate work and doctoral research. You end up a thoroughgoing ignoramus on everything in the world except for one subdivisional sliver of nothing.

"On the other hand, if you guard your mind carefully and keep it blank of any clutter of information till maturity is reached, filling it only with intelligence and training it only in clear thinking, you then have a powerful instrument at your disposal and you can become a science writer."

Nimmo received his first assignment at the age of twenty-five, after he had completed his apprenticeship and been out in the field for less than three months. It came in the shape of a clotted manuscript whose language would impart no glimmering of understanding to any reader, however qualified, without careful study and some inspired guesswork. Nimmo took it apart and put it together again (after five long and exasperating interviews with the authors, who were biophysicists), making the language taut and meaningful and smoothing the style to a pleasant gloss.

"Why not?" he would say tolerantly to his nephew, who countered his strictures on degrees by berating him with his readiness to hang on the fringes of science. "The fringe is important. Your scientists can't write. Why should they be expected to? They aren't expected to be grand masters at chess or virtuosos at the violin, so why expect them to know how to put words together? Why not leave that for specialists, too?

"Good Lord, Jonas, read your literature of a hundred years ago. Discount the fact that the science is out of date and that some of the expressions are out of date. Just try to read it and make sense out of it. It's just jaw-cracking, amateurish. Pages are published uselessly; whole articles which are either noncomprehensible or both."

"But you don't get recognition, Uncle Ralph," protested young Foster, who was getting ready to start his college career and was rather starry-eyed about it. "You could be a terrific researcher."

"I get recognition," said Nimmo. "Don't think for a minute I don't. Sure, a biochemist or a strato-meteorologist won't give me the time of day, but they pay me well enough. Just find out what happens when some first-class chemist finds the Commission has cut his year's allowance for science writing. He'll fight harder for enough funds to afford me, or someone like me, than to get a recording ionograph."

He grinned broadly and Foster grinned back. Actually, he was proud of his paunchy, round-faced, stub-fingered uncle, whose vanity made him brush his fringe of hair futilely over the desert on his pate and made him dress like an unmade haystack because such negligence was his trademark. Ashamed, but proud, too.

And now Foster entered his uncle's cluttered apartment in no mood at all for grinning. He was nine years older now and so was Uncle Ralph. For nine more years, papers in every branch of science had come to him for polishing and a little of each had crept into his capacious mind.

Nimmo was eating seedless grapes, popping them into his mouth one at a time. He tossed a bunch to Foster who caught them by a hair, then bent to retrieve individual grapes that had torn loose and fallen to the floor.

"Let them be. Don't bother," said Nimmo carelessly. "Someone comes in here to clean once a week. What's up? Having trouble with your grant application write-up?"

"I haven't really got into that yet."

"You haven't? Get a move on, boy. Are you waiting for me to offer to do the final arrangement?"

"I couldn't afford you, Uncle."

"Aw, come on. It's all in the family. Grant me all popular publication rights and no cash need change hands."

Foster nodded. "If you're serious, it's a deal."

"It's a deal."

It was a gamble, of course, but Foster knew enough of Nimmo's science writing to realize it could pay off. Some dramatic discovery of public interest on primitive man or on a new surgical technique, or on any branch of spationautics could mean a very cash-attracting article in any of the mass media of communication.

It was Nimmo, for instance, who had written up, for scientific consumption, the series of papers by Bryce and co-workers that elucidated the fine structure of two cancer viruses, for which job he asked the picayune payment of fifteen hundred dollars, provided popular publication rights were included. He then wrote up, exclusively, the same work in semidramatic form for use in trimensional video for a twenty-thousand-dollar advance plus rental royalties that were still coming in after five years.

Foster said bluntly, "What do you know about neutrinics, Uncle?"

"Neutrinics?" Mimmo's small eyes looked surprised. "Are you working in that? I thought it was pseudo-gravitic optics."

"It is p.g.o. I just happen to be asking about neutrinics."

"That's a devil of a thing to be doing. You're stepping out of line. You know that, don't you?"

"I don't expect you to call the Commission because I'm a little curious about things."

"Maybe I should before you get into trouble. Curiosity is an occupational danger with scientists. I've watched it work. One of them will be moving quietly along on a problem, then curiosity leads him up a strange creek. Next thing you know they've done so little on their proper problem, they can't justify for a project renewal. I've seen more——"

"All I want to know," said Foster patiently, "is what's been passing through your hands lately on neutrinics."

Nimmo leaned back, chewing at a grape thoughtfully. "Nothing. Nothing ever. I don't recall ever getting a paper on neutrinics."

"What!" Foster was openly astonished. "Then who does get the work?"

"Now that you ask," said Nimmo, "I don't know. Don't recall anyone talking about it at the annual conventions. I don't think much work is being done there."

"Why not?"

"Hey, there, don't bark. I'm not doing anything. My guess would be——"

Foster was exasperated. "Don't you know?"

"Hmp. I'll tell you what I know about neutrinics. It concerns the applications of neutrino movements and the forces involved——"

"Sure. Sure. Just as electronics deals with the applications of electron movements and the forces involved, and pseudo-gravitics deals with the applications of artificial gravitational fields. I didn't come to you for that. Is that all you know?"

"And," said Nimmo with equanimity, "neutrinics is the basis of time viewing and that *is* all I know."

Foster slouched back in his chair and massaged one lean cheek with great intensity. He felt angrily dissatisfied. Without formulating it explicitly in his own mind, he had felt sure, somehow, that Nimmo would come up with some late reports, bring up interesting facets of modern neutrinics, send him back to Potterley able to say that the elderly historian was mistaken, that his data was misleading, his deductions mistaken.

Then he could have returned to his proper work.

But now . . .

He told himself angrily: So they're not doing much work in the field. Does that make it deliberate suppression? What if neutrinics is a sterile discipline? Maybe it is. I don't know. Potterley doesn't. Why waste the intellectual resources of humanity on nothing? Or the work might be secret for some legitimate reason. It might be . . .

The trouble was, he had to know. He couldn't leave things as they were now. *He couldn't!*

He said, "Is there a text on neutrinics, Uncle Ralph? I mean a clear and simple one. An elementary one."

Nimmo thought, his plump cheeks puffing out with a series of sighs. "You ask the damnedest questions. The only one I ever heard of was Sterbinski and somebody. I've never seen it, but I viewed something about it once. . . . Sterbinski and LaMarr, that's it."

"Is that the Sterbinski who invented the chronoscope?"

"I think so. Proves the book ought to be good."

"Is there a recent edition? Sterbinski died thirty years ago."

Nimmo shrugged and said nothing.

"Can you find out?"

They sat in silence for a moment, while Nimmo shifted his bulk to the creaking tune of the chair he sat on. Then the science writer said, "Are you going to tell me what this is all about?"

"I can't. Will you help me anyway, Uncle Ralph? Will you get me a copy of the text?"

"Well, you've taught me all I know on pseudo gravitics. I should be grateful. Tell you what—I'll help you on one condition."

"Which is?"

The older man was suddenly very grave. "That you be careful, Jonas. You're obviously way out of line whatever you're doing. Don't blow up your career just because you're curious about something you haven't been assigned to and which is none of your business. Understand?"

Foster nodded, but he hardly heard. He was thinking furiously.

A full week later, Ralph Nimmo eased his rotund figure into Jonas Foster's on-campus two-room combination and said, in a hoarse whisper, "I've got something."

"What?" Foster was immediately eager.

"A copy of Sterbinski and LaMarr." He produced it, or rather a corner of it, from his ample topcoat.

Foster almost automatically eyed door and windows to make sure they were closed and shaded respectively, then held out his hand.

The film case was flaking with age, and when he cracked it the film was faded and growing brittle. He said sharply, "Is this all?"

"Gratitude, my boy, gratitude!" Nimmo sat down with a grunt, and reached into a pocket for an apple.

"Oh, I'm grateful, but it's so old."

"And lucky to get it at that. I tried to get a film run from the Congressional Library. No go. The book was restricted."

"Then how did you get this?"

"Stole it." He was biting crunchingly around the core. "New York Public."

"What?"

"Simple enough. I had access to the stacks, naturally. So I stepped over a chained railing when no one was around, dug this up, and walked out with it. They're very trusting out there. Meanwhile, they won't miss it in years. . . . Only you'd better not let anyone see it on you, nephew."

Foster stared at the film as though it were literally hot.

Nimmo discarded the core and reached for a second apple. "Funny thing, now. There's nothing more recent in the whole field of neutrinics. Not a monograph, not a paper, not a progress note. Nothing since the chronoscope."

"Uh-huh," said Foster absently.

Foster worked evenings in the Potterley home. He could not trust his own on-campus rooms for the purpose. The evening work grew more real to him than his own grant applications. Sometimes he worried about it but then that stopped, too.

His work consisted, at first, simply in viewing and reviewing the text film. Later it consisted in thinking (sometimes while a section of the book ran itself off through the pocket projector, disregarded).

Sometimes Potterley would come down to watch, to sit with prim, eager eyes, as though he expected thought processes to solidify and become visible in all their convolutions. He interfered in only two ways. He did not allow Foster to smoke and sometimes he talked.

It wasn't conversation talk, never that. Rather it was a low-voiced monologue with which, it seemed, he scarcely expected to command attention. It was much more as though he were relieving a pressure within himself.

Carthage! Always Carthage!

Carthage, the New York of the ancient Mediterranean. Carthage, commercial empire and queen of the seas. Carthage, all that Syracuse and Alexandria pretended to be. Carthage, maligned by her enemies and inarticulate in her own defense.

She had been defeated once by Rome and then driven out of Sicily and Sardinia, but came back to more than recoup her losses by new dominions in Spain, and raised up Hannibal to give the Romans sixteen years of terror.

In the end, she lost again a second time, reconciled herself to fate and built again with broken tools a limping life in shrunken territory, succeeding so well that jealous Rome deliberately forced a third war. And then Carthage, with nothing but bare hands and tenacity, built weapons and forced Rome into a two-year war that ended only with complete destruction of the city, the inhabitants throwing themselves into their flaming houses rather than surrender.

"Could people fight so for a city and a way of life as bad as the ancient writers painted it? Hannibal was a better general than any Roman and his soldiers were absolutely faithful to him. Even his bitterest enemies praised him. There was a Carthaginian. It is fashionable to say that he was an atypical Carthaginian, better than the others, a diamond placed in garbage. But then why was he so faithful to Carthage, even to his death after years of exile? They talk of Moloch——"

Foster didn't always listen but sometimes he couldn't help himself and he shuddered and turned sick at the bloody tale of child sacrifice.

But Potterley went on earnestly, "Just the same, it isn't true. It's a twenty-five-hundred-year-old canard started by the Greeks and Romans. They had their own slaves, their crucifixions and torture, their gladiatorial contests. They weren't holy. The Moloch story is what later ages would have called war propaganda, the big lie. I can prove it was a lie. I can prove it and, by Heaven, I will—I will——"

He would mumble that promise over and over again in his earnestness.

Mrs. Potterley visited him also, but less frequently, usually on Tuesdays and Thursdays when Dr. Potterley himself had an evening course to take care of and was not present.

She would sit quietly, scarcely talking, face slack and doughy, eyes blank, her whole attitude distant and withdrawn.

The first time, Foster tried, uneasily, to suggest that she leave.

She said tonelessly, "Do I disturb you?"

"No, of course not," lied Foster restlessly. "It's just that—that——" He couldn't complete the sentence.

She nodded, as though accepting an invitation to stay. Then she opened a cloth bag she had brought with her and took out a quire of vitron sheets which she proceeded to weave together by rapid, delicate movements of a pair of slender, tetra-faceted depolarizers, whose battery-fed wires made her look as though she were holding a large spider.

One evening, she said softly, "My daughter, Laurel, is your age."

Foster started, as much at the sudden unexpected sound of speech as at the words. He said, "I didn't know you had a daughter, Mrs. Potterly."

"She died. Years ago."

The vitron grew under the deft manipulations into the uneven shape of some garment Foster could not yet identify. There was nothing left for him to do but mutter inanely, "I'm sorry."

Mrs. Potterley sighed. "I dream about her often." She raised her blue, distant eyes to him.

Foster winced and looked away.

Another evening she asked, pulling at one of the vitron sheets to loosen its gentle clinging to her dress, "What is time viewing anyway?"

That remark broke into a particularly involved chain of thought, and Foster said snappishly, "Dr. Potterley can explain."

"He's tried to. Oh, my, yes. But I think he's a little impatient with me. He calls it chronoscopy most of the time. Do you actually see things in the past, like the trimensionals? Or does it just make little dot patterns like the computer you use?"

Foster stared at his hand computer with distaste. It worked well enough, but every operation had to be manually controlled and the answers were obtained in code. Now if he could use the school computer . . . Well, why dream, he felt conspicuous enough, as it was, carrying a hand computer under his arm every evening as he left his office.

He said, "I've never seen the chronoscope myself, but I'm under the impression that you actually see pictures and hear sound."

"You can hear people talk, too?"

"I think so." Then, half in desperation, "Look here, Mrs. Potterley, this must be awfully dull for you. I realize you don't like to leave a guest all to himself, but really, Mrs. Potterley, you mustn't feel compelled——"

"I don't feel compelled," she said. "I'm sitting here, waiting."

"Waiting? For what?"

She said composedly, "I listened to you that first evening. The time you first spoke to Arnold. I listened at the door."

He said, "You did?"

"I know I shouldn't have, but I was awfully worried about Arnold. I had a notion he was going to do something he oughtn't and I wanted to hear what. And then when I heard——" She paused, bending close over the vitron and peering at it.

"Heard what, Mrs. Potterley?"

"That you wouldn't build a chronoscope."

"Well, of course not."

"I thought maybe you might change your mind."

Foster glared at her. "Do you mean you're coming down here hoping I'll build a chronoscope, waiting for me to build one?"

"I hope you do, Dr. Foster. Oh, I hope you do."

It was as though, all at once, a fuzzy veil had fallen off her face, leaving all her features clear and sharp, putting color into her cheeks, life into her eyes, the vibrations of something approaching excitement into her voice.

"Wouldn't it be wonderful," she whispered, "to have one? People of the past could live again. Pharoahs and kings and—just people. I hope you build one, Dr. Foster. I really—hope——"

She choked, it seemed, on the intensity of her own words and let the vitron sheets slip off her lap. She rose and ran up the basement stairs, while Foster's eyes followed her awkwardly fleeing body with astonishment and distress.

It cut deeper into Foster's nights and left him sleepless and painfully stiff with thought. It was almost a mental indigestion.

His grant requests went limping in, finally, to Ralph Nimmo. He scarcely had any hope for them. He thought numbly: They won't be approved.

If they weren't, of course, it would create a scandal in the department and probably mean his appointment at the university would not be renewed, come the end of the academic year.

He scarcely worried. It was the neutrino, the neutrino, only the neutrino. Its trail curved and veered sharply and led him breathlessly along uncharted pathways that even Sterbinski and LaMarr did not follow.

He called Nimmo. "Uncle Ralph, I need a few things. I'm calling from off the campus."

Nimmo's face in the video plate was jovial, but his voice was sharp. He said, "What you need is a course in communication. I'm having a hell of a time pulling your application into one intelligible piece. If that's what you're calling about——"

Foster shook his head impatiently. "That's *not* what I'm calling about. I need these." He scribbled quickly on a piece of paper and held it up before the receiver.

Nimmo yiped. "Hey, how many tricks do you think I can wangle?"

"You can get them, Uncle. You know you can."

Nimmo reread the list of items with silent motions of his plump lips and looked grave.

"What happens when you put those things together?" he asked. Foster shook his head. "You'll have exclusive popular publication rights to whatever turns up, the way it's always been. But please don't ask any questions now."

"I can't do miracles, you know."

"Do this one. You've got to. You're a science writer, not a research man. You don't have to account for anything. You've got friends and connections. They can look the other way, can't they, to get a break from you next publication time?"

"Your faith, nephew, is touching. I'll try."

Nimmo succeeded. The material and equipment were brought over late one evening in a private touring car. Nimmo and Foster lugged it in with the grunting of men unused to manual labor.

Potterley stood at the entrance of the basement after Nimmo had left. He asked softly, "What's this for?"

Foster brushed the hair off his forehead and gently massaged a sprained wrist. He said, "I want to conduct a few simple experiments."

"Really?" The historian's eyes glittered with excitement.

Foster felt exploited. He felt as though he were being led along a dangerous highway by the pull of pinching fingers on his nose; as though he could see the ruin clearly that lay in wait at the end of the path, yet walked eagerly and determinedly. Worst of all, he felt the compelling grip on his nose to be his own.

It was Potterley who began it, Potterley who stood there now, gloating; but the compulsion was his own.

Foster said sourly, "I'll be wanting privacy now, Potterley. I can't have you and your wife running down here and annoying me."

He thought: If that offends him, let him kick me out. Let him put an end to this.

In his heart, though, he did not think being evicted would stop anything.

But it did not come to that. Potterley was showing no signs of offense. His mild gaze was unchanged. He said, "Of course, Dr. Foster, of course. All the privacy you wish."

Foster watched him go. He was left still marching along the highway, perversely glad of it and hating himself for being glad.

He took to sleeping over on a cot in Potterley's basement and spending his weekends there entirely.

During that period, preliminary word came through that his grants (as doctored by Nimmo) had been approved. The Department Head brought the word and congratulated him.

Foster stared back distantly and mumbled, "Good. I'm glad," with so little conviction that the other frowned and turned away without another word.

Foster gave the matter no further thought. It was a minor point, worth no notice. He was planning something that really counted, a climactic test for that evening.

One evening, a second and third and then, haggard and half beside himself with excitement, he called in Potterley.

Potterley came down the stairs and looked about at the homemade gadgetry. He said, in his soft voice, "The electric bills are quite high. I don't mind the expense, but the City may ask questions. Can anything be done?"

It was a warm evening, but Potterley wore a tight collar and a semi-jacket. Foster, who was in his undershirt, lifted bleary eyes and said shakily, "It won't be for much longer, Dr. Potterley. I've called you down to tell you something. A chronoscope can be built. A small one, of course, but it can be built."

Potterley seized the railing. His body sagged. He managed a whisper. "Can it be built here?"

"Here in the basement," said Foster wearily.

"Good Lord. You said——"

"I know what I said," cried Foster impatiently. "I said it couldn't be done. I didn't know anything then. Even Sterbinski didn't know anything."

Potterley shook his head. "Are you sure? You're not mistaken, Dr. Foster? I couldn't endure it if——"

Foster said, "I'm not mistaken. Damn it, sir, if just theory had been enough, we could have had a time viewer over a hundred years ago, when the neutrino was first postulated. The trouble was, the original investigators considered it only a mysterious particle without mass or charge that could not be detected. It was just something to even up the bookkeeping and save the law of conservation of mass energy."

He wasn't sure Potterley knew what he was talking about. He didn't care. He needed a breather. He had to get some of this out of his clotting thoughts. . . . And he needed background for what he would have to tell Potterley next.

He went on. "It was Sterbinski who first discovered that the neutrino broke through the space-time cross-sectional barrier, that it traveled through time as well as through space. It was Sterbinski who first devised a method for stopping neutrinos. He invented a neutrino recorder and learned how to interpret the pattern of the neutrino stream. Naturally, the stream had been affected and deflected by all the matter it had passed through in its passage through time, and the deflections could be analyzed and converted into the images of the matter that had done the deflecting. Time viewing was possible. Even air vibrations could be detected in this way and converted into sound."

Potterley was definitely not listening. He said, "Yes. Yes. But when can you build a chronoscope?"

Foster said urgently, "Let me finish. Everything depends on the method used to detect and analyze the neutrino stream. Sterbinski's method was difficult and roundabout. It required mountains of energy. But I've studied pseudo-gravitics, Dr. Potterley, the science of artificial gravitational fields. I've specialized in the behavior of light in such fields. It's a new science. Sterbinski knew nothing of it. If he had, he would have seen—anyone would have—a much better and more efficient method of detecting neutrinos using a pseudo-gravitic field. If I had known more neutrinics to begin with, I would have seen it at once."

Potterley brightened a bit. "I knew it," he said. "Even if they stop research in neutrinics there is no way the government can be sure that discoveries in other segments of science won't reflect knowledge on neutrinics. So much for the value of centralized direction of science. I thought this long ago, Dr. Foster, before you ever came to work here."

"I congratulate you on that," said Foster, "but there's one thing——"

"Oh, never mind all this. Answer me. Please. When can you build a chronoscope?"

"I'm trying to tell you something, Dr. Potterley. A chronoscope won't do you any good." (This is it, Foster thought.)

Slowly, Potterley descended the stairs. He stood facing Foster. "What do you mean? Why won't it help me?"

"You won't see Carthage. It's what I've got to tell you. It's what I've been leading up to. You can never see Carthage."

Potterley shook his head slightly. "Oh, no, you're wrong. If you have the chronoscope, just focus it properly——"

"No, Dr. Potterley. It's not a question of focus. There are random factors affecting the neutrino stream, as they affect all subatomic particles. What we call the uncertainty principle. When the stream is recorded and interpreted, the random factor comes out as fuzziness, or 'noise' as the communications boys speak of it. The further back in time you penetrate, the more pronounced the fuzziness, the greater the noise. After a while, the noise drowns out the picture. Do you understand?"

"More power," said Potterley in a dead kind of voice.

"That won't help. When the noise blurs out detail, magnifying detail magnifies the noise, too. You can't see anything in a sun-burned film by enlarging it, can you? Get this through your head, now. The physical nature of the universe sets limits. The random thermal motions of air molecules set limits to how weak a sound can be detected by any instrument. The length of a light wave or of an electron wave sets limits to the size of objects that can be seen by any instrument. It works that way in chronoscopy, too. You can only time view so far."

"How far? How far?"

Foster took a deep breath. "A century and a quarter. That's the most."

"But the monthly bulletin the Commission puts out deals with ancient history almost entirely." The historian laughed shakily. "You must be wrong. The government has data as far back as 3000 B.C."

"When did you switch to believing them?" demanded Foster, scornfully. "You began this business by proving they were lying; that no historian had made use of the chronoscope. Don't you see why now? No historian, except one interested in contemporary history, could. No chronoscope can possibly see back in time further than 1920 under any conditions."

"You're wrong. You don't know everything," said Potterley.

"The truth won't bend itself to your convenience either. Face it. The government's part in this is to perpetuate a hoax."

"Why?"

"I don't know why."

Potterley's snubby nose was twitching. His eyes were bulging. He pleaded, "It's only theory, Dr. Foster. Build a chronoscope. Build one and try."

Foster caught Potterley's shoulders in a sudden, fierce grip. "Do you think I haven't? Do you think I would tell you this before I had checked it every way I knew? I *have* built one. It's all around you. Look!"

He ran to the switches at the power leads. He flicked them on, one by one. He turned a resistor, adjusted other knobs, put out the cellar lights. "Wait. Let it warm up."

There was a small glow near the center of one wall. Potterley was gibbering incoherently, but Foster only cried again, "Look!"

The light sharpened and brightened, broke up into a light-and-dark pattern. Men and women! Fuzzy. Features blurred. Arms and legs mere streaks. An old-fashioned ground car, unclear but recognizable as one of the kind that had once used gasoline-powered internal-combustion engines, sped by.

Foster said, "Mid-twentieth century, somewhere. I can't hook up an audio yet so this is soundless. Eventually, we can add sound. Anyway, mid-twentieth is almost as far back as you can go. Believe me, that's the best focusing that can be done."

Potterley said, "Build a larger machine, a stronger one. Improve your circuits."

"You can't lick the Uncertainty Principle, man, any more than you can live on the sun. There are physical limits to what can be done."

"You're lying. I won't believe you. I——"

A new voice sounded, raised shrilly to make itself heard.

"Arnold! Dr. Foster!"

The young physicist turned at once. Dr. Potterley froze for a long moment, then said, without turning, "What is it, Caroline? Leave us."

"No!" Mrs. Potterley descended the stairs. "I heard. I couldn't help hearing. Do you have a time viewer here, Dr. Foster? Here in the basement?"

"Yes, I do, Mrs. Potterley. A kind of time viewer. Not a good one. I can't get sound yet and the picture is darned blurry, but it works."

Mrs. Potterley clasped her hands and held them tightly against her breast. "How wonderful. How wonderful."

"It's not at all wonderful," snapped Potterley. "The young fool can't reach further back than——"

"Now, look," began Foster in exasperation. . . .

"Please!" cried Mrs. Potterley. "Listen to me. Arnold, don't you see that as long as we can use it for twenty years back, we can see Laurel once again? What do we care about Carthage and ancient times? It's Laurel we can see. She'll be alive for us again. Leave the machine here, Dr. Foster. Show us how to work it."

Foster stared at her then at her husband. Dr. Potterley's face had gone white. Though his voice stayed low and even, its calmness was somehow gone. He said, "You're a fool!"

Caroline said weakly, "Arnold!"

"You're a fool, I say. What will you see? The past. The dead past. Will Laurel do one thing she did not do? Will you see one thing you haven't seen? Will you live three years over and over again, watching a baby who'll never grow up no matter how you watch?"

His voice came near to cracking, but held. He stepped closer to her, seized her shoulder and shook her roughly. "Do you know what will happen to you if you do that? They'll come to take you away because you'll go mad. Yes, mad. Do you want mental treatment? Do you want to be shut up, to undergo the psychic probe?"

Mrs. Potterley tore away. There was no trace of softness or vagueness about her. She had twisted into a virago. "I want to see my child, Arnold. She's in that machine and I want her."

"She's *not* in the machine. An image is. Can't you understand? An image! Something that's not real!"

"I want my child. Do you hear me?" She flew at him, screaming, fists beating. *"I want my child."*

The historian retreated at the fury of the assault, crying out. Foster moved to step between them, when Mrs. Potterley dropped, sobbing wildly, to the floor.

Potterley turned, eyes desperately seeking. With a sudden heave, he snatched at a Lando-rod, tearing it from its support, and whirling away before Foster, numbed by all that was taking place, could move to stop him.

"Stand back!" gasped Potterley, "or I'll kill you. I swear it."

He swung with force, and Foster jumped back.

Potterley turned with fury on every part of the structure in the cellar, and Foster, after the first crash of glass, watched dazedly.

Potterley spent his rage and then he was standing quietly amid shards and splinters, with a broken Lando-rod in his hand. He said to Foster in a whisper, "Now get out of here! Never come back! If any of this cost you anything, send me a bill and I'll pay for it. I'll pay double."

Foster shrugged, picked up his shirt and moved up the basement stairs. He could hear Mrs. Potterley sobbing loudly, and, as he turned at the head of the stairs for a last look, he saw Dr. Potterley bending over her, his face convulsed with sorrow.

Two days later, with the school day drawing to a close, and Foster looking wearily about to see if there were any data on his newly approved projects that he wished to take home, Dr. Potterley appeared once more. He was standing at the open door of Foster's office.

The historian was neatly dressed as ever. He lifted his hand in a gesture that was too vague to be a greeting, too abortive to be a plea. Foster stared stonily.

Potterley said, "I waited till five, till you were . . . May I come in?"

Foster nodded.

Potterley said, "I suppose I ought to apologize for my behavior. I was dreadfully disappointed; not quite master of myself. Still, it was inexcusable."

"I accept your apology," said Foster. "Is that all?"

"My wife called you, I think."

"Yes, she has."

"She has been quite hysterical. She told me she had but I couldn't be quite sure——"

"She has called me."

"Could you tell me—would you be so kind as to tell me what she wanted?"

"She wanted a chronoscope. She said she had some money of her own. She was willing to pay."

"Did you—make any commitments?"

"I said I wasn't in the manufacturing business."

"Good," breathed Potterley, his chest expanding with a sigh of relief. "Please don't take any calls from her. She's not—quite——"

"Look, Dr. Potterley," said Foster, "I'm not getting into any domestic quarrels, but you'd better be prepared for something. Chronoscopes can be built by anybody. Given a few simple parts that can be bought through some etherics sales center, it can be built in the home workshop. The video part, anyway."

"But no one else will think of it beside you, will they? No one has."

"I don't intend to keep it secret."

"But you can't publish. It's illegal research."

"That doesn't matter any more, Dr. Potterley. If I lose my grants, I lose them. If the university is displeased, I'll resign. It just doesn't matter."

"But you can't do that!"

"Till now," said Foster, "you didn't mind my risking loss of grants and position. Why do you turn so tender about it now? Now let me explain something to you. When you first came to me, I believed in organized and directed research; the situation as it existed, in other words. I considered you an intellectual anarchist, Dr. Potterley, and dangerous. But, for one reason or another, I've been an anarchist myself for months now and I have achieved great things.

"Those things have been achieved not because I am a brilliant scientist. Not at all. It was just that scientific research had been directed from above and holes were left that could be filled in by anyone who looked in the right direction. And anyone might have if the government hadn't actively tried to prevent it.

"Now understand me. I still believe directed research can be useful. I'm not in favor of a retreat to total anarchy. But there must be a middle ground. Directed research can retain flexibility. A scientist must be allowed to follow his curiosity, at least in his spare time."

Potterley sat down. He said ingratiatingly, "Let's discuss this, Foster. I appreciate your idealism. You're young. You want the moon. But you can't destroy yourself through fancy notions of what research must consist of. I got you into this. I am responsible and I blame myself bitterly. I was acting emotionally. My interest in Carthage blinded me and I was a damned fool."

Foster broke in. "You mean you've changed completely in two days? Carthage is nothing? Government suppression of research is nothing?"

"Even a damned fool like myself can learn, Foster. My wife taught me something. I understand the reason for government suppression of neutrinics now. I didn't two days ago. And, understanding, I approve. You saw the way my wife reacted to the news of a chronoscope in the basement. I had envisioned a chronoscope used for research purposes. All *she* could see was the personal pleasure of returning neurotically to a personal past, a dead past. The pure researcher, Foster, is in the minority. People like my wife would outweigh us.

"For the government to encourage chronoscopy would have meant that everyone's past would be visible. The government officers would be subjected to blackmail and improper pressure, since who on Earth has a past that is absolutely clean? Organized government might become impossible."

Foster licked his lips. "Maybe the government has some justification in its own eyes. Still, there's an important principle involved here. Who knows what other scientific advances are being stymied because scientists are being stifled into walking a narrow path? If the chronoscope becomes the terror of a few politicians, it's a price that must be paid. The public must realize that science must be free and there is no more dramatic way of doing it than to publish my discovery, one way or another, legally or illegally."

Potterley's brow was damp with perspiration, but his voice remained even. "Oh, not just a few politicians, Dr. Foster. Don't think that. It would be my terror, too. My wife would spend her time living with our dead daughter. She would retreat fruther from reality. She would go mad living the same scenes over and over. And not just my terror. There would be others like her. Children searching for their dead parents or their own youth. We'll have a whole world living in the past. Midsummer madness."

Foster said, "Moral judgments can't stand in the way. There isn't one advance at any time in history that mankind hasn't had the ingenuity to pervert. Mankind must also have the ingenuity to prevent. As for the chronoscope, your delvers into the dead past will get tired soon enough. They'll catch their loved parents in some of the things their loved parents did and they'll lose their enthusiasm for it all. But all this is trivial. With me, it's a matter of important principle."

Potterley said, "Hang your principle. Can't you understand men and women as well as principle? Don't you understand that my wife will live through the fire that killed our baby? She won't be able to help herself. I know her. She'll follow through each step, trying to prevent it. She'll live it over and over again, hoping each time that it won't happen. How many times do you want to kill Laurel?" A huskiness had crept into his voice.

A thought crossed Foster's mind. "What are you really afraid she'll find out, Dr. Potterley? What happened the night of the fire?"

The historian's hands went up quickly to cover his face and they shook with his dry sobs. Foster turned away and stared uncomfortably out the window.

Potterley said after a while, "It's a long time since I've had to think of it. Caroline was away. I was baby-sitting. I went into the baby's bedroom midevening to see if she had kicked off the bedclothes. I had my cigarette with me . . . I smoked in those days. I must have stubbed it out before putting it in the ashtray on the chest of drawers. I was always careful. The baby was all right. I returned to the living room and fell asleep before the video. I awoke, choking, surrounded by fire. I don't know how it started."

"But you think it may have been the cigarette, is that it?" said Foster. "A cigarette which, for once, you forgot to stub out?"

"I don't know. I tried to save her, but she was dead in my arms when I got out."

"You never told your wife about the cigarette, I suppose."

Potterley shook his head. "But I've lived with it."

"Only now, with a chronoscope, she'll find out. Maybe it wasn't the cigarette. Maybe you did stub it out. Isn't that possible?"

The scant tears had dried on Potterley's face. The redness had subsided. He said, "I can't take the chance . . . But it's not just myself, Foster. The past has its terrors for most people. Don't loose those terrors on the human race."

Foster paced the floor. Somehow, this explained the reason for Potterley's rabid, irrational desire to boost the Carthaginians, deify them, most of all disprove the story of their fiery sacrifices to Moloch. By freeing them of the guilt of infanticide by fire, he symbolically freed himself of the same guilt.

So the same fire that had driven him on to causing the construction of a chronoscope was now driving him on to the destruction.

Foster looked sadly at the older man. "I see your position, Dr. Potterley, but this goes above personal feelings. I've got to smash this throttling hold on the throat of science."

Potterley said, savagely, "You mean you want the fame and wealth that goes with such a discovery."

"I don't know about the wealth, but that, too, I suppose. I'm no more than human."

"You won't suppress your knowledge?"

"Not under any circumstances."

"Well, then——" and the historian got to his feet and stood for a moment, glaring.

Foster had an odd moment of terror. The man was older than he, smaller, feebler, and he didn't look armed. Still . . .

Foster said, "If you're thinking of killing me or anything insane like that, I've got the information in a safety-deposit vault where the proper people will find it in case of my disappearance or death."

Potterley said, "Don't be a fool," and stalked out.

Foster closed the door, locked it and sat down to think. He felt silly. He had no information in any safety-deposit vault, of course. Such a melodramatic action would not have occurred to him ordinarily. But now it had.

Feeling even sillier, he spent an hour writing out the equations of the application of pseudo-gravitic optics to neutrinic recording, and some diagrams for the engineering details of construction. He sealed it in an envelope and scrawled Ralph Nimmo's name over the outside.

He spent a rather restless night and the next morning, on the way to school, dropped the envelope off at the bank, with appropriate instructions to an official, who made him sign a paper permitting the box to be opened after his death.

He called Nimmo to tell him of the existence of the envelope, refusing querulously to say anything about its contents.

He had never felt so ridiculously self-conscious as at that moment.

That night and the next, Foster spent in only fitful sleep, finding himself face to face with the highly practical problem of the publication of data unethically obtained.

The *Proceedings of the Society for Pseudo-Gravitics,* which was the journal with which he was best acquainted, would certainly not touch any paper that did not include the magic footnote: "The work described in this paper was made possible by Grant No. so-and-so from the Commission of Research of the United Nations."

Nor, doubly so, would the *Journal of Physics."*

There were always the minor journals who might overlook the nature of the article for the sake of the sensation, but that would require a little financial negotiation on which he hesitated to embark. It might, on the whole, be better to pay the cost of publishing a small pamphlet for general distribution among scholars. In that case, he would even be able to dispense with the services of a science writer, sacrificing polish for speed. He would have to find a reliable printer. Uncle Ralph might know one.

He walked down the corridor to his office and wondered anxiously if perhaps he ought to waste no further time, give himself no further chance to lapse into indecision and take the risk of calling Ralph from his office phone. He was so absorbed in his own heavy thoughts that he did not notice that his room was occupied until he turned from the clothes closet and approached his desk.

Dr. Potterley was there and a man whom Foster did not recognize.

Foster stared at them. "What's this?"

Potterley said, "I'm sorry, but I had to stop you."

Foster continued staring. "What are you talking about?"

The stranger said, "Let me introduce myself." He had large teeth, a little uneven, and they showed prominently when he smiled. "I am Thaddeus Araman, Department Head of the Division of Chronoscopy. I am here to see you concerning information brought to me by Professor Arnold Potterley and confirmed by our own sources——"

Potterley said breathlessly, "I took all the blame, Dr. Foster. I explained that it was I who persuaded you against your will into unethical practices. I have offered to accept full responsibility and punishment. I don't wish you harmed in any way. It's just that chronoscopy must not be permitted!"

Araman nodded. "He has taken the blame as he says, Dr. Foster, but this thing is out of his hands now."

Foster said, "So? What are you going to do? Blackball me from all consideration for research grants?"

"This is in my power," said Araman.

"Order the university to discharge me?"

"That, too, is in my power."

"All right, go ahead. Consider it done. I'll leave my office now, with you. I can send for my books later. If you insist, I'll leave my books. Is that all?"

"Not quite," said Araman. "You must engage to do no further research in chronoscopy, to publish none of your findings in chronoscopy and, of course, to build no chronoscope. You will remain under surveillance indefinitely to make sure you keep that promise."

"Supposing I refuse to promise? What can you do? Doing research out of my field may be unethical, but it isn't a criminal offense."

"In the case of chronoscopy, my young friend," said Araman patiently, "it is a criminal offense. If necessary, you will be put in jail and kept there."

"Why?" shouted Foster. "What's magic about chronoscopy?"

Araman said, "That's the way it is. We cannot allow further developments in the field. My own job is, primarily, to make sure of that, and I intend to do my job. Unfortunately, I had no knowledge, nor did anyone in the department, that the optics of pseudo-gravity fields had such immediate application to chronoscopy. Score one for general ignorance, but henceforward research will be steered properly in that respect, too."

Foster said, "That won't help. Something else may apply that neither you nor I dream of. All science hangs together. It's one piece. If you want to stop one part, you've got to stop it all."

"No doubt that is true," said Araman, "in theory. On the practical side, however, we have managed quite well to hold chronoscopy down to the original Sterbinski level for fifty years. Having caught you in time, Dr. Foster, we hope to continue doing so indefinitely. And we wouldn't have come this close to disaster, either, if I had accepted Dr. Potterley at something more than face value."

He turned toward the historian and lifted his eyebrows in a kind of humorous self-deprecation. "I'm afraid, sir, that I dismissed you as a history professor and no more on the occasion of our first interview. Had I done my job properly and checked on you, this would not have happened."

Foster said abruptly, "Is anyone allowed to use the government chronoscope?"

"No one outside our division under any pretext. I say that since it is obvious to me that you have already guessed as much. I warn you, though, that any repetition of that fact will be a criminal, not an ethical, offense."

"And your chronoscope doesn't go back more than a hundred twenty-five years or so, does it?"

"It doesn't."

"Then your bulletin with its stories of time viewing ancient times is a hoax?"

Araman said coolly, "With the knowledge you now have, it is obvious you know that for a certainty. However, I confirm your remark. The monthly bulletin is a hoax."

"In that case," said Foster, "I will not promise to suppress my knowledge of chronoscopy. If you wish to arrest me, go ahead. My defense at the trial will be enough to destroy the vicious card house of directed research and bring it tumbling down. Directing research is one thing; suppressing it and depriving mankind of its benefits is quite another."

Araman said, "Oh, let's get something straight, Dr. Foster. If you do not co-operate, you will go to jail directly. You will *not* see a lawyer, you will *not* be charged, you will *not* have a trial. You will simply stay in jail."

"Oh, no," said Foster, "you're bluffing. This is not the twentieth century, you know."

There was a stir outside the office, the clatter of feet, a high-pitched shout that Foster was sure he recognized. The door crashed open, the lock splintering, and three intertwined figures stumbled in.

As they did so, one of the men raised a blaster and brought its butt down hard on the skull of another.

There was a whoosh of expiring air, and the one whose head was struck went limp.

"Uncle Ralph!" cried Foster.

Araman frowned. "Put him down in that chair," he ordered, "and get some water.

Ralph Nimmo, rubbing his head with a gingerly sort of disgust, said, "There was no need to get rough, Araman."

Araman said, "The guard should have been rough sooner and kept you out of here, Nimmo. You'd have been better off."

"You know each other?" asked Foster.

"I've had dealings with the man," said Nimmo, still rubbing. "If he's here in your office, nephew, you're in trouble."

"And you, too," said Araman angrily. "I know Dr. Foster consulted you on neutrinics literature."

Nimmo corrugated his forehead, then straightened it with a wince as though the action had brought pain. "So?" he said. "What else do you know about me?"

"We will know everything about you soon enough. Meanwhile, that one item is enough to implicate you. What are you doing here?"

"My dear Dr. Araman," said Nimmo, some of his jauntiness restored, "day after yesterday, my jackass of a nephew called me. He had placed some mysterious information——"

"Don't tell him! Don't say anything!" cried Foster.

Araman glanced at him coldly. "We know all about it, Dr. Foster. The safety-deposit box has been opened and its contents removed."

"But how can you know——" Foster's voice died away in a kind of furious frustration.

"Anyway," said Nimmo, "I decided the net must be closing around him and, after I took care of a few items, I came down to tell him to get off this thing he's doing. It's not worth his career."

"Does that mean you know what he's doing?" asked Araman.

"He never told me," said Nimmo, "but I'm a science writer with a hell of a lot of experience. I know which side of an atom is electronified. The boy, Foster, specializes in pseudo-gravitic optics and coached me on the stuff himself. He got me to get him a textbook on neutrinics and I kind of skip-viewed it myself before handing it over. I can put the two together. He asked me to get him certain pieces of physical equipment, and that was evidence, too. Stop me if I'm wrong, but my nephew has built a semiportable, low-power chronoscope. Yes, or—yes?"

"Yes." Araman reached thoughtfully for a cigarette and paid no attention to Dr. Potterley (watching silently, as though all were a dream) who shied away, gasping, from the white cylinder. "Another mistake for me. I ought to resign. I should have put tabs on you, too, Nimmo, instead of concentrating too hard on Potterley and Foster. I didn't have much time of course and you've ended up safely here, but that doesn't excuse me. You're under arrest, Nimmo."

"What for?" demanded the science writer.

"Unauthorized research."

"I wasn't doing any. I can't, not being a registered scientist. And even if I did, it's not a criminal offense."

Foster said savagely, "No use, Uncle Ralph. This bureaucrat is making his own laws."

"Like what?" demanded Nimmo.

"Like life imprisonment without trial."

"Nuts," said Nimmo. "This isn't the twentieth cen——"

"I tried that," said Foster. "It doesn't bother him."

"Well, nuts," shouted Nimmo. "Look here, Araman. My nephew and I have relatives who haven't lost touch with us, you know. The professor has some also, I imagine. You can't just make us disappear. There'll be questions and a scandal. This *isn't* the twentieth century. So if you're trying to scare us, it isn't working."

The cigarette snapped between Araman's fingers and he tossed it away violently. He said, "Damn it, I don't know *what* to do. It's never been like this before. . . . Look! You three fools know nothing of what you're trying to do. You understand nothing. Will you listen to me?"

"Oh, we'll listen," said Nimmo grimly.

(Foster sat silently, eyes angry, lips compressed. Potterley's hands writhed like two intertwined snakes.)

Araman said, "The past to you is the dead past. If any of you have discussed the matter, it's dollars to nickels you've used that phrase. The dead past. If you knew how many times I've heard those three words, you'd choke on them, too.

"When people think of the past, they think of it as dead, far away and gone, long ago. We encourage them to think so. When we report time viewing, we always talk of views centuries in the past, even though you gentlemen know seeing more than a century or so is impossible. People accept it. The past means Greece, Rome, Carthage, Egypt, the Stone Age. The deader the better.

"Now you three know a century or a little more is the limit, so what does the past mean to you? Your youth. Your first girl. Your dead mother. Twenty years ago. Thirty years ago. Fifty years ago. The deader the better. . . . But when does the past really begin?"

He paused in anger. The others stared at him and Nimmo stirred uneasily.

"Well," said Araman, "when did it begin? A year ago? Five minutes ago? One second ago? Isn't it obvious that the past begins an instant ago? The dead past is just another name for the living present. What if you focus the chronoscope in the past of one-hundredth of a second ago? Aren't you watching the present? Does it begin to sink in?"

Nimmo said, "Damnation."

"Damnation," mimicked Araman. "After Potterley came to me with his story night before last, how do you suppose I checked up on both of you? I did it with the chronoscope, spotting key moments to the very instant of the present."

"And that's how you knew about the safety-deposit box?" said Foster.

"And every other important fact. Now what do you suppose would happen if we let news of a home chronoscope get out? People might start out by watching their youth, their parents and so on, but it wouldn't be long before they'd catch on to the possibilities. The housewife will forget her poor, dead mother and take to watching her neighbor at home and her husband at the office. The businessman will watch his competitor; the employer his employee.

"There will be no such thing as privacy. The party line, the prying eye behind the curtain will be nothing compared to it. The video stars will be closely watched at all times by everyone. Every man his own peeping Tom and there'll be no getting away from the watcher. Even darkness will be no escape because chronoscopy can be adjusted to the infrared and human figures can be seen by their own body heat. The figures will be fuzzy, of course, and the surroundings will be dark, but that will make the titillation of it all the greater, perhaps. . . . Hmp, the men in charge of the machine now experiment sometimes in spite of the regulations against it."

Nimmo seemed sick. "You can always forbid private manufacture——"

Araman turned on him fiercely. "You can, but do you expect it to do good? Can you legislate successfully against drinking, smoking, adultery or gossiping over the back fence? And this mixture of nosiness and prurience will have a worse grip on humanity than any of those. Good Lord, in a thousand years of trying we haven't even been able to wipe out the heroin traffic and you talk about legislating against a device for watching anyone you please at any time you please that can be built in a home workshop."

Foster said suddenly, "I won't publish."

Potterley burst out, half in sobs, "None of us will talk. I regret——"

Nimmo broke in. "You said you didn't tab me on the chronoscope, Araman."

"No time," said Araman wearily. "Things don't move any faster on the chronoscope than in real life. You can't speed it up like the film in a book viewer. We spent a full twenty-four hours trying to catch the important moments during the last six months of Potterley and Foster. There was no time for anything else and it was enough."

"It wasn't," said Nimmo.

"What are you talking about?" There was a sudden infinite alarm on Araman's face.

"I told you my nephew, Jonas, had called me to say he had put important information in a safety-deposit box. He acted as though he were in trouble. He's my nephew. I had to try to get him off the spot. It took a while, then I came here to tell him what I had done. I told you when I got here, just after your man conked me, that I had taken care of a few items."

"What? For Heaven's sake——"

"Just this: I sent the details of the portable chronoscope off to half a dozen of my regular publicity outlets."

Not a word. Not a sound. Not a breath. They were all past any demonstration.

"Don't stare like that," cried Nimmo. "Don't you see my point? I had popular publication rights. Jonas will admit that. I knew he couldn't publish scientifically in any legal way. I was sure he was planning to publish illegally and was preparing the safety-deposit box for that reason. I thought if I put through the details prematurely, all the responsibility would be mine. His career would be saved. And if I were deprived of my science-writing license as a result, my exclusive possession of the chronometric data would set me up for life. Jonas would be angry, I expected that, but I could explain the motive and we would split the take fifty-fifty. . . . Don't stare at me like that. How did I know——"

"Nobody knew anything," said Araman bitterly, "but you all just took it for granted that the government was stupidly bureaucratic, vicious, tyrannical, given to suppressing research for the hell of it. It never occurred to any of you that we were trying to protect mankind as best we could."

"Don't sit there talking," wailed Potterley. "Get the names of the people who were told——"

"Too late," said Nimmo, shrugging. "They've had better than a day. There's been time for the word to spread. My outfits will have called any number of physicists to check my data before going on with it and they'll call one another to pass on the news. Once scientists put neutrinics and pseudo-gravitics together, home chronoscopy becomes obvious. Before the week is out, five hundred people will know how to build a small chronoscope and how will you catch them all?" His plump cheeks sagged. "I suppose there's no way of putting the mushroom cloud back into that nice, shiny uranium sphere."

Araman stood up. "We'll try, Potterley, but I agree with Nimmo. It's too late. What kind of world we'll have from now on, I don't know, I can't tell, but the world we know has been destroyed completely. Until now, every custom, every habit, every tiniest way of life has always taken a certain amount of privacy for granted, but that's all gone now."

He saluted each of the three with elaborate formality.

"You have created a new world among the three of you. I congratulate you. Happy goldfish bowl to you, to me, to everyone, and may each of you fry in hell forever. Arrest rescinded."

The Dying Night

Part 1

It was almost a class reunion, and though it was marked by joylessness, there was no reason as yet to think it would be marred by tragedy.

Edward Talliaferro, fresh from the Moon and without his gravity legs yet, met the other two in Stanley Kaunas's room. Kaunas rose to greet him in a subdued manner. Battersley Ryger merely sat and nodded.

Talliaferro lowered his large body carefully to the couch, very aware of its unusual weight. He grimaced a little, his plump lips twisting inside the rim of hair that surrounded his mouth on lip, chin, and cheek.

They had seen one another earlier that day under more formal conditions. Now for the first time they were alone, and Talliaferro said, "This is a kind of occasion. We're meeting for the first time in ten years. First time since graduation, in fact."

Ryger's nose twitched. It had been broken shortly before that same graduation and he had received his degree in astronomy with a bandage disfiguring his face. He said grumpily, "Anyone ordered champagne? Or something?"

Talliaferro said, "Come on! First big interplanetary astronomical convention in history is no place for glooming. And among friends, too!"

Kaunas said suddenly, "It's Earth. It doesn't feel right. I can't get used to it." He shook his head but his look of depression was not detachable. It remained.

Talliaferro said, "I know. I'm so heavy. It takes all the energy out of me. At that, you're better off than I am, Kaunas. Mercurian gravity is 0.4 normal. On the Moon, it's only 0.16." He interrupted Ryger's beginning of a sound by saying, "And on Ceres they use pseudo-grav fields adjusted to 0.8. You have no problem at all, Ryger."

The Cerian astronomer looked annoyed, "It's the open air. Going outside without a suit gets me."

"Right," agreed Kaunas, "and letting the sun beat down on you. Just letting it."

Talliaferro found himself insensibly drifting back in time. They had not changed much. Nor, he thought, had he himself. They were all ten years older, of course. Ryger had put on some weight and Kaunas's thin face had grown a bit leathery, but he would have recognized either if he had met him without warning.

He said, "I don't think it's Earth getting us. Let's face it."

Kaunas looked up sharply. He was a little fellow with quick, nervous movements of his hands. He habitually wore clothes that looked a shade too large for him.

He said, "Villiers! I know. I think about him sometimes." Then, with an air of desperation, "I got a letter from him."

Ryger sat upright, his olive complexion darkening further and said with energy, "You did? When?"

"A month ago."

Ryger turned to Talliaferro. "How about you?"

Talliaferro blinked placidly and nodded.

Ryger said, "He's gone crazy. He claims he's discovered a practical method of mass-transference through space. ——He told you two also? ——That's it, then. He was always a little bent. Now he's broken."

He rubbed his nose fiercely and Talliaferro thought of the day Villiers had broken it.

For ten years, Villiers had haunted them like the vague shadow of a guilt that wasn't really theirs. They had gone through their graduate work together, four picked and dedicated men being trained for a profession that had reached new heights in this age of interplanetary travel.

The Observatories were opening on the other worlds, surrounded by vacuum, unblurred by air.

There was the Lunar Observatory, from which Earth and the inner planets could be studied; a silent world in whose sky the home-planet hung suspended.

Mercury Observatory, closest to the sun, perched at Mercury's north pole, where the terminator moved scarcely at all, and the sun was fixed on the horizon and could be studied in the minutest detail.

Ceres Observatory, newest, most modern, with its range extending from Jupiter to the outermost galaxies.

There were disadvantages, of course. With interplanetary travel still difficult, leaves would be few, anything like normal life virtually impossible, but this was a lucky generation. Coming scientists would find the fields of knowledge well-reaped and, until the invention of an interstellar drive, no new horizon as capacious as this one would be opened.

Each of these lucky four, Talliaferro, Ryger, Kaunas, and Villiers, was to be in the position of a Galileo, who by owning the first real telescope, could not point it anywhere in the sky without making a major discovery.

But then Romero Villiers had fallen sick and it was rheumatic fever. Whose fault was that? His heart had been left leaking and limping.

He was the most brilliant of the four, the most hopeful, the most intense—and he could not even finish his schooling and get his doctorate.

Worse than that, he could never leave Earth; the acceleration of a spaceship's take-off would kill him.

Talliaferro was marked for the Moon, Ryger for Ceres, Kaunas for Mercury. Only Villiers stayed behind, a life-prisoner of Earth.

They had tried telling their sympathy and Villiers had rejected it with something approaching hate. He had railed at them and cursed them. When Ryger lost his temper and lifted his fist, Villiers had sprung at him, screaming, and had broken Ryger's nose.

Obviously Ryger hadn't forgotten that, as he caressed his nose gingerly with one finger.

Kaunas's forehead was an uncertain washboard of wrinkles. "He's at the Convention, you know. He's got a room in the hotel—405."

"*I* won't see him," said Ryger.

"He's coming up here. He said he wanted to see us. I thought—— He said nine. He'll be here any minute."

"In that case," said Ryger, "if you don't mind, I'm leaving." He rose.

Talliaferro said, "Oh, wait a while. What's the harm in seeing him?"

"Because there's no point. He's mad."

"Even so. Let's not be petty about it. Are you afraid of him?"

"Afraid!" Ryger looked contemptuous.

"Nervous, then. What is there to be so nervous about?"

"I'm not nervous," said Ryger.

"Sure you are. We all feel guilty about him, and without real reason. Nothing that happened was our fault." But he was speaking defensively and he knew it.

And when, at that point, the door signal sounded, all three jumped and turned to stare uneasily at the barrier that stood between themselves and Villiers.

The door opened and Romero Villiers walked in. The others rose stiffly to greet him, then remained standing in embarrassment, without one hand being raised.

He stared them down sardonically.

He's changed, thought Talliaferro.

He had. He had shrunken in almost every dimension. A gathering stoop made him seem even shorter. The skin of his scalp glistened through thinning hair, the skin on the back of his hands was ridged crookedly with bluish veins. He looked ill. There seemed nothing to link him to the memory of the past except for his trick of shading his eyes with one hand when he stared intently and, when he spoke, the even, controlled baritone of his voice.

He said, "My friends! My space-trotting friends! We've lost touch."

Talliaferro said, "Hello, Villiers."

Villiers eyed him. "Are you well?"

"Well enough."

"And you two?"

Kaunas managed a weak smile and a murmur. Ryger snapped, "All right, Villiers. What's up?"

"Ryger, the angry man," said Villiers. "How's Ceres?"

"It was doing well when I left. How's Earth?"

"You can see for yourself," but Villiers tightened as he said that.

He went on, "I am hoping that the reason all three of you have come to the Convention is to hear my paper day after tomorrow."

"Your paper? What paper?" asked Talliaferro.

"I wrote you all about it. My method of mass-transference."

Ryger smiled with one corner of his mouth. "Yes, you did. You didn't say anything about a paper, though, and I don't recall that you're listed as one of the speakers. I would have noticed it if you had been."

"You're right. I'm not listed. Nor have I prepared an abstract for publication."

Villiers had flushed and Talliaferro said soothingly, "Take it easy, Villiers. You don't look well."

Villiers whirled on him, lips contorted. "My heart's holding out, thank you."

Kaunas said, "Listen, Villiers, if you're not listed or abstracted——"

"*You* listen. I've waited ten years. You have the jobs in space and I have to teach school on Earth, but I'm a better man than any of you or all of you."

"Granted——" began Talliaferro.

"And I don't want your condescension either. Mandel witnessed it. *I* suppose you've heard of Mandel. Well, he's chairman of the astronautics division at the Convention and I demonstrated mass-transference for him. It was a crude device and it burnt out after one use but—— Are you listening?"

"We're listening," said Ryger coldly, "for what that counts."

"He'll let me talk about it my way. You bet he will. No warning. No advertisement. I'm going to spring it at them like a bombshell. When I give them the fundamental relationships involved it will break up the Convention. They'll scatter to their home labs to check on me and build devices. And they'll find it works. I made a live mouse disappear at one spot in my lab and appear in another. Mandel witnessed it."

He stared at them, glaring first at one face, then at another. He said, "You don't believe me, do you?"

Ryger said, "If you don't want advertisement, why do you tell us?"

"You're different. You're my friends, my classmates. You went out into space and left me behind."

"That wasn't a matter of choice," objected Kaunas in a thin, high voice.

Villiers ignored that. He said, "So I want you to know *now*. What will work for a mouse will work for a human. What will move something ten feet across a lab will move it a million miles across space. I'll be on the Moon, *and* on Mercury, *and* on Ceres and anywhere I want to go. I'll match every one of you and more. And I'll have done more for astronomy just teaching school and thinking, than all of you with your observatories and telescopes and cameras and spaceships."

"Well," said Talliaferro, "I'm pleased. More power to you. May I see a copy of the paper?"

"Oh, no." Villiers' hands clenched close to his chest as though he were holding phantom sheets and shielding them from observation. "You wait like everyone else. There's only one copy and no one will see it till I'm ready. Not even Mandel."

"One copy," cried Talliaferro. "If you misplace it——"

"I won't. And if I do, it's all in my head."

"If you——" Talliaferro almost finished that sentence with "die" but stopped himself. Instead, he went on after an almost imperceptible pause, "——have any sense, you'll scan it at least. For safety's sake."

"No," said Villiers, shortly. "You'll hear me day after tomorrow. You'll see the human horizon expanded at one stroke as it never has been before."

Again he stared intently at each face. "Ten years," he said. "Good-by."

"He's mad," said Ryger explosively, staring at the door as though Villiers were still standing before it.

"Is he?" said Talliaferro thoughtfully. "I suppose he is, in a way. He hates us for irrational reasons. And, then, not even to scan his paper as a precaution——"

Talliaferro fingered his own small scanner as he said that. It was just a neutrally colored, undistinguished cylinder, somewhat thicker and somewhat shorter than an ordinary pencil. In recent years, it had become the hallmark of the scientist, much as the stethoscope was that of the physician and the micro-computer that of the statistician. The scanner was worn in a jacket pocket, or clipped to a sleeve, or slipped behind the ear, or swung at the end of a string.

Talliaferro sometimes, in his more philosophical moments, wondered how it was in the days when research men had to make laborious notes of the literature or file away full-sized reprints. How unwieldy!

Now it was only necessary to scan anything printed or written to have a micro-negative which could be developed at leisure. Talliaferro had already recorded every abstract included in the program booklet of the Convention. The other two, he assumed with full confidence, had done likewise.

Talliaferro said, "Under the circumstances, refusal to scan is mad."

"Space!" said Ryger hotly. "There is no paper. There is no discovery. Scoring one on us would be worth any lie to him."

"But then what will he do day after tomorrow?" asked Kaunas.

"How do I know? He's a madman."

Talliaferro still played with his scanner and wondered idly if he ought to remove and develop some of the small slivers of film that lay stored away in its vitals. He decided against it. He said, "Don't underestimate Villiers. He's a brain."

"Ten years ago, maybe," said Ryger. "Now he's a nut. I propose we forget him."

He spoke loudly, as though to drive away Villiers and all that concerned him by the sheer force with which he discussed other things. He talked about Ceres and his work—the radio-plotting of the Milky Way with new radioscopes capable of the resolution of single stars.

Kaunas listened and nodded, then chimed in with information concerning the radio emissions of sunspots and his own paper, in press, on the association of proton storms with the gigantic hydrogen flares on the sun's surface.

Talliaferro contributed little. Lunar work was unglamorous in comparison. The latest information on long-scale weather forecasting through direct observation of terrestrial jet-streams would not compare with radioscopes and proton storms.

More than that, his thoughts could not leave Villiers. Villiers *was* the brain. They all knew it. Even Ryger, for all his bluster, must feel that if mass-transference were at all possible then Villiers was a logical discoverer.

The discussion of their own work amounted to no more than an uneasy admission that none of them had come to much. Talliaferro had followed the literature and knew. His own papers had been minor. The others had authored nothing of great importance.

None of them—face the fact—had developed into space-shakers. The colossal dreams of school days had not come true and that was that. They were competent routine workmen. No less. Unfortunately, no more. They knew that.

Villiers would have been more. They knew that, too. It was that knowledge, as well as guilt, which kept them antagonistic.

Talliaferro felt uneasily that Villiers, despite everything, was yet to *be* more. The others must be thinking so, too, and mediocrity could grow quickly unbearable. The mass-transference paper would come to pass and Villiers would be the great man after all, as he was always fated to be apparently, while his classmates, with all their advantages, would be forgotten. Their role would be no more than to applaud from the crowd.

He felt his own envy and chagrin and was ashamed of it, but felt it none the less.

Conversation died, and Kaunas said, his eyes turning away, "Listen, why don't we drop in on old Villiers?"

There was a false heartiness about it, a completely unconvincing effort at casualness. He added, "No use leaving bad feelings—unnecessarily——"

Talliaferro thought: He wants to make sure about the mass-transference. He's hoping it *is* only a madman's nightmare so he can sleep tonight.

But he was curious himself, so he made no objection, and even Ryger shrugged with ill grace and said, "Hell, why not?"

It was a little before eleven then.

Talliaferro was awakened by the insistent ringing of his door signal. He hitched himself to one elbow in the darkness and felt distinctly outraged. The soft glow of the ceiling indicator showed it to be not quite four in the morning.

He cried out, "Who is it?"

The ringing continued in short, insistent spurts.

Growling, Talliaferro slipped into his bathrobe. He opened the door and blinked in the corridor light. He recognized the man who faced him from the trimensionals he had seen often enough.

Nevertheless, the man said in an abrupt whisper, "My name is Hubert Mandel."

"Yes, sir," said Talliaferro. Mandel was one of the Names in astronomy, prominent enough to have an important executive position with the World Astronomical Bureau, active enough to be Chairman of the Astronautics section here at the Convention.

It suddenly struck Talliaferro that it was Mandel for whom Villiers claimed to have demonstrated mass-transference. The thought of Villiers was somehow a sobering one.

Mandel said, "You are Dr. Edward Talliaferro?"

"Yes, sir."

"Then dress and come with me. It is very important. It concerns a mutual acquaintance."

"Dr. Villiers?"

Mandel's eyes flickered a bit. His brows and lashes were so fair as to give those eyes a naked, unfringed appearance. His hair was silky-thin, his age about fifty.

He said, "Why Villiers?"

"He mentioned you last evening. I don't know any other mutual acquaintance."

Mandel nodded, waited for Talliaferro to finish slipping into his clothes, then turned and led the way. Ryger and Kaunas were waiting in a room one floor above Talliaferro's. Kaunas's eyes were red and troubled. Ryger was smoking a cigarette with impatient puffs.

Talliaferro said, "We're all here. Another reunion." It fell flat.

He took a seat and the three stared at one another. Ryger shrugged.

Mandel paced the floor, hands deep in his pockets. He said, "I apologize for any inconvenience, gentlemen, and I thank you for your co-operation. I would like more of it. Our friend, Romero Villiers, is dead. About an hour ago, his body was removed from the hotel. The medical judgment is heart failure."

There was a stunned silence. Ryger's cigarette hovered halfway to his lips, then sank slowly without completing its journey.

"Poor devil," said Talliaferro.

"Horrible," whispered Kaunas hoarsely. "He was——" His voice played out.

Ryger shook himself. "Well, he had a bad heart. There's nothing to be done."

"One little thing," corrected Mandel quietly. "Recovery."

"What does that mean?" asked Ryger sharply.

Mandel said, "When did you three see him last?"

Talliaferro spoke. "Last evening. It turned out to be a reunion. We all met for the first time in ten years. It wasn't a pleasant meeting, I'm sorry to say. Villiers felt he had cause for anger with us, and he was angry."

"That was—when?"

"About nine, the first time."

"The first time?"

"We saw him again later in the evening."

Kaunas looked troubled. "He had left angrily. We couldn't leave it at that. We had to try. It wasn't as if we hadn't all been friends at one time. So we went to his room and——"

Mandel pounced on that. "You were all in his room?"

"Yes," said Kaunas, surprised.

"About when?"

"Eleven, I think." He looked at the others. Talliaferro nodded.

"And how long did you stay?"

"Two minutes," put in Ryger. "He ordered us out as though we were after his paper." He paused as though expecting Mandel to ask what paper, but Mandel said nothing. He went on. "I think he kept it under his pillow. At least he lay across the pillow as he yelled at us to leave."

"He may have been dying then," said Kaunas, in a sick whisper.

"Not then," said Mandel shortly. "So you probably all left fingerprints."

"Probably," said Talliaferro. He was losing some of his automatic respect for Mandel and a sense of impatience was returning. It *was* four in the morning, Mandel or no. He said, "Now what's all this about?"

"Well, gentlemen," said Mandel, "there's more to Villiers' death than the fact of death. Villiers' paper, the only copy of it as far as I know, was stuffed into the cigarette flash-disposal unit and only scraps of it were left. I've never seen or read the paper, but I knew enough about the matter to be willing to swear in court if necessary that the remnants of unflashed paper in the disposal unit were of the paper he was planning to give at this Convention. ——You seem doubtful, Dr. Ryger."

Ryger smiled sourly. "Doubtful that he was going to give it. If you want my opinion, sir, he was mad. For ten years he was a prisoner of Earth and he fantasied mass-transference as escape. It was all that kept him alive probably. He rigged up some sort of fraudulent demonstration. I don't say it was deliberate fraud. He was probably madly sincere, and sincerely mad. Last evening was the climax. He came to our rooms—he hated us for having escaped Earth—and triumphed over us. It was what he had lived for for ten years. It may have shocked him back to some form of sanity. He knew he couldn't actually give the paper; there was nothing to give. So he burnt it and his heart gave out. It *is* too bad."

Mandel listened to the Cerian astronomer, wearing a look of

sharp disapproval. He said, "Very glib, Dr. Ryger, but quite wrong. I am not as easily fooled by fraudulent demonstrations as you may believe. Now according to the registration data, which I have been forced to check rather hastily, you three were his classmates at college. Is that right?"

They nodded.

"Are there any other classmates of yours present at the Convention?"

"No," said Kaunas. "We were the only four qualifying for a doctorate in astronomy that year. At least he would have qualified except——"

"Yes, I understand," said Mandel. "Well, then, in that case one of you three visited Villiers in his room one last time at midnight."

There was a short silence. Then Ryger said coldly, "Not I." Kaunas, eyes wide, shook his head.

Talliaferro said, "What are you implying?"

"One of you came to him at midnight and insisted on seeing his paper. I don't know the motive. Conceivably, it was with the deliberate intention of forcing him into heart failure. When Villiers collapsed, the criminal, if I may call him so, was ready. He snatched the paper which, I might add, probably *was* kept under his pillow and scanned it. Then he destroyed the paper itself in the flash-disposal, but he was in a hurry and destruction wasn't complete."

Ryger interrupted. "How do you know all this? Were you a witness?"

"Almost," said Mandel. "Villiers was not quite dead at the moment of his first collapse. When the criminal left, he managed to reach the phone and call my room. He choked out a few phrases, enough to outline what had occurred. Unfortunately I was not in my room; a late conference kept me away. However, my recording attachment taped it. I always play the recording tape back whenever I return to my room or office. Bureaucratic habit. I called back. He was dead."

"Well, then," said Ryger, "who did he say did it?"

"He didn't. Or if he did, it was unintelligible. But one word rang out clearly. It was 'classmate.'"

Talliaferro detached his scanner from its place in his inner jacket pocket and held it out toward Mandel. Quietly he said, "If you would like to develop the film in my scanner, you are welcome to do so. You will not find Villiers' paper there."

At once, Kaunas did the same, and Ryger, with a scowl, joined.

Mandel took all three scanners and said dryly, "Presumably, whichever one of you has done this has already disposed of the piece of exposed film with the paper on it. However——"

Talliaferro raised his eyebrows. "You may search my person or my room."

But Ryger was still scowling, "Now wait a minute, wait one bloody minute. Are you the police?"

Mandel stared at him. "Do you *want* the police? Do you want a scandal and a murder charge? Do you want the Convention disrupted and the System press to make a holiday out of astronomy and astronomers? Villiers' death might well have been accidental. He *did* have a bad heart. Whichever one of you was there may well have acted on impulse. It may not have been a premeditated crime. If whoever it is will return the negative, we can avoid a great deal of trouble."

"Even for the criminal?" asked Talliaferro.

Mandel shrugged. "There may be trouble for him. I will not promise immunity. But whatever the trouble, it won't be public disgrace and life imprisonment, as it might be if the police are called in."

Silence.

Mandel said, "It is one of you three."

Silence.

Mandel went on, "I think I can see the original reasoning of the guilty person. The paper would be destroyed. Only we four knew of the mass-transference and only I had ever seen a demonstration. Moreover you had only his word, a madman's word perhaps, that I had seen it. With Villiers dead of heart failure and the paper gone, it would be easy to believe Dr. Ryger's theory that there was no mass-transference and never had been. A year or two might pass and our criminal, in possession of the mass-transference data, could reveal it little by little, rig experiments, publish careful papers, and end as the apparent discoverer with all that would imply in terms of money and renown. Even his own classmates would suspect nothing. At most they would believe that the long-past affair with Villiers had inspired him to begin investigations in the field. No more."

Mandel looked sharply from one face to another. "But none of that will work now. Any of the three of you who comes through with mass-transference is proclaiming himself the criminal. I've seen the demonstration; I know it is legitimate; I know that one of you possesses a record of the paper. The information is therefore useless to you. Give it up then."

Silence.

Mandel walked to the door and turned again, "I'd appreciate it if you would stay here till I return. I won't be long. I hope the guilty one will use the interval to consider. If he's afraid a confession will lose him his job, let him remember that a session with police may lose him his liberty *and* cost him the Psychic Probe." He hefted the three scanners, looked grim and somewhat in need of sleep. "I'll develop these."

Kaunas tried to smile. "What if we make a break for it while you're gone?"

"Only one of you has reason to try," said Mandel. "I think I can rely on the two innocent ones to control the third, if only out of self-protection."

He left.

It was five in the morning. Ryger looked at his watch indignantly. "A hell of a thing. I want to sleep."

"We can curl up here," said Talliaferro philosophically. "Is anyone planning a confession?"

Kaunas looked away and Ryger's lip lifted.

"I didn't think so." Talliaferro closed his eyes, leaned his large head back against the chair and said in a tired voice, "Back on the Moon, they're in the slack season. We've got a two-week night and then it's busy, busy. Then there's two weeks of sun and there's nothing but calculations, correlations and bull-sessions. That's the hard time. I hate it. If there were more women, if I could arrange something permanent——"

In a whisper, Kaunas talked about the fact that it was still impossible to get the entire Sun above the horizon and in view of the telescope on Mercury. But with another two miles of track soon to be laid down for the Observatory—move the whole thing, you know, tremendous forces involved, solar energy used directly—it might be managed. It *would* be managed.

Even Ryger consented to talk of Ceres after listening to the low murmur of the other voices. There was the problem there of the two hour rotation period, which meant the stars whipped across the sky at an angular velocity twelve times that in Earth's sky. A net of three light scopes, three radio scopes, three of everything, caught the fields of study from one another as they whirled past.

"Could you use one of the poles?" asked Kaunas.

"You're thinking of Mercury and the Sun," said Ryger impatiently. "Even at the poles, the sky would still twist, and half of it would be forever hidden. Now if Ceres showed only one face to the Sun, the way Mercury does, we could have a permanent night sky with the stars rotating slowly once in three years."

The sky lightened and it dawned slowly.

Talliaferro was half asleep, but he kept hold of half-consciousness firmly. He would not fall asleep and leave the others awake. Each of the three, he thought, was wondering, "Who? Who?"—except the guilty one, of course.

Talliaferro's eyes snapped open as Mandel entered again. The sky, as seen from the window, had grown blue. Talliaferro was glad the window was closed. The hotel was air-conditioned, of course, but windows could be opened during the mild season of the year by those Earthmen who fancied the illusion of fresh air. Talliaferro, with Moon-vacuum on his mind, shuddered at the thought with real discomfort.

Mandel said, "Have any of you anything to say?"

They looked at him steadily. Ryger shook his head.

Mandel said, "I have developed the film in your scanners, gentlemen, and viewed the results." He tossed scanners and developed slivers of film on to the bed. "Nothing! ——You'll have trouble sorting out the film, I'm afraid. For that I'm sorry. And now there is still the question of the missing film."

"If any," said Ryger, and yawned prodigiously.

Mandel said, "I would suggest we come down to Villiers' room, gentlemen."

Kaunas looked startled. "Why?"

Talliaferro said, "Is this psychology? Bring the criminal to the scene of the crime and remorse will wring a confession from him?"

Mandel said, "A less melodramatic reason is that I would like to have the two of you who are innocent help me find the missing film of Villers' paper."

"Do you think it's there?" asked Ryger challengingly.

"Possibly. It's a beginning. We can then search each of your rooms.

The symposium on Astronautics doesn't start till tomorrow at 10 A.M. We have till then."

"And after that?"

"It may have to be the police."

They stepped gingerly into Villiers' room. Ryger was red, Kaunas pale. Talliaferro tried to remain calm.

Last night they had seen it under artificial lighting with a scowling, disheveled Villiers clutching his pillow, staring them down, ordering them away. Now there was the scentless odor of death about it.

Mandel fiddled with the window-polarizer to let more light in, and adjusted it too far, so that the eastern Sun slipped in.

Kaunas threw his arm up to shade his eyes and screamed, "The Sun!" so that all the others froze.

Kaunas's face showed a kind of terror, as though it were his Mercurian sun that he had caught a blinding glimpse of.

Talliaferro thought of his own reaction to the possibility of open air and his teeth gritted. They were all bent crooked by their ten years away from Earth.

Kaunas ran to the window, fumbling for the polarizer, and then the breath came out of him in a huge gasp.

Mandel stepped to his side. "What's wrong?" and the other two joined them.

The city lay stretched below them and outward to the horizon in broken stone and brick, bathed in the rising sun, with the shadowed portions toward them. Talliaferro cast it all a furtive and uneasy glance.

Kaunas, his chest seemingly contracted past the point where he could cry out, stared at something much closer. There, on the outer window sill, one corner secured in a trifling imperfection, a crack in the cement, was an inch-long strip of milky-gray film, and on it were the early rays of the rising sun.

Mandel, with an angry, incoherent cry, threw up the window and snatched it away. He shielded it in one cupped hand, staring out of hot and reddened eyes.

He said, "Wait here!"

There was nothing to say. When Mandel left, they sat down and stared stupidly at one another.

Mandel was back in twenty minutes. He said quietly (in a voice that gave the impression, somehow, that it was quiet only because its owner had passed far beyond the raving stage), "The corner in the crack wasn't overexposed. I could make out a few words. It is Villiers' paper. The rest is ruined; nothing can be salvaged. It's gone."

"What next?" said Talliaferro.

Mandel shrugged wearily. "Right now, I don't care. Mass-transference is gone until someone as brilliant as Villiers works it out again. I shall work on it but I have no illusions as to my own capacity. With it gone, I suppose you three don't matter, guilty or not. What's the difference?" His whole body seemed to have loosened and sunk into despair.

But Talliaferro's voice grew hard. "Now, hold on. In your eyes, any of the three of us might be guilty. I, for instance. You are a big man in the field and you will never have a good word to say for me. The general idea may arise that I am incompetent or worse. I will not be ruined by the shadow of guilt. Now let's solve this thing."

"I am no detective," said Mandel wearily.

"Then call in the police, damn it."

Ryger said, "Wait a while, Tal. Are you implying that I'm guilty?"

"I'm saying that I'm innocent."

Kaunas raised his voice in fright. "It will mean the Psychic Probe for each of us. There may be mental damage——"

Mandel raised both arms high in the air. "Gentlemen! Gentlemen! Please! There is one thing we might do short of the police; and you are right, Dr. Talliaferro, it would be unfair to the innocent to leave this matter here."

They turned to him in various stages of hostility. Ryger said, "What do you suggest?"

"I have a friend named Wendell Urth. You may have heard of him, or you may not, but perhaps I can arrage to see him tonight."

"What if you can?" demanded Talliaferro. "Where does that get us?"

"He's an odd man," said Mandel hesitantly, "very odd. And very brilliant in his way. He has helped the police before this and he may be able to help us now."

Part 2

Edward Talliaferro could not forbear staring at the room and its occupant with the greatest astonishment. It and he seemed to exist in isolation, and to be part of no recognizable world. The sounds of Earth were absent in this well-padded, windowless nest. The light and air of Earth had been blanked out in artificial illumination and conditioning.

It was a large room, dim and cluttered. They had picked their way across a littered floor to a couch from which book-films had been brusquely cleared and dumped to one side in a tangle.

The man who owned the room had a large, round face on a stumpy, round body. He moved quickly about on his short legs, jerking his head as he spoke until his thick glasses all but bounced off the thoroughly inconspicuous nubble that served as a nose. His thick-lidded, somewhat protuberant eyes gleamed in myopic good nature at them all, as he seated himself in his own chair-desk combination, lit directly by the one bright light in the room.

"So good of you to come, gentlemen. Pray excuse the condition of my room." He waved stubby fingers in a wide-sweeping gesture. "I am engaged in cataloguing the many objects of extraterrological interest I have accumulated. It is a tremendous job. For instance——"

He dodged out of his seat and burrowed in a heap of objects beside the desk till he came up with a smoky-gray object, semitranslucent and roughly cylindrical. "This," he said, "is a Callistan object that may be a relic of intelligent nonhuman entities. It is not decided. Not more than a dozen have been discovered and this is the most perfect single specimen I know of."

He tossed it to one side and Talliaferro jumped. The plump man stared in his direction and said, "It's not breakable." He sat down again, clapsed his pudgy fingers tightly over his abdomen and let them pump slowly in and out as he breathed. "And now what can I do for you?"

Hubert Mandel had carried through the introductions and Talliaferro was considering deeply. Surely it was a man named Wendell Urth who had written a recent book entitled *Comparative Evolutionary Processes on Water-Oxygen Planets,* and surely this could not be the man.

He said, "Are you the author of *Comparative Evolutionary Processes,* Dr. Urth?"

A beatific smile spread across Urth's face, "You've read it?"

"Well, no, I haven't, but——"

Urth's expression grew instantly censorious. "Then you should. Right now. Here, I have a copy——"

He bounced out of his chair again and Mandel cried at once, "Now wait, Urth, first things first. This is serious."

He virtually forced Urth back into his chair and began speaking rapidly as though to prevent any further side issues from erupting. He told the whole story with admirable word-economy.

Urth reddened slowly as he listened. He seized his glasses and shoved them higher up on his nose. "Mass-transference!" he cried.

"I saw it with my own eyes," said Mandel.

"And you never told me."

"I was sworn to secrecy. The man was—peculiar. I explained that."

Urth pounded the desk. "How could you allow such a discovery to remain the property of an eccentric, Mandel? The knowledge should have been forced from him by Psychic Probe, if necessary."

"It would have killed him," protested Mandel.

Bur Urth was rocking back and forth with his hands clasped tightly to his cheeks. "Mass-transference. The only way a decent, civilized man should travel. The only possible way. The only conceivable way. If I had known. If I could have been there. But the hotel is nearly thirty miles away."

Ryger, who listened with an expression of annoyance on his face, interposed, "I understand there's a flitter line direct to Convention Hall. It could have gotten you there in ten minutes."

Urth stiffened and looked at Ryger strangely. His cheeks bulged. He jumped to his feet and scurried out of the room.

Ryger said, "What the devil?"

Mandel muttered, "Damn it. I should have warned you."

"About what?"

"Dr. Urth doesn't travel on any sort of conveyance. It's a phobia. He moves about only on foot."

Kaunas blinked about in the dimness. "But he's an extraterrologist, isn't he? An expert on life forms of other planets?"

Talliaferro had risen and now stood before a Galatic Lens on a pedestal. He stared at the inner gleam of the star systems. He had never seen a Lens so large or so elaborate.

Mandel said, "He's an extraterrologist, yes, but he's never visited any of the planets on which he is expert and he never will. In thirty years, I doubt if he's ever been more than a mile from this room."

Ryger laughed.

Mandel flushed angrily. "You may find it funny, but I'd appreciate your being careful what you say when Dr. Urth comes back."

Urth sidled in a moment later. "My apologies, gentlemen," he said in a whisper. "And now let us approach our problem. Perhaps one of you wishes to confess."

Talliaferro's lips quirked sourly. This plump, self-imprisoned ex-traterrologist was scarcely formidable enough to force a confession from anyone. Fortunately, there would be no need of his detective talents, if any, after all.

Talliaferro said, "Dr. Urth, are you connected with the police?"

A certain smugness seemed to suffuse Urth's ruddy face. "I have no official connection, Dr. Talliaferro, but my unofficial relationships are very good indeed."

"In that case, I will give you some information which you can carry to the police."

Urth drew in his abdomen and hitched at his shirttail. It came free, and slowly he polished his glasses with it. When he was quite through and had perched them precariously on his nose once more, he said, "And what is that?"

"I will tell you who was present when Villiers died and who scanned his paper."

"You have solved the mystery?"

"I've thought about it all day. I think I've solved it." Talliaferro rather enjoyed the sensation he was creating.

"Well, then?"

Talliaferro took a deep breath. This was not going to be easy to do, though he had been planning it for hours. "The guilty man," he said, "is obviously Dr. Hubert Mandel."

Mandel stared at Talliaferro in sudden, hard-breathing indignation. "Look here, Doctor," he began, loudly, "if you have any basis for such a ridiculous——"

Urth's tenor voice soared above the interruption. "Let him talk, Hubert, let us hear him. You suspected him and there is no law that forbids him to suspect you."

Mandel fell angrily silent.

Talliaferro, not allowing his voice to falter, said, "It is more than just suspicion, Dr. Urth. The evidence is perfectly plain. Four of us knew about mass-transference, but only one of us, Dr. Mandel, had actually seen a demonstration. He *knew* it to be a fact. He *knew* a paper on the subject existed. We three knew only that Villiers was more or less unbalanced. Oh, we might have thought there was just a chance. We visited him at eleven, I think, just to check on that, though none of us actually said so—but he just acted crazier than ever."

"Check special knowledge and motive then on Dr. Mandel's side. Now, Dr. Urth, picture something else. Whoever it was who confronted Villiers at midnight, saw him collapse, and scanned his paper (let's keep him anonymous for a moment) must have been terribly startled to see Villiers apparently come to life again and to hear him talking into the telephone. Our criminal, in the panic of the moment, realized one thing: he must get rid of the one piece of incriminating material evidence.

"He had to get rid of the undeveloped film of the paper and he had to do it in such a way that it would be safe from discovery so that he might pick it up once more if he remained unsuspected. The outer window sill was ideal. Quickly he threw up Villiers' window, placed the strip of film outside, and left. Now, even if Villiers survived or if his telephoning brought results, it would be merely Villiers' word against his own and it would be easy to show that Villiers was unbalanced."

Talliaferro paused in something like triumph. This would be irrefutable.

Wendell Urth blinked at him and wiggled the thumbs of his clasped hands so that they slapped against his ample shirt front. He said, "And the significance of all that?"

"The significance is that the window was thrown open and the film placed in open air. Now Ryger has lived for ten years on Ceres, Kaunas on Mercury, I on the Moon—barring short leaves and not many of them. We commented to one another several times yesterday on the difficulty of growing acclimated to Earth.

"Our work-worlds are each airless objects. We never go out in the open without a suit. To expose ourselves to unenclosed space is unthinkable. None of us could have opened the window without a severe inner struggle. Dr. Mandel, however, has lived on Earth exclusively. Opening a window to him is only a matter of a bit of muscular exertion. He could do it. We couldn't. Ergo, he did it."

Talliaferro sat back and smiled a bit.

"Space, that's it!" cried Ryger, with enthusiasm.

"That's not it at all," roared Mandel, half rising as though tempted to throw himself at Talliaferro. "I deny the whole miserable fabrication. What about the record I have of Villiers' phone call? He used the word 'classmate.' The entire tape makes it obvious——"

"He was a dying man," said Talliaferro. "Much of what he said you admitted was incomprehensible. I ask you, Dr. Mandel, without having heard the tape, if it isn't true that Villiers' voice is distorted past recognition."

"Well——" said Mandel in confusion.

"I'm sure it is. There is no reason to suppose, then, that you might not have rigged up the tape in advance, complete with the damning word 'classmates.'"

Mandel said, "Good Lord, how would I know there were classmates at the Convention? How would I know they knew about the mass-transference?"

"Villiers might have told you. I presume he did."

"Now, look," said Mandel, "you three saw Villiers alive at eleven. The medical examiner, seeing Villiers' body shortly after 3 A.M. declared he had been dead at least two hours. That was certain. The time of death, therefore, was between 11 P.M. and 1 A.M. I was at a late conference last night. I can prove my whereabouts, miles from the hotel, between 10:00 and 2:00 by a dozen witness no one of whom anyone can possibly question. Is that enough for you?"

Talliaferro paused a moment. Then he went on stubbornly, "Even so. Suppose you got back to the hotel by 2:30. You went to Villiers' room to discuss his talk. You found the door open, or you had a duplicate key. Anyway, you found him dead. You seized the opportunity to scan the paper——"

"And if he were already dead, and couldn't make phone calls, why should I hide the film?"

"To remove suspicion. You may have a second copy of the film safe in your possession. For that matter, we have only your own word that the paper itself was destroyed."

"Enough. Enough," cried Urth. "It is an interesting hypothesis, Dr. Talliaferro, but it falls to the ground of its own weight."

Talliaferro frowned. "That's your opinion, perhaps——"

"It would be anyone's opinion. Anyone, that is, with the power of human thought. Don't you see that Hubert Mandel did too much to be the criminal?"

"No," said Talliaferro.

Wendell Urth smiled benignly. "As a scientist, Dr. Talliaferro, you undoubtedly know better than to fall in love with your own theories to the exclusion of facts and reasoning. Do me the pleasure of behaving similarly as a detective.

"Consider that if Dr. Mandel had brought about the death of Villiers and faked an alibi, or if he had found Villiers dead and taken advantage of that, how little he would really have had to do! Why scan the paper or even pretend that anyone had done so? He could simply have taken the paper. Who else knew of its existence? Nobody, really. There is no reason to think Villiers told anyone else about it. Villiers was pathologically secretive. There would have been every reason to think that he told no one.

"No one knew Villiers was giving a talk, except Dr. Mandel. It wasn't announced. No abstract was published. Dr. Mandel could have walked off with the paper in perfect confidence.

"Even if he had discovered that Villiers had talked to his classmates about the matter, what of it? What evidence would his classmates have except the word of one whom they are themselves half willing to consider a madman.

"By announcing instead that Villiers' paper had been destroyed, by declaring his death to be not entirely natural, by searching for a scanned copy of the film—in short by everything Dr. Mandel has done—he has aroused a suspicion that only he could possibly have aroused when he need only have remained quiet to have committed a perfect crime. If he were the criminal, he would be more stupid, more colossally obtuse than anyone I have ever known. And Dr. Mandel, after all, is none of that."

Talliaferro thought hard but found nothing to say.

Ryger said, "Then who did do it?"

"One of you three. That's obvious."

"But which?"

"Oh, that's obvious, too. I knew which of you was guilty the moment Dr. Mandel had completed his description of events."

Talliaferro stared at the plump extraterrologist with distaste. The bluff did not frighten him, but it was affecting the other two. Ryger's lips were thrust out and Kaunas's lower jaw had relaxed moronically. They looked like fish, both of them.

He said, "Which one, then? Tell us."

Urth blinked. "First, I want to make it perfectly plain that the important thing is mass-transference. It can still be recovered."

Mandel, scowling still, said querulously, "What the devil are you talking about, Urth?"

"The man who scanned the paper probably looked at what he was scanning. I doubt that he had the time or presence of mind to read it, and if he did, I doubt if he could remember it—consciously. However, there is the Psychic Probe. If he even glanced at the paper, what impinged on his retina could be Probed."

There was an uneasy stir.

Urth said at once, "No need to be afraid of the Probe. Proper handling is safe, particularly if a man offers himself voluntarily. When damage is done, it is usually because of unnecessary resistance, a kind of mental tearing, you know. So if the guilty man will voluntarily confess, place himself in my hands——"

Talliaferro laughed. The sudden noise rang out sharply in the dim quiet of the room. The psychology was so transparent and artless.

Wendell Urth looked almost bewildered at the reaction and stared earnestly at Talliaferro over his glasses. He said, "I have enough influence with the police to keep the Probing entirely confidential."

Ryger said savagely, "I didn't do it."

Kaunas shook his head.

Talliaferro disdained any answer.

Urth sighed. "Then I will have to point out the guilty man. It will be traumatic. It will make things harder." He tightened the grip on his belly and his fingers twitched. "Dr. Talliaferro pointed out that the film was hidden on the outer window sill so that it might remain safe from discovery and from harm. I agree with him."

"Thank you," said Talliaferro dryly.

"However, why should anyone think that an outer window sill is a particularly safe hiding place? The police would certainly look there. Even in the absence of the police it was discovered. Who would tend to consider anything outside a building as particularly safe? Obviously, some person who has lived a long time on an airless world and has had it drilled into him that no one goes outside an enclosed place without detailed precautions.

"To someone on the Moon, for instance, anything hidden outside a Lunar Dome would be comparatively safe. Men venture out only rarely and then only on specific business. So he would overcome the hardship of opening a window and exposing himself to what he would subconsciously consider a vacuum for the sake of a safe hiding place. The reflex thought, 'Outside an inhabited structure is safe,' would do the trick."

Talliaferro said between clenched teeth, "Why do you mention the moon, Dr. Urth?"

Urth said blandly, "Only as an example. What I've said so far applies to all three of you. But now comes the crucial point, the matter of the dying night."

Talliaferro frowned. "You mean the night Villiers died?"

"I mean any night. See here, even granted that an outer window sill was a safe hiding place, which of you would be mad enough to consider it a safe hiding place *for a piece of unexposed film?* Scanner film isn't very sensitive, to be sure, and is made to be developed under all sorts of hit-and-miss conditions. Diffuse nighttime illumination wouldn't seriously affect it, but diffuse daylight would ruin it in a few minutes, and direct sunlight would ruin it at once. Everyone knows that."

Mandel said, "Go ahead, Urth. What is this leading to?"

"You're trying to rush me," said Urth, with a massive pout. "I want you to see this clearly. The criminal wanted, above all, to keep the film safe. It was his only record of something of supreme value to himself and to the world. Why would he put it where it would inevitably be ruined by the morning sun? ——Only because he did not expect the morning sun ever to come. He thought the night, so to speak, was immortal.

"But nights *aren't* immortal. On Earth, they die and give way to daytime. Even the six-month polar night is a dying night eventually. The nights on Ceres last only two hours; the nights on the Moon last two weeks. They are dying nights, too, and Drs. Talliaferro and Ryger know that day must always come."

Kaunas was on his feet. "But wait——"

Wendell Urth faced him full. "No longer any need to wait, Dr. Kaunas. Mercury is the only sizable object in the Solar System that turns only one face to the sun. Even taking libration into account, fully three-eighths of its surface is true dark-side and never sees the sun. The Polar Observatory is at the rim of that dark-side. For ten years, you have grown used to the fact that nights are immortal, that a surface in darkness remains eternally in darkness, and so you entrusted unexposed film to Earth's night, forgetting in your excitement that night must die——"

Kaunas stumbled forward. "Wait——"

Urth was inexorable. "I am told that when Mandel adjusted the polarizer in Villiers' room, you screamed at the sunlight. Was that your ingrained fear of Mercurian sun, or your sudden realization of what sunlight meant to your plans? You rushed forward. Was that to adjust the polarizer or to stare at the ruined film?"

Kaunas fell to his knees. "I didn't mean it. I wanted to speak to him, only to speak to him, and he screamed and collapsed. I thought he was dead and the paper was under his pillow and it all just followed. One thing led on to another and before I knew it, I couldn't get out of it anymore. But I meant none of it. I swear it."

They had formed a semicircle about him and Wendell Urth stared at the moaning Kaunas with pity in his eyes.

An ambulance had come and gone. Talliaferro finally brought himself to say stiffly to Mandel, "I hope, sir, there will be no hard feelings for anything said here."

And Mandel had answered, as stiffly, "I think we had all better forget as much as possible of what has happened during the last twenty-four hours."

They were standing in the doorway, ready to leave, and Wendell Urth ducked his smiling head, and said, "There's the question of my fee, you know."

Mandel looked startled.

"Not money," said Urth at once. "But when the first mass-transference setup for humans is established, I want a trip arranged for me."

Mandel continued to look anxious. "Now, wait. Trips though outer space are a long way off."

Urth shook his head rapidly. "Not outer space. Not at all. I would like to step across to Lower Falls, New Hampshire."

"All right. But why?"

Urth looked up. To Talliaferro's outright surprise, the extraterrologist's face wore an expression compounded of shyness and eagerness.

Urth said, "I once—quite a long time ago—knew a girl there. It's been many years—but I sometimes wonder——"

Afterword

Some readers may realize that this story, first published in 1956, has been overtaken by events. In 1965, astronomers discovered that Mercury does not keep one side always to the Sun, but has a period of rotation of about fifty-four days, so that all parts of it are exposed to sunlight at one time or another.

Well, what can I do except say that I wish astronomers would get things right to begin with?

And I certainly refuse to change the story to suit their whims.

Anniversary

The annual ritual was all set.

It was the turn of Moore's house this year, of course, and Mrs. Moore and the children had resignedly gone to her mother's for the evening.

Warren Moore surveyed the room with a faint smile. Only Mark Brandon's enthusiasm kept it going at the first, but he himself had come to like this mild remembrance. It came with age, he supposed; twenty additional years of it. He had grown paunchy, thin-haired, soft-jowled, and—worst of all—sentimental.

So all the windows were polarized into complete darkness and the drapes were drawn. Only occasional stipples of wall were illuminated, thus celebrating the poor lighting and the terrible isolation of that day of wreckage long ago.

There were spaceship rations in sticks and tubes on the table and, of course, in the center an unopened bottle of sparkling green Jabra water, the potent brew that only the chemical activity of Martian fungi could supply.

Moore looked at his watch. Brandon would be here soon; he was never late for this occasion. The only thing that disturbed him was the memory of Brandon's voice on the tube: "Warren, I have a surprise for you this time. Wait and see. Wait and see."

Brandon, it always seemed to Moore, aged little. The younger man had kept his slimness, and the intensity with which he greeted all in life, to the verge of his fortieth birthday. He retained the ability to be in high excitement over the good and in deep despair over the bad. His hair was going gray, but except for that, when Brandon walked up and down, talking rapidly at the top of his voice about anything at all, Moore didn't even have to close his eyes to see the panicked youngster on the wreck of the *Silver Queen*.

The door signal sounded and Moore kicked the release without turning around. "Come, Mark."

It was a strange voice that answered, though; softly, tentatively, "Mr. Moore?"

Moore turned quickly. Brandon was there, to be sure, but only in the background, grinning with excitement. Someone else was standing before him; short, squat, quite bald, nut-brown and with the feel of space about him.

Moore said wonderingly, "Mike Shea—*Mike Shea,* by all space."

They pounded hands together, laughing.

Brandon said, "He got in touch with me through the office. He remembered I was with Atomic Products—"

"It's been *years,*" said Moore. "Let's see, you were on Earth twelve years ago—"

"He's never been here on an anniversary," said Brandon. "How about that? He's retiring now. Getting out of space to a place he's buying in Arizona. He came to say hello before he left—stopped off at the city just for that—and I was sure he came for the anniversary. 'What anniversary?' says the old jerk."

Shea nodded, grinning. "He said you made a kind of celebration out of it every year."

"You bet," said Brandon enthusiastically, "and this will be the first one with all three of us here, the first *real* anniversary. It's twenty years, Mike; twenty years since Warren scrambled over what was left of the wreck and brought us down to Vesta."

Shea looked about. "Space ration, eh? That's old home week to me. And Jabra. Oh, sure, I remember . . . twenty years. I never give it a thought and now, all of a sudden, it's yesterday. Remember when we got back to Earth finally?"

"Do I!" said Brandon. "The parades, the speeches. Warren was the only real hero of the occasion and we kept saying so, and they kept paying no attention. Remember?"

"Oh, well," said Moore. "We were the first three men ever to survive a spaceship crash. We were unusual and anything unusual is worth a celebration. These things are irrational."

"Hey," said Shea, "any of you remember the songs they wrote? That marching one? 'You can sing of routes through Space and the weary maddened pace of the—' "

Brandon joined in with his clear tenor and even Moore added his voice to the chorus so that the last line was loud enough to shake the drapes. "On the *wreck* of the *Silver* Que-e-en," they roared out, and ended laughing wildly.

Brandon said, "Let's open the Jabra for the first little sip. This one bottle has to last all of us all night."

Moore said, "Mark insists on complete authenticity. I'm surprised he doesn't expect me to climb out the window and human-fly my way around the building."

"Well, now, that's an idea," said Brandon.

"Remember the last toast we made?" Shea held his empty glass before him and intoned, " 'Gentlemen, I give you the year's supply of good old H$_2$O *we used to have.*' Three drunken bums when we landed. Well, we were kids. I was thirty and I thought I was old. And now," his voice was suddenly wistful, "they've retired me."

"Drink!" said Brandon. "Today you're thirty again, and we remember the day on the *Silver Queen* even if no one else does. Dirty, fickle public."

Moore laughed. "What do you expect? A national holiday every year with space ration and Jabra the ritual food and drink?"

"Listen, we're still the only men ever to survive a spaceship crash and now look at us. We're in oblivion."

"It's pretty good oblivion. We had a good time to begin with and the publicity gave us a healthy boost up the ladder. We are doing well, Mark. And so would Mike Shea be if he hadn't wanted to return to space."

Shea grinned and shrugged his shoulder. "That's where I like to be. I'm not sorry, either. What with the insurance compensation I got, I have a nice piece of cash now to retire on."

Brandon said reminiscently, "The wreck set back Trans-space Insurance a real packet. Just the same, there's still something missing. You say '*Silver Queen*' to anyone these days and he can only think of Quentin, if he can think of anyone."

"Who?" said Shea.

"Quentin. Dr. Horace Quentin. He was one of the non-survivors on the ship. You say to anyone, 'What about the three men who survived?' and they'll just stare at you. 'Huh?' they'll say."

Moore said calmly, "Come, Mark, face it. Dr. Quentin was one of the world's great scientists and we three are just three of the world's nothings."

"We survived. We're still the only men on record to survive."

"So? Look, John Hester was on the ship, and he was an important scientist too. Not in Quentin's league, but important. As a matter of fact, I was next to him at the last dinner before the rock hit us. Well, just because Quentin died in the same wreck, Hester's death was drowned out. No one ever remembers Hester died on the *Silver Queen*. They only remember Quentin. We may be forgotten too, but at least we're alive."

"I tell you what," said Brandon after a period of silence during which Moore's rationale had obviously failed to take, "we're marooned again. Twenty years ago today, we were marooned off Vesta. Today, we're marooned in oblivion. Now here are the three of us back together again at last, and what happened before can happen again. Twenty years ago, Warren pulled us down to Vesta. Now let's solve this new problem."

"Wipe out the oblivion, you mean?" said Moore. "Make ourselves famous?"

"Sure. Why not? Do you know of any better way of celebrating a twentieth anniversary?"

"No, but I'd be interested to know where you expect to start. I don't think people remember the *Silver Queen* at all, except for Quentin, so you'll have to think of some way of bringing the wreck back to mind. That's just to begin with."

Shea stirred uneasily and a thoughtful expression crossed his blunt countenance. "Some people remember the *Silver Queen*. The insurance company does, and you know that's a funny thing, now that you bring up the matter. I was on Vesta about ten-eleven years ago, and I asked if the piece of wreck we brought down was still there and they said sure, who would cart it away? So I thought I'd take a look at it and shot over by reaction motor strapped to my back. With Vestan gravity, you know, a reaction motor is all you need. Anyway, I didn't get to see it except from a distance. It was circled off by force field."

Brandon's eyebrows went sky-high. "Our *Silver Queen*? For what reason?"

"I went back and asked how come? They didn't tell me and they said they didn't know I was going there. They said it belonged to the insurance company."

Moore nodded. "Surely. They took over when they paid off. I signed a release, giving up my salvage rights when I accepted the compensation check. You did too, I'm sure."

Brandon said, "But why the force field? Why all the privacy?"

"I don't know."

"The wreck isn't worth anything even as scrap metal. It would cost too much to transport it."

Shea said, "That's right. Funny thing, though; they were bringing pieces back from space. There was a pile of it there. I could see it and it looked like just junk, twisted pieces of frame, you know. I asked about it and they said ships were always landing and unloading more scrap, and the insurance company had a standard price for any piece of the *Silver Queen* brought back, so ships in the neighborhood of Vesta were always looking. Then, on my last voyage in, I went to see the *Silver Queen* again and that pile was a lot bigger."

"You mean they're still looking?" Brandon's eyes glittered.

"I don't know. Maybe they've stopped. But the pile was bigger than it was ten-eleven years ago so they were still looking then."

Brandon leaned back in his chair and crossed his legs. "Well, now, that's very queer. A hard-headed insurance company is spending all kinds of money, sweeping space near Vesta, trying to find pieces of a twenty-year-old wreck."

"Maybe they're trying to prove sabotage," said Moore.

"After twenty years? They won't get their money back even if they do. It's a dead issue."

"They may have quit looking years ago."

Brandon stood up with decision. "Let's ask. There's something funny here and I'm just Jabrified enough and anniversaried enough to want to find out."

"Sure," said Shea, "but ask who?"

"Ask Multivac," said Brandon.

Shea's eyes opened wide. "Multivac! Say, Mr. Moore, do you have a Multivac outlet here?"

"Yes."

"I've never seen one, and I've always wanted to."

"It's nothing to look at, Mike. It looks just like a typewriter. Don't confuse a Multivac outlet with Multivac itself. I don't know anyone who's seen Multivac."

Moore smiled at the thought. He doubted if ever in his life he would meet any of the handful of technicians who spent most of their working days in a hidden spot in the bowels of Earth tending a mile-long super-computer that was the repository of all the facts known to man, that guided man's economy, directed his scientific research, helped make his political decisions, and had millions of circuits left over to answer individual questions that did not violate the ethics of privacy.

Brandon said as they moved up the power ramp to the second floor, "I've been thinking of installing a Multivac, Jr., outlet for the kids. Homework and things, you know. And yet I don't want to make it just a fancy and expensive crutch for them. How do you work it, Warren?"

Moore said tersely. "They show me the questions first. If I don't pass them, Multivac does not see them."

The Multivac outlet was indeed a simple typewriter arrangement and little more.

Moore set up the co-ordinates that opened his portion of the planet-wide network of circuits and said, "Now listen. For the record, I'm against this and I'm only going along because it's the anniversary and because I'm just jackass enough to be curious. Now how ought I to phrase the question?"

Brandon said, "Just ask: Are pieces of the wreck of the *Silver Queen* still being searched for in the neighborhood of Vesta by Trans-space Insurance? It only requires a simple yes or no."

Moore shrugged and tapped it out, while Shea watched with awe.

The spaceman said, "How does it answer? Does it talk?"

Moore laughed gently, "Oh, no. I don't spend *that* kind of money. This model just prints the answer on a slip of tape that comes out that slot."

A short strip of tape did come out as he spoke. Moore removed it and, after a glance, said, "Well, Multivac says yes."

"Hah!" cried Brandon. "Told you. Now ask why."

"Now that's silly. A question like that would obviously be against privacy. You'll just get a yellow state-your-reason."

"Ask and find out. They haven't made the search for the pieces secret. Maybe they're not making the reason secret."

Moore shrugged. He tapped out: Why is Trans-space Insurance conducting its *Silver Queen* search-project to which reference was made in the previous question?

A yellow slip clicked out almost at once: *State Your Reason For Requiring The Information Requested.*

"All right," said Brandon unabashed. "You tell it we're the three survivors and have a right to know. Go ahead. Tell it."

Moore tapped that out in unemotional phrasing and another

yellow slip was pushed out at them: *Your Reason Is Insufficient. No Answer Can Be Given.*

Brandon said, "I don't see they have a right to keep that secret."

"That's up to Multivac," said Moore. "It judges the reasons given it and if it decides the ethics of privacy is against answering, that's it. The government itself couldn't break those ethics without a court order, and the courts don't go against Multivac once in ten years. So what are you going to do?"

Brandon jumped to his feet and began the rapid walk up and down the room that was so characteristic of him. "All right, then let's figure it out for ourselves. It's something important to justify all their trouble. We're agreed they're not trying to find evidence of sabotage, not after twenty years. But Trans-space must be looking for *something*, something so valuable that it's worth looking for all this time. Now what could be that valuable?"

"Mark, you're a dreamer," said Moore.

Brandon obviously didn't hear him. "It can't be jewels or money or securities. There just couldn't be enough to pay them back for what the search has already cost them. Not if the *Silver Queen* were pure gold. What would be more valuable?"

"You can't judge value, Mark," said Moore. "A letter might be worth a hundredth of a cent as wastepaper and yet make a difference of a hundred million dollars to a corporation, depending on what's in the letter."

Brandon nodded his head vigorously. "Right. Documents. Valuable papers. Now who would be most likely to have papers worth billions in his possession on that trip?"

"How could anyone possibly say?"

"How about Dr. Horace Quentin? How about that, Warren? He's the one people remember because he was so important. What about the papers he might have had with him? Details of a new discovery, maybe. Damn it, if I had only seen him on that trip, he might have told me something, just in casual conversation, you know. Did *you* ever see him, Warren?"

"Not that I recall. Not to talk to. So casual conversation with me is out too. Of course, I might have passed him at some time without knowing it."

"No, you wouldn't have," said Shea, suddenly thoughtful. "I think I remember something. There was one passenger who never left his cabin. The steward was talking about it. He wouldn't even come out for meals."

"And that was Quentin?" said Brandon, stopping his pacing and staring at the spaceman eagerly.

"It might have been, Mr. Brandon. It might have been him. I don't know that anyone *said* it was. I don't remember. But it must have been a big shot, because on a spaceship you don't fool around bringing meals to a man's cabin unless he *is* a big shot."

"And Quentin was *the* big shot on the trip," said Brandon, with satisfaction. "So he had something in his cabin. Something very important. Something he was concealing."

"He might just have been space sick," said Moore, "except that—" He frowned and fell silent.

"Go ahead," said Brandon urgently. "You remember something too?"

"Maybe. I told you I was sitting next to Dr. Hester at the last dinner. He was saying something about hoping to meet Dr. Quentin on the trip and not having any luck."

"Sure," cried Brandon, "because Quentin wouldn't come out of his cabin."

"He didn't *say* that. We got to talking about Quentin, though. Now what was it he said?" Moore put his hands to his temples as though trying to squeeze out the memory of twenty years ago by main force. "I can't give you the exact words, of course, but it was something about Quentin being very theatrical or a slave of drama or something like that, and they were heading out to some scientific conference on Ganymede and Quentin wouldn't even announce the title of his paper."

"It all fits." Brandon resumed his rapid pacing. "He had a new, great discovery, which he was keeping absolutely secret, because he was going to spring it on the Ganymede conference and get maximum drama out of it. He wouldn't come out of his cabin because he probably thought Hester would pump him—and Hester would, I'll bet. And then the ship hit the rock and Quentin was killed. Transspace Insurance investigated, got rumors of this new discovery and figured that if they gained control of it they could make back their losses and plenty more. So they took ownership of the ship and have been hunting for Quentin's papers among the pieces ever since."

Moore smiled, in absolute affection for the other man. "Mark, that's a beautiful theory. The whole evening is worth it, just watching you make something out of nothing."

"Oh, yeah? Something out of nothing? Let's ask Multivac again. I'll pay the bill for it this month."

"It's all right. Be my guest. If you don't mind, though, I'm going to bring up the bottle of Jabra. I want one more little shot to catch up with you."

"Me, too," said Shea.

Brandon took his seat at the typewriter. His fingers trembled with eagerness as he tapped out: What was the nature of Dr. Horace Quentin's final investigations?

Moore had returned with the bottle and glasses, when the answer came back, on white paper this time. The answer was long and the print was fine, consisting for the most part of references to scientific papers in journals twenty years old.

Moore went over it. "I'm no physicist, but it looks to me as though he was interested in optics."

Brandon shook his head impatiently. "But all that is published. We want something he had not published yet."

"We'll never find out anything about that."

"The insurance company did."

"That's just your theory."

Brandon was kneading his chin with an unsteady hand. "Let me ask Multivac one more question."

He sat down again and tapped out: Give me the name and tube number of the surviving colleagues of Dr. Horace Quentin from among those associated with him at the University on whose faculty he served.

"How do you know he was on a University faculty?" asked Moore.

"If not, Multivac will tell us."

A slip popped out. It contained only one name.

Moore said, "Are you planning to call the man?"

"I sure am," said Brandon. "Otis Fitzsimmons, with a Detroit tube number. Warren, may I—"

"Be my guest, Mark. It's still part of the game."

Brandon set up the combination on Moore's tube keyboard. A woman's voice answered. Brandon asked for Dr. Fitzsimmons and there was a short wait.

Then a thin voice said, "Hello." It sounded old.

Brandon said, "Dr. Fitzsimmons, I'm representing Trans-space Insurance in the matter of the late Dr. Horace Quentin—"

"For heaven's sake, Mark," whispered Moore, but Brandon held up a sharply restraining hand.

There was a pause so long that a tube breakdown began to seem possible and then the old voice said, "After all these years? Again?"

Brandon snapped his fingers in an irrepressible gesture of triumph. But he said smoothly, almost glibly, "We're still trying to find out, Doctor, if you have remembered further details about what Dr. Quentin might have had with him on that last trip that would pertain to his last unpublished discovery."

"Well"—there was an impatient clicking of the tongue—"I've told you, I don't know. I don't want to be bothered with this again. I don't know that there was *anything*. The man hinted, but he was always hinting about some gadget or other."

"What gadget, sir?"

"I tell you I don't know. He used a name once and I told you about that. I don't think it's significant."

"We don't have the name in our records, sir."

"Well, you should have. Uh, what was that name? An optikon, that's it."

"With a K?"

"C or K. I don't know or care. Now, please, I do not wish to be disturbed again about this. Good-bye." He was still mumbling querulously when the line went dead.

Brandon was pleased.

Moore said, "Mark, that was the stupidest thing you could have done. Claiming a fraudulent identity on the tube is illegal. If he wants to make trouble for you—"

"Why should he? He's forgotten about it already. But don't you see, Warren? Trans-space has been asking him about this. He kept saying he'd explained all this before."

"All right. But you'd assumed that much. What else do you know?"

"We also know," said Brandon, "that Quentin's gadget was called an optikon."

"Fitzsimmons didn't sound certain about that. And even so, since we already know he was specializing in optics toward the end, a name like optikon does not push us any further forward."

"And Trans-space Insurance is looking either for the optikon or for papers concerning it. Maybe Quentin kept the details in his hat and just had a model of the instrument. After all, Shea said they were picking up metal objects. Right?"

"There was a bunch of metal junk in the pile," agreed Shea.

"They'd leave that in space if it were papers they were after. So that's what we want, an instrument that might be called on optikon."

"Even if all your theories were correct, Mark, and we're looking for an optikon, the search is absolutely hopeless now," said Moore flatly. "I doubt that more than ten per cent of the debris would remain in orbit about Vesta. Vesta's escape velocity is practically nothing. It was just a lucky thrust in a lucky direction and at a lucky velocity that put our section of the wreck in orbit. The rest is gone, scattered all over the Solar System in any conceivable orbit about the Sun."

"They've been picking up pieces," said Brandon.

"Yes, the ten per cent that managed to make a Vestan orbit out of it. That's all."

Brandon wasn't giving up. He said thoughtfully, "Suppose it *were* there and they hadn't found it. Could someone have beat them to it?"

Mike Shea laughed. "We were right there, but we sure didn't walk off with anything but our skins, and glad to do that much. Who else?"

"That's right," agreed Moore, "and if anyone else picked it up, why are they keeping it a secret?"

"Maybe they don't know what it is."

"Then how do we go about—" Moore broke off and turned to Shea, "What did you say?"

Shea looked blank. "Who, me?"

"Just now, about us being there." Moore's eyes narrowed. He shook his head as though to clear it, then whispered, "Great Galaxy!"

"What is it?" asked Brandon tensely. "What's the matter, Warren?"

"I'm not sure. You're driving me mad with your theories; so mad, I'm beginning to take them seriously, I think. You know, we *did* take some things out of the wreck with us. I mean besides our clothes and what personal belongings we still had. Or at least I did."

"What?"

"It was when I was making my way across the outside of the wreckage—space, I seem to be there now, I see it so clearly— I picked up some items and put them in the pocket of my spacesuit. I don't know why; I wasn't myself, really. I did it without thinking. And then, well, I held on to them. Souvenirs, I suppose. I brought them back to Earth."

"Where are they?"

"I don't know. We haven't stayed in one place, you know."

"You didn't throw them out, did you?"

"No, but things do get lost when you move."

"If you didn't throw them out, they must be somewhere in this house."

"If they didn't get lost. I swear I don't recall seeing them in fifteen years."

"What were they?"

Warren Moore said, "One was a fountain pen, as I recall; a real antique, the kind that used an ink-spray cartridge. What gets me, though, is that the other was a small field glass, not more than about six inches long. You see what I mean? A field glass?"

"An optikon," shouted Brandon. "Sure!"

"It's just a coincidence," said Moore, trying to remain level-headed. "Just a curious coincidence."

But Brandon wasn't having it. "A coincidence, nuts! Trans-space couldn't find the optikon on the wreck and they couldn't find it in space because you had it all along."

"You're crazy."

"Come on, we've got to find the thing now."

Moore blew out his breath. "Well, I'll look, if that's what you want, but I doubt that I'll find it. Okay, let's start with the storage level. That's the logical place."

Shea chuckled. "The logical place is usually the worst place to look." But they all headed for the power ramp once more and the additional flight upward.

The storage level had a musty, unused odor to it. Moore turned on the precipitron. "I don't think we've precipitated the dust in two years. That shows you how often I'm up here. Now, let's see—if it's anywhere at all, it would be in with the bachelor collection. I mean the junk I've been hanging on to since bachelor days. We can start here."

Moore started leafing through the contents of plastic collapsibles while Brandon kept peering anxiously over his shoulder.

Moore said, "What do you know? My college yearbook. I was a sonist in those days; a real bug on it. In fact, I managed to get a voice recording with the picture of every senior in this book." He tapped its cover fondly. "You could swear there was nothing there but the usual trimensional photos, but each one has an imprisoned—"

He grew aware of Brandon's frown and said, "Okay, I'll keep looking."

He gave up on the collapsibles and opened a trunk of heavy, old-fashioned woodite. He separated the contents of the various compartments.

Brandon said, "Hey, is that it?"

He pointed to a small cylinder that rolled out on the floor with a small clunk.

Moore said, "I don't— Yes! That's the pen. There it is. And here's the field glass. Neither one works, of course. They're both broken. At least, I suppose the pen's broken. Something's loose and rattles in it. Hear? I wouldn't have the slightest idea about how to fill it so I can check whether it really works. They haven't even made ink-spray cartridges in years."

Brandon held it under the light. "It has initials on it."

"Oh? I don't remember noticing any."

"It's pretty worn down. It looks like J.K.Q."

"Q.?"

"Right, and that's an unusual letter with which to start a last name. This pen might have belonged to Quentin. An heirloom he kept for luck or sentiment. It might have belonged to a great-grandfather in the days when they used pens like this; a great-grandfather called Jason Knight Quentin or Judah Kent Quentin or something like that. We can check the names of Quentin's ancestors through Multivac."

Moore nodded. "I think maybe we should. See, you've got me as crazy as you are."

"And if this is so, it proves you picked it up in Quentin's room. So you picked up the field glass there too."

"Now hold it. I don't remember that I picked them both up in the same place. I don't remember the scrounging over the outside of the wreck that well."

Brandon turned the small field glass over and over under the light. "No initials here."

"Did you expect any?"

"I don't see anything, in fact, except this narrow joining mark here." He ran his thumbnail into the fine groove that circled the glass near its thicker end. He tried to twist it unsuccessfully. "One piece." He put it to his eye. "This thing doesn't work."

"I told you it was broken. No lenses—"

Shea broke in. "You've got to expect a little damage when a spaceship hits a good-sized meteor and goes to pieces."

"So even if this were it," said Moore, pessimistic again, "if this were the optikon, it would not do us any good."

He took the field glass from Brandon and felt along the empty rims. "You can't even tell where the lenses belonged. There's no groove I can feel into which they might have been seated. It's as if there never— *Hey!*" He exploded the syllable violently.

"Hey what?" said Brandon.

"The name! The name of the thing!"

"Optikon, you mean?"

"Optikon, I don't mean! Fitzsimmons, on the tube, called it an optikon and we thought he said 'an optikon.'"

"Well, he did," said Brandon.

"Sure," said Shea. "I heard him."

"You just thought you heard him. He said 'anoptikon.' Don't you get it? Not 'an optikon,' two words, 'anoptikon,' one word."

"Oh," said Brandon blankly. "And what's the difference?"

"A hell of a difference. 'An optikon' would mean an instrument with lenses, but 'anoptikon,' one word, has the Greek prefix 'an-' which means 'no.' Words of Greek derivation use it for 'no.' Anarchy means 'no government,' anemia means 'no blood,' anonymous means 'no name,' and anoptikon means—"

"No lenses," cried Brandon.

"Right! Quentin must have been working on an optical device without lenses and this may be it and it may not be broken."

Shea said, "But you don't see anything when you look through it."

"It must be set to neutral," said Moore. "There must be some way of adjusting it." Like Brandon, he placed it in both hands and tried to twist it about that circumscribing groove. He placed pressure on it, grunting.

"Don't break it," said Brandon.

"It's giving. Either it's supposed to be stiff or else it's corroded shut." He stopped, looked at the instrument impatiently, and put it to his eye again. He whirled, unpolarized a window and looked out at the lights of the city."

"I'll be dumped in space," he breathed.

Brandon said, "What? What?"

Moore handed the instrument to Brandon wordlessly. Brandon put it to his eyes and cried out sharply, "It's a telescope."

Shea said at once, "Let me see."

They spent nearly an hour with it, converting it into a telescope with turns in one direction, a microscope with turns in the other.

"How does it work?" Brandon kept asking.

"I don't know," Moore kept saying. In the end he said, "I'm sure it involves concentrated force fields. We are turning against considerable field resistance. With larger instruments, power adjustment will be required."

"It's a pretty cute trick," said Shea.

"It's more than that," said Moore. "I'll bet it represents a completely new turn in theoretical physics. It focuses light without lenses, and it can be adjusted to gather light over a wider and wider area without any change in focal length. I'll bet we could duplicate the five-hundred-inch Ceres telescope in one direction and an electron microscope in the other. What's more, I don't see any chromatic aberration, so it must bend light of all wavelengths equally. Maybe it bends radio waves and gamma rays also. Maybe it distorts gravity, if gravity is some kind of radiation. Maybe—"

"Worth money?" asked Shea, breaking in dryly.

"All kinds if someone can figure out how it works."

"Then we don't go to Trans-space Insurance with this. We go to a lawyer first. Did we sign these things away with our salvage rights or didn't we? You had them already in your possession before signing the paper. For that matter, is the paper any good if we didn't know what we were signing away? Maybe it might be considered fraud."

"As a matter of fact," said Moore, "with something like this, I don't know if any private company ought to own it. We ought to check with some government agency. If there's money in it—"

But Brandon was pounding both fists on his knees. "To *hell* with the money, Warren. I mean, I'll take any money that comes my way but that's not the important thing. We're going to be famous, man, famous! Imagine the story. A fabulous treasure lost in space. A giant corporation combing space for twenty years to find it and all the time we, the forgotten ones, have it in our possession. Then, on the twentieth anniversary of the original loss, we find it again. If this thing works, if anoptics becomes a great new scientific technique, they'll *never* forget us."

Moore grinned, then started laughing. "That's right. You did it, Mark. You did just what you set out to do. You've rescued us from being marooned in oblivion."

"We all did it," said Brandon. "Mike Shea started us off with the necessary basic information. I worked out the theory, and you had the instrument."

"Okay. It's late, and the wife will be back soon, so let's get the ball rolling right away. Multivac will tell us which agency would be appropriate and who—"

"No, no," said Brandon. "Ritual first. The closing toast of the anniversary, please, and with the appropriate change. Won't you oblige, Warren?" He passed over the still half-full bottle of Jabra water.

Carefully, Moore filled each small glass precisely to the brim. "Gentlemen," he said solemnly, "a toast." The three raised the glasses in unison. "Gentlemen, I give you the *Silver Queen* souvenirs *we used to have.*"

The Billiard Ball

James Priss—I suppose I ought to say Professor James Priss, though everyone is sure to know whom I mean even without the title—always spoke slowly.

I know. I interviewed him often enough. He had the greatest mind since Einstein, but it didn't work quickly. He admitted his slowness often. Maybe it was *because* he had so great a mind that it didn't work quickly.

He would say something in slow abstraction, then he would think, and then he would say something more. Even over trivial matters, his giant mind would hover uncertainly, adding a touch here and then another there.

Would the Sun rise tomorrow, I can imagine him wondering. What do we mean by "rise"? Can we be certain that tomorrow will come? Is the term "Sun" completely unambiguous in this connection?

Add to this habit of speech a bland countenance, rather pale, with no expression except for a general look of uncertainty; gray hair, rather thin, neatly combed; business suits of an invariably conservative cut; and you have what Professor James Priss was—a retiring person, completely lacking in magnetism.

That's why nobody in the world, except myself, could possibly suspect him of being a murderer. And even I am not sure. After all, he *was* slow-thinking; he was *always* slow-thinking. Is it conceivable that at one crucial moment he managed to think quickly and act at once?

It doesn't matter. Even if he murdered, he got away with it. It is far too late now to try to reverse matters and I wouldn't succeed in doing so even if I decided to let this be published.

Edward Bloom was Priss's classmate in college, and an associate, through circumstance, for a generation afterward. They were equal in age and in their propensity for the bachelor life, but opposites in everything else that mattered.

Bloom was a living flash of light; colorful, tall, broad, loud, brash, and self-confident. He had a mind that resembled a meteor strike in the sudden and unexpected way it could seize the essential. He was no theoretician, as Priss was; Bloom had neither the patience for it, nor the capacity to concentrate intense thought upon a single abstract point. He admitted that; he boasted of it.

What he did have was an uncanny way of seeing the application of a theory; of seeing the manner in which it could be put to use. In the cold marble block of abstract structure, he could see, without apparent difficulty, the intricate design of a marvelous device. The block would fall apart at his touch and leave the device.

It is a well-known story, and not too badly exaggerated, that nothing Bloom ever built had failed to work, or to be patentable, or to be profitable. By the time he was forty-five, he was one of the richest men on Earth.

And if Bloom the Technician were adapted to one particular matter more than anything else, it was to the way of thought of Priss the Theoretician. Bloom's greatest gadgets were built upon Priss's greatest thoughts, and as Bloom grew wealthy and famous, Priss gained phenomenal respect among his colleagues.

Naturally it was to be expected that when Priss advanced his Two-Field Theory, Bloom would set about at once to build the first practical anti-gravity device.

My job was to find human interest in the Two-Field Theory for the subscribers to *Tele-News Press,* and you get that by trying to deal with human beings and not with abstract ideas. Since my interviewee was Professor Priss, that wasn't easy.

Naturally, I was going to ask about the possibilities of anti-gravity, which interested everyone; and not about the Two-Field Theory, which no one could understand.

"Anti-gravity?" Priss compressed his pale lips and considered. "I'm not entirely sure that it is possible, or ever will be. I haven't—uh—worked the matter out to my satisfaction. I don't entirely see whether the Two-Field equations would have a finite solution, which they would have to have, of course; if—" And then he went off into a brown study.

I prodded him. "Bloom says he thinks such a device can be built."

Priss nodded. "Well, yes, but I wonder. Ed Bloom has had an

amazing knack at seeing the unobvious in the past. He has an unusual mind. It's certainly made him rich enough."

We were sitting in Priss's apartment. Ordinary middle-class. I couldn't help a quick glance this way and that. Priss was not wealthy.

I don't think he read my mind. He saw me look. And I think it was on *his* mind. He said, "Wealth isn't the usual reward for the pure scientist. Or even a particularly desirable one."

Maybe so, at that, I thought. Priss certainly had his own kind of reward. He was the third person in history to win two Nobel Prizes, and the first to have both of them in the sciences and both of them unshared. You can't complain about that. And if he wasn't rich, neither was he poor.

But he didn't sound like a contented man. Maybe it wasn't Bloom's wealth alone that irked Priss; maybe it was Bloom's fame among the people of Earth generally; maybe it was the fact that Bloom was a celebrity wherever he went, whereas Priss, outside scientific conventions and faculty clubs, was largely anonymous.

I can't say how much of all this was in my eyes or in the way I wrinkled the creases in my forehead, but Priss went on to say, "But we're friends, you know. We play billiards once or twice a week. I beat him regularly."

(I never published that statement. I checked it with Bloom, who made a long counterstatement that began: "He beats *me* at billiards. That jackass—" and grew increasingly personal thereafter. As a matter of fact, neither one was a novice at billiards. I watched them play once for a short while, after the statement and counterstatement, and both handled the cue with professional aplomb. What's more, both played for blood, and there was no friendship in the game that I could see.)

I said, "Would you care to predict whether Bloom will manage to build an anti-gravity device?"

"You mean would I commit myself to anything? Hmm. Well, let's consider, young man. Just what do we mean by anti-gravity? Our conception of gravity is built around Einstein's General Theory of Relativity, which is now a century and a half old but which, within its limits, remains firm. We can picture it—"

I listened politely. I'd heard Priss on the subject before, but if I was to get anything out of him—which wasn't certain—I'd have to let him work his way through in his own way.

"We can picture it," he said, "by imagining the Universe to be a flat, thin, superflexible sheet of untearable rubber. If we picture mass as being associated with weight, as it is on the surface of the Earth, then we would expect a mass, resting upon the rubber sheet, to make an indentation. The greater the mass, the deeper the indentation.

"In the actual Universe," he went on, "all sorts of masses exist, and so our rubber sheet must be pictured as riddled with indentations. Any object rolling along the sheet would dip into and out of the indentations it passed, veering and changing direction as it did so. It is this veer and change of direction that we interpret as demonstrating the existence of a force of gravity. If the moving object comes close enough to the center of the indentation and is moving slowly enough, it gets trapped and whirls round and round that indentation. In the absence of friction, it keeps up that whirl forever. In other words, what Isaac Newton interpreted as a force, Albert Einstein interpreted as geometrical distortion."

He paused at this point. He had been speaking fairly fluently—for him—since he was saying something he had said often before. But now he began to pick his way.

He said, "So in trying to produce anti-gravity, we are trying to alter the geometry of the Universe. If we carry on our metaphor, we are trying to straighten out the indented rubber sheet. We could imagine ourselves getting under the indenting mass and lifting it upward, supporting it so as to prevent it from making an indentation. If we make the rubber sheet flat in that way, then we create a Universe—or at least a portion of the Universe—in which gravity doesn't exist. A rolling body would pass the non-indenting mass without altering its direction of travel a bit, and we could interpret this as meaning that the mass was exerting no gravitational force. In order to accomplish this feat, however, we need a mass equivalent to the indenting mass. To produce anti-gravity on Earth in this way, we would have to make use of a mass equal to that of Earth and poise it above our heads, so to speak."

I interrupted him. "But your Two-Field Theory—"

"Exactly. General Relativity does not explain both the gravitational field and the electromagnetic fields in a single set of equations. Einstein spent half his life searching for that single set—for a Unified Field Theory—and failed. All who followed Einstein also failed. I, however, began with the assumption that there were two fields that could not be unified and followed the consequences, which I can explain, in part, in terms of the 'rubber sheet' metaphor."

Now we came to something I wasn't sure I had ever heard before. "How does that go?" I asked.

"Suppose that, instead of trying to lift the indenting mass, we try to stiffen the sheet itself, make it less indentable. It would contract, at least over a small area, and become flatter. Gravity would weaken, and so would mass, for the two are essentially the same phenomenon in terms of the indented Universe. If we could make the rubber sheet completely flat, both gravity and mass would disappear altogether.

"Under the proper conditions, the electromagnetic field could be made to counter the gravitational field, and serve to stiffen the indented fabric of the Universe. The electromagnetic field is tremendously stronger than the gravitational field, so the former could be made to overcome the latter."

I said uncertainly, "But you say 'under the proper conditions.' Can those proper conditions you speak of be achieved, Professor?"

"That is what I don't know," said Priss thoughtfully and slowly. "If the Universe were really a rubber sheet, its stiffness would have to reach an infinite value before it could be expected to remain completely flat under an indenting mass. If that is also so in the real Universe, then an infinitely intense electromagnetic field would be required and that would mean anti-gravity would be impossible."

"But Bloom says—"

"Yes, I imagine Bloom thinks a finite field will do, if it can be properly applied. Still, however ingenious he is," and Priss smiled narrowly, "we needn't take him to be infallible. His grasp on theory is quite faulty. He—he never earned his college degree, did you know that?"

I was about to say that I knew that. After all, everyone did. But there was a touch of eagerness in Priss's voice as he said it and I looked up in time to catch animation in his eye, as though he were delighted to spread that piece of news. So I nodded my head as if I were filing it for future reference.

"Then you would say, Professor Priss," I prodded again, "that Bloom is probably wrong and that anti-gravity is impossible?"

And finally Priss nodded and said, "The gravitational field can be weakened, of course, but if by anti-gravity we mean a true zero-gravity field—no gravity at all over a significant volume of space—then I suspect anti-gravity may turn out to be impossible, despite Bloom."

And I had, after a fashion, what I wanted.

I wasn't able to see Bloom for nearly three months after that, and when I did see him he was in an angry mood.

He had grown angry at once, of course, when the news first broke concerning Priss's statement. He let it be known that Priss would be invited to the eventual display of the anti-gravity device as soon as it was constructed, and would even be asked to participate in the demonstration. Some reporter—not I, unfortunately—caught him between appointments and asked him to elaborate on that and he said:

"I'll have the device eventually; soon, maybe. And you can be there, and so can anyone else the press would care to have there. And Professor James Priss can be there. He can represent Theoretical Science and after I have demonstrated anti-gravity, he can adjust his theory to explain it. I'm sure he will know how to make his adjustments in masterly fashion and show exactly why I couldn't possibly have failed. He might do it now and save time, but I suppose he won't."

It was all said very politely, but you could hear the snarl under the rapid flow of words.

Yet he continued his occasional game of billiards with Priss and when the two met they behaved with complete propriety. One could tell the progress Bloom was making by their respective attitudes to the press. Bloom grew curt and even snappish, while Priss developed an increasing good humor.

When my umpteenth request for an interview with Bloom was finally accepted, I wondered if perhaps that meant a break in Bloom's quest. I had a little daydream of him announcing final success to *me*.

It didn't work out that way. He met me in his office at Bloom Enterprises in upstate New York. It was a wonderful setting, well away from any populated area, elaborately landscaped, and covering as much ground as a rather large industrial estblishment. Edison at his height, two centuries ago, had never been as phenomenally successful as Bloom.

But Bloom was not in a good humor. He came striding in ten

minutes late and went snarling past his secretary's desk with the barest nod in my direction. He was wearing a lab coat, unbottoned.

He threw himself into his chair and said, "I'm sorry if I've kept you waiting, but I didn't have as much time as I had hoped." Bloom was a born showman and knew better than to antagonize the press, but I had the feeling he was having a great deal of difficulty at that moment in adhering to this principle.

I made the obvious guess. "I am given to understand, sir, that your recent tests have been unsuccessful."

"Who told you that?"

"I would say it was general knowledge, Mr. Bloom."

"No, it isn't. Don't say that, young man. There is no general knowledge about what goes on in my laboratories and workshops. You're stating the Professor's opinions, aren't you? Priss's, I mean."

"No, I'm—"

"Of course you are. Aren't you the one to whom he made that statement—that anti-gravity is impossible?"

"He didn't make the statement that flatly."

"He never says anything flatly, but it was flat enough for him, and not as flat as I'll have his damned rubber-sheet Universe before I'm finished."

"Then does that mean you're making progress, Mr. Bloom?"

"You know I am," he said with a snap. "Or you should know. Weren't you at the demonstration last week?"

"Yes, I was."

I judged Bloom to be in trouble or he wouldn't be mentioning that demonstration. It worked but it was not a world beater. Between the two poles of a magnet a region of lessened gravity was produced.

It was done very cleverly. A Mössbauer-Effect Balance was used to probe the space between the poles. If you've never seen an M-E Balance in action, it consists primarily of a tight monochromatic beam of gamma rays shot down the low-gravity field. The gamma rays change wavelength slightly but measurably under the influence of the gravitational field and if anything happens to alter the intensity of the field, the wavelength-change shifts correspondingly. It is an extremely delicate method for probing a gravitational field and it worked like a charm. There was no question but that Bloom had lowered gravity.

The trouble was that it had been done before by others. Bloom, to be sure, had made use of circuits that greatly increased the ease with which such an effect had been achieved—his system was typically ingenious and had been duly patented—and he maintained that it was by this method that anti-gravity would become not merely a scientific curiosity but a practical affair with industrial applications.

Perhaps. But it was an incomplete job and he didn't usually make a fuss over incompleteness. He wouldn't have done so this time if he weren't desperate to display *something*.

I said, "It's my impression that what you accomplished at that preliminary demonstration was 0.82 *g,* and better than that was achieved in Brazil last spring."

"That so? Well, calculate the energy input in Brazil and here, and then tell me the difference in gravity decrease per kilowatthour. You'll be surprised."

"But the point is, can you reach 0 *g*—zero gravity? That's what Professor Priss thinks may be impossible. Everyone agrees that merely lessening the intensity of the field is no great feat."

Bloom's fist clenched. I had the feeling that a key experiment had gone wrong that day and he was annoyed almost past endurance, Bloom hated to be balked by the Universe.

He said, "Theoreticians make me sick." He said it in a low, controlled voice, as though he were finally tired of not saying it, and he was going to speak his mind and be damned. "Priss has won two Nobel Prizes for sloshing around a few equations, but what has he done with it? Nothing! I *have* done something with it and I'm going to do more with it, whether Priss likes it or not.

"*I'm* the one people will remember. *I'm* the one who gets the credit. He can keep his damned title and his Prizes and his kudos from the scholars. Listen, I'll tell you what gripes him. Plain oldfashioned jealousy. It kills him that I get what I get for doing. He wants it for *thinking*.

"I said to him once—we play billiards together, you know—"

It was at this point that I quoted Priss's statement about billiards and got Bloom's counterstatement. I never published either That was just trivia.

"We play billiards," said Bloom, when he had cooled down, "and I've won my share of games. We keep things friendly enough. What the hell—college chums and all that—though how he got through, I'll never know. He made it in physics, of course, and in math, but he got a bare pass—out of pity, I think—in every humanities course he ever took."

"You did not get your degree, did you, Mr. Bloom?" That was sheer mischief on my part. I was enjoying his eruption.

"I quit to go into business, damn it. My academic average, over the three years I attended, was a strong B. Don't imagine anything else, you hear? Hell, by the time Priss got his Ph.D., I was working on my second million."

He went on, clearly irritated, "Anyway, we were playing billiards and I said to him, 'Jim, the average man will never understand why you get the Nobel Prize when I'm the one who gets the results. Why do you need two? Give me one!' He stood there, chalking up his cue, and then he said in his soft namby-pamby way, 'You have two billions, Ed. Give me one.' So you see, he wants the money."

I said, "I take it you don't mind his getting the honor?"

For a minute I thought he was going to order me out, but he didn't. He laughed instead, waved his hand in front of him, as though he were erasing something from an invisible blackboard in front of him. He said, "Oh, well, forget it. All that is off the record. Listen, do you want a statement? Okay. Things didn't go right today and I blew my top a bit, but it will clear up. I think I know what's wrong. And if I don't, I'm going to know.

"Look, you can say that I say that we *don't* need infinite electromagnetic intensity; we *will* flatten out the rubber sheet; we *will* have zero gravity. And when we get it, I'll have the damndest demonstration you ever saw, exclusively for the press and for Priss, and you'll be invited. And you can say it won't be long. Okay?"

Okay!

I had time after that to see each man once or twice more. I even saw them together when I was present at one of their billiard games. As I said before, both of them were *good*.

But the call to the demonstration did not come as quickly as all that. It arrived six weeks less than a year after Bloom gave me his statement. And at that, perhaps it was unfair to expect quicker work.

I had a special engraved invitation, with the assurance of a cocktail hour first. Bloom never did things by halves and he was planning to have a pleased and satisfied group of reporters on hand. There was an arrangement for trimensional TV, too. Bloom felt completely confident, obviously; confident enough to be willing to trust the demonstration in every living room on the planet.

I called up Professor Priss, to make sure he was invited too. He was.

"Do you plan to attend, sir?"

There was a pause and the professor's face on the screen was a study in uncertain reluctance. "A demonstration of this sort is most unsuitable where a serious scientific matter is in question. I do not like to encourage such things."

I was afraid he would beg off, and the dramatics of the situation would be greatly lessened if he were not there. But then, perhaps, he decided he dared not play the chicken before the world. With obvious distaste he said, "Of course, Ed Bloom is not really a scientist and he must have his day in the sun. I'll be there."

"Do you think Mr. Bloom can produce zero gravity, sir?"

"Uh . . . Mr. Bloom sent me a copy of the design of his device and . . . and I'm not certain. Perhaps he can do it, if . . . uh . . . he says he can do it. Of course"—he paused again for quite a long time—"I think I would like to see it."

So would I, and so would many others.

The staging was impeccable. A whole floor of the main building at Bloom Enterprises—the one on the hilltop—was cleared. There were the promised cocktails and a splendid array of hors d'oeuvres, soft music and lighting, and a carefully dressed and thoroughly jovial Edward Bloom playing the perfect host, while a number of polite and unobtrusive menials fetched and carried. All was geniality and amazing confidence.

James Priss was late and I caught Bloom watching the corners of the crowd and beginning to grow a little grim about the edges. Then Priss arrived, dragging a volume of colorlessness in with him, a drabness that was unaffected by the noise and the absolute splendor (no other word would describe it—or else it was the two martinis glowing inside me) that filled the room.

Bloom saw him and his face was illuminated at once. He bounced across the floor, seized the smaller man's hand and dragged him to the bar.

"Jim! Glad to see you! What'll you have? Hell, man, I'd have called it off if you hadn't showed. Can't have this thing without the star, you know." He wrung Priss's hand. "It's your theory, you know. We poor mortals can't do a thing without you few, you damned *few* few, pointing the way."

He was being ebullient, handing out the flattery, because he could afford to do so now. He was fattening Priss for the kill.

Priss tried to refuse a drink, with some sort of mutter, but a glass was pressed into his hand and Bloom raised his voice to a bull roar.

"Gentlemen! A moment's quiet, please. To Professor Priss, the greatest mind since Einstein, two-time Nobel Laureate, father of the Two-Field Theory, and inspirer of the demonstration we are about to see—even if he didn't think it would work, and had the guts to say so publicly."

There was a distinct titter of laughter that quickly faded out and Priss looked as grim as his face could manage.

"But now that Professor Priss is here," said Bloom, "and we've had our toast, let's get on with it. Follow me, gentlemen!"

The demonstration was in a much more elaborate place than had housed the earlier one. This time it was on the top floor of the building. Different magnets were involved—smaller ones, by heaven —but as nearly as I could tell, the same M-E Balance was in place.

One thing was new, however, and it staggered everybody, drawing much more attention than anything else in the room. It was a billiard table, resting under one pole of the magnet. Beneath it was the companion pole. A round hole, about a foot across, was stamped out of the very center of the table and it was obvious that the zero-gravity field, if it was to be produced, would be produced through that hole in the center of the billiard table.

It was as though the whole demonstration had been designed, surrealist fashion, to point up the victory of Bloom over Priss. This was to be another version of their everlasting billiards competition and Bloom was going to win.

I don't know if the other newsmen took matters in that fashion, but I think Priss did. I turned to look at him and saw that he was still holding the drink that had been forced into his hand. He rarely drank, I knew, but now he lifted the glass to his lips and emptied it in two swallows. He stared at that billiard ball and I needed no gift of ESP to realize that he took it as a deliberate snap of fingers under his nose.

Bloom led us to the twenty seats that surrounded three sides of the table, leaving the fourth free as a working area. Priss was carefully escorted to the seat commanding the most convenient view. Priss glanced quickly at the trimensional cameras which were now working. I wondered if he were thinking of leaving but deciding that he couldn't in the full glare of the eyes of the world.

Essentially, the demonstration was simple; it was the production that counted. There were dials in plain view that measured the energy expenditure. There were others that transferred the M-E Balance readings into a position and a size that were visible to all. Everything was arranged for easy trimensional viewing.

Bloom explained each step in a genial way, with one or two pauses in which he turned to Priss for a confirmation that had to come. He didn't do it often enough to make it obvious, but just enough to turn Priss upon the spit of his own torment. From where I sat I could look across the table and see Priss on the other side.

He had the look of a man in Hell.

As we all know, Bloom succeeded. The M-E Balance showed the gravitational intensity to be sinking steadily as the electromagnetic field was intensified. There were cheers when it dropped below the 0.52 g mark. A red line indicated that on the dial.

"The 0.52 g mark, as you know," said Bloom confidently, "represents the previous record low in gravitational intensity. We are now lower than that at a cost in electricity that is less than ten per cent what it cost at the time that mark was set. And we will go lower still."

Bloom—I think deliberately, for the sake of the suspense—slowed the drop toward the end, letting the trimensional cameras switch back and forth between the gap in the billiard table and the dial on which the M-E Balance reading was lowering.

Bloom said suddenly, "Gentlemen, you will find dark goggles in the pouch on the side of each chair. Please put them on now. The zero-gravity field will soon be established and it will radiate a light rich in ultraviolet."

He put goggles on himself, and there was a momentary rustle as others went on too.

I think no one breathed during the last minute, when the dial reading dropped to zero and held fast. And just as that happened a cylinder of light sprang into existence from pole to pole through the hole in the billiard table.

There was a ghost of twenty sighs at that. Someone called out, "Mr. Bloom, what is the reason for the light?"

"It's characteristic of the zero-gravity field," said Bloom smoothly, which was no answer, of course.

Reporters were standing up now, crowding about the edge of the table. Bloom waved them back. "Please, gentlemen, stand clear!"

Only Priss remained sitting. He seemed lost in thought and I have been certain ever since that it was the goggles that obscured the possible significance of everything that followed. I didn't see his eyes. I couldn't. And that meant neither I nor anyone else could even begin to make a guess as to what was going on behind those eyes. Well, maybe we couldn't have made such a guess, even if the goggles hadn't been there, but who can say?

Bloom was raising his voice again. "Please! The demonstration is not yet over. So far, we've only repeated what I have done before. I have now produced a zero-gravity field and I have shown it can be done practically. But I want to demonstrate something of what such a field can do. What we are going to see next will be something that has never been seen, not even by myself. I have not experimented in this direction, much as I would have liked to, because I have felt that Professor Priss deserved the honor of—"

Priss looked up sharply. "What—what—"

"Professor Priss," said Bloom, smiling broadly, "I would like you to perform the first experiment involving the interaction of a solid object with a zero-gravity field. Notice that the field has been formed in the center of a billiard table. The world knows your phenomenal skill in billiards, Professor, a talent second only to your amazing aptitude in theoretical physics. Won't you send a billiard ball into the zero-gravity volume?"

Eagerly he was handing a ball and cue to the professor. Priss, his eyes hidden by the goggles, stared at them and only very slowly, very uncertainly, reached out to take them.

I wonder what his eyes were showing. I wonder, too, how much of the decision to have Priss play billiards at the demonstration was due to Bloom's anger at Priss's remark about their periodic game, the remark I had quoted. Had I been, in my way, responsible for what followed?

"Come, stand up, Professor," said Bloom, "and let me have your seat. The show is yours from now on. Go ahead!"

Bloom seated himself, and still talked, in a voice that grew more organlike with each moment. "Once Professor Priss sends the ball into the volume of zero gravity, it will no longer be affected by Earth's gravitational field. It will remain truly motionless while the Earth rotates about its axis and travels about the Sun. In this latitude, and at this time of day, I have calculated that the Earth, in its motions, will sink downward. We will move with it and the ball will stand still. To us it will seem to rise up and away from the Earth's surface. Watch."

Priss seemed to stand in front of the table in frozen paralysis. Was it surprise? Astonishment? I don't know. I'll never know. Did he make a move to interrupt Bloom's little speech, or was he just suffering from an agonized reluctance to play the ignominious part into which he was being forced by his adversary?

Priss turned to the billiard table, looking first at it, then back at Bloom. Every reporter was on his feet, crowding as closely as possible in order to get a good view. Only Bloom himself remained seated, smiling and isolated. He, of course, was not watching the table, or the ball, or the zero-gravity field. As nearly as I could tell through the goggles, he was watching Priss.

Priss turned to the table and placed his ball. He was going to be the agent that was to bring final and dramatic triumph to Bloom and make himself—the man who said it couldn't be done—the goat to be mocked forever.

Perhaps he felt there was no way out. Or perhaps—

With a sure stroke of his cue, he set the ball into motion. It was not going quickly, and every eye followed it. It struck the side of the table and caromed. It was going even slower now as though Priss himself were increasing the suspense and making Bloom's triumph the more dramatic.

I had a perfect view, for I was standing on the side of the table opposite from that where Priss was. I could see the ball moving toward the glitter of the zero-gravity field and beyond it I could see those portions of the seated Bloom which were not hidden by that glitter.

The ball approached the zero-gravity volume, seemed to hang on the edge for a moment, and then was gone, with a streak of light, the sound of a thunderclap, and the sudden smell of burning cloth.

We yelled. We all yelled.

I've seen the scene on television since—along with the rest of the world. I can see myself in the film during that fifteen-second period of wild confusion, but I don't really recognize my face.

Fifteen seconds!

And then we discovered Bloom. He was still sitting in the chair, his arms still folded, but there was a hole the size of a billiard ball through forearm, chest, and back. The better part of his heart, as it later turned out under autopsy, had been neatly punched out.

They turned off the device. They called in the police. They dragged off Priss, who was in a state of utter collapse. I wasn't much better off, to tell the truth, and if any reporter then on the scene ever tried to say he remained a cool observer of that scene, then he's a cool liar.

It was some months before I got to see Priss again. He had lost some weight but seemed well otherwise. Indeed, there was color in his cheeks and an air of decision about him. He was better dressed than I had ever seen him to be.

He said, "I know what happened *now*. If I had had time to think, I would have known then. But I am a slow thinker, and poor Ed Bloom was so intent on running a great show and doing it so well that he carried me along with him. Naturally, I've been trying to make up for some of the damage I unwittingly caused."

"You can't bring Bloom back to life," I said soberly.

"No, I can't," he said, just as soberly. "But there's Bloom Enterprises to think of, too. What happened at the demonstration, in full view of the world, was the worst possible advertisement for zero gravity, and it's important that the story be made clear. That is why I have asked to see *you*."

"Yes?"

"If I had been a quicker thinker, I would have known Ed was speaking the purest nonsense when he said that the billiard ball would slowly rise in the zero-gravity field. It *couldn't* be so! If Bloom hadn't despised theory so, if he hadn't been so intent on being proud of his own ignorance of theory, he'd have known it himself.

"The Earth's motion, after all, isn't the only motion involved, young man. The Sun itself moves in a vast orbit about the center of the Milky Way Galaxy. And the Galaxy moves too, in some not very clearly defined way. If the billiard ball were subjected to zero gravity, you might think of it as being unaffected by any of these motions and therefore of suddenly falling into a state of absolute rest—when there is no such thing as absolute rest."

Priss shook his head slowly. "The trouble with Ed, I think, was that he was thinking of the kind of zero gravity one gets in a spaceship in free fall, when people float in mid-air. He expected the ball to float in mid-air. However, in a spaceship, zero gravity is not the result of an absence of gravitation, but merely the result of two objects, a ship and a man within the ship, falling at the same rate, responding to gravity in precisely the same way, so that each is motionless with respect to the other.

"In the zero-gravity field produced by Ed, there was a flattening of the rubber-sheet Universe, which means an actual loss of mass. Everything in that field, including molecules of air caught within it, and the billiard ball I pushed into it, was completely massless as long as it remained with it. A completely massless object can move in only one way."

He paused, inviting the question. I asked, "What motion would that be?"

"Motion at the speed of light. Any massless object, such as a neutrino or a photon, must travel at the speed of light as long as it exists. In fact, light moves at that speed only because it is made up of photons. As soon as the billiard ball entered the zero-gravity field and lost its mass, it too assumed the speed of light at once and left."

I shook my head. "But didn't it regain its mass as soon as it left the zero-gravity volume?"

"It certainly did, and at once it began to be affected by the gravitational field and to slow up in response to the friction of the air and the top of the billiard table. But imagine how much friction it would take to slow up an object the mass of a billiard ball going at the speed of light. It went through the hundred-mile thickness of our atmosphere in a thousandth of a second and I doubt that it was slowed more than a few miles a second in doing so, a few miles out of 186,282 of them. On the way, it scorched the top of the billiard table, broke cleanly through the edge, went through poor Ed and the window too, punching out neat circles because it had passed through before the neighboring portions of something even as brittle as glass had a chance to split and splinter.

"It is extremely fortunate we were on the top floor of a building set in a countrified area. If we were in the city, it might have passed through a number of buildings and killed a number of people. By now that billiard ball is off in space, far beyond the edge of the Solar System and it will continue to travel so forever, at nearly the speed of light, until it happens to strike an object large enough to stop it. And then it will gouge out a sizable crater."

I played with the notion and was not sure I liked it. "How is that possible? The billiard ball entered the zero-gravity volume almost at a standstill. I saw it. And you say it left with an incredible quantity of kinetic energy. Where did the energy come from?"

Priss shrugged. "It came from nowhere! The law of conservation of energy only holds under the conditions in which general relativity is valid; that is, in an indented-rubber-sheet universe. Wherever the indentation is flattened out, general relativity no longer holds, and energy can be created and destroyed freely. That accounts for the radiation along the cylindrical surface of the zero-gravity volume. That radiation, you remember, Bloom did not explain, and, I fear, could not explain. If he had only experimented further first; if he had only not been so foolishly anxious to put on his show—"

"What accounts for the radiation, sir?"

"The molecules of air inside the volume. Each assumes the speed of light and comes smashing outward. They're only molecules, not billiard balls, so they're stopped, but the kinetic energy of their motion is converted into energetic radiation. It's continuous because new molecules are always drifting in, and attaining the speed of light and smashing out."

"Then energy is being created continuously?"

"Exactly. And that is what we must make clear to the public. Anti-gravity is not primarily a device to lift spaceships or to revolutionize mechanical movement. Rather, it is the source of an endless supply of free energy, since part of the energy produced can be diverted to maintain the field that keeps that portion of the Universe flat. What Ed Bloom invented, without knowing it, was not just anti-gravity, but the first successful perpetual-motion machine of the first class—one that manufactures energy out of nothing."

I said slowly, "Any one of us could have been killed by that billiard ball, is that right, Professor? It might have come out in any direction."

Priss said, "Well, massless photons emerge from any light source at the speed of light in any direction; that's why a candle casts light in all directions. The massless air molecules come out of the zero-gravity volume in all directions, which is why the entire cylinder radiates. But the billiard ball was only one object. It could have come out in any direction, but it had to come out in some one direction, chosen at random, and the chosen direction happened to be the one that caught Ed."

That was it. Everyone knows the consequences. Mankind had free energy and so we have the world we have now. Professor Priss was placed in charge of its development by the board of Bloom Enterprises, and in time he was as rich and famous as ever Edward Bloom had been. And Priss still has two Nobel Prizes in addition.

Only . . .

I keep thinking. Photons smash out from a light source in all directions because they are created at the moment and there is no reason for them to move in one direction more than in another. Air molecules come out of a zero-gravity field in all directions because they enter it in all directions.

But what about a single billiard ball, entering a zero-gravity field from one particular direction? Does it come out in the same direction or in any direction?

I've inquired delicately, but theoretical physicists don't seem to be sure, and I can find no record that Bloom Enterprises, which is the only organization working with zero-gravity fields, has ever experimented in the matter. Someone at the organization once told me that the uncertainty principle guarantees the random emersion of an object entering in any direction. But then why don't they try the experiment?

Could it be, then . . .

Could it be that for once Priss's mind had been working quickly? Could it be that, under the pressure of what Bloom was trying to do to him, Priss had suddenly seen everything? He had been studying the radiation surrounding the zero-gravity volume. He might have realized its cause and been certain of the speed-of-light motion of anything entering the volume.

Why, then, had he said nothing?

One thing is certain. *Nothing* Priss would do at the billiard table could be accidental. He was an expert and the billiard ball did exactly what he wanted it to. I was standing right there. I saw him look at Bloom and then at the table as though he were judging angles.

I watched him hit that ball. I watched it bounce off the side of the table and move into the zero-gravity volume, heading in one particular direction.

For when Priss sent that ball toward the zero-gravity volume—and the tri-di films bear me out—it was *already* aimed directly at Bloom's heart!

Accident? Coincidence?

. . . Murder?

Afterword

A friend of mine after reading the above story suggested I change the title to "Dirty Pool." I have been tempted to do so but have refrained, for it seems too flippant a title for so grave a story—or perhaps I am just corroded with jealousy at not having thought of it first.

But in either case, now that all the stories in this volume have been gone over, and I have experienced the memories to which each gave rise, all I can say is, "Gee, it's great to be a science fiction writer."

Mirror Image

The Three Laws of Robotics

1: *A robot may not injure a human being or, through inaction, allow a human being to come to harm.*

2: *A robot must obey the orders given it by human beings except where such orders would conflict with the First Law.*

3: *A robot must protect its own existence as long as such protection does not conflict with the First or Second Laws.*

Lije Baley had just decided to relight his pipe, when the door of his office opened without a preliminary knock, or announcement, of any kind. Baley looked up in pronounced annoyance and then dropped his pipe. It said a good deal for the state of his mind that he left it lie where it had fallen.

"R. Daneel Olivaw," he said, in a kind of mystified excitement. "Jehoshaphat! It *is* you, isn't it?"

"You are quite right," said the tall, bronzed newcomer, his even features never flicking for a moment out of their accustomed calm. "I regret surprising you by entering without warning, but the situation is a delicate one and there must be as little involvement as possible on the part of the men and robots even in this place. I am, in any case, pleased to see you again, friend Elijah."

And the robot held out his right hand in a gesture as thoroughly human as was his appearance. It was Baley who was so unmanned by his astonishment as to stare at the hand with a momentary lack of understanding.

But then he seized it in both his, feeling its warm firmness. "But Daneel, *why?* You're welcome any time, but—What is this situation that is a delicate one? Are we in trouble again? Earth, I mean?"

"No, friend Elijah, it does not concern Earth. The situation to which I refer as a delicate one is, to outward appearances, a small thing. A dispute between mathematicians, nothing more. As we happened, quite by accident, to be within an easy Jump of Earth—"

"This dispute took place on a starship, then?"

"Yes, indeed. A small dispute, yet to the humans involved astonishingly large."

Baley could not help but smile. "I'm not surprised you find humans astonishing. They do not obey the Three Laws."

"That is, indeed, a shortcoming," said R. Daneel, gravely, "and I think humans themselves are puzzled by humans. It may be that you are less puzzled than are the men of other worlds because so many more human beings live on Earth than on the Spacer worlds. If so, and I believe it is so, you could help us."

R. Daneel paused momentarily and then said, perhaps a shade too quickly, "And yet there are rules of human behavior which I have learned. It would seem, for instance, that I am deficient in etiquette, by human standards, not to have asked after your wife and child."

"They are doing well. The boy is in college and Jessie is involved in local politics. The amenities are taken care of. Now tell me how you come to be here."

"As I said, we were within an easy Jump of Earth," said R. Daneel, "so I suggested to the captain that we consult you."

"And the captain agreed?" Baley had a sudden picture of the proud and autocratic captain of a Spacer starship consenting to make a landing on Earth—of all worlds—and to consult an Earthman—of all people.

"I believe," said R. Daneel, "that he was in a position where he would have agreed to anything. In addition, I praised you very highly; although, to be sure, I stated only the truth. Finally, I agreed to conduct all negotiations so that none of the crew, or passengers, would need to enter any of the Earthman cities."

"And talk to any Earthman, yes. But what has happened?"

"The passengers of the starship, *Eta Carina,* included two mathematicians who were traveling to Aurora to attend an interstellar conference on neurobiophysics. It is about these mathematicians, Alfred Barr Humboldt and Gennao Sabbat, that the dispute centers. Have you perhaps, friend Elijah, heard of one, or both, of them?"

"Neither one," said Baley, firmly. "I know nothing about mathematics. Look, Daneel, surely you haven't told anyone I'm a mathematics buff or—"

"Not at all, friend Elijah. I know you are not. Nor does it matter, since the exact nature of the mathematics involved is in no way relevant to the point at issue."

"Well, then, go on."

"Since you do not know either man, friend Elijah, let me tell you that Dr. Humboldt is well into his twenty-seventh decade—Pardon me, friend Elijah?"

"Nothing. Nothing," said Baley, irritably. He had merely muttered to himself, more or less incoherently, in a natural reaction to the extended life-spans of the Spacers. "And he's still active, despite his age? On Earth, mathematicians after thirty or so . . ."

Daneel said, calmly; "Dr. Humboldt is one of the top three mathematicians, by long-established repute, in the galaxy. Certainly he is still active. Dr. Sabbat, on the other hand, is quite young, not yet fifty, but he has already established himself as the most remarkable new talent in the most abstruse branches of mathematics."

"They're both great, then," said Baley. He remembered his pipe and picked it up. He decided there was no point in lighting it now and knocked out the dottle. "What happened? Is this a murder case? Did one of them apparently kill the other?"

"Of these two men of great reputation, one is trying to destroy that of the other. By human values, I believe this may be regarded as worse than physical murder."

"Sometimes, I suppose. Which one is trying to destroy the other?"

"Why, that, friend Elijah, is precisely the point at issue. Which?"

"Go on."

"Dr. Humboldt tells the story clearly. Shortly before he boarded the starship, he had an insight into a possible method for analyzing neural pathways from changes in microwave absorption patterns of local cortical areas. The insight was a purely mathematical technique of extraordinary subtlety, but I cannot, of course, either understand or sensibly transmit the details. These do not, however, matter. Dr. Humboldt considered the matter and was more convinced each hour that he had something revolutionary on hand, something that would dwarf all his previous accomplishments in mathematics. Then he discovered that Dr. Sabbat was on board."

"Ah. And he tried it out on young Sabbat?"

"Exactly. The two had met at professional meetings before and knew each other thoroughly by reputation. Humboldt went into it with Sabbat in great detail. Sabbat backed Humboldt's analysis completely and was unstinting in his praise of the importance of the discovery and of the ingenuity of the discoverer. Heartened and reassured by this, Humboldt prepared a paper outlining, in summary, his work and, two days later, prepared to have it forwarded subetherically to the co-chairmen of the conference at Aurora, in order that he might officially establish his priority and arrange for possible discussion before the sessions were closed. To his surprise, he found that Sabbat was ready with a paper of his own, essentially the same as Humboldt's, and Sabbat was also preparing to have it subetherized to Aurora."

"I suppose Humboldt was furious."

"Quite!"

"And Sabbat? What was his story?"

"Precisely the same as Humboldt's. Word for word."

"Then just what is the problem?"

"Except for the mirror-image exchange of names. According to Sabbat, it was he who had the insight, and he who consulted Humboldt; it was Humboldt who agreed with the analysis and praised it."

"Then each one claims the idea is his and that the other stole it. It doesn't sound like a problem to me at all. In matters of scholarship, it would seem only necessary to produce the records of research, dated and initialed. Judgment as to priority can be made from that. Even if one is falsified, that might be discovered through internal inconsistencies."

"Ordinarily, friend Elijah, you would be right, but this is mathematics, and not in an experimental science. Dr. Humboldt claims to have worked out the essentials in his head. Nothing was put in writing until the paper itself was prepared. Dr. Sabbat, of course, says precisely the same."

"Well, then, be more drastic and get it over with, for sure. Subject each one to a pyschic probe and find out which of the two is lying."

R. Daneel shook his head slowly, "Friend Elijah, you do not understand these men. They are both of rank and scholarship, Fellows of the Imperial Academy. As such, they cannot be subjected to trial of professional conduct except by a jury of their peers—their professional peers—unless they personally and voluntarily waive that right."

"Put it to them, then. The guilty man won't waive the right because he can't afford to face the psychic probe. The innocent man will waive it at once. You won't even have to use the probe."

"It does not work that way, friend Elijah. To waive the right in such a case—to be investigated by laymen—is a serious and perhaps irrecoverable blow to prestige. Both men steadfastly refuse to waive the right to special trial, as a matter of pride. The question of guilt, or innocence, is quite subsidiary."

"In that case, let it go for now. Put the matter in cold storage until you get to Aurora. At the neurobiophysical conference, there will be a huge supply of professional peers, and then—"

"That would mean a tremendous blow to science itself, friend Elijah. Both men would suffer for having been the instrument of scandal. Even the innocent one would be blamed for having been party to a situation so distasteful. It would be felt that it should have been settled quietly out of court at all costs."

"All right. I'm not a Spacer, but I'll try to imagine that this attitude makes sense. What do the men in question say?"

"Humboldt agrees thoroughly. He says that if Sabbat will admit theft of the idea and allow Humboldt to proceed with transmission of the paper—or at least its delivery at the conference, he will not press charges. Sabbat's misdeed will remain secret with him; and, of course, with the captain, who is the only other human to be party to the dispute."

"But young Sabbat will not agree?"

"On the contrary, he agreed with Dr. Humboldt to the last detail —with the reversal of names. Still the mirror-image."

"So they just sit there, stalemated?"

"Each, I believe, friend Elijah, is waiting for the other to give in and admit guilt."

"Well, then, wait."

"The captain has decided this cannot be done. There are two alternatives to waiting, you see. The first is that both will remain stubborn so that when the starship lands on Aurora, the intellectual scandal will break. The captain, who is responsible for justice on board ship will suffer disgrace for not having been able to settle the matter quietly and that, to him, is quite insupportable."

"And the second alternative?"

"Is that one, or the other, of the mathematicians will indeed admit to wrongdoing. But will the one who confesses do so out of actual guilt, or out of a noble desire to prevent the scandal? Would it be right to deprive of credit one who is sufficiently ethical to prefer to lose that credit than to see science as a whole suffer? Or else, the guilty party will confess at the last moment, and in such a way as to make it appear he does so only for the sake of science, thus escaping the disgrace of his deed and casting its shadow upon the other. The captain will be the only man to know all this but he does not wish to spend the rest of his life wondering whether he has been a party to a grotesque miscarriage of justice."

Baley sighed. "A game of intellectual chicken. Who'll break first as Aurora comes nearer and nearer? Is that the whole story now, Daneel?"

"Not quite. There are witnesses to the transaction."

"Jehoshaphat! Why didn't you say so at once. *What* witnesses?

"Dr. Humboldt's personal servant—"

"A robot, I suppose."

"Yes, certainly. He is called R. Preston. This servant, R. Preston, was present during the initial conference and he bears out Dr. Humboldt in every detail."

"You mean he says that the idea was Dr. Humboldt's to begin with; that Dr. Humboldt detailed it to Dr. Sabbat; that Dr. Sabbat praised the idea, and so on."

"Yes, in full detail."

"I see. Does that settle the matter or not? Presumably not."

"You are quite right. It does not settle the matter, for there is a second witness. Dr. Sabbat also has a personal servant, R. Idda, another robot of, as it happens, the same model as R. Preston, made, I believe, in the same year in the same factory. Both have been in service equal times."

"An odd coincidence—very odd."

"A fact, I am afraid, and it makes it difficult to arrive at any judgment based on obvious differences between the two servants."

"R. Idda, then, tells the same story as R. Preston?"

"Precisely the same story, except for the mirror-image reversal of the names."

"R. Idda stated, then, that young Sabbat, the one not yet fifty"— Lije Baley did not entirely keep the sardonic note out of his voice; he himself was not yet fifty and he felt far from young—"had the idea to begin with; that he detailed it to Dr. Humboldt, who was loud in his praises, and so on."

"Yes, friend Elijah."

"And one robot is lying, then."

"So it would seem."

"It should be easy to tell which. I imagine even a superficial examination by a good roboticist—"

"A roboticist is not enough in this case, friend Elijah. Only a qualified robopsychologist would carry weight enough and experience enough to make a decision in a case of this importance. There is no one so qualified on board ship. Such an examination can be performed only when we reach Aurora—"

"And by then the crud hits the fan. Well, you're here on Earth. We can scare up a robopsychologist, and surely anything that happens on Earth will never reach the ears of Aurora and there will be no scandal."

"Except that neither Dr. Humboldt, nor Dr. Sabbat, will allow his servant to be investigated by a robopsychologist of Earth. The Earthman would have to—" He paused.

Lije Baley said stolidly, "He'd have to touch the robot."

"These are old servants, well thought of—"

"And not to be sullied by the touch of Earthman. Then what do you want me to do, damn it?" He paused, grimacing. "I'm sorry, R. Daneel, but I see no reason for your having involved me."

"I was on the ship on a mission utterly irrelevant to the problem at hand. The captain turned to me because he had to turn to someone. I seemed human enough to talk to, and robot enough to be a safe recipient of confidences. He told me the whole story and asked what I would do. I realized the next Jump could take us as easily to Earth as to our target. I told the captain that, although I was at as much a loss to resolve the mirror-image as he was, there was on Earth one who might help."

"Jehoshaphat!" muttered Baley under his breath.

"Consider, friend Elijah, that if you succeed in solving this puzzle, it would do your career good and Earth itself might benefit. The matter could not be publicized, of course, but the captain is a man of some influence on his home world and he would be grateful."

"You just put a greater strain on me."

"I have every confidence," said R. Daneel, stolidly, "that you already have some idea as to what procedure ought to be followed."

"Do you? I suppose that the obvious procedure is to interview the two mathematicians, one of whom would seem to be a thief."

"I'm afraid, friend Elijah, that neither one will come into the city. Nor would either one be willing to have you come to them."

"And there is no way of forcing a Spacer to allow contact with an Earthman, no matter what the emergency. Yes, I understand that, Daneel—but I was thinking of an interview by closed-circuit television."

"Nor that. They will not submit to interrogation by an Earthman."

"Then what do they want of me? Could I speak to the robots?"

"They would not allow the robots to come here, either."

"Jehoshaphat, Daneel. *You've* come."

"That was my own decision. I have permission, while on board ship, to make decisions of that sort without veto by any human being but the captain himself—and he was eager to establish the contact. I, having known you, decided that television contact was insufficient. I wished to shake your hand."

Lije Baley softened. "I appreciate that, Daneel, but I still honestly wish you could have refrained from thinking of me at all in this case. Can I talk to the robots by television at least?"

"That, I think, can be arranged."

"Something, at least. That means I would be doing the work of a robopsychologist—in a crude sort of way."

"But you are a detective, friend Elijah, not a robopsychologist."

"Well, let it pass. Now before I see them, let's think a bit. Tell me: is it possible that both robots are telling the truth? Perhaps the conversation between the two mathematicians was equivocal. Perhaps it was of such a nature that each robot could honestly believe its own master was proprietor of the idea. Or perhaps one robot heard only one portion of the discussion and the other another portion, so that each could suppose its own master was proprietor of the idea."

"That is quite impossible, friend Elijah. Both robots repeat the conversation in identical fashion. And the two repetitions are fundamentally inconsistent."

"Then it is absolutely certain that one of the robots is lying?"

"Yes."

"Will I be able to see the transcript of all evidence given so far in the presence of the captain, if I should want to?"

"I thought you would ask that and I have copies with me."

"Another blessing. Have the robots been cross-examined at all, and is that cross-examination included in the transcript?"

"The robots have merely repeated their tales. Cross-examination would be conducted only by robopsychologists."

"Or by myself?"

"You are a detective, friend Elijah, not a—"

"All right, R. Daneel. I'll try to get the Spacer psychology straight. A detective can do it because he isn't a robopsychologist. Let's think further. Ordinarily a robot will not lie, but he will do so if necessary to maintain the Three Laws. He might lie to protect, in legitimate fashion, his own existence in accordance with the Third Law. He is more apt to lie if that is necessary to follow a legitimate order given him by a human being in accordance with the Second Law. He is most apt to lie if that is necessary to save a human life, or to prevent harm from coming to a human in accordance with the First Law."

"Yes."

"And in this case, each robot would be defending the professional reputation of his master, and would lie if it were necessary to do so. Under the circumstances, the professional reputation would be nearly equivalent to life and there might be a near-First-Law urgency to the lie."

"Yet by the lie, each servant would be harming the professional reputation of the other's master, friend Elijah."

"So it would, but each robot might have a clearer conception of the value of its own master's reputation and honestly judge it to be greater than that of the other's. The lesser harm would be done by his lie, he would suppose, than by the truth."

Having said that, Lije Baley remained quiet for a moment. Then he said, "All right, then, can you arrange to have me talk to one of the robots—to R. Idda first, I think?"

"Dr. Sabbat's robot?"

"Yes," said Baley, dryly, "the young fellow's robot."

"It will take me but a few minutes," said R. Daneel. "I have a micro-receiver outfitted with a projector. I will need merely a blank wall and I think this one will do if you will allow me to move some of these film cabinets."

"Go ahead. Will I have to talk into a microphone of some sort?"

"No, you will be able to talk in an ordinary manner. Please pardon me, friend Elijah, for a moment of further delay. I will have to contact the ship and arrange for R. Idda to be interviewed."

"If that will take some time, Daneel, how about giving me the transcripted material of the evidence so far."

Lije Baley lit his pipe while R. Daneel set up the equipment, and leafed through the flimsy sheets he had been handed.

The minutes passed and R. Daneel said, "If you are ready, friend Elijah, R. Idda is. Or would you prefer a few more minutes with the transcript?"

"No," sighed Baley, "I'm not learning anything new. Put him on and arrange to have the interview recorded and transcribed."

R. Idda, unreal in two-dimensional projection against the wall, was basically metallic in structure—not at all the humanoid creature that R. Daneel was. His body was tall but blocky, and there was very little to distinguish him from the many robots Baley had seen, except for minor structural details.

Baley said, "Greetings, R. Idda."

"Greetings, sir," said R. Idda, in a muted voice that sounded surprisingly humanoid.

"You are the personal servant of Gennao Sabbat, are you not?"

"I am sir."

"For how long, boy?"

"For twenty-two years, sir."

"And your master's reputation is valuable to you?"

"Yes, sir."

"Would you consider it of importance to protect that reputation?"

"Yes, sir."

"As important to protect his reputation as his physical life?"

"No, sir."

"As important to protect his reputation as the reputation of another."

R. Idda hesitated. He said, "Such cases must be decided on their individual merit, sir. There is no way of establishing a general rule."

Baley hesitated. These Spacer robots spoke more smoothly and intellectually than Earth-models did. He was not at all sure he could outthink one.

He said, "If you decided that the reputation of your master were more important than that of another, say, that of Alfred Barr Humboldt, would you lie to protect your master's reputation?"

"I would, sir."

"Did you lie in your testimony concerning your master in his controversy with Dr. Humboldt?"

"No, sir."

"But if you were lying, you would deny you were lying in order to protect that lie, wouldn't you?"

"Yes, sir."

"Well, then," said Baley, "let's consider this. Your master, Gennao Sabbat, is a young man of great reputation in mathematics, but he is a young man. If, in this controversy with Dr. Humboldt, he had succumbed to temptation and had acted unethically, he would suffer a certain eclipse of reputation, but he is young and would have ample time to recover. He would have many intellectual triumphs ahead of him and men would eventually look upon this plagiaristic attempt as the mistake of a hot-blooded youth, deficient in judgment. It would be something that would be made up for in the future.

"If, on the other hand, it were Dr. Humboldt who succumbed to temptation, the matter would be much more serious. He is an old man whose great deeds have spread over centuries. His reputation has been unblemished hitherto. All of that, however, would be forgotten in the light of this one crime of his later years, and he would have no opportunity to make up for it in the comparatively short time remaining to him. There would be little more that he could accomplish. There would be so many more years of work ruined in Humboldt's case than in that of your master and so much less opportunity to win back his position. You see, don't you, that Humboldt faces the worse situation and deserves the greater consideration?"

There was a long pause. Then R. Idda said, with unmoved voice, "My evidence was a lie. It was Dr. Humboldt whose work it was, and my master has attempted, wrongfully, to appropriate the credit."

Baley said, "Very well, boy. You are instructed to say nothing to anyone about this until given permission by the captain of the ship. You are excused."

The screen blanked out and Baley puffed at his pipe. "Do you suppose the captain heard that, Daneel?"

"I am sure of it. He is the only witness, except for us."

"Good. Now for the other."

"But is there any point to that, friend Elijah, in view of what R. Idda has confessed?"

"Of course there is. R. Idda's confession means nothing."

"Nothing?"

"Nothing at all. I pointed out that Dr. Humboldt's position was the worse. Naturally, if he were lying to protect Sabbat, he would switch to the truth as, in fact, he claimed to have done. On the other hand, if he were telling the truth, he would switch to a lie to protect Humboldt. It's still mirror-image and we haven't gained anything."

"But then what will we gain by questioning R. Preston?"

"Nothing, if the mirror-image were perfect—but it is not. After all, one of the robots *is* telling the truth to begin with, and one *is* lying to begin with, and that is a point of asymmetry. Let me see R. Preston. And if the transcription of R. Idda's examination is done, let me have it.

The projector came into use again. R. Preston stared out of it; identical with R. Idda in every respect, except for some trivial chest design.

Baley said, "Greetings, R. Preston." He kept the record of R. Idda's examination before him as he spoke.

"Greetings, sir," said R. Preston. His voice was identical with that of R. Idda.

"You are the personal servant of Alfred Barr Humboldt are you not?"

"I am, sir."

"For how long, boy?"

"For twenty-two years, sir."

"And your master's reputation is valuable to you?"

"Yes, sir."

"Would you consider it of importance to protect that reputation?"

"Yes, sir."

"As important to protect his reputation as his physical life?"

"No, sir."

"As important to protect his reputation as the reputation of another?"

R. Preston hesitated. He said, "Such cases must be decided on their individual merit, sir. There is no way of establishing a general rule."

Baley said, "If you decided that the reputation of your master were more important than that of another, say, that of Gennao Sabbat, would you lie to protect your master's reputation?"

"I would, sir."

"Did you lie in your testimony concerning your master in his controversy with Dr. Sabbat?"

"No, sir."

"But if you were lying, you would deny you were lying, in order to protect that lie, wouldn't you?"

"Yes, sir."

"Well, then," said Baley, "let's consider this. Your master, Alfred Barr Humboldt, is an old man of great reputation in mathematics, but he is an old man. If, in this controversy with Dr. Sabbat, he had succumbed to temptation and had acted unethically, he would suffer a certain eclipse of reputation, but his great age and his centuries of accomplishments would stand against that and would win out. Men would look upon this plagiaristic attempt as the mistake of a perhaps-sick old man, no longer certain in judgment.

"If, on the other hand, it were Dr. Sabbat who had succumbed to temptation, the matter would be much more serious. He is a young man, with a far less secure reputation. He would ordinarily have centuries ahead of him in which he might accumulate knowledge and achieve great things. This will be closed to him, now, obscured by one mistake of his youth. He has a much longer future to lose than your master has. You see, don't you, that Sabbat faces the worse situation and deserves the greater consideration?"

There was a long pause. Then R. Preston said, with unmoved voice, "My evidence was as I—"

At that point, he broke off and said nothing more.

Baley said, "Please continue, R. Preston."

There was no response.

R. Daneel said, "I am afraid, friend Elijah, that R. Preston is in stasis. He is out of commission."

"Well, then," said Baley, "we have finally produced an asymmetry. From this, we can see who the guilty person is."

"In what way, friend Elijah?"

"Think it out. Suppose you were a person who had committed no crime and that your personal robot were a witness to that. There would be nothing you need do. Your robot would tell the truth and bear you out. If, however, you were a person who *had* committed the crime, you would have to depend on your robot to lie. That would be a somewhat riskier position, for although the robot would lie, if necessary, the greater inclination would be to tell the truth, so that the lie would be less firm than the truth would be. To prevent that, the crime-committing person would very likely have to *order* the robot to lie. In this way. First Law would be strengthened by Second Law; perhaps very substantially strengthened."

"That would seem reasonable," said R. Daneel.

"Suppose we have one robot of each type. One robot would switch from truth, unreinforced, to the lie, and could do so after some hesitation, without serious trouble. The other robot would switch from the lie, *strongly reinforced,* to the truth, but could do so only at the risk of burning out various positronic-track-ways in his brain and falling into stasis."

"And since R. Preston went into stasis—"

"R. Preston's master, Dr. Humboldt, is the man guilty of plagiarism. If you transmit this to the captain and urge him to face Dr. Humboldt with the matter at once, he may force a confession. If so, I hope you will tell me immediately."

"I will certainly do so. You will excuse me, friend Elijah? I must talk to the captain privately."

"Certainly. Use the conference room. It is shielded."

Baley could do no work of any kind in R. Daneel's absence. He sat in uneasy silence. A great deal would depend on the value of his analysis, and he was acutely aware of his lack of expertise in robotics.

R. Daneel was back in half an hour—very nearly the longest half hour of Baley's life.

There was no use, of course, in trying to determine what had happened from the expression of the humanoid's impassive face. Baley tried to keep his face impassive.

"Yes, R. Daneel?" he asked.

"Precisely as you said, friend Elijah. Dr. Humboldt has confessed. He was counting, he said, on Dr. Sabbat giving way and allowing Dr. Humboldt to have this one last triumph. The crisis is over and you will find the captain grateful. He has given me permission to tell you that he admires your subtlety greatly and I believe that I, myself, will achieve favor for having suggested you."

"Good," said Baley, his knees weak and his forehead moist now that his decision had proven correct, "but Jehoshaphat, R. Daneel, don't put me on the spot like that again, will you?"

"I will try not to, friend Elijah. All will depend, of course, on the importance of a crisis, on your nearness, and on certain other factors. Meanwhile, I have a question—"

"Yes?"

"Was it not possible to suppose that passage from a lie to the truth was easy, while passage from the truth to a lie was difficult? And in that case, would not the robot in stasis have been going from a truth to a lie, and since R. Preston was in stasis, might one not have drawn the conclusion that it was Dr. Humboldt who was innocent and Dr. Sabbat who was guilty?"

"Yes, R. Daneel. It was possible to argue that way, but it was the other argument that proved right. Humboldt did confess, didn't he?"

"He did. But with arguments possible in both directions, how could you, friend Elijah, so quickly pick the correct one?"

For a moment, Baley's lips twitched. Then he relaxed and they curved into a smile. "Because, R. Daneel, I took into account human reactions, not robotic ones. I know more about human beings than about robots. In other words, I had an idea as to which mathematician was guilty before I ever interviewed the robots. Once I provoked an asymmetric response in them, I simply interpreted it in such a way as to place the guilt on the one I already believed to be guilty. The robotic response was dramatic enough to break down the guilty man; my own analysis of human behavior might not have been sufficient to do so."

"I am curious to know what your analysis of human behavior was?"

"Jehoshaphat, R. Daneel; think, and you won't have to ask. There is another point of asymmetry in this tale of mirror-image besides the matter of true-and-false. There is the matter of the age of the two mathematicians; one is quite old and one is quite young."

"Yes, of course, but what then?"

"Why, this. I can see a young man, flushed with a sudden, startling and revolutionary idea, consulting in the matter an old man whom he has, from his early student days, thought of as a demigod in the field. I can *not* see an old man, rich in honors and used to triumphs, coming up with a sudden, startling and revolutionary idea, consulting a man centuries his junior whom he is bound to think of as a young whippersnapper—or whatever term a Spacer would use. Then, too, if a young man had the chance, would he try to steal the idea of a revered demigod? It would be unthinkable. On the other hand, an old man, conscious of declining powers, might well snatch at one last chance of fame and consider a baby in the field to have no rights he was bound to observe. In short, it was not conceivable that Sabbat steal Humboldt's idea; and from both angles, Dr. Humboldt was guilty."

R. Daniel considered that for a long time. Then he held out his hand. "I must leave now, friend Elijah. It was good to see you. May we meet again soon."

Baley gripped the robot's hand, warmly, "If you don't mind, R. Daneel," he said, "not too soon."